Bo Balder

THE WAN

Bo Balder

THE WAN

PINK
NARCISSUS
PRESS

THE WAN
©2016 Bo Balder

Cover illustration & design by Duncan Eagleson

Published by Pink Narcissus Press
pinknarc.com

Library of Congress Control Number: 2015944333
ISBN: 978-1-939056-10-8
First trade paperback edition: January 2016

CHAPTER 1

Frog's mother-in-law had divvied out no rice in her bowl, for the second morning in a row. It couldn't mean anything good. Frog straightened her aching back and snuck a look at where her husband was working. The young men were plaiting finger-thick withies into the tall horned ribs that would support the new woven longhouse. She and the other women wove the walls in between the spaced beams; this would be a twelve-horn longhouse, the biggest she'd ever seen. Two whole sections more than the eight-horn house floating on its own little island over there.

As far as she could see, the village didn't need the space. After all, not many babies had been born the last few years; however, the village elders had become convinced that it was the Ancestors punishing them for not giving the Ancestors a new meetinghouse.

The old reed mat she sat on was soaked and pricked her feet. Frog slid her hair back over her face and continued twining supple reeds into an airy wickerwork wall, which would provide both privacy and fresh air.

Her hand jerked when a razor-sharp reed cut her finger, straight through the thick layer of callus on her hands. It wasn't fair. She was one of the best weavers of the village in spite of not having been born to the craft. She should be working on the front with the women of proven fertility, creating the elaborate spirals and intricate waves of the village's signature knots. Because she didn't have a living baby, or a belly filled with one, she got the scut work, the walls between two already finished side beams. Mostly plain weaving, with only a simplified version of the village's crest in the middle.

Her empty rice bowl crowned a series of slights that had been accumulating for weeks. Mallard hadn't called her to the married couples' huts even once; he didn't speak to her anymore, and now his mother had skipped Frog's bowl. How would she live if nobody gave her food? If they let her, she could live off the land, but with all eyes on her, that was not an option. And going into the swamp, where the Ghast lived, was too dangerous.

In her life before Mallard had bedded her and taken her to his rice-farmers' village, she had served as the lowly slave of a trader, slogging up and down the roads between the marsh villages and Black Shores on the other end of the Rim. The trader had preferred to beat her instead of feeding her from his meager proceeds. Frog had learned to find edible roots and frogs in the marsh, crickets and mice and guinea pigs in the Rim mountains. She knew how to steal plantains from jungle fields and could skinny up a palm tree on the coast.

But here in New Rice Fields, the people thought wild food was haram, evil poisonous food for Ghast and Wan, and prided themselves on eating only what they grew on their own fields. Foolishness, but she'd gladly accustomed herself to it for Mallard's sake. If not for him, she'd still be traveling with the merchant, waiting for her daily beating while he got drunk.

Footsteps slapped up and she plaited harder, licking her cut finger all the time to keep the blood from staining the fresh green weave. The men were trooping off to take the afternoon siesta. Most of them greeted their wives or complimented them on their handiwork. Frog kept her eyes cast down, but she couldn't help recognizing Mallard's step. A pang of love and lust shot through her at the sight of his strong brown calves. He said nothing. He didn't even pause.

She bit her lip to keep from crying out and blinked hard to get rid of her unwelcome tears. The other women working by her side would be laughing and watching, waiting for an opening to taunt her. She would have taken care of the babies while the women worked in the fields, but the stranger in their midst caused only fear and resentment. Maybe they'd wished to have Mallard for themselves, with his shiny copper skin and heavy swinging ponytail.

Her belly cramped. If nobody fed her, she would starve. Or she could leave. She could forage enough to live on in the marsh, but for what purpose, all alone and unwanted? She'd rather die than find the merchant again, and be rented out and worked like a dog for never a kind word. She had no choice—she never had. Once again, she had to stay and bear anything Mallard and his mother dished out.

***

Ing licked the sheen of moisture seeping down the cave wall. It tasted of obsidian with a coating of chalk and brine. The exact place she marked yesterday.

Her companions shuffled their feet and whispered to each other, apparently unaware of the importance of the occasion—and not doing what she'd told them to a dozen times before. She wanted to ream out their sorry asses, but she knew that would only make things worse. How did it go again? Praise first, then reinforce the commands.

"Good work so far, guys. They saw you, they sent out a hunting party. You remember what to do next?" she asked.

Harpa nodded, but she didn't quite believe him. A man of many promises and few results. Tembo shrugged. In spite of the highly reflective whiteness of his face, she couldn't see his expression well enough in the cave's semi-darkness. With a sigh, she broke off two ring fingers—again—and fed them one each. Their stances righted as the knowledge sped through their bodies.

"I lead him off," Harpa said.

"I lure the others away from the leader when he follows Harpa."

Finally. "Now off you go. I can smell the humans coming."

They loped off, two dancing white outlines in the gloom.

She groped along the rough stone of the cave wall until she found a natural path between the stony stalagmite teeth on the cave floor. The perfect spot for an ambush.

Hunkering down, she ran the rope over the shallow footpath, ready to pull it taut and snare her prey. Her elbow banged against a stalactite—invisible in the darkness. She winced, shoulders stiffening against the pain she expected to shoot up through her funny bone. There was no pain. No more pain, no more cramps or shivers or fevers. Except those that the human mind generated. Even a couple of centuries of being a Wan didn't stop the mind from trying out million-years old reptile reflexes.

This was her last chance. Every time in the past century when Ing thought she found the right person, they had always disappointed her after the transformation to Wan was complete. She'd tried for intelligence, for creativity, for craftsmanship, for endurance or aggressiveness. They'd all listened, nodded their heads in agreement, and then wandered off in pursuit of their own happiness.

What did that say about humanity? Were they all shortsighted fools? Maybe. What did it tell her about her own ability to choose the right person? Probably that it sucked. So this time, she'd picked someone chosen not by herself, but by the population of White City. The Stadholder, the ruler. She'd seen him from afar many times. A tall, husky fellow with mahogany skin under iridescent silk scarves, a great prow of a nose, and a deep, happy voice. She bit her lip. He might not be so happy after she'd turned and captured him. What if happiness was the vital ingredient that made people trust him? Only one way to find out.

Ing's sigh echoed around the cave wall. Sadness and a sense of futility gathered in her from time to time, when the enormity of her dreams overwhelmed her. Ing knew the bad thoughts intimately because they occurred at great frequency. She forced these thoughts into a pinky finger. She snapped it off and tossed it away. There. No more grief and despair.

She straightened her spine and flexed her shoulders. She shouldn't have been sitting hunched up like that. She'd need her limberness and speed when her helpers led the prey past. They were idiots and fools, and she had no guarantee that they would carry out her wishes even after she fed them the instructions three times over. She gripped the rope in her remaining fingers. The stumps itched, already growing back.

Faint shouts and the slapping of feet echoed through the passage. She sniffed the air. The salty wind brought the sweat of excited men, with the strongest male scent in front. That would be Firdaus, the Stadholder. He led, others followed.

"Firdaus! You got it, I saw it hit!" an overexcited young human voice screeched, closer than she'd expected.

"I'll take the first one, you go after the other!" Firdaus' baritone answered, panting.

He was the one.

She inched closer, ready to tauten the rope after her hare passed.

***

Firdaus pounded after the Wan warrior along the steep cave floor, deeper into the tunnels. His breath sawed in his lungs. After a dry season of cold and inactivity, he wasn't in the best shape to hunt, but that was the heart of the matter. He had to lead the hunting party. He had to prove his power and virility, demonstrate his fitness to be the Stadholder of White City for another year.

In spite of the stitch in his left side, he increased his speed. The sticky salt in the air made him suspect that the desperate beast was leading him back to the sea.

Bamboo tapped on rock. He'd landed an obsidian-bladed spear in his prey's left eye and one in its ear socket. The more the cave ceiling jogged those spears, the more they would work themselves into the monster's brain. The glowapple around Firdaus' neck created a circle of dusk around him. Further ahead was only darkness. The creature's wheezes rasped against the tunnel walls, signaling that it was tiring.

Firdaus transferred his last spear to his throwing hand and hefted it over his shoulder.

"Heya!" he shouted.

His shins cannoned into an invisible rope. His legs went out from under him, shooting him headlong onto the sharp rocky floor covered with warm slime, blood, fish guts, and other offal. His shins smarted and stung.

Light flared up, a dozen times brighter than his fading glowapple.

A white apparition towered above him. A Wan.

Firdaus' breath hissed out of him. The flame in the creature's hand underlit a visage of black shadows and gray flesh, long teeth and dead-fish eyes. Winged arms beat up and down while it uttered a curse he couldn't hear through the blood roaring in his ears. A real Wan, risen from the black swamp to drag him down into its watery lair and devour him.

"Firdaus Eyvindurson!" a voice thundered, echoing off the walls, slamming into his ears with hammers of sound.

Every child learned of the Wan at their nurses' knees. Of their beauty, great in spite of their unnatural white skin. They'd tempt you with their singing and their promises of wealth and immortality. They'd lure you into their underground halls in the marshes, and no one had ever returned alive. And if somebody did, everyone he knew would be dead and gone. Plenty of reason to kill the Wan on sight when they ventured out of the Maze.

This one wasn't beautiful or alluring. He wouldn't be snared as easily as the foolish young men in the nursery tales. Firdaus had people to take care of. Hilm, Boon, his younger children, the soft arms of his lovers waiting for him, ten thousand hungry citizens watching the sky for omens about his fate.

He scrambled to get his feet back under him on the slippery, uneven cave floor, the Wan's white hairless shins right in front of his face. They reeked of mold and dank cellars. He lifted his head, but no matter how hard he blinked, he couldn't see past the bright light the figure carried. A cold paw gripped his elbow and hoisted his arm up. Firdaus lunged for the shadowed neck; a hard pale limb cuffed him in the face. He fell back, stunned.

Something pierced the fleshy part of his thumb. His mouth opened in shock. A white hand jammed a slimy fish-shaped thing into his mouth. He spat it out, gagging from the taste. Whitefish. What the prophet?

"What do you want?" he asked when his mouth was clear.

He swiped at a white leg, but it danced out of reach on dainty, human-looking feet. Firdaus overreached and smacked his nose on the rocky ground. When he scrabbled onto painful knees, inky darkness stared back, his night-sight lost because of the brief flash of light.

The creature was gone, as if it had never been there.

The Wan had known his name. What did that mean? He rubbed his thumb where the creature had stung it. Had it tasted him and found him not to its liking? Rumours abounded about the Wan feasting on newborn flesh. Its odour still hung in the air. A reminder to get away before it returned for another bite.

He groped around in the dark until he found the spear. His hands shoved a pebble that clanked instead of scraping. His fingers felt straight lines, the smooth coolness of metal. An ancestral object, a six-sided star with a grooved hole in the middle. An omen. A good one, he hoped. He shoved it onto his thumb and stumbled forward, hand and spear held out while his eyes adjusted back to the dim dapple of light.

After the murky tunnels, the cloudlight seemed as bright and evil as the Wan's torch. The other hunters waited for him, their hands as empty of Wan ears as his. He clambered up the steep cliff to his father's old villa in silence.

The second hunting party lounged around small fires in one of the seaside rooms, the orange flames almost invisible in the daylight. A precious substance called "glarse" filled the windows, shielding the fires from the sea wind. Glarse was full of shining lights and reflections at night, but in daylight, you could see through it as if it wasn't there. Nobody knew how to make it anymore.

"Heya, huntfellows," he called out. "I winged it, but it got away."

They crowded around him, asking excited questions. His milkbrother, Ali, led the raggle-taggle of hunters and fishermen in a rousing cheer. People struggled up, stiff from waiting, eager to take their turn. Firdaus let it wash over him, wondering why he hadn't told the rest of the tale. They deserved to know everything, didn't they? Yet he couldn't bring himself to mention the creature speaking his name in a human voice, the sting that throbbed in the fleshy base of his thumb. He'd tell Ali, later, when they were alone.

The relief party trotted off with their axes, knives, and bows, fresh glowapples ready. Their spines were straight and their steps light. Not telling them about the Wan who'd trapped and bitten him was the right decision. He'd think on what it meant, sleep on it, but first he wanted a cup of something hot and a moment of rest.

A chilly draft from the open door tautened his sweaty skin and stung his scrapes. His knees were ripped and bloody from the fall, his palms and arms up to the elbows in grazes, red against the deep brown. He couldn't find the whitefish sting amidst the cuts, although the pain lanced deep with every movement of his thumb.

His son Awayo came tottering up to him as fast as his little legs allowed. He stretched out his fat little arms to be picked up.

"Abba owie?"

Firdaus hunkered down and let the little boy kiss away the pain on his scraped palms.

He squatted by the fire, Awayo's little body cuddled up against him. Thank the prophet for Awayo's health; his skin shone a rich blue-black like his mother's, and the boy was fat and lively, without coughing blood and wasting away like Firdaus' eldest son Boon. No amount of stroking holy ancestral syringes along Boon's arm had helped.

Firdaus accepted a cup of coffee that had boiled too

long. Hanako, Awayo's mother, bit her lip when he grimaced at the taste. The little groove of worry between her elegant black eyebrows deepened. Osma, the one-year old, sucked on his thumb, half asleep on his mother's lap, while baby Zuzana suckled half-heartedly on an empty breast. It was good of her to come down here and help out with the camp, with three children to look after. It was her way of making up to him for the rift that had grown between them since he'd taken up with Kem. Thank the Ancestors Hanako wasn't making him choose anymore; he didn't want to lose either of the women.

He downed the coffee in one gulp since it had cooled quickly in the leather cup, and stood up to stretch his stiffening muscles. He reckoned he was close on thirty years now. His bones hadn't felt right since that cold winter two years ago.

"Let me clean those cuts up for you," Hanako said, but she made no movement towards her pack.

"Just scrapes."

He sighed. The first mutters about his failings as a Stadholder had started after the not-rainy-enough season last year. Crops were meager, rice paddies abandoned because they had dried out. The ruler of the city embodied the fertility of the land, and if the land failed, it must be due to him, in spite of his twelve children and the care with which he ruled his city. The people would sacrifice the life of a failing leader to appease the Ancestors.

As the Stadholder, he was supposed to look further ahead than this year's crop, but it seemed no one shared his worries. Everybody was so sure that things would be normal again soon, but what if they weren't? He rubbed his eyes, stinging from the smoky seaweed fire. He went outside to clamber onto the prickly basalt spine that led down to the city.

The black, pockmarked cliffs sloped down until they met the white bulbous rock that formed White City's foundation. The two towers of Stack Palace thrust into the sky on top of the low, wide buildings that formed the Palace first floor. The outer walls of the city glowed peach from the slanting rays of cloudlight. If you looked at it from out here, the city shone like a beacon of friendliness and civilization in a sea of hungry vastness.

He lifted his eyes to look to the north. Beyond the city, across the lagoon, beyond the rice fields, floated the hazy green depths of the Maze. In the shifting marshes lived the misshapen Ghast, creatures of legend, and the fairer but equally terrifying Wan. The Wan they hunted must have come from there. Maybe the second hunting party would have more luck than the first. He shivered and tore his gaze back to the city.

From the onion bulb of the Singing Tower peeking out from behind Stack Palace, the Stentor would be singing the cloudwane greeting. He'd heard that chant all the days of his life, and the idea that his lovely city might fall to famine tasted bitter in his mouth. He tossed the coffee dregs away and squatted at the edge of the tiny stream to wash the cup.

***

Ing bent down and picked up the squashed remnant of the whitefish from the tunnel floor. Eat it? No, it would add mass, which she didn't need, without carrying any useful information. She licked it just in case, but although it was old, it tasted boring. Whitefish didn't lead interesting lives. She pulled the hood of her cloak tighter around her face and walked off as fast as she could, through the tunnel exiting on the other side of the cliff, near the Rim Pass road. She needed to be back in her quarters under the city before daylight.

The Stadholder would be sleeping high above her in the tower made of old saucer modules, Stack Palace as they called it nowadays. He'd been so tall in person, the dark brown hand grasping at her shins so big, with such long fingers. He was nowhere near as full-bellied as she remembered from public appearances. Even the Stadholder must have been feeling the scarcity of winter.

She allowed a smile to relax her mouth. Her plan had worked perfectly. The small bite of the whitefish was so insignificant that Firdaus Eyvindurson would have forgotten it a second later. Soon he would start to show the first symptoms.

The last light of the day caught her hand in its glare, as white as the fish she'd picked up before. She pulled a fold of the cloak over it and hurried on.

CHAPTER 2

Frog crouched a few lengths away from Mallard's bower. He'd forbidden her to sleep on his mat, but hadn't told her where else to go. When he slept, she'd sneak closer and lie against the reed curtain that was let down against the season's river wind. The cloudsky was still bright, but here between the bowers the shadows deepened enough to hide her from the casual eye.

Her stomach clenched. She needed to eat something soon. Already standing up made her weak and dizzy. The village stores of rice were locked up in the great hall, where the unmarried men slept. She could cut out a piece of wicker wall and steal some, but that would only work once, and everyone would know she'd done it.

The new mat she'd just woven for Mallard groaned a little, the fibers still green and full of juice. Mallard padded out, wearing his best tapa skirt. She could almost feel the skirt's silky thinness under her hand, perfect after days and days of beating it just so. If she left the village, she would take that and other samples of her craft along.

Where was Mallard going? He loped to the village square. Lost in her misery, Frog hadn't noticed the big fires being stoked. The blaze would make the dusk outside the circle seem like darkness. She inched to the edge of the square. Everybody was present. Even old Gander had been carried out on his litter. Something important must be going on.

Mallard stood up. His mother, Gannet, hung a necklace of withered, browned flowers around his neck. It looked like it had once been a marriage garland. Frog's heart thumped in her chest. She didn't need to get any closer; Gannet might lisp due to her missing teeth, but the old woman's lungs worked just fine.

"Mallard, son of Loon and Gannet," Gannet said with a ringing voice. "What is it that you ask?"

"I, Mallard, wish to break my marriage to the woman Frog, of no known clan and parentage, on grounds of infertility."

Frog stuffed her hand in her mouth to keep from crying out. It wasn't fair. She wanted babies as much as Mallard, more! So much more.

"Elders, do you assent to Mallard's request?" Gannet asked.

Frog couldn't distinguish the individual murmurs, but clearly everybody agreed. Nobody would take her side. She'd never deceived herself about being liked by the other women, but realizing how much she stood apart from them still hurt. She didn't belong to any clan, no powerful elders would defend her.

"All say aye. With these hands I break the marriage bond." Gannet stepped forward, snapped the wilted remnant of Frog's marriage in two and tossed it into the fire. The flames didn't even flicker.

Frog half turned to go and cry her heart out somewhere far away from here, when a woman rose. Plover, the mother of two living children, Lark and Duck, and a dozen stillborn or deceased ones. Duck had recently become a woman.

"Gannet, mother of Mallard. I, Plover, ask for your son's hand in marriage for my daughter Duck."

Blood sprang into Frog's mouth. No. No wonder her mother in law hadn't fed her in days, no wonder everybody avoided meeting her eyes. They had all known.

Duck, a slender young girl barely into womanhood stood beside Mallard, her belly already bulging with early pregnancy. Mallard was marrying her for her proven fertility. A sensible action everyone would approve, except if you were the cast-off bride. Frog hadn't been paying enough attention to the eddies and whirls of village life around her, or she would have known.

She stole off, although the urge to cry had gone. If she

was no longer Mallard's wife, she wasn't part of the village. Nobody would feed her or take her in. Maybe she could beg a little food off the men in exchange for bedsports, but she didn't want to return to that life. Better chance the freedom of the Maze.

She entered Mallard's bower—his, although she'd built it with her own hands—, found an old nettle bag and started to put her things in. A small earthen lamp, tinderbox, a carved wooden cup she'd stolen from the merchant who'd owned her for so long, a wooden knife, her tapa skirts, a bone needle and thread, a little woven box with trinkets and pretty pebbles.

A rough hand yanked her up by the upper arm. "Out of my bower, woman. You have no place here!" Mallard's voice growled in her ear.

"Yes, yes, I'm going, just a moment," Frog said without looking up. "Let me go, I was just packing."

Duck tittered in the door opening.

The next moment Frog landed hard on her nose on the packed earth floor. Through the ringing in her ears, she heard Duck's giggles and Mallard's boastful pronouncements. She managed to work her elbows under her chest and forced herself upright.

Duck and Mallard pawed through her small hoard. Duck gathered some in her skirt, but most of them she ignored. Mallard caught Frog's eye and held up her needle in his hand. With a wink, he broke it in two.

Duck lightly slapped his forearm. "That was a good needle, silly."

"I'll get you better ones," Mallard promised.

He'd talked like that to Frog, before. She'd seen him for the first time early in the morning, when the mist was still on the paddies, swinging his scythe. His coppery skin gleamed, and his muscles moved so nicely beneath it. She'd had to come out of hiding and touch that pretty pretty skin. Mallard had taken her there in the wet rice field, with the cloudlight beating down upon them and nobody had ever been that nice to her, ever. Until he stopped.

"This is our bower now," Mallard said to Duck. "Frog, get out of my house."

"I was leaving!" she snapped.

She shouldn't have, because he cuffed her again. Thick dark blood dripped from her nose onto her breasts, and her lip felt huge.

"Don't go too far. I would have drowned you, but mother wants to sell you," he said. "We won't tell the buyer that you're barren. And stupid."

Duck rubbed her rounded belly demonstratively.

Frog slunk out.

***

The cloudlight scorched the back of Firdaus' neck as he ascended the Temple steps. His bare feet danced on the hot stone, but he was the Stadholder, feet in the earth for strength, head in the air for wisdom, hands touching his people, rod bestowing fruitfulness. No sandals for him.

His hand ached and felt swollen twice its usual size, but when he peeked into his wrap, it appeared normal enough. It had been a week, though. Should he risk letting a physician examine it? A Stadholder couldn't afford to appear slow to heal.

His elder sister Aranaz stepped outside, cool and composed in an elegant tapa scarf and wide straw hat. "Dear Assembly members, we shall proceed to the Physician's Temple, where I have arranged refreshments for all of you."

Situated on the opposite side of Stack Palace, the bilious yellow bulk of the Physicians' Temple defied common sense and the upkeep abilities of the Physicians' Guild. His sister kept trying to drum up support to repair the North Corner, where the fancy glazed bricks had cracked and tumbled down, ruining the symmetry of the façade. So far, he'd managed to quash that drive, because he could think of dozens of better ways to spend the labor than repairing the lumbering edifice. For example, building trade ships or digging new rice fields.

The coolness of the Temple's echoing interior was most welcome. Tall narrow windows let in slants of light, too high up to reach and heat up the floor. Against a background of colorful friezes depicting the Ancestors' heroic and improbable adventures, their statues ranked all around the great atrium. They were slightly over life size, but lifted into awesome proportions by their black stone pedestals. Their clothing was heavily adorned with metal depicted in lifelike detail in the stone, along with strange gray bandoliers made of a stiff substance that looked like cloth but wasn't woven, and that couldn't be reforged like metal. The Ancestors must have been wealthy beyond imagining. Some of them looked a bit like present-day people, but others had the strangest taste in personal styling. Their skin color had bleached over the century into washy pinks and tans, and their hair and eyes were blue and yellow and red. Firdaus couldn't imagine wanting to wear a red wig.

He joined the group of politely attentive guild masters. Aranaz demonstrated her medicinal craft on a live patient, a strapping young man with an infected wound on his leg. The patient's face was gray with pain and fear, two blotches of bright color staining his cheekbones. Firdaus leaned forward to have a look at the leg. A machete wound, he guessed. A rotten stench rose from it, and dark stripes ran up to the young man's groin. Firdaus was no physician, but he didn't think the patient stood much chance of surviving. Firdaus' hand throbbed in response to the man's moans.

"When we get a case this serious," Aranaz said, appearing oblivious of the frightened eyes of the patient upon her, "we ask the Ancestors' favor with the exact incantation for this kind of case. And of course the holy syringes must be prepared."

At Aranaz' nod, an apprentice offered her a covered tray. Aranaz swept away the silken covering to reveal the row of gleaming syringes, the last remnants of their Ancestors' fabled medicine. She picked one up, thumb on the plunger, holding it up to the light so the Ancestors would take notice. She snapped it with finger and thumb and approached the patient. The apprentice broke into chanting. Aranaz wafted the syringe over the suppurating wound.

Would it do the poor patient any good? It had never worked for Boon's cough.

Aranaz tapped Firdaus' elbow, waking him out of his reverie and causing more spikes of pain to shoot through his hand.

"Brother, I have something to show you and the good men and women of the council," Aranaz said loudly.

Firdaus flinched. Just as the light outside dizzied him, the sound of voices reverberated in his head for minutes on end. Aranaz inclined her head in the direction of the nurseries and after a hesitation, he followed. She lifted the bead hangings separating the nursery from the main hospital and motioned him through.

"Look," she said.

Firdaus looked, but saw nothing special. The row of wicker cots suspended from the ceiling was quiet, the floor was swept. He smelled no shit or vomit. Aranaz kept a neat hospital. Everything seemed peaceful.

"Look inside," Aranaz said with more emphasis.

With his twelve-fold experience of newborns, Firdaus was loath to disturb any sleeping baby, even the little unwanted foundlings, but he tiptoed to the nearest cot and peeked inside. Nothing.

He spread his arms to Aranaz.

"Look in all of them," she repeated.

"What for? There's nothing to see," he said.

"Exactly, brother. Where are all the babies?"

Firdaus raised his brows but her words intrigued him. He trod between the silent cots and checked. All empty.

"You're right, that is odd. Where are the foundlings? Are they being raised somewhere else?" he asked. A terrible thought struck him. His breath fluted from his throat. "The Wan took them?"

First, they had poisoned the Stadholder, and now they were dealing White City the deathblow.

Aranaz clucked her tongue. "You men have Wan on your mind all the time? I'm sure it's fun chasing them around the countryside, but it would be nice if you brought in actual proof instead of nothing." Someone tittered.

She smiled, but quickly pulled her face back in stern lines. "People are disappearing, and I need to autopsy a Wan for the portents in its stomach. But I called you here to tell you that Meena found First Midwife's accounts, and I have the yearly birth tallies." The First Midwife had been ill for a long time, and Firdaus had asked her deputy Meena for the census figures to confirm his suspicions about the city population. Why was Aranaz butting in on his business? "Last year one-hundred-and-six babies were born, of whom forty-seven lived."

Gasps sounded behind his back from the Assembly members were standing right behind him. Forty-seven? Far worse than he'd feared. The number should have been at least four times that, or more to keep the population intact. The silence endured, magnifying the small sounds of normal morning business in the temple. The apprentices chanted on at the far end. A sacrificial chicken screeched as the thwack of a heavy knife thudded down.

It was hard to believe that no one had noticed the lack of babies, but if it was true, this could be the most serious problem yet. Failing crops were grains of rice compared to widespread barrenness. He couldn't throw money or invention at it, because nobody knew what caused infertility in healthy young people. Aranaz as Chief Physician would have to plead with the Ancestors for their spiritual assistance.

"What's the cause of it?" he asked Meena Midwife, who stood beside Aranaz, looking guilty, as well she might. He'd counted her as an ally.

Meena shrugged. "We don't know, sire. We can see that it's the poor who are affected the most."

"They're probably killing their babies because they don't have the means to feed them," First Rice Merchant said.

"Perhaps. But we keep track of who's pregnant, too. Not enough pregnancies."

"Firdaus," Aranaz said over Meena's answer. "What have you to say for yourself? Does not the City reflect the Stadholder? What do these missing babies say about your quality as a ruler?"

Firdaus head reeled from the unexpected blow. "What?" He looked at the Assembly Members to check if they'd heard the same accusation. Most of them looked shocked, but some of them creased their eyes in calculation.

"I repeat, dear brother, what have you done? In what way have you brought this misfortune on our heads? How will we survive without children?"

Firdaus wanted to protest that it could hardly be his fault. Wasn't he a man with twelve children, eleven of them healthy and thriving? But such a defense wouldn't placate his opportunistic sister or power hungry Guild Masters.

The Butchers sided with him, as did the Reederers, Peatcutters, Farmers, Fishers and Shrimpnetters. Sadly, most of these good people were reckoned uncouth marsh dwellers in the eyes of the city craftsmen. Someone like old Grebe the farmer looked out of place among the other guild heads, tall, imposing men and women who never went hungry for a day. Grebe was small and wizened, and when he spoke in public, his ribs went in and out over his concave belly in agitation. Not to mention the fact that he had no matronymic and no proper ancestral name.

Firdaus drew himself up. "Beloved sister, valued Assembly Members. Believe me, now that this serious matter has come to my attention, I will do whatever lies in my power to find the cause of this terrible situation and remedy it. Haven't I always guided you wisely? Hasn't White City weathered many storms under my leadership?"

Several voices ayed him, and he saw more Assembly Members nodding. Yana, head of the Weavers, ignored him, while Meena, the cheerful Midwife gave him an apologetic smile. The shoulders of the Leatherers, Bakers and Woodcrafts dripped with silk and metal, and they accorded him no more than a nod.

"I built new ships when the harbor silted. I had new

rice fields dug when the old ones dried up. Are these not the actions of a true Stadholder, an Ancestor-given ruler?"

The ayes rang around in his head, tolling like bells at a funeral. His hand throbbed and he was afraid he'd fall over, he was that dizzy. Were they right? Maybe his luck had turned, and the bite by that Wan had been the first omen of his downfall. He didn't want to cause harm to White City, but what if he was already doing it?

He slid his hand deeper under his robe. This meant he couldn't risk asking a physician for a diagnosis and a curative chant. He couldn't let anyone know that he wasn't healing up right from a little cut like that. People would think he had bad blood, and he didn't need more trouble on top of his sister's accusation.

The pain in his hand vexed Firdaus long into the night. When he finally dozed off, Boon's phlegmy coughing woke him up. Firdaus had Boon sleep in his own bed so he could keep an eye on the sick little boy. The boy's sticklike fingers slid over his thumb and squeezed it.

"I'm sorry," Boon whispered.

Firdaus kissed his hair. "Go back to sleep."

He didn't fall back asleep. His hand ached. Boon either coughed, which made it impossible to doze off, or he was silent, which made Firdaus break out in a sweat of fatherly worry. The boy was emaciated, and the skin of the hand clenched around Firdaus' brown thumb was gray in comparison. If only Boon had grabbed the other hand instead of his sore thumb.

When Boon finally fell into a deep sleep, Firdaus eased himself out of bed. With all the tumult in his life, a relaxing visit to Kem Shauvansdottir seemed like an excellent idea.

He fished a batik wrap from a chair and padded down to his mistress' quarters. He walked past a saucer section where the light vines had stopped bearing glowapples, but his feet knew the way. The slapping of his bare soles on the cold floor changed from sharp and echoey to muted, and the relative warmth of the bamboo planks beneath his feet told him he was on the connecting bridge between saucers.

He squinched his eyes shut against the glowapple around the corner. It was brighter than normal. Strange.

He tiptoed up the groaning stairs to Kem's family's rooms. He rattled the bead curtain that screened her room from passing gazes, to give her the chance to kick her sisters and maids from the bed. "Kem? Blacker than the rainy night, rounder than the belly of the behemoth?"

Kem giggled, and after a few moments of cloth rustling, called him in. She displayed her ample self in a flattering position on her bed, one leg drawn up and her famous breasts turned towards him, two magnificent globes of purple-brown flesh. He climbed onto the foot of the big bed and crawled towards her. His knees slithered away on the orange-sweet and red-hot silk sheets and he grabbed the ornamented wooden side of the bed.

"How am I going to sport on this?" he grumbled. "I need leverage."

"Who said we were going to have sport?" Kem said. "Is that a way to start a conversation?"

"I think I started with poetry," Firdaus said and clasped a soft round thigh.

He bent down to plant a kiss on her soft belly and she giggled again, sinking back into her pillows. Firdaus leaned on his right hand and almost blacked out from the pain shooting up to his armpit. Prophet's balls, that hurt. Kem rubbed her head against his shoulder. The short curly tufts of hair tickled his skin. True hair, his mother used to call it, to distinguish it from his own thick glossy curls that were merely passable.

"You smell funny, baby," Kem said.

"The children have been crawling into my bed all winter," Firdaus said. "You never noticed before?"

"Hm," she said and offered up her pouty lips to be kissed.

Firdaus closed his eyes. This was what heaven was supposed to be like, cavorting in a bed with the biggest, most beautiful woman he knew. "Let's make ourselves a little fat baby of our own, what do you say?"

Kem pushed him off and crawled to the other side of

the bed.

She didn't want his child? "What did I say?"

Kem's smooth forehead contorted in concern. She held her perfumed hand to her nose. "You're sick. You smell funny and you taste like something died on your tongue. You should go to the temple."

"I'm... fine!" Firdaus said, but he made the mistake to use both hands to gesticulate.

Kem grabbed his sore hand and turned it over. "Your fingers are like hot sausages."

Firdaus wrenched his hand out of hers. His head swam, and he disentangled his legs from her spice-scarlet sheets. "I'll be fine. I'll get back to you when I'm not so lacking in fragrance and health."

"Honeydew, I didn't mean it like that!"

Firdaus hurried away from her, knowing she was too lazy to run after him. He found the one bathroom where the glowapples grew very bright, and usually had three ripe ones on the vine at the same time. He went in, eyes shut against the unbearable brightness of the light. Did he look as bad as he feared?

He opened his eyes and hastily closed them again. The afterimage of a demonic face burned against his eyelids. He peered through the lashes of one eye. His skin was as pale as cinnamon, his eyes yellow and bloodshot, staring like a dying goat's.

He could no longer deny the fear and suspicion that had grown along with the pain in his arm. The Wan creature in the caves had caused this. Poisoned him.

Turned him into a Wan.

CHAPTER 3

Ing wriggled around the corner of the air duct. Her quarry had eluded her all day by stomping up and down the palace like a maddened ram, oversetting all the daily rhythms she knew so well. She pressed her nose against the dusty old air vent and looked into the mirror where Firdaus was dabbing stuff onto his face. What the hell was he doing? The greasy stuff he was rubbing in came from an old wooden box. Somebody's make-up, she guessed.

Firdaus' face stared back at her from the mirror, yellow as marsh kale. His tongue had bleached to a timid chicken color instead of its usual purplish-pink hue. His teeth seemed less white, and the bags beneath his eyes pouched out, squashy as bruised grapes. His hair was a shade darker than his skin, tan against the saffron.

The man was whitening up, finally. He seemed to be taking a long time to turn into a Wan. Ing wished for the relevant data about previous Wannings at her fingertips, but all she had these days was hard copy, writing on stacks of half-baked clay tablets, for god's sake. She couldn't re-member her own Wanning, centuries ago. It had destroyed parts of her natural and all of her external memory, as well as turning her into a bigger and smarter version of a mushroom. Since that time, she'd had to make do with papyrus, clay tablets, and wooden engravings. And those were sitting in big stacks in her quarters below the city. Oh, for the days of her youth, back on Earth, with every fact known to mankind easily within reach on the Web.

Below, Firdaus rubbed the greasy brown stuff on his face. Did he really think that would hide his yellow skin, his pale eyes, and the other signs of Wanning? The transformation process would make him sick and disoriented, even before it turned him into a bleached version of himself. This pathetic make-up job was a sure sign of debilitation.

He unpicked all his braids, cornrows they'd called them back home. His hair stood out like dandelion fluff around his head, spiraling away from his scalp for seven or eight inches. Nice hair. Firdaus worked the grease through his curls, oiling every kinky strand. The grease didn't make it quite as black as it had been, but it wasn't a bad try. Ing was keeping an eye on him in case he tried suicide or running away, but the camouflage attempt indicated he was trying to fight it. Denial, the first stage of grief.

When he'd covered his whole body with the grease, he looked almost like the old Firdaus, big, shiny and brown.

A scrawny little man hurried in, an eager smile on his narrow face. The angle at which he entered suggested to Ing that he'd been hiding right next to the door. Had he seen Firdaus in all his pale glory? The small man was rubbing his hands as if he was cold, and his modest one-stripe ribands hung crooked over his pale gold chest. He always seemed to hang around Firdaus. To her Wan nose, Firdaus was starting to smell pretty good, which probably meant human beings found him stinky.

"Firdaus, what can I do for you? Need help with a poem?" Ali looked over his shoulder and put his face close to Firdaus. "How is the hand?"

"It's fine. I need your help. I want you to find me a good house in the Dark Quarter and buy it for me without anyone knowing about it," Firdaus said.

Ali goggled at him. "Whatever for? You live in the palace, my Lord. Why would you want to leave that for the dirt and discomfort of the Dark Quarter? Are you sick? You look a little off."

Firdaus winked at him, still staring at his own reflection in the mirror, and therefore right in Ing's line of sight. "Really, I'm fine. I just need some private place where nobody in the palace can find me. Get it?"

"Ah. I see. What's going on with you and Kem? The

rumors are that there's trouble?"

"There is," Firdaus said. "Don't tell anyone, though."

"My discretion is assured. How good does the house need to be?"

"Good," Firdaus said. "I know the glowapples all wither and die in the Dark Quarter, but I want a living compost seat, and all the normal amenities. So I can occupy myself if I have to wait. You know."

Ali patted Firdaus' shoulder. "I'll take care of it, Firdaus."

Ing nodded to herself as they left the bathroom, one of the few original rooms still working properly, with living glowapple vines, running water and a functioning nano-toilet.

Getting out of the palace was an excellent idea, both from Firdaus' point of view and from hers. People would be less likely to notice his changing color and scent, and he'd be more accessible to her in an ordinary house. She couldn't remember what had made her shipmates stack the Landers on top of each other, and she'd never understand why the Stadholders insisted on living in it, but it sure made keeping track of Firdaus hell. In the Dark Quarter, she could just crawl through the dead sewer lines and enter every house that way. She'd better get back and start digging through her clay tablets for that data on Wanning intervals. Clay tablets weren't bad, they didn't rot like papyrus and weren't expensive like vellum, but retrieving data was a nightmare. She'd resorted to keeping a separate indexing system scratched on the walls of her rooms, like a medieval librarian.

***

The pirogue kissed the new floating docks. Firdaus flinched from habit, but in truth, his hand no longer bothered him that much. Now, he ached all over. His limbs felt like water, and everything he saw had a fuzzy halo.

In spite of starting out for the Blessing of the Sea before cloud wax, the fishing fleet arrived home at midmorning, the day worryingly bright for Firdaus to be outdoors. The fishermen had caught a few net loads of pinkies, still flashing bold color in the bow, carmine, rose, salmon. They sold on the market for seasoning, dried and strung on a necklace like beads.

At the bottom of the steps up to the city, his eldest daughter Hilm ran into his arms. The first stab of joy dribbled away into misery when he saw the contrast between their colors as her thin arms hugged his waist, cinnamon against the dull brown of his make-up. They'd always been of one skin. Hilm didn't seem to be aware of this difference, and led him by the hand up to the palace. She'd grown during this one day away, if that was possible. So clever and thoughtful, his little Gentleness. She was still skinny and gawky with adolescence, her breasts no more than nubs, but he expected that within months she'd have half the city aching to get into her trousers.

"Did you have a good trip, Abba?" Hilm asked. "You look tired."

"It was fine. We had a proper catch of pinkies on the way back. I'll ask Chang to string some for you."

He slid his hand on her neck, under her thick curly sheaf of hair, and rubbed his thumb over the little groove at her nape. His heart skipped a beat. Should he be touching his daughter, now that he was becoming a Wan? But no, he felt no desire to murder or eat her. Old wives' tales, all of them.

They climbed up the four body lengths to the old quays. It felt like fifteen to Firdaus. The arms of the old jetty, for all their razor sharpness and ruler straightness, ran uselessly over mud flats for almost a mile. Digging the new canal from the river mouth to the sea had been his father's great feat of engineering, and sometimes Firdaus suspected he'd become Stadholder floating on the city's memory of his father's work. It must have been a sight for years on end, getting the black and orange mud out, bucket for bucket. The mounds of dried mud still lined the canal, crouching on the banks like striped beasts out of legend.

A drum roll of footsteps and a quivering of the old connecting bridge announced the arrival of many people.

Who would be visiting the docks in such numbers on the brink of the noon hour? Half the Assembly, apparently, and his sister.

His milkbrother Ali walked up first, holding a steaming towel. "You look a little sweaty, Sire. Let me wipe your face for you."

A terrible suspicion gripped Firdaus. Had Ali seen him, the other day, putting on his makeup?

Firdaus ducked. He grabbed Ali's hand to keep the propheting towel away from his face, but although he was a head taller and always had been the stronger, his arm flexed like putty. The illness was making him weak and slow. The hot, lemony-smelling towel landed on his face and Ali gave it a thorough swipe over his forehead and nose before Firdaus managed to push him off.

A collective gasp went through the gathering. Meena Midwife reeled back from him, hands up as if warding evil. Ali stepped away. Aranaz looked on, a tight cold grimace around her lips. Hilm stood like a statue, her eyes showing white around the brown.

It felt as if everyone could see straight through his cloak and his paint, right to the whiteness of his very bones. The horror on their faces! His lips turned into wood, imprisoning his words.

"Dear Brother," Aranaz said loudly, swiveling on her heels to catch the eyes of the Assembly members. "What terrible thing has happened to you?"

Firdaus' eyes rolled back in his head in a futile attempt to assess the damage. The towel had fallen on the paving in front of him, streaked dark brown. His face probably looked as bad as he thought it did. His throat felt as dry as a ball of cotton fluff. They'd caught him out. Now, of all times. In front of his own daughter, right smack in front of the whole propheting Assembly.

He refused to answer Aranaz and damn himself. How could Ali have done this, the man he'd trusted more than anyone in the world? Firdaus knew he should step up, take control of the situation, but his throat closed up like a fist and refused to let him speak.

"I'm very much afraid, honorable Assembly members," Aranaz went on, pulling her face into dignified regret, "that the worst possible fate has befallen our Stadholder." She bowed her head. "Our city is without a ruler."

The Assembly members, Firdaus was glad to see, were too dumbstruck to think through the political implications. Ali wasn't stunned, however. It wasn't his place to speak, not even in an Assembly session this informal, but he stood and lifted Aranaz' hand over her head. "The city has you, my lady."

Firdaus flinched.

"Abba!" Hilm screamed.

Ali grabbed her by the arms and prevented her from running up to Firdaus.

The first murmurs of assent started, punctuated by Hilm's sobs. The Assembly members drew away from him like a receding tide and eddied in a confused clot around his sister. Aranaz stood unmoving in the doorway, spine ramrod straight, forcing her face into a moue of sadness, but Firdaus knew it was all false.

"Sheriffs. Kill him," she said.

Hilm's wail cut the air like an obsidian blade.

The Assembly members avoided his gaze. Farmer Grebe murmured a shy goodbye, but First Rice Merchant elbowed him in the side. "Don't talk to it. A Wan will eat your wife and children if you look in its eyes."

That hurt. From Your Majesty to It in sixty counts. He swallowed away his distress. He tried to catch Hilm's gaze, but she was sobbing on Ali's chest.

The Sheriffs, who'd stood silently behind Aranaz, now slammed down their spears, hemming him in with six shafts interlocking like a star. What did they think they were going to do? It was hard to believe these fierce boys would actually prick their spears into him. He'd known them from the cradle, handpicked them from the ulama courts or the hunting parties, and now they refused to meet his gaze.

The ulama court. Quan had a fabulous long throw— but he always, always flinched when the bat came close.

Firdaus dove forward, wrenching the spear up into Quan's face. The boy lost his nerve; his grip on the spear loosened and Firdaus dove through the gap.

He landed hard on his shoulder and only the sharp edge of fear racing through him enabled him to stand up and run. The Assembly scattered before him like hens and he stumbled away from the docks and the guards with their spears.

"Kill him!" Aranaz screeched.

"Daddy!" Hilm cried.

A terrific blow slammed into his back and threw him against the nearest house. He rebounded and ran straight on without looking back.

Betrayed, uncovered, revealed as a monster in the eyes of his child, in the eyes of people he counted as friends.

He couldn't have expected to hide his disease over the long run, but to be renounced by his own sister and his own milkbrother... He and Aranaz had never been playmates, and he could understand her jealousy about him being picked to be Stadholder over her, but Ali! They'd been inseparable as ducklings from the same nest, going everywhere together, drinking from the same breast, sleeping in the same bed for the first twelve years of their life. How could Ali?

Firdaus' own breath was the loudest thing to be heard as he ran through the empty streets.

The few citizens around at this hottest hour of the day gaped at him. He crossed King's Plaza, and careened into the deserted Dark Quarter, through Nightlight Street to the old gate. His wooden soles clanked on the dusty white soil of the streets. He was amazed at his own strength and speed. Could he be outrunning the guards?

The disused North Gate came into view. He yanked at the rope loop holding the thick bamboo doors shut, stumbled and fell six feet down into the mud. He crawled back to his knees, the breath knocked out of him. In spite of that, he felt fit and strong and ready to run another mile. He looked back at the open gate. None of his pursuers had arrived yet, but it wouldn't take a military mastermind to guess where he'd go. He had to keep moving.

He took his first step into the gluey sludge, away from everyone he had ever known or loved, away from White City.

CHAPTER 4

Someone nibbled at Firdaus' finger. Hmmm, Kem? He pried open one gummy eye and blinked hard to clear the ochre gunk from it. A broken spring pricked his back, and the nibbling was a little bit too insistent. As if Kem was taking actual bites from his fingertip, which was taking love too far. He jerked the hand towards him and levered himself up. With a wet, sucking sound his face came unstuck from the gloppy pillow he was lying on. No pillow. No bed. Just mud and reeds and the hot white sky glaring down at him.

The nibbling continued. He wiped his eyes with the heel of his hand and now he could see from the other eye as well. A whitefish had attached itself to his finger and blithely continued to eat. The peculiar thing was that it smelled amazing. Whitefish was food for the poor, to be consumed only in direst need, because of its bland texture and unappetizing smell. It was better used in cheap paper or to stiffen textiles. But today it smelled like warm, toasty bread with a hint of caraway, perhaps a trifle salty and sprinkled with oil? Yum!

He took a bite of its tail and a complex sensation filled his mouth, spreading across his tongue and shooting up to his brain. Countless days and years had flickered across the whitefish's uneventful life down here in the mud, its days spent eating and eating and wishing for more food. Firdaus blinked and stared at the tailless creature. For a moment there, he'd imagined he was the whitefish. He couldn't resist taking another bite.

The world felt huge and impenetrable, yet cool and clean as he sliced through the water. The cloudsky frowned down at him, too close, his skin stretched out and floppy. The mud tasted red and orange, but he preferred the blueness of the water flavor. Firdaus shook himself like a dog, to get his brain and his muscles working again. His body resettled around him like a comfy old cloak and he blew out a relieved breath. What a strange experience. He'd never felt like an ox haunch or a rice kernel after eating one of those. How was the whitefish different? He inspected the trace of slime the thing had left on his palm

Sadly, before Firdaus sent it to whitefish heaven, the creature had devoured the tip of his left middle finger. It didn't bleed or hurt, it was more like the phantom pain he felt when his children hurt themselves.

He pinched himself. He was wasting precious thinking time by staring at his peculiar new finger. Life had moved so fast, his thoughts hadn't caught up to it yet. His worst fears had come to pass. He was no longer Stadholder of White City. How had that happened? Ali must have suspected something. He must have told Aranaz, and together... Tears welled up in his eyes and he swatted them away. He refused to cry over those traitors.

In some ways, it was even a relief to be free of the burdens of ruling the city, although being a Wan loomed huge and troubling. He would never chair an assembly again. The crowds would never cheer him at the Spring Festival or the Blessing of the Rice. What would the rest of his life be like?

He rubbed aching eyes.

A small turn of his neck away, the city perched on its hill, pale and proud and full of people he loved. As easy as it might seem right now to let his Stadholderdom slip away, he couldn't let go of his children. One never stopped being a father, not even facedown in stinky mud. Who would look after them now? Their mothers? Yes, if they could. If Aranaz wanted to kill his children, she would, and nothing he could do about it. He didn't think she would, though. A barren woman needed children to solidify her position, and the most likely scenario was that she'd adopt them, pretend they were hers.

He propped himself up on his elbow. He had to be reunited with his children. Live with them again. He needed to hold their wriggly little bodies, see them take their first steps, start running and talking. He needed to see Hilm become a mother, he ached to hold Boon's hand when he died and to teach the little ones their marks. But how? He was a white freak, a thing strange and fearsome enough to give his children nightmares. He slapped his hand in the orange mud and succeeded in splashing a drop in his eye. Great.

The white creature that had doomed him had sprung its trap in the caves near the city, which meant there were Wan nearby. He wished he'd seen his executioner's face. He'd like to throttle the life out of it to pay it for ruining his life. It was a monstrous thought. He was a monster now. He would crawl away and hide his ugly white face from humanity. Maybe instead of keeping away from the monsters, he should join them.

Firdaus turned his face away from the city that shimmered white and desirable on the edges of his vision. No more thoughts of what he had lost. He shaded his eyes and stared north. There. The Maze. That's where he had to go. To find the underground halls of the Wan and become one of them. Regroup before he returned to his children.

From where he was standing, all the way back to the city, the gullies and channels of the great river delta showed muddy bottoms, the water not deep enough for the rafts and flatboats. He spotted a small speck on the dike road above him, trundling his way. The speck resolved into an ox-drawn cart and a human figure leading it.

Firdaus dove down on his face among the reeds and water lilies and speckled soap weed. Again. He'd be invisible, muddy as he was. The cart passed him by with a creaking of bone wheels, ox-sniffles and farts, the low chant of the ox girl charming her animals into walking. Slap slap went her feet. Maybe he could get his children out like that. Hilm could play the ox-girl, Boon would lie on the cart; the older ones would keep the young ones silent. Firdaus mentally struck the youngest children off the list. Hanako would never let them go, and the baby was still breastfed. That still left nine children. How would he feed them?

He peeked up to see if the coast was clear. Mud splashed near his face. A paradile? He rolled over and up on his feet in seconds. A white-faced woman swaddled in a big cloak stood at the foot of the dike, looking miraculously clean and cool for someone standing in the silty mire. A Wan woman.

Firdaus opened his mouth to scream, but no sound came out. His heart raced in his chest and he rubbed his aching ribs. He must have strained a muscle with that aborted scream. This was ridiculous. He was a Wan himself now. She might be an envoy from the mighty Wan Queen.

The woman pushed her cloak off her head and shoulders. The cloudlight glinted on her smooth bone-white hair. She opened her mouth, no fangs, and said something else, but Firdaus couldn't comprehend the words.

She talked? Firdaus closed his eyes. Stupid. Now that he was a Wan himself, of course they knew him and of course they talked. He opened his eyes again and took in the woman. Her face was odd in a way he couldn't quite pinpoint, but nothing like the terrible creature he'd seen on the hunt, or the horned women of legend. Her hair was straight, her figure tall but slight. She must have been Wanned quite young, he assumed, with her un-creased face and a body with none of the signs of motherhood. A bright blue cloth hugged her trim hips and he couldn't help imagining taking it off her and having bedsports with her. She smelled good, too. Very good. Nothing like the toadstool reek of the monster in the cave.

The woman waited, looking down on him from a clump of reeds. She crossed her arms and lifted her eyebrows.

"How have you been, Stadholder?"

She knew him? Being known by his enemies was like a

cold bucket of water in the face. He felt naked, vulnerable, knowing nothing about them in return.

He hid his fears behind the useful mask of politeness. "Thank you. I am as well as can be expected. Who are you, my child? Were you one of my loyal subjects when this happened to you?"

The broad smile that formed on her face wasn't reassuring.

"Very royal," she snorted. "Don't bother, though. I know who you are, but I'm not one of your subjects. I might be your ally."

She talked like a wise old Guild mother, in spite of her youthful looks. It was curiously attractive, and Firdaus took a step closer to her.

"Ally?" Firdaus said. "Do you rule the Wan? And ally to what cause? Will you aid me in regaining my city?"

The woman recrossed her arms and shifted to the other hip. "Yes, and no."

She was nuts. He'd just said it to get a rise out of her. He'd never rule White City again. Would he?

Firdaus approached another step. She was very annoying, but the combination of feistiness and her smell aroused him even more. He imagined taking that cream-tipped little breast in his mouth and... no, no, not biting it off. Of course not. Maybe he shouldn't have eaten that whitefish. He didn't just look strange; he was thinking uncomfortable new thoughts. He wanted to remain himself, the person who'd never ever bite someone in anger.

The woman held up her hand. "Don't come any closer. I know exactly what you're feeling, but you're going to have to contain yourself. I'm not your breakfast."

Firdaus drew himself up. "I have no idea what you're talking about. But you're a personable..."

"Not that either. Let's start again, huh? I say, Good morning, Stadholder Firdaus, my name is Ing. And then you say, Good morning, Ing, how pleasant to meet you."

"Good morning, Ing." Firdaus paused. "What's your mother's name?"

Ing shrugged. "I don't remember."

How was that possible? "I'm Firdaus Eyvindurson. What have people been calling you all your life? Were you a foundling?"

Ing waved a narrow white hand. "With my people, we used our father's name to identify ourselves. My full name is Giok Siu Ing."

He'd never heard of people using their fathers' names. How could they be sure who their father was? "Which part of that is your father's name, then?"

"Giok."

"So you'd be Ing Gioksdottir. What guild do you belong to?"

She grinned that disconcerting grin again. "When I was young, we had a guild called Mycologists. I belonged to that."

"How old are you then? You talk old, but you look young."

"We Wan don't age, Firdaus. As you will find out in due time. I'm hundreds of years old."

Amazing. She didn't look it. "So you remember my father and grandmother when they were Stadholders?"

"I do. And further back, too. I remember a time when there weren't Stadholders."

She laid a hand on his arm and Firdaus reeled, dizzy from the wonderful smell. Like the whitefish, only magnified a hundred times.

"I want..." he started, unable to find words for his desire.

"Shut up and lie down. There's another cart. We've been standing around here too long. Get down in that gully there."

She dragged him into another, deeper gully, one ridge of reed-topped islands further away from the causeway.

"We need to get away from the city, but we can't travel now. There's too much traffic on the road, and people who're looking our way could spot us easily."

"You must take me to the strongholds of the Wan," Firdaus said. "I need to gather an army and retake the city."

"If you want my help, you have to listen to me and do as I say. You don't know enough about us to gain the trust of the other Wan. I'll teach you what you need to know. Now get your head down."

***

When the Stentor called the cloudwane-hour from the Singing Tower, Ing shook Firdaus awake. He opened suspiciously alert eyes at once. Had he been feigning sleep for some reason? Evading her conversation? She'd never been great at small talk. She'd been sent to soft skills courses almost every year back home, but relating to people had never quite sunk in. She wasn't a mycologist for nothing. Members of the Fungi Kingdom never talked back or complained about lack of attention.

She plodded in the direction of the road, careful to step from clump to clump. The twilight drained the color from the yellowish haram species and the green halal ones alike. Sometimes Ing wished she'd spent less of her former life looking down at fungi, molds, and slimes, and had looked up a little more often at the blue sky of her home world. She missed color. Sometimes she'd break a root or plant open, just for the flash of bright orange from a carrot, or magenta from a beet, because she couldn't eat non-native foods anymore. The vegetable dyes the people here used looked dull to her eyes, and even the remnants of color the settlers had left had dimmed over the centuries. If she could create a bright dye, she would have made a fortune. But she had no time for schemes like that, she had a world to save.

"Where are we going?" he asked.

"To the Queen Mound. It's time to introduce you to the biggest Ghast you've ever seen."

"A Ghast! I don't want to have anything to with them. I want to find the other Wan."

Ing looked back, but Firdaus hadn't budged from his muddy resting place.

"Come, lazybones. I plan on making good time to-night."

"Why would I trust you?"

"Follow me and you'll learn things that might be to your advantage. Come on. You don't want to fall in Aranaz' hands again, do you?"

"I never thought I'd leave my children," Firdaus said. He heaved his filthy bulk out of the mud, releasing a puff of peaty stench, and trod onto a cord grass clump. "Ow! Those reeds are sharp."

"Cord grasses, not reeds. And they can't hurt you anymore. The memory of pain will go away eventually, because it's not real. Nothing like that can hurt us."

Firdaus followed, muttering, stumbling, losing his balance. Great clunky oaf. He should do something about his center of gravity. Gain mass in the lower body. Given his newness, he seemed to be doing quite well with the cravings he must be feeling.

"Mistress Gioksdottir," he started, "I've been trying to reckon under whose reign you were born. Three hundred years would be Stadholder Anastasia?"

"Call me Ing, please. No, not Anastasia. I was already old when she was Stadholder. I actually don't know how old I am. When I was made into a Wan, something happened to me that made me lose a large part of my memory. The Wanning destroyed my memory storage implants, and I had a lot of stuff stored there. I might be four hundred years old. But I'd like to know more precisely. Can you name all the Stadholders and tell me exactly how long they reigned?"

Firdaus wide shoulders shrugged. "I can recite all the reigns, but we always assume Stadholders reign a score of years."

Ing sighed. "That's not very accurate. I wish I hadn't lost all my records. Twice they all broke; and before that, I tried it with reed paper, but it rotted."

"What did you expect here in the swamp?" Firdaus said. "We only make that for trade."

Once they were on the road, the walking went faster, and Firdaus set a hefty pace with his long legs. Ing shrugged mentally and walked at the pace she found most comfortable. Firdaus wasn't going to go anywhere without her.

"How's the yearning, Stadholder?"

"Thanks for reminding me," he growled. "I'll keep away from you."

"I promise you will have plenty of opportunities to exchange mass at the Queen Mound."

"Is that the city of the Ghast?"

"No city, Firdaus. Ghast have no cities."

"Hm."

Ing halted. The road continued on here as a reed and willow-bough walkway, and by her calculations, they should have arrived at the first ring of rice paddies already. She saw no neat fields dotted with fresh green shoots, or huts, or any other sign of human habitation. "Did we pass the fields without noticing?"

"No," Firdaus said. "We had to give up the closest paddies a long time ago, maybe ten years or so. Have you been away from the city?"

"No. I haven't been out of the city in twenty or thirty years. I get caught up in my research."

Firdaus grunted. Ing couldn't stop herself from going on. "I've been cataloguing this world's plant species for hundreds of years now. Did you know that the rushes that cool your floor in summer are actually twenty different species of rush? We only brought the one saline-tolerant species, but in the past three hundred year they've mutated into all those varieties. How about that!"

"Fascinating," Firdaus said.

"Sorry," Ing said. "Not your thing, plants."

What had gotten into her? The man was a potential ally, a tool, not a hot date.

"Why are you helping me? Is that a sideline from the plant thing?"

"In a way. I think–" Ing halted. She'd never formulated her goals in simple terms before. "Humanity is having a hard time on this world. Birth rates are dropping. I want to save you. Us. I think humanity is destined to live on as Wan."

"Now you've confused me," Firdaus said. "You want to

save us by exterminating us?"

"Well, if you put it that way. But I believe that Wan are still human. I'm a Wan, you're a Wan. Has it changed you?"

"Now that I'm not so sick anymore, it feels as if it hasn't changed me that much," Firdaus said. "Yet." He looked her up and down. "I don't know about you. You're very strange. You don't look like anybody I know, and you talk about strange things in a strange way. And why are you meddling with us? Why don't you go back to your own island and meddle with your kinsmen?"

Ing's eyebrows rose. "I can't go back. We dismantled the ship, and we stacked the Landers in the middle of the city we made! How could I go back?"

"Ing, with all respect, the things you say don't match. The words you use mean nothing. Are you talking about the palace? And you made the city?"

"Me and the rest of the crew."

Ing pointed to the sky above. "You know what the sun is, right?"

"I've never seen it, but people say it shines behind the clouds."

"Exactly. And this we stand on,"—she stamped hard on the wobbly walkway and her foot crashed through the rotting reed-bundles—"is a planet, circling around the sun. We came from another sun, with another planet circling it."

She checked out Firdaus' face. His forehead was furrowed, but he didn't look bored. "You with me so far?"

"I don't know. So the Wan arrived here from another 'pannet?'"

Ing barely prevented herself from stamping through the walkway again. "No! Not the Wan! The people! Humanity!"

Firdaus stared back, refusing to get it. Why was she even bothering to inform this primitive? He only lived in a city because his forefathers had been kind enough to build one for him, not because of hard work or technological prowess.

She walked on. Barbarians. No, that was unfair. No one, however intelligent, could understand these concepts cold from the farmyard. They had taken humanity centuries, if not millennia, to develop. She'd have to find a better way to tell him.

"Ing!" Firdaus called out. "You wanted to stop at the rice paddies? Here they are."

Ing blew out a frustrated breath and forced herself to walk back and look where Firdaus pointed. A small, makeshift floating jetty almost hidden under tall stands of flowering reeds lay alongside the walkway, tied to a surprisingly robust willow. Ing had long assumed it was too brackish here for willows. They must have adapted.

"What did you want at Far Fields?"

Ing rolled her eyes. "Steal a boat, what else? We can hardly walk to Queen Mound."

"If you say so. But we can't just steal a boat. That's criminal."

"Who cares?"

"I care!" Firdaus exploded. "Do you know how often I have to mediate disputes about property? Neighbors stealing clothing, and food, and boats from each other? That's robbery. People could die without a boat to get fresh water and trade rice and catch fish."

"It's for our mission. Which is important. Who cares about one fisherman if we can save humanity?"

"You're a madwoman who says she wants to save humanity. What does the fisherman care? What do I care?"

"You want your children to live? You better listen to me."

That shut him up.

***

Firdaus waded through the waist-deep channel that separated the walkway from the paddies. His feet cringed every time he sank down in the squishy, unpleasantly organic mud at the bottom. He knew too well what kind of organic matter kept the Maze green. And besides, the water was infested with paradiles. Nobody wanted to meet a paradile. What was he doing, following this crazy woman with her crazy talk about suns and Ghast and mounds? Visiting the Ghast sounded even worse than consorting with Wan. Meeting one kind of creepy man-eating creature, not to mention becoming one, was enough weirdness for an entire lifetime.

He unhooked his eating knife from his belt and held it poised over the half-rotted nettle twine that tied the little boat to the sagging dock. Ing had pointed out that no one had been using it in a long time, what with the water in the bottom, but those were flimsy justifications for stealing. Could he cut through this cord and sever himself not only from the physical White City, but from all it stood for? The obsidian blade trembled from indecision.

Yes. He must.

The cord parted with a sigh and Firdaus tried to roll aboard the boat from his crouched position in the channel. The boat rocked and he fell back with a loud splash. Ing hissed at him and the temptation to hiss back and throw something at her was huge. He'd known her for a few hours and already she brought out the worst in him.

He crawled onto the prickly grasses bordering the shallow channel and pulled the pirogue towards him. Balancing madly on the narrow benches, because one foot on the fragile reed bottom would cause a leak, he cast off and paddled, weaving and lurching towards Ing. She stepped aboard without a word or a wobble and folded herself on the narrow bench in front of him. She plied the paddle and the craft picked up speed.

"You do that well," Firdaus said.

"Hundreds of years of practice," she answered.

There she went again. She rubbed his nose in her otherness every second sentence. Why did she do that, if she wanted him as an ally? Never mind. He'd win her over yet.

"Tell me how you do it."

She sighed. "I know how to do it, not how to talk about it." But after a grudging silence, she did start talking. "Listen to the boat's rhythm. If you put the paddle in cross-wise when she's still surging, you'll effectively brake her. Watch me do it and learn how to feel it. Paddle in as silently as you can, because that means the least water resistance."

He couldn't see where he was going. The scenery of flat sheets of water and clumps of reeds or grasses, dotted now and then by struggling trees, remained unchanged. The night sky above them shone cloud gray, giving an illusion of light but no real illumination.

Ing talked on. Once you asked her about something, and kept your mouth shut, everything she knew about the subject ran out without stopping. Firdaus let her voice lull him into a light trance underscored by their rhythmic movements.

Now that he was freed of his fear of paradile mouths, Ing's scent consumed his attention. Every movement of her arms wafted a snatch of smell towards him, nothing like the sweaty odor from his friends and family. Kem and he could work up rivers of sweat and lubrication in their bouts of sport, but that smelled of salt and fish and semen. Ing smelled of cinnamon one moment, the next of cardamom or fresh bread, all sweet spicy scents, food scents, mouth-watering scents.

Firdaus now knew what made Wan different.

Because what he wanted to do to Ing wasn't fuck her, but eat her.

CHAPTER 5

The new morning upended a bucket of light over the marsh. It tinted the permanent haze rose and salmon, a ghostly school of pinkies floating over the green plumes and topaz rosettes of the vegetation. The horizontal rays skipped over the water and blinded Firdaus. He turned his eyes westwards, away from the light and from Ing. The lower-lying sheets of water still reflected blackness.

"Are we going to hide now?" he asked.

"No, why?"

"I thought we were traveling by night to avoid being seen."

Ing sighed a little cranky sigh. "We were. But now we're far enough from the city not to fear discovery."

"People could still send notice to the city."

"Sure they could! And then when it finally arrived there, days from now, who would take action and send out a search party?"

She was right. The Sheriffs had jurisdiction in the city, but they seldom went out into the swamp. Once, when Firdaus was about eleven, a crazed wife murderer had fled out into the Maze, but he wasn't pursued. Everybody figured he'd be eaten by a paradile. Maybe the man was still alive, turned into a Wan?

A chill ran down his back at the idea of being presumed dead. He felt naked, as if until now Aranaz' gaze had been pressing against his spine and keeping him upright. This wasn't an adventure that was going to end with soapy baths and kisses like after a boyhood prank. This was going to last forever.

The thought jolted him. How forever?

"Will I live as long as you, Ing?" he asked.

"Probably. No old age or disease is going to kill you now. Nothing seems to kill the Wan, except other Wan, or Ghast."

If he would live forever, what would he do with his life? He could picture being a grandfather, wise and old and spoiling his great-great-grandchildren, but after that? He'd never met anyone that old, except Ing, but she didn't count. She wasn't old, just odd.

And before the advent of great-grandchildren, first he needed to raise his children. Who he might never see again. He should not be sidetracked by this woman. Securing the health and happiness of his children was his goal.

A spiral of smoke escaped from the low-hanging fog blanket.

"There," he pointed. "That must be New Rice Fields."

"Good. Let's head over there," Ing said.

"We're not going to stop by, are we? These people will know we're Wan. We'd be stoned, they'd send for the Sheriffs..."

"We need a servant. Extra hands when crossing the river."

"So the lair of the Wan is across the river?" he asked.

Ing didn't answer. He wasn't surprised.

"If we're so strong, why can't we paddle ourselves? What is the servant really for? An offering to the Queen?"

Ing shrugged. "We can use someone to wash our clothes and make our fire."

The idea of clean clothes appealed, as well as someone else paddling the pirogue. He could travel in some style, to impress the Queen of the Ghast with a suitable retinue. He gritted his teeth and gave in. For now.

"Will they welcome us?" he asked. "Us being Wan and all?"

"Now you think of that?" Ing said. He already knew her well enough to imagine the sneer she wore on her face right now. "I think they will. They will have encountered Wan before, and perhaps realized we're not always dangerous."

They paddled on quietly. The fronds of the papyrus stands surrounding the village spread out like lacy parasols, and a low murmur of people talking and fire crackling emerged, quite distinct from the chirping insects and lapping water that hummed the background song of the swamp.

"You greet them," Ing said. "You know how to do that without alarming them."

At least she knew how weird she was.

They halted to don their mud-stiff, crinkle-dried cloaks and then paddled on to the gap in the papyrus border that was both harbor and dock in these poor hinterlands. Pink orchids nodded on slender stems between the papyrus umbrellas. The village consisted of little islands with irregular circles of reed huts, most of them wall-less, surrounding a big woven structure crowned with curly sheep horns. The mulberry trees and sallows that ringed the place were only man high, indicating that it was a recent settlement. Flies and nettles, as well as his nose, told Firdaus to skirt the midden and take the right fork to the village center. Some inhabitants lay curled up like seed-pods in their hammocks; others poked sleepily at dung fires.

He coughed and waited until the old crone tending the fire deigned to notice him. Empty dugs dangled on her chest, her arms and thighs wattled with crepey skin. Her eyes widened at the sight of them. One stringy arm sent the younger fire-tenders scurrying away.

The woman got up with the help of her crooked willow stick and waddled over to him.

"Good morning to you, traveler! What brings you to New Fields?" She lisped the sentence into mush.

"Good morning, my good woman. We are traveling to, the, um, to cross the river. We need an extra pair of hands on the paddle. Could you provide us with a sturdy servant?"

"Not too sturdy, Firdaus," Ing murmured against his back. Her breath tickled his back and gave him a frisson of pleasure. "We don't want him to be stronger than the two of us."

He couldn't answer her with the woman in front of him, but he had little fear of being able to buy a good strong servant. Those they'd keep for themselves, for the rice planting and harvesting and the thousand other physical tasks of village life.

The woman folded her arms over her sagging belly and pursed her lips. "Well. That's a question we don't get asked a lot. Well. Sit down and have a cup of tea. Least we can do. I'll ask my husband if he has any ideas about selling servants. Well, well. You been traveling by night, then?"

She gestured to a stack of moldy bark mats close to the fire and shuffled off to one of the huts with its side shutters down, presumably to find the husband.

Firdaus handed Ing one of the mats and sat down himself. His thighs and back protested a bit after the long night of paddling, but he wasn't a fraction as sore as he might have expected.

A stick-thin young girl came over and handed them clay cups with lukewarm tea. The taste was so astringent his throat refused to swallow it down.

"Only pretend to drink!" Ing whispered. "We can't drink anything but pure water."

"Why? Don't Wan need food to live?"

"We do, but not like them. You have no digestive system anymore, Firdaus. Any opening in your skin will do."

***

Her mother-in-law poked her with her walking stick. Frog pretended to wake and sat up.

Gannet loomed over her, rotting breath pumping out of her nearly toothless mouth. "Get up, girl. Now. Look lively."

The hour was just after cloud dawn, normally Frog's favorite time of day, when everything looked new, and the shadows were long and sharp. Anything could still happen in the morning. But being locked away in the close dark hut, reeking of generations of monthly flow, made her logy. The woven walls distorted the light, so she never knew quite what time of day it was.

What did Gannet want? Were they going to sacrifice her to the Ancestors, as they had threatened? Kill her, cast her out? She might almost welcome any change, after weeks in the hut, with nothing to do, listless from lack of food.

She stumbled out into the village square. Not many people were up and about yet. She heard whispers from the family bowers she passed, but she held her head down and ignored them. Gannet prodded her to stand before two tall, cloaked strangers. Her parents, come to tell her she was a long-lost Stadholder scion?

Her breath hiccupped when she saw their white faces, and their great white feet protruding from their fancy clothes. Dead people. Ancestors? No. Just Wan. She'd never seen them herself, but she knew of them.

Gannet offered her to them, as a slave for sale. Maybe Frog would leap up and kill her right now. They had never paid a wooden groat for her, she'd just found them on her own, and now they were selling her as if she was their slave? It wasn't fair.

The white man came up to her and touched her eyes and mouth. He smelled a little funny, spice from his cloak and haram herbs from his breath, but his fingers almost made her cry; they were so sweet and sure and soft. Nobody had touched her in weeks. Nobody had ever touched her as kindly as that.

She snuck a look at his face. His brow was creased and his full lips pressed shut while he checked her for disease or weakness. It was a stern, noble face, but he had these nice smiley wrinkles near his eyes. A man's face, only bleached like rice flour. She wanted to feel if his curly white hair felt as soft as it looked. Did she want them to buy her? Oh yes. Already she knew being his slave would be better than clinging to the fringes of village life.

She pretended not to hear the bartering, but they were offering two woods and the most beautiful piece of cloth she'd ever seen, a narrow strip of rainbow hues and fabulous shine. The villagers made their own cloth from tapa bark, but they didn't know how to dye beautiful colors like this. She was worth that much?

She pushed out her breasts a little to see if the white man noticed them, and yes, he did.

The other white person was a woman with mean eyes and a harsh voice. "Frog, go get your paddles!" she said and Frog waited a moment before obeying.

She'd wanted the white man to be the leader, but he released her after the white woman's command. She scuttled to the hut and gathered her meager possessions. Mussel knife, leather cup, her digger, the old bedmat they'd given her, while taking her own beautiful new one, tinderbox... It was gone. Someone had sneaked in and stolen it while she was being sold. Maybe she should feel lucky to have anything left. If she ever returned to this village, she was going to take their babies away. They deserved it.

***

Ing rubbed her eyes. The smoky fires and the stench all around her gave her a headache. How did pampered palace boy stand it? Those people stank. Their midden stank, their flesh, their food, their fire. They were drenched in offal and they didn't even care! This was why she hadn't left the city in so long. It might be peopled by primitives who barely managed to stay afloat at subsistence level, but at least it had waste removal, and the people in the city washed themselves and their clothes.

It made sense to gather excrement for fertilizer. They needed something to feed the halal plants, which would die if they had to subsist on this alien soil, but did the villagers have to put the fucking midden in the fucking middle of the village square? Her feet sank into the squishy ground, pushing up brown water. All earthlike organic matter smelled the same to her these days.

And look at these people. Half-rotted bark aprons, chewing with their mouths open, someone in the hut behind her making love, where everybody could hear it!

Not to mention the girl they were trying to sell to Firdaus. She must be the village black sheep, being cast out for some stupid taboo she'd broken. Or whatever. Maybe she'd been sleeping with the headman and his wife didn't like it. Not that she cared what kind of character the wretch had. Ing only needed her for a short time.

Firdaus grabbed the girl around the waist. Frog endured it stolidly. Her dirty brown skin glowed compared to Firdaus' matte white hide. It hadn't acquired the satiny luster of a mature Wan yet.

Firdaus was ogling the girl's breasts as if they were ripe fruit he was going to devour. He hadn't gotten it into his thick head yet that Wan and humans didn't match that way anymore. He'd find out soon enough.

"Come," Ing said, when Firdaus seemed lost in the contemplation of the nubile flesh under his hands. "We have a ways to travel yet. Frog, where is the paddle we were promised?"

The girl scuttled off to one of the reed-screened huts and returned with a sturdy paddle and a hastily rolled bundle of bark cloth and cord.

Ing wrote herself a mental memo to set the girl to rope making at the next camp. That would come in useful. Ing had left the city as she was, not even taking the time to outfit herself for travel. No clay jars and wooden presses for specimens. She told herself it didn't matter. This journey was devoted to training Firdaus.

***

Firdaus maneuvered the girl Frog between himself and Ing as they boarded the pirogue. Her narrow brown back was the perfect barrier to hide Ing from view and her strong sweaty scent hid Ing's spice cake allure. He enjoyed seeing the slight movements of Frog's haunches while she plied her oar. As promised, Frog was a strong paddler. At least, she was at first. After a few hours of rowing, which hardly dented his own energy, she started to flag and he could hear her stomach rumble from where he sat. Ing gave no indication of stopping, but he could feel the current tug at his paddle. Frog would need a rest before they attempted the river.

The marsh's patchwork of dappled green and yellow shifted slowly. It lost most of the green, the halal foods

Firdaus had once identified as edible, and transformed into a tapestry of chartreuse and pale gray leaves, with the asymmetrical shapes of all haram plants.

"Ing, what will Frog eat?" he called out.

"There'll still be fish and frogs tonight," she said. "She must catch and smoke extra for the next days."

Frog flicked him a glance from her large dark eyes, lashes waving gracefully shut when she caught his answering gaze. Firdaus decided he would have sport with her tonight.

When the cloudlight started to lengthen from the west, tingeing the sky with sad beery smears, Ing abruptly halted her paddling. Frog's paddle crashed into Ing's, and Firdaus' knees came into pleasant contact with Frog's warm springy backside.

"We're stopping here!" Ing announced.

"What for? There's still an hour of light," Firdaus said.

"I've spotted some rare plants. I have to identify them."

Ing scrabbled off board, rocking the pirogue so hard that water sloshed over the gunwales. She bent to the ground and disappeared, mumbling, behind a stand of translucent mauve vegetable swords. Firdaus pricked his paddle into a clump of ocher, fleshy-leaved plants and hauled the boat closer to shore. He held the boat steady.

"After you, Frog," he said.

She giggled.

He was in for tonight, he figured.

Frog waited, head bowed, for his orders. Her submissiveness stirred Firdaus loins, but he didn't want to conduct his sport under Ing's disapproving eyes.

"You may go and gather yourself some food."

Frog trembled in confusion. "But, sir, don't you and the lady need food?"

"We don't. Go on."

Frog unearthed a sharpened coney shoulderblade from her pack and scurried to the waterside. With the little tool, she dug up white and purple speckled roots, and a few pale green ones. Orchid and sweet flag. Firdaus remembered their taste, sweet and chewy, delicious when stewed with fish, but today they just seemed plants, not food.

Frog saw his look and immediately surrendered her harvest. Firdaus sniffed the roots, but his body didn't signal that he wanted them.

"They're yours," he said.

She peeped at him from under her thick lashes as she gnawed at the raw, tough root. "Can I make a fire to roast them?" she asked.

Bold little lass! If he fed her for a few days and cleaned her up, she'd be a regular charmer.

"Fetch dry plants for the fire, and afterwards you can wash our clothes."

Frog pouted but set to work diligently enough. She built a small, furiously smoky fire and set water to boil in her leather kettle. Firdaus offered his loincloth and cloak for her to wash.

She fluttered her eyes as he removed it and clapped her hand before her mouth. "You have no hair down there!"

Firdaus gaped. It must have fallen out sometime during their trek through the marsh. How easily he had accepted never needing to void! He touched his head to reassure himself that his hair was still there. It hadn't fallen out, although he could tell it was muddy and matted. He was so used to the old mirrors in the palace to signal his need for washing and combing that he'd forgotten about his appearance. All right, he'd take a bath as well.

"Ing, are there paradiles here?"

Ing lurched out of the bushes and trampled across the designated campsite, sniffing a couple of orange bulbs, eyes to the ground. "Of course there are," she said. "Catch one if you can, will you? You're probably starving." From her pack all kinds of haram fronds and stems dangled. Whatever did she need them for?

Firdaus swallowed. The closest he'd ever seen a paradile was forty feet away, on a hunting party with his father. The paradile had taken a whole leg off one of the rowers before mysteriously disappearing.

"Sure," he said, trying for a nonchalance he didn't feel.

He sat down on the waterside. The floating island wobbled beneath his buttocks. He wasn't sure the water was any deeper than at the edge of the marsh, but the idea that wide, patient jaws waited under the wallow of mud made him hesitate. He wouldn't have gone in, if the two women hadn't been watching him. He wanted to be fresh for Frog, too. Show her how a Stadholder made bedsport. He would have to wash off some of Frog's human stink. At first, it was intoxicating, but after a while, it got a bit much.

Okay. There he went. Firdaus slid in, expecting slippery mud between his toes, but he felt no bottom and plummeted down. Down he went, the color of the water before his astonished eyes changing from beer to ink in seconds. He kicked his feet and worked his arms to stop his sinking. What in paradise was going on? He wasn't going up. He wasn't. He kicked harder. Finally, when it seemed he'd been sinking for minutes, the flicker of light above him, mimicking the cloudy sky by night, turned brighter.

A band of fear gripped his chest. He could still make it. He wriggled and twisted around his axis, grabbing handfuls of water, hauling himself towards the light. His foot hit something solid, and he'd kicked off against it before his slow brain realized it had to be a paradile, waiting for just such an opportunity. His mouth opened in a scream of shock and rage and he felt his midriff buck as he tried to reverse his breath halfway down his lungs. He paddled his legs, harder, flailing his arms, yelling out in the water. One of his legs was strangely heavy and unwieldy. His voice sounded far away and low. He couldn't feel his leg anymore. Oh, god, it had eaten his leg!

Firdaus shot out of the water in mid-scream. His voice bubbled out into the air, accompanied by streams of water from his mouth. He struck out to the shore, shamefully a mere six feet away, and slithered onto soggy land.

"Firdaus!" Ing called. "Are you okay?"

"A paradile!" he panted. He felt nothing, though. "I'm all right. I'm fine."

"Where is your foot?" Frog asked. Her voice quivered and she stuffed her fingers into her mouth.

"What foot?"

His left leg stopped about four inches below the knee. Firdaus blinked. It wasn't true. The leg must be covered with greens or something. He slid his fingers down the leg, and was shocked anew when his fingers confirmed what his eyes saw. The leg just stopped. The edges of the flesh were rough, springy, but not wet. The stump had no blood, no pain, nothing. Firdaus sat up, and bent the leg up towards his face. It resembled a marble statue, not a human leg. There were no different textures or colors, just uniform whiteness.

Where had his bone and muscle gone?

CHAPTER 6

"Okay, I'm going to get that leg back," Ing said. "Go on, Frog, get back to your work. This is not a problem."

Ing unsheathed her knife and dove into the water like a pearl diver, straight and perfect, hardly disturbing the water.

"The lady is going to kill the paradile?" Frog asked.

Firdaus pinched himself. How could he feel so numb and calm about his propheting foot getting bit off? He tried to shock his feelings into overdrive. Look at that foot. He was never going to walk again. He was going to die here in this marsh. Ing would leave him behind, and the paradile would get the rest of him.

That Ing was a cool one.

Frog sat frozen in horror, hands working in her mouth, staring at his foot.

"Get going, girl," he said. "You heard what the lady said."

"I don't know what to do!" she wailed. "I should bind your wound. But there's no blood!"

His feelings in a clamshell. He rested his back against the spongy trunk of a giant ochre fern tree and kept his eyes on the dark water. Ing had disappeared, leaving only widening circles on the surface. Frog gave a muffled sob and went back to her washing.

Firdaus let himself be soothed by the rhythmic sounds of the wet linen getting soaked and wrung and slapped against the woody base of a stand of reed stalks. Occasionally, the rhythm paused and Frog's hand would steal to a root she'd hidden in a patch of yellow leaves to gnaw off a bite. Stealing food, that's what she thought she was doing. Firdaus didn't need food. Soon he wouldn't need anything.

With a plop, Ing's sleek pale head surfaced. With her white hair plastered to invisibility against her scalp, she resembled a faded statue, with the hard planes of flesh sloping down from her almond eyes to her pointy chin. Firdaus stared, fascinated.

"Firdaus, get off your butt and help me haul this thing on land!" Ing shouted, unfazed by the atmosphere of paralysis and despair.

Frog assumed the command to be directed at her as well and scrambled to the water's edge, which had become muddied and crumbling from repeated use. Firdaus roused himself and crawled over on his knees. The movement didn't hurt at all. His heart filled with sudden hope. Maybe it was all a bad dream. Maybe he'd wake up in his comfortable bed, surrounded on all sides by sweetly breathing children.

Ing lugged an enormous white thing to shore. It took all of Firdaus strength, and Frog's assistance, to heave it partway on land.

Ing hauled herself up on land. "Got him," she said, and stretched her arms as far as they would go. "Big nasty critter. Now we will eat, Firdaus. Eat and discover what that means."

She rolled over. At the back of her muscled thigh, a big chunk was missing. He couldn't feel the impact of the wound because of the lack of blood, no colors to emphasize the seriousness, no moaning and thrashing and panic.

"Ing. You're hurt," he said. His voice sounded small and petulant.

She shrugged. "Yeah. That's okay."

The paradile twitched. Firdaus looked closer and saw it had only half a jaw. Had Ing cut off the lower half? Clever, that. Without the lower jaw, the upper was just a big chunk of thrashing muscle and bone.

Ing climbed to her knees and started sawing on one of the legs. It broke off halfway, leaving the exact kind of wound he and Ing had, bone white, jagged edged, but not oozing or wet. Ing handed him the short, flipper-like leg, the claws roughly defined and irregular. "Eat. It'll tide you over until I get your leg out of its stomach."

It should have been revolting, but in truth, the smell rising from the wet paradile leg made Firdaus' mouth water. He averted his gaze from Frog's horrified and astounded face and bit into the white, crunchy meat. His tongue curled around it like a lover and a sensation of imminent joy seeped through his mouth. More. He chewed and bit, bit and chewed. His flesh tingled and buzzed, waves crashing against him, harder and harder until he was engulfed in a breaker that lapped away his defenses and dissolved him into a million shining particles of spume.

***

Ing watched Firdaus twitch and shiver in his first flesh dream, while she gnawed on a bit of paradile jaw herself. She was always sparing with food, because she didn't want to accrete too much mass and be unable to move around easily. But she could afford to gain some right now, what with the paradile taking a bite out of her, Firdaus to convince, and tribute to pay to the Queen Mound later.

Frog crept off and returned with a reed strung full of dead namesakes. The roasting frog flesh smelled delicious, but in a distant way, like perfume or flowers. Frog kept shooting Ing nervous glances as she ate, apparently expecting Ing to take the food away from her. Poor thing. She'd must have been abused as well as starved. Not that rice farmers ever had excess food, but the black eyes and the cringing seemed to indicate something more than that.

Ing put away the chunk of paradile, whose flesh didn't have any new sensations to offer her anyway, and scooted over to Frog.

Frog held out her half-gnawed frog leg, but Ing waved it away. Time for some anthropological questioning. Not what she was trained for, but someone had to do it.

"Frog, why did they sell you?"

Frog started crying.

"I won't punish you, Frog. You've been a good servant to us so far. Tell me."

Frog hugged her skinny arms closer over her protruding ribs, although the night could hardly be called cool. "My husband cast me out for barrenness."

Ing's memory shot back to the endless boring moments at the dreary village. Yes. That's what had been different. No babies crying. No small children playing in the mud.

"I'm sorry. But maybe it's your husband's fault?"

Frog shook her head. "Mallard lay with Duck, and she got with child."

It wasn't hard evidence, but it was the best she would get.

"What about the rest of the village? What happened to their babies?"

Frog shrugged. "I guess that was my fault, too. Mother-in-law only bears dead or wrong babies, and none of Mallard's sisters or cousins has had a child. We're cursed."

That was odd. Alarming, even. It confirmed Ing's worst suspicions. Humanity wasn't going to make it on this hostile world. It had found a way to strike back at the invaders. The colonists were all genetically engineered for health, strong teeth, easy birthing, everything to give them as good a life as possible without technology or medical care. This wouldn't happen without an outside cause.

Another thought struck her. "Have you been eating properly?"

Frog looked at her as if she was mad. "It's spring. Everyone's been hungry. Frogs hiding. Whitefish most days."

"You know you shouldn't be eating haram food," Ing said. "It'll fill your belly, but it won't sustain you."

"You think I don't know that? We're not stupid, even if we're not fancy city people with cotton dresses and bellies full of rice and behemoth!"

Eating whitefish or paradile, or the local vegetables, didn't feed one, the human body being unable to break down and use the alien proteins and cellulose. That wasn't new. Might it actually be poisonous? In that case, maybe humans could assimilate some of it, but the rest built up in the tissue and resulted in infertility?

Ing groped after the hump of paradile. She'd eaten enough to replenish the hole in her thigh but she needed to stock up more mass for the Queen Mound, who would demand her pound of fleshy information.

***

Firdaus swam through the familiar channels of his home, moving sluggishly this far away from the cold, fast-moving water. Here he was safe and warm and dark. Above his head, the force of his passage shook the dry world. He was old and had grown massive over the years, accumulated one whitefish at a time. He hooked his tail around the thick root of the living island above him and hung suspended in the rich slow water, full of interesting smells that seeped through the roots. Scents that told him about cloud shine and crunchy leaves, rootlets moving and groping for nutrients, leaves trembling in tender winds or being eaten by small hard jaws.

He was hungry. The whitefish that had once been so plentiful had left his waters. But if the waters had become as full of whitefish as they had been before, they would not have fed his craving for something different. He dreamed of being even bigger, of crawling onto the land and opening his jaws wide for the food to walk in and become part of him. He knew, though, that he could not move on land, that his legs hurt when they had to bear his weight on the dry.

He caressed his snout with his tail. He nibbled on it, perfunctorily, because it was his own flesh and would bring him nothing new to savor. His tail slapped harder. Hey. He twisted around, trying to find the other paradile's tail that was slapping him.

"Firdaus! Wake up!" someone shouted and Firdaus corkscrewed up from his safe murky depth to the bright dry world.

He blinked. Ing was shouting in his face. The world wasn't bright at all; it was the usual darkness near the ground, with the false illumination of gray clouds above his head.

He opened his mouth and was surprised when speech came out. "I dreamed I was a paradile."

Prophet, that sounded dumb. A child fibbing to his mother about why he'd fallen asleep in the middle of his chores.

"Of course you did," Ing said. "You ate part of it, didn't you? That's what our flesh does. It transfers memories and thoughts. You can have a little bit more, but not too much. You shouldn't eat down the food chain. It'll make you stupid."

He felt stupid enough already. Her explanation made no sense at all. He sat up and fell over again. His balance was off. Oh. His foot. His foot!

The panic he'd expected earlier hit his stomach, but in an odd, buffered way. It was like a memory of something that had happened years ago.

"How's that foot going?" Ing asked. "We're gonna be paddling for another couple of days, but after that it should be ready to walk on."

Firdaus could only gape. "What?"

"Do I have to say everything twice? That foot of yours needs to grow back. Focus on it."

"But it can't... I don't know how..." Firdaus stammered, but his fingers were tracing the rim of the break already, fueled by the wild hope it was true.

The edge felt different, less rough, as if skin was smoothing over the chewed-off bits.

Firdaus lifted his eyes to Ing's. "Is that why you were so calm? It's going to grow back?"

Ing nodded. "Yep. Isn't that nifty? You need mass, of course, which is why I went after the paradile. Here."

She held out a long white thing. When he took it from her hands, it resolved into a humanoid leg with the foot still attached. His own foot. Firdaus braced himself for nausea, or disgust of some kind, but his only response was saliva. That was wrong. Gross. He was chewing a toe before he could decide not to, and it felt right. Not as

overwhelming as the paradile flesh, which had transported
him into improbable, lucid paradile dreams, but meaning-
ful and affirming. He was taking back what was his. The
world went away for a few moments and when it re-
solidified, he had devoured his foot and a third of his
lower leg.

Ing looked on with an approving smile that gave him
gooseflesh up his back. Firdaus studied the leg for signs of
tampering. How could he tell if she'd already taken a bite
from it? She had no right to do that. His flesh was his and
his alone! Maybe if he was so attracted to her edibility, she
might feel the same about him? Of course, that had been
her purpose all along. She was going to take him into her
lair and devour him. She'd better think twice, then. He was
double her weight and she was only a woman.

Ing noticed his scrutiny and raised a thin white eyebrow.

Firdaus forced himself to smile and nod. "Thanks.
This is great."

"I know."

He dropped the leg and cast an eye to the sky, to see if
it was still worth getting some sleep before dawn. A light
touch on his arm reminded him of Frog's presence. She
supported herself on one elbow on her reed mat, displaying her breasts and hips to best advantage. Apparently,
she still found him attractive, even footless. Her flesh, dark
in the gray gloom of night, sent out little waves of
fragrance to him, timed with her heartbeat. Also, that mat
would be more comfortable to lie on than the soggy
ground of the floating island.

He crawled over to Frog and she shifted aside to allow
him to repose at least part of his body on her narrow mat.
The flesh of their thighs met, knees bumped and Firdaus
left his worries and unpleasant new life behind. Frog's
hand closed over his rod and he inhaled so profoundly he
shuddered. Here, he was in his natural habitat, a woman's
bedroom, and he knew exactly what to do. The lightness of
that idea made the looming darkness of his present life
seem bigger and darker than before, but he thrust that

notion aside. He had a woman to please and astound.

Frog lifted her legs for him and he dove in, too shaken and stirred to stick to his plan of pleasuring her first. His body fell into its natural rhythms, rooting around in Frog's soft drenched flesh, and time stopped.

When Frog burst into her third peak, Firdaus started to get worried. He felt no approaching brink of joy. He was a master in the art of postponing his own release, prolonging the woman's pleasure and his own, but something felt wrong all the same. The sensation of Frog's honeypot enclosing his rod was pleasant, but no more than that. Frog's sighs and moans gratified him, certainly, but in the end a man wanted to shoot out his soul for his own satisfaction.

He rolled off her. Frog curled up into a ball, sighed once, and was asleep. Firdaus lay on his back and stared at the shifting night sky. Ing must have heard his every groan and gasp. She would know if this inability was permanent, or just a hiccup. He vowed never to ask her. There must be Wan men in the Queen's hall he could consult.

⁕

Before dawn broke the next day, Ing woke Firdaus up and told him to get moving. They were close to the river and needed the early start to make the crossing before dark. Firdaus peeled himself away from Frog's naked buttocks. She was so warm and pliant. He would have liked another bout of sport with her before leaving, but Ing was in a hurry and the memory of last night's failure rang a warning bell.

Frog flexed luxuriously as Firdaus stood up to swing his arms and stretch his back. His body didn't give any of the signs he'd expected after lying on clammy ground all night, not a twinge of back pain or stiffness. Perhaps being a Wan did have its perks. Frog batted her eyelashes at him and stroked the cotton of his cloak with reverent hands. To his own eyes, it was much faded and wrinkled after only a few days in the marshes, but it was probably the most expensive garment the poor girl had ever seen. He took it from her hands and wrapped it around his shoulders.

"Frog. Go dig up roots. We have no time to rest all day," Ing said, and Frog scuttled off.

The scuttling was unattractive, but it did give him a good view of her curvy backside as she bent down to find the now-scarce orchid and sweet flag roots. She seemed sleeker than she'd been, as if these days of rowing were less hard on her than her former life. Such was the peasant's lot.

He stepped on board without rocking the boat or losing his balance. He was getting quite adept on the water.

After an hour or so of paddling in widening channels, while the floating islands became smaller and yellower as halal foliage diminished further, the vista of the open river appeared behind the last stand of sword plants.

Frog gasped. Firdaus could understand her awe. He'd seen the river before, on trips with his father in the royal ketch, but seated in this flimsy bamboo boat it seemed larger and more imposing. A flat sheet of silvery water flowed straight past them, empty of island or growth. The water seemed silky smooth, but his arms felt the strength of the flow he was paddling against.

"Okay," Ing said. "Now we paddle hard, and long. No stopping until we reach the other side, no resting, no mistakes. If we stop, the flow will carry us out and we'll be on our way to the ocean before we know it. The current would smash us against the reef barrier. Go!"

Hours fled by. The other side of the river looked as far away as before.

"Are we moving at all?" Firdaus asked Ing.

"Of course we are. But most of our effort is spent laterally."

He fell silent again. Frog's paddling was becoming erratic.

"Frog. Rest for a few minutes and eat something," he said.

Frog shot him a gratful glance and fell onto her little stash of roots and frogs. They hadn't even given her time to roast them, he realized with a tiny stab of guilt.

When Frog was rested, Firdaus took a few moments to ingest a bite of paradile flesh. Not that he felt hungry, but because he thought he should. The remnant of his own leg stared at him with reproof, but he didn't feel up to eating more of it.

He looked straight down through the clear water that pulled at them with invisible, infinitely strong arms, and he thought he saw black at the bottom. No mud, no fish, nothing.

"Where are the fish?" he said. "I'm sure there used to be whitefish near the Rim before."

"I don't know. But you're right, there are fewer whitefish than there used to be. Good observation."

They paddled on. Although the riverbank seemed close, it still took an hour or more to reach the other side. Then they had to find a creek to enter, and navigate through smaller channels until they found an island that looked large enough to bear their weight.

***

Ing sank down on the ground, not caring that it was wet and squishy. She felt broken and old. Her Wan body wasn't exhausted, but her human spirit was failing. The monotony and the burning light had chipped down her defenses and left her quivering and exposed to the relentless silver glare of the clouds.

A thud next to her, and then another.

"Give Frog some water," Ing said without opening her eyes.

Firdaus grunted and she heard him shuffling and splashing around. The sound traveled through the springy mass of turf and roots and mosses that made up the island. Thunk went his heavy step, a deeper thunk when he knelt down, minute shiftings as he lifted up Frog's head and almost inaudible trickling as some of the water missed Frog's mouth. Frog coughed weakly and stirred. Good. Ing had no use for a dead girl.

Ing must have fallen asleep then, because the next thing she knew, a cool gray dawn surrounded her. She felt disinclined to get up and paddle on, but she wanted an end to the journey. Things needed to be done, alliances made, Stadholders persuaded. Onwards!

Firdaus and Frog lay entwined on Frog's tiny sleeping mat, curled around each other like a brown slug and its thicker whiter mate. Firdaus must still be trying to act like a human man. She suppressed a snort.

She checked the water surrounding their little island. It contained enough whitefish for her needs. She prodded the others awake with her foot. When they were seated beside the breakfast fire, with Firdaus roasting yellowtail and frogs for the sluggish Frog, Ing started her spiel.

"Did you guys know that whitefish and paradile are the same kind of creature?"

They answered with vague grunts. She didn't care about that. Nobody ever wanted to listen to this except other biologists, but it was vital that they understand before visiting the Mound.

"The whitefish are the young. When they are old enough, their skin changes and they stick to one another. Those two whitefishes are the beginning of a much bigger creature, the paradile. One by one, they find other white-fishes to make them bigger. That's all they want, to accumulate mass. They can eat whitefish when they have grown a little older and bigger and their skin isn't so per-meable anymore. It's not eating like humans do, breaking down the flesh into an easy digestible soup."

Ing halted; no diversions into digestion, that was too hard for them.

"Firdaus! What did I just say?"

He sniffed but answered civilly enough. "Whitefish become paradiles."

"Very good. Then, when the paradiles are big enough, they start to turn smart. They get curious. They climb on land and grow legs after a while. Which makes them what?"

Firdaus frowned. "Huh?"

"Ghast!" Frog piped up.

She wasn't as stupid as she looked, Ing guessed. Never mind, this lecture wasn't for Frog. "You concentrate on eating, girl."

"I don't get it," Firdaus said. "If the whitefish, the paradiles, and the Ghast are one kind, how are the Wan made? I thought Ghast is what Wan change into after a while."

"Let me show you something," Ing said. She knelt down by the waterside and dangled her hand in the cool water. A sweet presence grazed her fingertips, and then a less appealing one. That one would do for Frog. She grabbed the whitefish behind its jaws.

"Look. No, look closer. See here? See the teeth?"

She held the fish before Firdaus. Frog tried to look over Firdaus' shoulder and Ing held the creature closer to Frog's face.

"What's so special about..."

Frog yelped. The whitefish had bitten her in the cheek. "Ow! Owowow!"

"Don't make a fuss, girl," Ing said.

The whitefish lay limp in her hand. Ing made to chuck it back into the marsh water but Firdaus held her hand. "Why is the fish dead?"

"Whitefish die when they bite people. They won't bite on their own accord, but they can be forced to if you press them hard enough against human flesh."

"So?"

Ing waited, checking Firdaus' face for signs of understanding. She couldn't dumb it down any further.

"You asked how Wan were made. I showed you."

Frog was the first to grasp the implications. Her howl would have scared away a regiment of paradiles. She launched herself at Ing and clenched her hands around Ing's neck. "I'm going to die! You killed me! I'm going to turn into a Wan!"

CHAPTER 7

Ing winked at Firdaus, most disconcertingly. Who winked while being strangled? But Ing's face maintained its half-amused, half-exasperated look while Frog wailed and groaned and gnashed her teeth, squeezing Ing's neck.

Firdaus couldn't get a handle on either woman's emotion. Time turned to sludge. His hands had been reaching for Frog's arms for an eternity, and he still hadn't managed to grab her and haul her off Ing. His emotions were as syrupy as his arms.

"You used Frog to demonstrate how a Wan is made?" he said, as if he still couldn't believe it. He already knew the answer, though.

Ing couldn't answer or even nod, because Frog was still wailing in her face and trying to dent in Ing's solid Wan flesh. Firdaus' slow arms finally grasped Frog's skinny brown ones and he lifted the screeching, sniveling girl off Ing and cradled her in his arms.

"Shh," he said. "Shh. I know how you feel, I do, I do. Shh. Just cry for now."

Firdaus' eyes met Ing's over Frog's heaving shoulders. Ing rubbed her neck and stared at him. What did she want? Did she expect him to take her part? What she'd done was callous and horrible. Ing scrambled upright and straightened her clothes with jagged pulls and twitches. It was almost as if Ing had wanted to be in his arms instead of Frog, strange as it might seem.

Ing stalked off and Firdaus released his tight hold on Frog. She wailed anew and hid her face against Firdaus' chest, her lank curls and damp dark skin like a stain on his heart. How could Ing have done this? Frog was not an important person, not even to him, but she'd been a young woman, who might have been pretty with a few months of good food and repeated washing. The only life she'd known was work hard, bear lots of babies, and die young. She wasn't ready to live like a Wan, a shunned and unnatural creature. Living for centuries, like Ing.

He sighed and patted Frog's shaking shoulders again. Maybe it would be the most merciful thing to kill her right now? While she was still human? He'd never killed anyone before.

"Frog?" he said.

Frog wailed.

He patted her hand. "Frog. Stop. Crying isn't going to change anything."

She lifted her blotched, swollen face. Her yellowy sclera were dotted with red blood. "Kill her for me? You have to avenge me."

Kill Ing? Yes, Ing had done wrong, but killing her wouldn't set anything right. Frog couldn't be changed back. "First we must find out why she did this. Why she's doing all of this, taking me along, all those cryptic mutterings of hers. Then I'll decide what to do to her."

Frog beat his chest with her fist. "No!" she ground out. "I want her dead."

"I am the Stadholder, and I will decide what happens. Promise me not to kill her until I give you permission."

She gaped. "You're not the Stadholder! He's not white. The Stadholder sits on his throne with his giant belly and all his wives and children. You're not him."

"I was him," Firdaus said. "Once. Before I turned into a Wan."

"She did it to you, too?" Frog brought her face close to his. "Let's kill her when she comes back," she whispered.

"No. I need to find out what she's up to. She promised me allies. I need to know more before I make my decision."

Frog stamped her foot on his good one. She didn't have much leverage, sitting on his lap, but the intent was clear. "Know, know! Who cares about knowing. I feel," and she beat her fist over her heart, "I feel in my heart I'm going to kill her. What else is there to know!"

"That's not knowledge. Frog, a Stadholder doesn't make hasty decisions. He weighs all the possibilities before he answers. He has to take care of all the people, not just himself or his lovers."

Frog subsided unexpectedly and lunged beneath his loincloth. She smiled. "I've been the lover of a Stadholder. How about that! You are large and wonderful, a real Stadholder." She squeezed him once more but didn't follow up on her overture.

"I'm hungry." She crawled over to the little pile of roots Ing had left for her, a clumsy apology if one wanted to read it that way. Maybe that's why she'd been named Frog. She never stood upright if she didn't have to, she crawled or rolled or hunched over as much as possible. She busied herself making a fire from the kindling they'd brought in the boat, fueled with dry tips from last year's reeds and sedges. She sang a children's song under her breath. Firdaus knew it so well he could easily supply the words.

"Yellow for staple, orange for sweet, red for sharp and green for fiber. Blue for poison, purple for wisdom."

Not that he'd ever seen a purple or blue plant or animal; according to the Physician's Guild, the Ancestors would bestow them when they felt the people deserved them. Ing would probably know enough about the hierarchy of food to lecture him for hours. A good reason not to ask her.

Muttering and splashing from the neighboring island announced Ing's return. She carried a makeshift basket of green reeds with heaps of weeds in them. Firdaus tensed, ready to restrain Frog if she was going to leap onto Ing again.

But Frog gave Ing a dark glance from over the pale pink salsify she was munching with open mouth, and left it at that, only turning her back on Ing demonstratively. It must be strange to be Frog, floating on a fog of emotions and never delving deeper to remember what else was there.

Ing raised an eyebrow to Firdaus, inviting him to

complicity over Frog's demeanor. Firdaus frowned at Ing. That he hadn't immediately jumped Ing's throat didn't mean he condoned what she'd done. He grabbed her arm and walked her out of hearing distance from Frog. "What the prophet did you think you were doing? Killing that poor girl just to make a point?"

Ing's face grimaced up at him. "Yes. A very important point. I need your help. I need you at my side to save all those people you care so much about! You have to know the score."

He shook her until her teeth rattled, but the excited grin never left her face.

"What do you care about the girl? She'd never have been your lover if you still were Stadholder. She's nothing, nobody, no power, no knowledge, no beauty. Expendable," Ing said.

"Frog may not have wit or beauty, but not everybody needs those. Without people like her to grow rice, where would the Stadholders and biologists be?" Firdaus said. Poor Frog.

Ing shrugged and leaned her face closer. Her eyes glittered and her breath smelled of persuasion. "Think about it, Firdaus! You could be a hero, the savior of mankind."

The pressure of Ing's feverish body against his and her fresh bread fragrance distracted him mightily. Now was not the time. Ing did have wit, too much of it, and although she wasn't beautiful, she was well made and straight. He could do worse than take her for a lover. Much worse. Her lips were close, the points of her breast, the faintest tinge darker than her smooth skin, pricked against his bare chest and he felt himself stirring. No.

He thrust her away from him and she smacked with a satisfying thud into the wet grass. Or rushes or sedges or whatever she chose to call them. Bitch.

"You're still telling me nothing. Is mankind in danger? Is my city in danger, my daughters? What are you talking about? You talk in riddles and weird words and you think I understand you? You're insane. I'm not going anywhere with you. Save the world on your own."

Her face fell comically, and she scrabbled in the dirt and churned weeds to get up. "Firdaus! Wait! It is important, believe me. Everybody will die unless you follow my plan! Please!"

Her urgency was both gratifying and unsettling. Here was mistress Ing, cocksure know-it-all, desperately needing his help. Common sense told him to stay aloof. She hadn't told him anything yet.

"Wait, Firdaus, wait. It's a complicated story. Let me tell it."

Firdaus nodded. He was the Stadholder; she would get fair hearing.

"I told you humankind was brought here by my fellow travelers. We brought everything we would need, a complete ecosystem designed for this water world. But when I woke up after my Wanning and calculated how long I'd been wandering witless in the Maze, our expectations hadn't come out. Population wasn't rising. Whole breeds hadn't survived. Dolphins, pigs, where are they now? Our mutated rice was a puny crop.

"I only recently discovered humanity, too, is affected. Lesser fertility and lots of other signs. We are not adapting to this world, Firdaus, we're losing the battle. If we don't act, humanity will die out."

Firdaus didn't want to agree with her, but years of worried Assembly sessions made her information strike a chord within him.

"Act how?" he asked.

Ing pushed herself up, holding one hand to the ground for balance. "The Wan are the answer. Somehow, the human personality and emotions survive when the mold starts to grow. Or maybe it mimics a virus more than a mold. The Wan body is virtually indestructible. We could survive as a race. Sure, we'd look different, but what do looks matter?"

Frog paused in her gobbling to sniff.

Firdaus wasn't sure what to think. Turn everyone into a Wan, because otherwise they would die? Farfetched.

"Ing, everybody dies. That's inevitable. We wouldn't be people if we were Wan. I don't like your idea."

"You think I like it? You can't know, but it's close to the abomination we fled from when we colonized this world, when everybody was uploading themselves and hastening the Singularity along."

Firdaus ignored her babblings. Every once in a while she'd say something that made sense, but most of it was sheer rubbish.

"Tell me in words I can understand, Ing," he said. "You don't have to dazzle me with your magic vocabulary. I believe you're centuries old and from somewhere else. It's obvious you're not like us. Tell me again why turning into Wan will save humankind?"

Ing rolled her eyes. "Because otherwise you'll die out. Slowly, from decreasing fertility. We need to get civilization going, so we can escape from here."

"Ing, I still don't get why we should be Wan. We won't be human anymore. Wan aren't able to have children, are they? I've never seen a baby Wan."

Ing scratched her head and shook it simultaneously. She looked deranged. "No. Yes. I'm as human as you are, as far as emotions and stuff are concerned."

Firdaus doubted that. She seemed more interested in plants and fish and unlikely tales than human company.

"Okay, Firdaus, let's make a deal. I take you to the Queen Mound, where you can see for yourself that the Ghast are not like the Wan. Believe me, Wan are very human compared to the strangeness of the Ghast. And think about it while we paddle. Your foot is almost re-grown already. I'm four hundred years old. Nothing would be able to harm or kill Wanned humanity. People who lived that long would have the time to relearn all the forgotten skills." Ing paused to take a breath, ready to continue in this vein for hours if her earlier behavior was any indication.

"Okay, enough. You're making my eyes cross. No more preaching. No more tricks. I'll go along, and I'll decide afterward if I believe you or not."

Frog vomited suddenly and noisily. Her last meal, pink and black roots, dripped down her chin and chest. She stared at it in horrified fascination. Firdaus hastened over to her.

"That's quick," Ing said, interest clear in her voice. "Usually takes a week to get to this stage."

"Shut up or die right now," Firdaus said between clenched teeth.

***

Ing chewed her lip as she watched her travel companions by the flickering light of the smoky fire. Frog hunched over, clutching her stomach, and Firdaus sat cross-legged beside her, wiping her forehead with a bit of moist sphagnum. Frog was descending with incredible rapidity towards Wanhood, and the speed was making her ill. She might not even survive, which would be a pity. Ing inched closer to the first heap of vomit to check it out. Barely chewed food that hadn't been inside Frog for long.

Frog moaned. "I'm going to die! Who's going to tell Mallard?"

Firdaus, more sensible than Ing had expected, didn't answer that. She doubted that the husband was expecting to hear anything from his ex-wife ever again.

A hesitant dawn lifted the gloom of night. Thick mists still clouded the marsh as far as they could see, covering the chartreuse and ochre-yellow of the native foliage with a silver veil.

It reminded her of her last look at Earth, no longer blue and white, but a patchy yellow, clouded in a haze of particles where the machines were eating the world itself in the uploaded humans' hurry to convert everything physical into thought. Everything except the machines that held their system-spanning minds. She and her friends had managed to come this far, to give warm, smelly, messy, fallible humanity a new chance. It must not end here. She wouldn't let it.

She stood up, and felt the same satisfaction that she'd felt in the four centuries since her Wanning. She wasn't stiff or tired in the slightest, not even after a sleepless night and hours spent sitting cross-legged on moist ground.

"We should go, Firdaus."

"Frog can't travel like this!"

"She can't paddle, but we can take her in the boat," Ing said. "We can't leave her, can we?"

Firdaus dithered, but at last he shrugged and doused the fire with the wet moss. Ing tossed her possessions in the boat, while Firdaus gathered Frog's pitiful bindle and carried the shivering girl into the pirogue.

Not far now. They might even make it tonight. Distances were hard to judge here in the Maze. The floating islands shifted constantly and only the distant peaks of the Rim kept her on course. Only the Queen Mound, perched on the foot of those mountains, never moved.

They paused at midday, sheltering under a stand of papyrus that threw stippled shadows with its feathery parasols. Firdaus said that Frog needed water and food. Ing doubted the last, but went and scouted out some of the salsify and calumny roots Frog liked so much. She held Frog's leather cup to her mouth, and the girl took a few mouthfuls before subsiding into feverish mutters again. Her dull mahogany skin was dappled by pale gold blotches.

"It was much slower and even with me," Firdaus said, touching one of the bigger patches with one long white finger.

Ing nodded. "I've never seen it take people like this, either. I wonder if it has to do with the amount of haram foods the poor eat."

"Poor people never get Wanned?" Firdaus said.

"Why Wan the boring and talentless? If people want company, they pick someone who has something to give. Designers, poets, artists. We don't need unskilled labor."

The Maze had shifted more than Ing had hoped, and at dusk the Queen Mound still wasn't visible. Ing checked their course against the Trident Peaks, delineated in ink against the graying clouds, but she was sure they were going in the right direction.

Firdaus lit a fire and they sat around it, not speaking much. Frog twitched and babbled in her delirium, and he couldn't think of anything to talk about without touching on tender subjects.

Ing stared in the fire, imagining what tomorrow would bring. Firdaus, awed and silenced by the strangeness of the Mound Queen. She knew the perfect way to win him over, but Firdaus wasn't ready to eat her persuasion yet, and neither could she risk him knowing too much.

Firdaus rolled over in his sleep, releasing a cloud of irresistible scent. Ing rummaged in her pack for the paradile haunch, but repacked it after a few bites. Hunger was her enemy. The urge to keep on eating was never far away, and that was one way she'd vowed never to go. If she let herself, she'd eat and eat until she couldn't bear her own weight anymore. Occasionally she dreamed of planting herself in the mud and growing bigger and bigger. Never. Her flesh might be Wan, but her mind was still human and it could control these alien cravings.

***

Firdaus pulled his oar. Frog was better than yesterday, but sat staring at nothing and dropped the paddle if he put it into her hands. Her skin was a pale buff now, her temporarily orange hair drooping down from her head in dejected ringlets. Behind her bowed head, a pale hump in the landscape could be seen against the dark mass of the Rim Mountains. Ing called the hump 'the Queen-Mound', their destination. It seemed like a great spot to start a city, though it lacked a river or sea harbor to make it truly attractive. As they moved closer, the hump grew startlingly fast into a massive hillock. It was almost white, the bald head of a giant submerged beneath the Maze.

The channels narrowed and became shallower. Once or twice, the pirogue's bottom scraped over sand or rock, a sure sign that the marsh was ending. After an hour of zigzagging through weed-choked channels, Ing called out to halt.

"We're continuing on foot after this."

Firdaus prodded Frog out of the boat.

Ing took him aside. "Can you order her to make a length of rope? We need to tie up the boat or it'll be gone when we return."

"Frog," he asked gently. "Can you make rope? You look like a girl who's good at weaving and rope making."

Frog's spine straightened infinitesimally. "I can."

"Can you do it now? Is there stuff here that you can use?"

Frog's dull eyes lifted and she looked around vaguely. She flapped her hand at a stand of yellow-and-black striped corkscrewing vegetation. "There. I'll get it."

Firdaus thought it best to keep an eye on her. Frog walked over to the plant, produced her small mussel knife after some limp rummaging in her pouch, and starting sawing off the tough stalks. It would take a while. Firdaus knelt down beside her and set a fresh sliver of obsidian in his carved wooden knife-hilt. He cut off four times as much as Frog did in the same amount of time.

Frog did something swift and magical with the stalk he'd cut off for her, and the strip of weed fell apart in two perfect even strands. She repeated her action, and soon she had a little heap of white and yellow-striped sliver-thin fibers. With a flick of her hand, she straightened out seven or nine of them and started braiding. Firdaus stared at her dancing hands. Watching someone practice their craft at this level always gave him joy, and the rope that coiled on the grass from Frog's nonchalant, minute movements seemed sturdy and incredibly even.

He left her to the weaving and walked back to Ing to consult her on the route. The stretch of marsh they'd have to cross was soggy and treacherous.

When Frog was done with the rope, Ing took it with an unfathomable look at Firdaus.

"Frog," coaxing her like a shy goat into a new pasture, "I want to tie us together so that if you stumble, Firdaus and I can drag you up."

Apparently Ing thought Frog might run. He would have thought she didn't care whether Frog lived or died. Maybe something gentle and caring hid deep inside Ing, usually overpowered by the maniac who thought she needed to save the world.

He didn't want it to need saving, but she was onto something. Maybe the Ancestors were angry with the world, and were punishing them by withholding sons and daughters. He just refused to swallow her solution.

Become Wan, every man and woman? Become as white and disgusting as himself? The color white didn't stand for all that was evil and corrupt for nothing. The white goat was for the altar, the whitefish was inedible. The world had a certain order, and to break that foreordained division between good and evil, to become haram as a whole person? Better that he kill himself right now than suffer his fellow citizens, not to mention his children, to follow his fate. Better to die.

Best to keep these thoughts to himself, watch and wait for the opportunity to thwart her plans.

Ing tied Frog to the both of them, and they started their trek to the edge of the marsh. Firdaus had cut himself a bamboo pole to test the wobbling ground for firmness. He needed it when he stepped onto a solid-seeming spot and his leg shot into a watery hole to the thigh. Frog stepped, uncaring, into every dodgy spot the marsh offered, and her piebald skin became crisscrossed with red from rope burn. Wise Ing, to tie her up.

They tramped through a forest of skinny bamboo stalks and squat ochre fern trees, whose thick boles were so soft a fist could punch a hole through them. The thick foliage hid the mound Ing had pointed out to him, and anyway Firdaus had to keep his eyes on his feet, alert for pitfalls hidden underneath the deceptively firm-looking yellow mosses and grasses.

His foot, accustomed to the give and tremble of the marsh, stomped hard on solid ground. Firdaus felt the shock through his spine and into his teeth. The bamboo and fern forest ended as abruptly.

His glance stuttered against the sudden enormity of the Queen Mound revealed in all its bone-white glory only a few hundred feet away. The ground was a mix of the white mud he knew from the city, the orange-tinged marsh ground and the black slag that crumbled off the

Rim mountains, swirling in dizzying patterns under his feet, leading his eye to the gaping black mouth that beckoned them inwards.

"I knew I could find the quickest way here," Ing said.

"Well done," Firdaus said with absentminded politeness. "Now what?"

"Now we go in, to talk to the Queen."

CHAPTER 8

"The Queen of the Ghast?" Firdaus asked.

"Not exactly. Or maybe, yes. She is the biggest of the mounds, and has eaten the most respect and wisdom of them all. Treat her as if she's a fellow ruler, and remember she's not human."

"Like me," Firdaus said, dejected at the thought of being related to a creature that lived in a dank cave, isolated at the farthest end of the Maze.

"Not like you or me!" Ing said and tugged hard at Frog's leash.

The poor thing stumbled and her eyes beseeched Firdaus for help. He would have given it if he knew how.

"Hold the leash for me," Ing said. "I'm going in first, to announce our presence. I won't be long."

Firdaus wound the rope about his fist. Ing draped her faded cotton cloak around her mud-splattered form and strode towards the entrance. Firdaus followed at a distance. The opening promised blackness, musty air, cheerless tunnels.

The next moment, his nose pushed against the side of the mound and his tongue scraped over an intriguing surface. How had he gotten here? He tried to worm the tip of his tongue between the minute bumps, to get at the goodness dissolving against it, but he couldn't quite reach it. Hints of nameless flavors vied on his tongue, formless memories and ancient hungers coursed through him, aimed straight at his spine.

A small yammer scrabbled for his attention and he peeled his face loose to deal with the disturbance. His foot connected with a heavy thing that clung to it.

Something yanked at his neck and he strained to reach the incredible taste again, tongue and hands and cock out.

"Firdaus!" Ing yelled. "Wake up!"

He lifted one arm to swat off the contender for the ambrosia, but then his eyes cleared and he was standing here, humping a hillock, a whimpering muddied Frog at his feet. Ing stared furiously into his face.

"Jesus, Firdaus, what have I been telling you? Eat the fucking paradile. You can't just eat from the Queen without offering something in exchange; otherwise she'll take all of you. And I'm no fan of Frog, but dragging her through the mud like a recalcitrant Dachshund is no solution."

The words dripped into his consciousness one by one. He forced his hands and tongue back down and blinked to regain his perspective. He'd been waiting a hundred steps away, as Ing had told him to, he was sure of it.

"What happened?" he asked.

"You're underfed and so when you got a whiff of the Queen's enticement, you fell for it. Why don't you just feed when I tell you to?"

"I'm taking that as a rhetorical question," Firdaus replied stiffly. "The rhetorical answer is, when you start explaining yourself better."

"Hmph." Ing strode off.

***

Ing entered the dark maw with slow and measured steps. It wouldn't do to surprise the Queen Mound. As a sessile entity, being surprised was her least favorite thing. Ing rapped on the walls to announce her presence, and waited in the dim interior while the sound travelled all through the Mound. Her eyes became accustomed to the gloom and she checked out the entrance hall. It had changed since her last visit. The ceiling was higher, and the floor was pitted and friable, so that with every step she took, her feet crashed through the surface and sent up clouds of pulverized Ghast stuff. Very wasteful of mass. The Queen she remembered would never have squandered a single grain of her flesh.

The irregular chamber walls, scoured in spirals as if they'd been carved with water, opened up to a dozen or more tunnels, some of them flush with the floor, others angling away downwards or upwards.

A light glowed up in one of the less steep downward passageways. Ing went in. She walked slowly, out of respect, but also because something in the atmosphere inside the tunnel was different. Off. Was it the lights? She'd always had to stumble in the darkness. Or the smell? It was too subtle for her to place it right away, but it stirred something inside her.

More light flared up and her mouth fell open. Oil lamps? In a Mound? That was new.

"My Queen?"

A blocky humanoid shape detached itself partway from the wall, a bleached sphinx moving ponderously closer to Bethlehem. Ing steeled herself to stay in place, but every fiber in her being screamed at her to run away from the approaching predator.

"Lady Ing. How do you like my lamps?" a voice made of gravel and ash rumbled all around her.

"I'm impressed," Ing said. "I didn't know you used lamps."

"It's a thing I learned from the Wan," the Queen said with satisfaction.

"I thought you kept aloof from the other Wan."

"Sometimes. But since you taught me how to use speech, I decided to try it out on our fellows, to see if you had not deceived me as to its use. It's not a thing we Ghast have ever needed before." The enormous, crudely hewn white hand gestured. "Give me your offering."

Ing dug into the roll of extra mass on her stomach, especially accumulated for this purpose, and tore it loose. She deposited the squab of flesh on the outstretched hand and it withdrew back into the wall. A shadowy opening emerged, becoming black and deeper millimeter by millimeter.

"Ah," the disembodied voice said.

Ing would never get used to the great Ghast creature

speaking and chewing, if that's what it did, at the same time.

"You withhold from me, Ing!" it said plaintively. "What is the danger you sense?"

"I don't know myself, your Majesty," Ing said. If she'd still had a heart, it would have been pounding. "I sense a danger to the humans, but I don't know what it is. Do you?"

"I?" the stone voice rumbled. "Not I. What do I care about the humans? I hold no friendship for them. They squat on my sister mound like overgrown paradiles, too dim to pay respect to what is bigger than they are."

"Indeed," Ing said. It was disturbing to hear the Queen voice the same sentiment about people that she herself harbored. She was still human at heart, wasn't she? It was the mind that counted, not the envelope of flesh, the avatar. As long as the avatar was truly flesh, not ones and zeros in a machine. "My thought is to make all the humans into Wan."

"Will you bring them to me so I can eat them?"

Ing's foot twitched. "Not all, majesty. Perhaps you can send walkers to collect them from time to time."

"Not many free walkers abroad any more, Ing. I've eaten most of them."

"Is that why you wish to eat more Wan?"

"One can never grow too large, can one?"

The Queen opened more smacking sniffling slits in the wall and inhaled deeply. "Hmmm. I taste a seasoning of newly made Wan. Did you bring him to me, or did you gobble him up yourself?"

"No, your Majesty, I bring him and another freshly made Wan. Maybe her flesh isn't ready for you to digest, though."

"I don't find them appetizing when they're that young," the Queen confessed. "They taste of mud and weeds, they do. They don't have enough experience to taste of interesting thoughts."

"Humans think when they're still mud," Ing said. "You might be surprised."

"I'll have a sniff, then, because you insist," the creature

rumbled. "Bring them to me."

Ing bowed, although she didn't know if the Queen had eaten enough Wan to interpret the human gesture.

She hurried back. She hoped recalcitrant Firdaus had listened to her and eaten something, so he wouldn't have to part with flesh that he would miss. He had made her spill snippets of information and that worried her. She thought she'd been cryptic enough to confound the Queen, who couldn't possibly see through Firdaus' own imperfect understanding of the facts she'd dangled before him. But it was still a risk.

Once in the entrance hall, she breathed easier. The burden of the Queen's regard slid from her shoulders. The strain of standing before a creature that alien, that different, that dangerous was incredible. Really, whatever Firdaus might think about the substance of Wan flesh being identical to that of Ghast flesh, it was their minds that made the Wan human.

***

Firdaus bent to help Frog up out of the dirt. She stared at his hand and sniffed it. Of course, she would soon feel the hunger for white flesh. On impulse, he broke off a fingertip and offered it to her.

She gobbled it up, chewed it a few times, surprise rising on her face, and then her eyes rolled away in a swoon. The only thing holding her up was her hand-knotted rope. Firdaus lowered her gently. He didn't know what to expect, how long he'd been out when he'd first eaten paradile flesh. His own leg, and his subsequent feedings on the paradile remnant, hadn't recreated the same intense trance state.

Frog sprawled back, utterly limp and relaxed. Her mouth was open and she snored a little through her wide nostrils. She opened her eyes and smiled beatifically.

"I'm a Stadholder. I have a dozen children."

Firdaus cut short his surprised guffaw. Frog never reacted the way he expected. Her skin had passed the saffron and cream stage and was now approaching rice flour. Her hair was cream at the parting, ocher in the middle and the ends were dipped in squid ink. Firdaus touched his own hair. The humid air made it hang lank and heavy down his back instead of curling away from his head as it did in the fresh sea breeze.

Frog's face fell back into its dejected folds. "I wish I had as many children as you have," she said miserably.

"Amazing!" Firdaus said. "You got all that from a fingertip? Do you know my children's names?"

Frog shook her head and wept a pink tear.

"Just try and see it like this," Firdaus said. "You slept with a Stadholder."

The gallantry seemed heavy-handed to him, but Frog's lips curved a bit.

"I slept with a Stadholder," she said, tasting the words and approving of their flavor. "I slept with a Stadholder!"

"You'll be dining out on that one for the rest of your life," Ing said sourly from behind them.

Firdaus jumped. "I didn't see you coming! You're back soon."

Ing ignored his attempt at pleasantry. "Did you eat?" she asked.

Would she ever stop? He'd strongly implied that he resented being ordered around. Did he have to spell it out? "Not yet."

She snarled and dived into their bundles. She muttered and rummaged around until she'd found the paradile hunks and the remnant of his own foot.

"Oh!" she exclaimed. "You should have eaten it, of course, but this can be your gift to the Queen. It's indubitably yours, but it contains only what you knew a week ago. Brilliant!"

She thrust the stump of foot into his hand. Firdaus took it and cradled it to his chest. He was going to give this away? His guts rebelled against it and he would have started eating if Ing wasn't keeping an eagle eye on him. When he nodded his assent, she rounded up on Frog. "Get up, girl."

Frog stumbled upright, swaying, her eyes still unfocused, but obedient. His kindness was wasted on a girl like Frog if she interpreted it as weakness. Look how readily she obeyed Ing. Frog was different from the strong, independent craftswomen he used to know, who knew their own worth and who interpreted kindness as no more than their due. Or his beloved children. He squared his shoulders. He was about to meet a fellow regnant; now was not the time to waste on sentimentalities.

Ing sniffed Frog, Frog's tongue snaked out to taste a string of Ing's hair. For a moment he wished he could have sport with them both.

He inspected his foot. Had Ing eaten from it? He couldn't tell. And he wasn't sure if it would give her a handle on his feelings. What kind of things did one learn from eating another creature? He dipped into his small stash of paradile memories and discovered that he knew how to sleep with his tail curled around the root of an island. Hm.

"Come," Ing said.

"Are we going to meet the other Wan here?"

"I told you, just the Queen."

"But she commands the Wan? Does she command you?"

"Oh, Firdaus, stop asking questions that'll be answered if you just wait ten minutes."

She seemed stressed and hurried. Firdaus pulled at Frog's rope and followed Ing into the vertical puddle of black ink that was the mouth entrance.

The scent was overwhelming. Simply breathing made Firdaus' head whirl with vast and unidentifiable imagery, longing, waiting, devouring, and then culminating into a fragmented unknown.

Frog whimpered and clung to his back. Firdaus gritted his teeth. He wanted to be left alone to think, to savor the billion different tastes and thoughts that swirled through the air. Tunnels gaped hungry maws at him, and from the pocked ceiling dangers threatened to drop upon his head.

"Frog, get your lamp," he said.

Frog crouched down and unpacked her little clay lamp

from her shabby bindle. She lit it without his command, which showed foresight on her part. Was he imagining it or was she more alert?

Light flared up, illuminating Ing's tight lips and creased forehead. "Did I tell you to bring light?" she said. "There's light in the, ah, throne room. The Queen might be offended if you diminish her lighting with your own."

"I'm not going into one of these lightless holes," Firdaus said. "Are you kidding? One of us could fall and never be seen again."

Ing sighed but gestured that they should follow.

Firdaus wound Frog's rope around one hand and took the oil lamp himself. It reeked and guttered, blocking the fascinating odor in the mound with the stink of fish oil and burning papyrus. His hand felt greasy from the dried but unbaked clay. A poor thing compared to the steady oil and cotton wick lamps in the palace, not to mention the fabulous glowapples the Ancestors had left behind.

His feet landed on gritty stuff. He'd expected echoes from his footsteps in this hollow hill, but the pitted surfaces dampened all sounds. The air grew drier and sucked the moisture from his skin with thousands of hungry mouths. Frog wailed wordlessly behind them and he steeled his heart against it. She needed a firm hand, not encouragement in her craven, superstitious ways.

"Douse the light," Ing said. "The Queen's chamber is right ahead."

Firdaus carefully squeezed the wick and pasted it to the side of the crumble-edged spout. He wanted to give it to a servant, Frog, to leave his hands free, and was left holding it anyway. No way to greet a Queen, carrying a light like a supplicant.

Ing squeezed past him, rucking up a full body goosebump as her smooth skin slid over his. He hoped Frog wouldn't be able to see it. He laid a hand on Ing's shoulder. She no longer felt cool to the touch but rather faintly warm.

Ing had been right to douse the lamp that soon. Now the faint flicker of light as they entered the big chamber seemed festive and bright. He blinked and took in the enormous vaulted space. The even whites and stone tints made it hard to determine the true height and size, but when his eyes got used to the light he saw subtle differences. Until man height, the walls were almost smooth, and colored by long pinkish stripes running parallel to the floor. Above his head, pocks and blisters scarred the surface of the walls and ceiling.

Firdaus saw no throne, no bright and terrible Queen to lure unwary travelers into her castle. A part of the wall moved, rock grinding over itself, stalactites shuddering and boulders rolling. He blinked and the jumble of rocks re-formed in his mind into a monstrous body crouched on the floor, partly attached to the wall, with on top a head like a statue's after centuries of wind and water, the features smudged in by a clumsy hand.

He bowed. "Your Majesty."

The crude mouth opened and his head swam with the glory of her visage. Mighty, ancient, the wisdom of ages girding her once agile limbs, the Queen's eyes inhaled his scent.

"Small person. What do you wish to be called?"

"Firdaus," he stammered. He wanted to run forward, throw himself upon her body and melt into it. Her glory would consume him and he would be one with her splendor forever.

A sound snatched him out of his fog. Frog sniveled against his leg. Must she always cling to the ground?

"Firdaus. Lady Ing tells me that you are Queen of the dead nests humans have built near the sea."

His mind stretched to bend around her alien concepts. Did she mean White City? Yes. He was Stadholder of White City. He had been Stadholder.

"No longer, Your Majesty. The humans took my throne away for being Wanned."

"Yes. Ing told me that. She suggests I do not devour you but walk side by side with you."

"Y-yes," he agreed.

"My sister's mound groans under the dead weight of

rocks and inedible flesh. You wish to rule the mud-colored walkers again. I wish to eat more of Ing's white walkers. Their poetry is new and interesting. From them I learned about sounds instead of flesh to speak with. I learned about lamps. I wish to taste more of their ideas."

A rough flat rock swung ponderously back and forth, gesturing while she talked in a parody of Ing. The content of her words was even less graspable than Ing's.

"The lamps are amazing, Your Majesty," Firdaus said.

He thought fast. The alliance she offered was not specific, but it made his skin crawl. It was the only offer on the table, so he wasn't saying no at this moment. But where was her court, where were her subjects?

"What is it that you can help me with?" he asked.

"Many of my siblings are still motile," she said. "For a taste of my wisdom, I can command them to walk to your city and destroy it."

No! His guts screamed. Not destroy his beloved city! And how could he be Stadholder if he had no subjects and no city? That wasn't what being a ruler was about.

"Your Majesty," he said, trying for humble, although he had no idea whether subtleties of tone meant anything to her, or if she could simply taste the air leaving his mouth and know everything about him. "I do not wish to destroy my city. Only the present Queen of the mud-walkers."

"Lady Ing, clarify," the Queen rumbled vastly, shaking his guts with nausea.

Ing elbowed Firdaus in the side and stepped up beside him. Her voice sounded different. Ing was afraid. That meant he should be, too.

"Majesty, let me explain. Firdaus graciously accepts your help in deposing the usurper Queen from his nest. A select group of your siblings would be most welcome in helping us when, and only when we request it. I'm sure that in return for being freed of oppression, a sufficient amount of newly made Wan would love to visit you in your Mound."

"This sound talking is confusing. Come here, person

Firdaus. We will exchange flesh and seal our bargain."

The seduction in her voice and scent pulled at him but the rational part of his brain urged caution. What would she learn from him if she ate him? Now he understood Ing's nagging to eat more, so he could spare some excess flesh for the Queen.

Trembling, he broke off a toe from the old paradile-bitten foot and placed it on the outstretched hand-rock.

"Are all former mud-persons this stingy, Lady Ing?" the Queen growled. The tremors of her voice traveled through his feet and sowed fear in his guts.

"Give more!" Ing hissed. "Give the whole leg."

He felt enormous reluctance to part with his own flesh. What would she learn from it? He feared to hand her priceless knowledge about humankind, but he saw no way around it. He handed the gnawed foot to the Queen.

"That's better," the omnipresent voice rang throughout the chamber. Rows of mouths opened and closed in time with the Queen's speech, as if the chamber itself was an extension of her body.

"How does she make the walls talk?" he muttered to Ing.

"Don't be stupid. She is the walls. The Mound is her body."

"Impossible!"

"The Ghast grow very big when they stop walking. Now shush."

The Queen rumbled. "Firdaus. Father of many children. I see you need two persons to make new ones. How bizarre. But if you fear for your children so much, give them over to my flesh and you can eat their memories and never be without them."

Never. Firdaus bit his cheek to stay the words that threatened to burst out. Being a Wan was both oddly tolerable and worse than he'd imagined, but he would do anything to keep his children from suffering the same fate.

"Take this bite of my memories, Firdaus Father. My kind does not make lamps and tools, but I have eaten many interesting experiences in my long life."

Firdaus took the fist-sized chunk of pumice-like flesh that lay on the hand and broke off a bite.

At first, the Queen had floated in ricewine-colored waters. Whitefish attached themselves to her, attracted by her bright, curious presence. When she grew teeth and a mouth, she devoured the siblings that came questing up to eat her, and gained many memories and much mass. Curiosity drove her to crawl onto land when she was still agile enough to lift herself up, and she grew legs to walk the yellow grasses. She ate as much as she could, and gave gifts of thoughtful flesh to other walkers. They gave big chunks of themselves in return, compelled by her poetry.

After a long while of learning and tasting and growing, she found a mound whose Queen was old and could no longer command every part of her own flesh. She crawled into a tunnel and started eating. She ate the old Queen from the inside out until it was her flesh that thrust out from the earth. Many seasons later, she met a walker who was not of her flesh, or her siblings, and yet she was. Her poetry was so strange the Queen returned to it again and again, desiring to eat more of the strange thoughts. The stranger wished to remain a walker, and the Queen allowed her to roam the land, as long as she brought new tastes for the Queen to savor.

The thought ended abruptly, with no reference to the present. Firdaus staggered. The Queen's memory poem tingled in his fingertips, made his soles experience every bump and idea in the floor.

"Go now," the Queen's voice thundered. "My walkers will enter your city at the turning of the year."

Firdaus clapped his hands over his ears. He staggered back, hampered by Frog clinging to his thighs and Ing's hand clamping his elbow. Out, out, he needed to be outside now. Ing pushed him, he yanked Frog up by her withers and they stumbled outside, away from the avalanche of the Queen's voice, the earthquake of her thoughts.

CHAPTER 9

They popped out of the mound like stoppers from an amphora into the steaming, chirping dusk.

Firdaus leaned against the rocky outcrop shadowing the door, but then realized he was still touching the Queen's integument. He stumbled away to find a more congenial support for his shaken body. He collapsed against the nearest stand of fern trees and rested his aching head against the spongy bole. Never again.

He opened slitted eyes. Ing stood tapping her foot in front of him, hands akimbo. He'd thought her strange and off-putting, but compared to the Queen's brand of vast mystery, Ing's human shape, and her very human impatience assured him of his own sanity.

Ing blew out a long breath. "Phew. She was very forceful today. I feel like throwing up."

Firdaus ignored her. Frog whined and licked at his hand.

They trudged back in sullen single file to where they'd left the pirogue, Ing in front, Firdaus in the middle, Frog dragging on her leash, for some reason reluctant to leave the presence of the Queen. Firdaus couldn't understand why. His own cravings for the Queen's flesh had left him, and a deep revulsion surrounded the queasy snippets of her thoughts rooting around in his brain.

Behind him, the pale bald hillock loomed unseen but full of menace as he walked, the burden of the Queen's attention pressing on his shoulders. He wasn't sure what had happened back there. He'd expected a court, a person on a throne. Not a talking hillock. Ing must have known it, and taken care not to disabuse him. She was as slippery as a handful of mud. Also, she seemed beholden to the Mound Queen, in some nebulous way he couldn't quite grasp.

"Firdaus?" Ing never lifted her hands from her hips. "The boat isn't here. Did you tie it up?"

He couldn't remember. He looked around the trampled rushes and the muddy bank where the boat had been moored. "Are you sure this is the spot?"

"Hello, there's the reeds Frog stripped for her rope. Of course I'm sure."

He dragged himself over to Frog and peered into the dark waters of the narrow weed-choked channel. It did look like the one they'd paddled up in, but then they all looked the same. "I can't remember if I tied it up or not. Maybe this isn't the spot."

"Maybe you think I don't remember that rare patch of succulents there, but I'm sure I did. Stop blathering and help me find the boat."

That was patently impossible. Without a boat, they had no hope of searching for one, let alone traversing the Maze. What would they do, swim or wade across channels in the blind hope they would find something?

"If we follow the current," Ing went on, crouching by the side of the water, "we will find the boat. It didn't wander off on its own."

The water was a flat sheet of obsidian. "It can't have drifted off," Firdaus said. "There's hardly any current. Someone must have stolen it."

"Oh, and who do you think lives here in the middle of nowhere?"

He stared at her angry face. "The Queen and her minions, who else?"

Ing shook her head. "Impossible. I don't think one of her walkers would recognize a boat."

Their eyes met. Frog.

"Frog?" Ing said in a honeyed voice that grated on Firdaus' every nerve. "Is there something you need to tell us about the boat?"

Frog stared sullenly at the muddy ground and refused to answer. Firdaus was sure she'd done it. The petty revenge of the powerless on the powerful, the kind of thing a disgruntled maid would do, spilling tealeaves in his slippers or soot on his bedding in a fit of pique.

"Never mind," he said. "It can't be undone. We'll have to find another way. Build a raft, maybe?"

Stands of stork-legged papyrus, bamboo, and sponge fern ringed the island. With nothing but their eating knives, it would take a long time to build something water-worthy. And crossing the swift-flowing river would be riskier on a raft.

"We could float down to the Gap and get ashore there?" Firdaus said when Ing remained silent, in deep thought.

"No," she said after a long while of pulling her lip. "We'll go the other way around, across the Rim. Over the East Pass and then return via the Rim Pass until we hit the road."

"Return to the city? Why?" he said. "I want you to take me to the other Wan. I need real allies, not just a creepy creature pretending to be a hill."

Ing bit her lip.

A sure sign she was going to tell him another lie. "The truth, please," he said.

"Firdaus, there are no Wan in the Maze. Just Ghast."

He shouldn't have been surprised by now, but he still was.

"Then what the propheting fuck did we come here for?" He waved his arms to encompass the Maze, stinking gently in the morning breeze, the Mound, the whole island.

"You needed to meet the Queen Mound."

"You said you were taking me to the Wan strongholds, to make alliances!"

"I never used those exact words," Ing said, and tried to put her hand on his arm. "I knew you had to experience this for yourself, or you would never have understood how strange the Ghast are, and how human the Wan."

She might be right about that, but that didn't mean he liked being lied to. He turned his back to her and crossed his arms. "So I'm still on my own? Just me, no allies?"

"You have me," Ing said. "And the other Wan live in White City."

His mind boggled. "What? Where? In the Dark Quarter?"

"No, underneath the city, in tunnels."

Firdaus had to sit down. The idea of Wan crawling under his feet his whole life was like maggots oozing over his pristine city. He took a deep breath and pushed himself up again. He wouldn't give her the satisfaction of seeing him off balance.

"So back to the City. To sneak around in secret. How many Wan are there? Enough to form an army?"

"Hundreds," Ing said, her eyes steady on his.

The answer was too glib, too soon. Something more she wasn't telling him?

"We have to take the East Pass, and return via Black Shore," Ing said, as if the argument was over.

"I'm not going anywhere until you explain what you're doing."

"Of course," Ing said, surprisingly agreeable. "I couldn't tell you before because I didn't want the Queen to know. She might not have accepted that old leg of yours. Here's the thing. Humankind is in danger of dying out. The people in the city, and in the Maze, are alarmingly less fertile than they're supposed to be. Possibly this planet's heavy radiation, in spite of the cloud cover, or the habit of eating whitefish in difficult winters. Our numbers—I mean the numbers of humanity—should have grown much more than they have. The city is dwindling, not growing. If we accept that being Wanned is the only way to survive, we can save civilization."

She'd hinted at these things before, but he hadn't understood her veiled allusions. He didn't want to believe it. Ing made herself sound like a hero, but she never mentioned the Queen Mound's role in all this.

"What about the babies?" Frog said, her voice still hoarse. Firdaus had almost forgotten her presence at his feet. "There wouldn't be any babies anymore."

Frog and her one-track mind. But she was right to ask

the question. "Well? How about babies, Ing?" he said. "Where would they come from?"

Ing shrugged. "They could adopt pets, I suppose. We wouldn't die, though. We could build a civilization. Keep some of the people for breeding stock."

And here she flat out contradicted herself. The people with the low birth rates would magically transform into prime breeding stock? She must think he was too stupid to understand her. Talking about people like they were cattle. Firdaus stared at her face, blithely going off into some imaginary revolting future, without a thought for the people involved, the deaths and the heartbreak. He understood her desire to save humanity, but turning them all into Wan wasn't saving them. It was condemnation. As long as death wasn't a certainty, he was going to keep on trying. It wouldn't happen in his generation, or his children's, although he found it hard to think ahead that far. There just had to be another solution.

Ing said they'd need a full day for the climb up to the pass. There was no place to spend the night on the way up, so they bedded down in their old campsite again.

Frog flung herself down on the ground. "I'm not going up there!" she sniveled. "Those mountains cut you like a knife. People aren't meant to go up there. It's where our Ancestors live."

That was a fun prospect, dragging Frog up there every step of the way.

Ing tied her to a fern tree. Firdaus was glad Ing was prepared to play the bad merchant to Frog, because he couldn't have borne the hurt, kicked look Frog threw at Ing. He went over to her. "It'll not be so bad, Frog. I'll be there to protect you from the spirits."

"You're not the Stadholder anymore," Frog said and turned her face away. "You're as bad as she is."

Firdaus tried to catch her eye, but when she remained stubborn, he tried to make himself as comfortable as he could in the spongy moss. He refused to humble himself for her. Little she-goat.

***

A pinch on her shoulder jerked Frog awake. A cold, sweet-smelling hand clapped over her mouth. Her struggles to free herself were in vain. The blurry white shape dissolved into Lady Ing glaring down at her. Frog opened her mouth to protest the treatment, but couldn't help giving the tempting skin a little lick.

"Pay attention!" Lady Ing hissed. "We're going back to the Mound Queen. You have an audience with her."

Frog nodded and the hand moved a finger's width away from her mouth, ready to clamp back down on it. She wouldn't scream, not after promising she'd keep still. She hadn't let go of her anger with Lady Ing, but the thought of standing up to her made Frog feel weak and squishy inside, and she just knew there was no point. She scrambled up on her knees, but the rope attached to Firdaus' hand jerked her back.

His broad shoulders and back were turned away from her, rounded in sleep. When she gently tugged the rope away from him, she took a secret sniff of his spicy skin. A man so sweet she wanted to eat all of him. The nibble she'd taken had only made her ache for more. If she was modest and obedient tomorrow, he might give her another chance.

She pushed herself upright and shuffled over to Ing, who stood like a tall white tree in the night, exuding impatience, although she didn't fidget or tap her feet.

"Rope," Ing said, and Frog handed over the free end.

Ing started walking. Frog waited until she felt the tug of the rope before she followed. Lady Ing always remained stern and stiff, no matter how quickly Frog obeyed, so she'd given up on pleasing her.

It was easy to see where they were going, in spite of the midnight gloom, because the path they'd trodden through the ochre and orange growth yesterday still showed up darker and wetter than the untouched patches. She could even smell the difference. The path steamed with acidic sap seeping out from the fleshy ochre moss, and a minty freshness dripped from the broken stalks of orange sweetgrass. Frog broke off a stalk to suck on as she'd done when she was a child, but the taste had changed. It tasted sweeter, but also duller. Not enough value in plant sap to tingle her mind, not like eating a bit of Firdaus.

Frog smiled into the night, sliding her hair before her face in case Ing had eyes in the back of her head. When she got back, she was going to wait until Ing slept and then squeeze Firdaus awake by his rod and have sport with him.

Sweetened by this dream, the walk seemed a short one. The bald hump of the Queen Mound glowed faintly against the backdrop of inky Rim Mountains. Frog's feet slowed without her volition. She didn't want to go in there again. She knew the stories. The Queen would never let her out, would force her to dance all night until her feet had worn down to her knees.

Ing yanked on the rope and Frog trotted on after her. She couldn't disobey Lady Ing, could she? She was mean and pinched Frog when Firdaus wasn't looking. But Firdaus hadn't bedded Ing; he bedded Frog. So there.

"Stop whining," Ing said, and Frog opened her mouth to deny the charge, but the sound she'd been hearing for a while, a low, desperate keening, stopped.

Ing hauled Frog close and pushed her in front. "Get in there."

Frog tried to dig her heels into the ground, but she was already inside, and the floor was hard and curious. Ing pushed her on her knees. What did Ing want? Did she want Frog to lick her between the legs, as some of the trader's customers had asked? She could do that, if she had to.

Ing grabbed her upper arm with two hands, placed her foot on Frog's thigh and twisted.

Frog screamed from shock and anger. It hurt. No, it didn't, not as much as it ought to. She writhed away from Ing's painful grasp, and the pain worsened. Something tore with a wet gasp and Frog fell to the floor.

Ing held up something long and thin and white, sniffing at it with her stupid narrow little nose. At one end of the tube, a clump of thicker stuff flapped limply, dotted with a crinkled circle of slightly darker cream that reminded Frog of something. She wanted to sit up, get back at Ing, but she couldn't.

Her arm was gone. Half her breast was gone. Frog screamed again, a thin powerless sound that fell dead in the large chamber. She wanted to scream louder, but only wheezing came out.

Ing kneeled down next to her and rummaged in Frog's bindle. She held up Frog's mussel knife and sawed through Frog's own braided rope.

"She's yours, my Queen," Ing said. "Enjoy."

She stepped over Frog's kicking legs and left.

Frog lifted her remaining hand and felt the spot where her arm should be. Jagged pulpy stuff under her fingertips, a clear break between smooth outer skin and her hard white innards. No blood, but the arm was still gone. Her breast! Her pretty breasts, that had caught both Mallard's and Firdaus' attention.

She could still cry, though, even if she had no arm and no blood and no pain. She sobbed without sound, her one arm before her face. Her tears leaked onto the eager ground, and it was as if the rock lifted itself up to receive her tears. Little hungry mouths sucked at her ear and her thigh. She rolled over. Up close, the white floor wasn't as smooth as her feet had imagined it. Dozens of small fissures crisscrossed it, friable layers like the inside of a rotten tree. Frog forgot to breathe and picked at a fissure with her fingernail. The nail wasn't as hard as she'd expected, and the ground not as soft. The nail broke off. The thin crescent flattened against the ridged floor, as if someone was sucking on it from beneath.

She scratched at it with her middle finger, but the nail sliver was disappearing fast, silvering until it was the exact color of the floor under it, and then, one eye blink, and it was gone. If she lay herself down long enough, the floor would eat her just like her fingernail. She could just stay here, let herself go, disappear into the waiting floor, become one with the great hollow creature she sensed around her.

The tears petered out. Frog pushed her one hand

against the floor to get up, but she flopped back down. That wasn't going to work. She drew up her knees, rolled onto them, and managed to get on her forehead as the third point of support, instead of her missing hand. Lying there with her face down made her feel clogged-up and sad. When she moved her forehead, the skin tore loose from the sucking floor. The skin of her knees, the same.

What would Ing tell Firdaus? She was going to make up some lie so he'd think Frog had run away from him. She couldn't allow that. She pushed herself off the floor, knees, forehead, elbow, and hand. For the second time she tore her face off the avid surface, leaving a layer of skin behind.

Firdaus! She'd find him and tell him all about lying mistress Ing.

CHAPTER 10

Firdaus opened his eyes in the silver morning and stretched until his muscles felt as supple as fresh noodles. He thought he might get up and make tea. Not to drink it, because he couldn't, but for the pleasure of holding a warm cup in his hand with his eyes on a fire. He remembered he didn't have a cup or tea, and sat up. His eyes lifted to the Rim Mountains, looming black and forbidding over the pool of mist that covered the Maze. It was going to be a long walk.

His gaze slid past Frog's tree. No Frog. He couldn't see her anywhere near the campsite either. He pushed himself upright and walked over to see where Frog had hidden herself. Behind the bole, he guessed. But the leash was frayed and dangled to the ground.

"Frog?" he yelled into the wall of vegetation around them, but he knew she was gone.

Ing stumbled up, still half asleep and grabbed his arm to lean against him. She straightened up, but left her hand in place. She hadn't acted this friendly and up-close before; she tended to keep a wide circle of personal space around herself.

"What?"

"Look!" Firdaus said, gesturing to the leash and the tree. "Frog's gone."

"Damn," she said, but she didn't seem alarmed.

"We have to find her. She's going to die, out there on her own."

"Is she?" Ing answered. "She lived in the Maze all her life. I think she knows better how to survive than you do, even if she wasn't Wanned. But she is, which means she doesn't need food, and pretty much nothing can kill her."

"A paradile could. A Ghast or a Wan could," Firdaus said. Poor Frog.

"She probably hid the boat somewhere and has taken off on it. We should have forced her to tell us. But we're never going to find her. She could have gone anywhere. She could be on the next island over and we'd never see her. What do we need her for, anyway?"

Firdaus gestured to the grim prison walls encircling them. "Carrying our stuff up there?"

She rubbed her hand on his elbow in a reassuring gesture. "We have no stuff. We need nothing. All we need is in here!" She tapped her temple. "Our wits are all we need!"

She practically skipped off and bent down to fasten her small but heavy knapsack. She'd filled it up with plants, for purposes unknown to him. Wan didn't eat, she'd said so herself. What had gotten into her? She seemed like a different person. Maybe the prospect of meeting the strange and frightening Queen of the mound had burdened her and made her sour and crabby. And now that she was free of it, her normal spirits had returned.

Still. Odd.

Firdaus tried to think up more reasons to wait for Frog, but he couldn't find any. She'd taken her stuff, the boat. She wasn't going to come back. He bent to his own pack. His arm felt light and unencumbered without the leash and Frog attached to it. It didn't feel right, to leave without Frog, but she'd left them first, hadn't she?

* * *

The ground under Ing's feet firmed up steadily. When she stopped at midday to look back, the Maze was cupped in the black hands of the surrounding mountains like a handful of chartreuse moss. If she squinched her eyes tight, she could see a white spot blinking close to the gap leading to the ocean. She remembered standing on this spot two hundred years ago or so. Back then the gap had bottled up the lagoon that flooded the lower-lying ground of the Maze, surrounding White City on all sides. Now the former lagoon no longer twinkled blue and pretty but was broken up by terracotta mudflats in a thousand small ponds. A dramatic drop in sea levels. Or maybe the atoll itself was rising out of the sea, but it didn't seem likely to happen at this speed.

Dropping sea levels was a new factor she'd have to integrate into her plans. Maybe it wasn't such a bad thing. The island would get bigger. The drowned continents of this world would become accessible to humanity. Once people had cultivated the land, they could turn their attention to mining and smithing. Technology would leap ahead.

Ing sighed and turned her gaze back to the real world, where she was walking barefoot behind a charismatic savage, to whom technology meant an obsidian chisel and looms no more than a hand-span wide. And yet this was a man who thought ahead, who tried to bring new ways to his city. She needed him as a bridgehead to sway the greater mass of Wan to her cause.

The path switchbacked up the mountains, barely discernable among the black volcanic spikes of the slope. Ing knew from experience how sharp the rocky fingers were and drew her cloak around herself. The cotton was thin and worn, but would protect her from the worst of the glass-like slivers.

"Use your cloak," she warned Firdaus. "We don't want that pretty hide sliced up, now do we? The mass would be wasted on the rock; it's never going to get any smarter."

She bit her lip. She could hear her own voice chirping on with maniacal perkiness and Firdaus wasn't a fool. If she let her new abilities to socialize show too much too soon, he'd get suspicious. Frog had been a stupid and annoying girl, but she'd been worth all the aggravation of dragging her whiny carcass along. Ing was assimilating the Frog flesh she'd eaten, and she could feel the difference it made in her contacts with Firdaus.

Frog had subconsciously known how to apply light touches to a man's skin, to hold her head just so, and Firdaus was already displaying a different attitude to Ing. It worked; it really worked. And, by now, Frog was no more than a trace memory in the vast mind of the Mound Queen. Frog's mind had contained so little that Ing wasn't afraid of adding to the Queen's knowledge.

It was long past noon when Ing saw Firdaus stagger and push his weight forward against a sudden wind. The pass. She struggled up the last few meters and stood beside him to take in the new vista displayed below them.

The mountains on this side sloped down to meet the sea, which was choppy and wild even from this height. In between, a darker green than the haram marsh vegetation stretched fingers upward to the black mountain rock, criss-crossed by paths and irrigation ditches. Tea and coffee plantations at the top, then cotton, rice, and beans at the bottom.

The town running down the hill in a long stripe of grass-covered bamboo huts looked both longer and wider than she remembered, and there certainly hadn't been docks out in the turquoise-and-white surf. She blinked to clear the overexposed picture from her brain and looked closer at the ships that were bobbing on the waves. A ketch and a scow, bigger types of boats than she'd remembered the fisher folk using.

"When's the last time you were here, Firdaus?" The wind danced around the glassy black needles that crowned the mountain, singing fluting songs of freedom.

"Ten years ago!" he shouted back. "Is that a dock down there?"

So it was new to him too. Maybe the new docks had caused the trade slump in White City.

She hooked her arm into his and brought her mouth close to his ear. "Let's approach cautiously. Maybe we can find out some stuff about those docks and what they've been trading."

Firdaus' neck quivered and the line of fine hairs on the edge of his jaw rose up. Oh. His body offered more interesting things to do than think about trade, but not here in this brutal wind. All for the cause, of course. She wasn't interested in Firdaus as a person, not really.

She nudged his shoulder. "Let's go," she breathed in his ear.

Firdaus nodded.

Ing sent a silent message of thanks to Frog. It was working. It had been worth the risk of alienating Firdaus.

***

Firdaus wished that the sharp winds scouring his face would enter his nose and give his brains a thorough scrub. The whole day had been one confusion after another. Was his imagination running off with him or was Ing showering him with little flirtations? He didn't want to respond to them, with Frog so recently gone, but the sad truth of it was that Ing was his kind of woman. Forceful, independent women turned him on. He did too much fathering and ruling with his children, his childish subjects, and his rudderless Assembly members, to want to repeat that in bed. Frog had been sweet, but she lacked the bite he craved in a woman.

His hand tightened on Ing's thin arm, and she smiled. "Not here, you idiot. We'd run ourselves through on the rocks."

Firdaus hadn't been anywhere near point yet, but it was quite endearing that Ing got it wrong. That was the woman he knew, a razor-sharp intellect, but a blunt object in human relationships.

"Later," he agreed.

Before they ducked into the strip of finely fronded larch forest on their way down, he threw one last look at the docks through a gap in the woods. They were building ships too, with the timber that should have gone to White City. Larch and palmwood only, soft, easily rotted stuff, but still. Motherless sons of goats.

The clouds' glare was at its hottest when at last they had descended down to rice field level. A stream joined the downward path and ran next to them, cooling the air until it disappeared into a small channel branching off to the side. A primitive wooden board served as a lock to prevent it from running its own course.

"Let's follow the irrigation channel," Firdaus said.

"That's where they'll be planting out the rice today."

"If you weren't a Stadholder, where would you be?" she said.

"A Book of Verses underneath the Bough, A Jug of Wine, a Loaf of Bread—and Thou," he said.

"Hey! That sounds familiar," she said. "Where did you learn that?"

"My father had a vellum book of poems that one of his Ancestors wrote," Firdaus said.

"I think not," Ing said. "He copied it, maybe. That's so illegal! We were supposed to hand down only oral knowledge. To make a true, fresh start."

"I don't understand why you sailed all the way here," Firdaus said. "If it was so much better in your land."

"We did everything virtual, as if we were in a play, Firdaus. Living and loving and leaving. Nothing was real anymore. Everything was pretend."

Firdaus lifted a hand to ward off her strange thoughts. "You never make any sense when you say stuff like that."

When the rhythmic singing of a planting song rang through the fern trees, Firdaus and Ing shrouded themselves in their cloaks. The farmers stood in knee-deep water, planting out bunches of young rice shoots in a newly flooded field. The planting song stopped and the workers straightened out of their stoops.

"Hello!" the plantmistress, the one who set the rhythm for the crew, called out to them. She hitched up her apron full of rice shoots, her big brown breasts wobbling with the effort. "Welcome, travelers! Where are you from?"

Firdaus looked at Ing. She nodded. "We're from Reed Village, on the other side of the Rim. May the clouds brighten your day!"

"Same to you too! Check out my cousin Mohamad's new tavern. He will look after you as if you were a Stadholder!"

"Thank you, plantmistress, we will."

The woman waved a friendly goodbye and gave a backwards nod to her workers. "And one two three, and here we go! Get your seedling and then bend down, root it in the ground and straighten up!"

The workers fell in with her. Firdaus thought with regret of the Rice Planting Feast in the City, which would now pass by without him. Everyone, young or old, rich or poor, streamed out of the city gates to help with the rice planting. The singing, the feasting and the bed sports afterward made it one of the high points of the year. He liked it better than Spring Blessing, because on Rice Planting he'd be standing next to his subjects, feet in the muddy flooded fields, getting his hands dirty with planting the new shoots. It wasn't always hard to be Stadholder.

Ing and Firdaus continued their descent over the elevated narrow dykes that served as paths through the fields, stepping down a level on bamboo-strengthened steps every hundred yards or so.

"Did you see how well fed these people looked?" Firdaus said. "When I compare that to Frog's village..."

Ing frowned. If she wasn't a Wan, she'd have a forehead like a plowed field. "I wonder why. The winter must have been as harsh on this side of the mountain. Worse, even, with winds straight from the sea. But they looked as if they never ate a whitefish in their lives."

"That is the only cause of ill health in Frog's village?"

"Not the only cause. Lack of food isn't helping. But eating whitefish will make it worse."

"They can fish in the open sea, I suppose," Firdaus said morosely. "All winter long. Get the dogfish when they winter here."

"Why don't your people fish, then?"

Firdaus shrugged. "Trade agreements. It used to be that the Black Shore people fished, and that we were the craftsmen, supplying them with cotton and silks and dyes. We don't have truly seaworthy boats. For that you need timber, not only bamboo and willow."

"So here they are, ill-dressed in their bark aprons, but with round bellies and healthy children. You should probably rethink your trade strategy."

"What strategy?" Firdaus said. "I will become Stadholder again, and then I will break them. Smash their boats and their smug faces."

"Don't be ridiculous, Firdaus. Did you see those people planting the new rice? Bark clothes, all of them. They grow cotton, but they need you to weave it for them. They probably just stuff it into their mattresses. This is your sales market, you idiot. You don't go about destroying your market; you go out and sell them stuff. Rich market, so make it so that some of those riches get back to you."

Firdaus flapped his hands in the air. It was impossible to find words to gainsay Ing. "You don't understand anything! It's not about getting rich, it's about honor and honoring promises."

Ing shrugged. "Your way will result in war and poverty for everyone. Where's the point in that?"

Firdaus managed to keep his dignity intact by not answering her absurd and insulting words.

***

Dusk forced them to camp on the soggy dyke around a less recently planted rice field. Ing refused to go into the adjoining village and ask for guest rights.

"They may not know about the Wan here," she said, pulling her fingers through a strand of hair as if that helped her think. The gesture reminded him of Frog. "But let's not force them to see us."

Ing spread a mat on the grassy underground. It might be less humid here than in the marshes, but it was also colder, the slope perpetually ruffled by a fresh sea breeze.

"Where did you get that mat?" he asked.

"Frog left it behind, I guess," Ing said, looking shifty and caught out.

"That's funny. She was so proud of her weaving and basketing skills," Firdaus said, fingering the frayed edge of the simple mat. "Not that they were anything much compared to those of a woman like Kem," he said, not without a tinge of bitterness. Kem would mock him mercilessly if she knew he'd deigned to sleep with a grubby little peasant girl.

"Which is why she left this worn old thing behind?" Ing said with a shrug. "She could always have made a new one whenever she wanted."

Not without access to a mulberry tree, a vat for boiling the fibers, and pounding tools. Firdaus didn't speak the words out loud. As with her blithely stealing the pirogue, Ing didn't have an eye for the time and energy things cost to make, and therefore how much their owners valued them. If they didn't have much value to her, she assumed it wouldn't have any to them. She had the attitude of a very rich woman. What had she said about where she came from? Islands far, far away? None of the islands he'd visited—no more than two; he admitted to being a homebody—boasted any riches of that exalted kind.

Ing lay down on the mat and cast him a look from under her eyelashes that made it clear she was inviting him to join her.

Firdaus hesitated. Her glowing white hips and breasts lured him through the folds of her loose cloak. She didn't have the majestic build of Kem, with breasts like sacks of rice, a soft, rounded belly and buttocks like pillows, but she did have the spirit he sought in a woman. He didn't know what made him waver. No reason to think of Frog anymore.

He knelt down beside the mat, to keep from hurting Ing's feelings. "I never had the idea you were interested in me that way."

Ing sighed and tossed her hair. It gleamed, and Firdaus had the sneaking suspicion she'd somehow found the time to brush it.

"The Maze air gives me a headache," she said. She patted the narrow mat. "Come, don't wait until it gets dark and we won't be able to see who we're sleeping with."

She parted the cloak further to reveal naked, invitingly opened thighs and Firdaus could no longer deny his flesh was leaping in answer. He crawled onto the mat and arranged his body between Ing's thighs. She gasped, as if she hadn't expected him to act that quickly. Her belly trembled nervously when he kissed it; her face was rapt.

She swallowed. "I'm... I'm going to show you what

sport between the Wan really means," she said, chin up.

Firdaus admired her bravery, because her quivering thighs and wavering voice betrayed how scared she was. He didn't know what about. She couldn't have gotten the idea that he was a violent or inconsiderate lover, and a woman four centuries old would hardly be an innocent in the sport of love.

She lay back and accepted his touches with gasps of surprise and joy, so Firdaus ignored her words. He showed her how an adept lover could pleasure a woman, even the first awkward time of getting to know one another. Ing was more than ready to accept him. He slid in, slowly, giving her time to change her mind. He started moving, but she surprised him again.

"Come closer," she said throatily. "Nibble on my earlobe."

Why not? Maybe it had some special significance for her. She reciprocated the gesture and mumbled, "Wait until I give the signal."

Firdaus stirred his hips around in her lush honeypot. When the mood gripped him, he pushed her knees up against her chest and pumped. Ing's head rolled back. Firdaus let go of the earlobe and hoisted her higher, so he could lay her open to his hands.

"No," she panted, "no, come back, you have to eat me."

He was more than willing to eat her, but although he could do many things, he couldn't ride and eat her simultaneously. He bent over, allowing her to set the pace, and sucked on her ear again.

Ing bit off his earlobe.

In surprise and shock, his teeth clamped down on hers and tore off the little cushion of flesh. He just had time to notice that Wan flesh was more brittle than human flesh and then the impact of Ing's gift hit his system.

He was Ing, he was young and still young and never again. She was surrounded by unhealthily pale people with narrow eyes like herself, thousands upon thousands of them all dressed in identical strange clothes. Then there were other people, dark-skinned ones and straw-haired ones that were yet no one. She tore across the skies in strange boats, and talked and talked all day long with her fingers in boxes, to things in her ear, while ceaseless music played and other people's lives rushed by. He saw his own city in ruins, no not in ruins, just being mapped out and built, by that same bunch of strange-looking people, not that their skin and hair and features were strange, just the combinations in which they wore them.

The picture inside his head started to glow like dried kelp catching fire, turning rosy then gold then white, and exploded in a thousand fragments like a fire raining ash until all was quiet.

Firdaus found himself lying spread-eagled on his back, ribcage heaving with exertion. Ing was straddling him, her eyes burning into him, panting like him, her hair straggling over her face like a madwoman's.

"Yes!" she said. "Yes! How did you like that?"

Firdaus tried to shape a word but his lips and tongue were numb. "Unh."

"This is how Wan truly communicate. We can share our feelings in a way that no human can. Wasn't it wonderful? Like nothing you ever felt before?"

Firdaus licked his lips. "Yes," he croaked out. "But there have to be feelings first."

Ing frowned. "You can't lie in the flesh. You feel something for me."

"Yes. No. I don't know yet."

"What did you learn?"

"I saw you as a child surrounded by people who look just like you. Is everyone on your island so pale-skinned?"

"You saw my childhood? I didn't mean to give you that," Ing said. Her triumphant hunter's pose, gloating over the lion she had slain, fled out of her. She slumped over him, hesitantly touched a hand to his lips. "Not to be stingy, but I have so little of those days left. What else did you see?"

"You, talking all the time. All the time, even when you were alone. What happened to you? You are so silent now."

Ing's whole body stiffened around him and she started to get up. Firdaus' hand shot out and stopped her. "What?"

"You have no right to judge me!" She struggled in his hands, her skin slippery with fear that he felt through the palms of his hands.

"I'm not judging you. I'm telling you what you made me feel."

"I don't want your pity, Firdaus. I'm not pitiable. I'm a survivor. I'm serving my ideals. I'm going to save humanity!"

Firdaus took a deep breath. "I believe you. Isn't that what you wanted?"

Ing cast her eyes down. "Yes. I did. I didn't mean for you to get all that stuff from my past."

"Why not? As you say, feelings exist. There is no shame in them."

Ing pressed her lips together. "I didn't mean my... feelings. Well, I did. It's been a while. I just want to have control over what I send you through the flesh."

Firdaus drew her down to kiss her. "Don't be so anxious. Enjoy the moment. Let me do my thing now."

***

"I always liked standing up here," Firdaus said, leaning over the broken parapet of the watchpost that adorned the Rim Pass. No one had been stationed here in his memory, although, to judge from the black marks, fires had been lit recently. Traders maybe, coming up to White City to offer tea and cotton and bits of interesting woods.

The black stone sheltering them looked different. Volcanic rock, he thought when he looked at it, and he even knew what a volcano was and why the island was an atoll, like a ring with the finger missing. Odd to feel that new knowledge seeping through him.

He craned his head to look at Ing, who was looking the other way, over the ocean. Had she deliberately introduced that thought into him when they'd sported last night? What did bedsports mean to her? Enjoyment, or an opportunity to indoctrinate him? He didn't know how to concentrate a thought or an idea into a bit of flesh, and he wondered if she intended to teach him. Yet, he could feel her gratitude for his attentions and her longing for them in his fingertips. Those were real.

He didn't regret making the journey. Ing had been right, he'd needed the perspective he'd gained by meeting the Ghast Queen and making love to Ing. Absence made him love his city the more, seeing it there foolishly perched on its own-self esteem, and with no clue that it would fall if it didn't change its ways. He'd always feared that it would, but now he had something tangible to offer. They'd have to overlook the fact that he was Wan. He'd be Stadholder again. When he and Ing had overthrown Aranaz with the help of the other Wan, they would rule together. They'd make more Wan to save humanity.

His thoughts stuttered. No. He didn't want to create new Wan. He didn't mind being one as much as before, but he didn't want anyone else to suffer what he'd seen Frog go through. Ing was different. She'd adapted to the long life, or maybe she'd never expected any other way. But humanity needed to stay human, warm and fallible and short-lived, otherwise what would be the point in surviving? Living and dying and laughter and crying, having babies and burying your parents. That was humanity, and not being sterile and powerful and life going on and on and on beyond meaning.

The view before him looked so beautiful, the steamy yellowy green of the Maze, slashed through by a silver ribbon of river. He looked for the gap that linked lagoon to sea, but all he saw was the black jagged fingers of stone reaching up. They were all fools in the city not to have attended to the harbor problem sooner. None of the other islands' big-bellied wooden boats would be able to get through it. He, no they, would have to build a new harbor on the outer side of the atoll. Maybe on the stretch of beach that linked the city to his villa, crowning the looming crag on the left of White City.

White City.

His city was white.

He leaned blindly backwards against the inimical rock

face to keep his knees from buckling. Think away the buildings on top, and it was a mound. Like the Queen Mound.

CHAPTER 11

Frog crept to the top of the mountain, clinging to the harsh rock like a crab venturing on land for the first time. Her body had started to balance itself out, which was good, but it did make her look so odd. A short thick club now hung from something that wasn't quite a shoulder, and her other arm had become thin and was starting to shorten. She touched her face with her good hand. It still felt normal. The hand checked her breasts. The right one had been torn in half, and she'd never forget Ing's shocked face when it happened. As if tearing a breast was so much worse than taking a person's arm.

She'd known Ing was jealous of her sporting with Firdaus, of course. Who wouldn't be? Every woman dreamed of being the Stadholder's consort. No, that wasn't true. She never had. She'd dreamed of being someone's wife, and having lots of babies. That was all. If life had given her that, she would have been the happiest person in the world. She wasn't greedy; she didn't ask much. The dream seemed modest to her now, but it had been too great an aspiration for a lowly, orphaned girl.

Firdaus had changed her. She'd become his lover, and nobody could ever take that away from her. It had really happened. The touch of a Stadholder had made her into something better and shinier than mere flesh. If only she hadn't been Wanned by that Ing, she just knew she would have given him many babies. The touch of a Stadholder.

Stupid Ing. Had she thought Frog would lie down and be eaten by that thing that called herself a Queen? Frog had waited as long as she dared and crept out of the mound. Ing's trail had been easy to follow.

The only sound here on top the world was the fluting of the wind. Frog crawled into the shelter and lifted her secret rock. There they were, the marks she'd made every time she came up here with her trader, made to sleep in the hardest coldest corner of the shelter. It seemed like it had happened to another person. Seven marks.

She couldn't wait any longer, or dusk would find her still on the mountain. Frog inched upright, clinging to the rock face to support her out-of-kilter body and peered harder. It was safe to follow them down now. She knew where they'd be going, that wasn't so hard. The city, of course. She'd seen it before, as she and her master and his train had been made to wait outside the walls. She wouldn't be so humble now, squatting in the dirt and expecting nothing. She'd find a way to get in this time.

***

The guard hurt Hilm's arm as he dragged her into Aunt Aranaz' throne room. Hilm arranged her features into maximum tearful childishness and faked a sob. The old leather of the throne seat creaked when Aranaz bent forward to take a better look at her.

"Dear niece."

Hilm scowled and crossed her arms over her breasts. Dried flakes fell off her filthy, mud-caked skirt. She knew Aunt Aranaz had deliberately not allowed her to clean up, so the difference between poised, fragrant Stadholder and dirty smelly child would be even greater.

"Dear Hilm. I know you're not happy about what happened to your father, but you must understand it was necessary. The people would never have been satisfied as long as he still was in the city. The Wan are foul beasts, haram in their very nature, and they don't belong with humankind."

Hilm pushed her chin further down. "Firdaus is still my father. I want to take care of him."

"My dear girl, although I don't doubt that he loved you very much when he was still alive, he isn't your father anymore. He's been changed into something unclean and dreadful."

"I don't believe you! He was still himself. He sounded just like the old abba."

"Hilm!" Aranaz said. "Did you not smell him that day on the docks? Did you not feel his hard, alien flesh?"

Hilm hung her head. "Can't he stay close by the city somewhere? Maybe in the villa? So we can live with him?"

"Brother-daughter, you haven't been listening to what I've been saying. Your father is to all intents and purposes dead. Perhaps his white, rotting body still roams around the Maze somewhere, but you will never find him out there. He's gone. The Maze is huge, and very dangerous. Didn't you realize that when you took your little brother out there? Don't you realize what those peasants do to pretty little girls like you?"

"I was fine," Hilm said. "Nothing happened." She had an adult along, but she knew better than to tell her aunt about Ali.

Aranaz gestured at her. Hilm wasn't going to meet her gaze.

"Fine. Look at you. You're as thin as a peasant. You went hungry. You're filthy. You are no more able to take care of your father than you're able to take care of yourself and your brother yet. Leave your father be. Allow yourself to forget him."

Hilm tried to be unimpressed. If she found her father, he would take care of her.

Aranaz took another tack. "Think of your little brothers and sisters. If you took the lead and acknowledged he was dead, their grief would fade away. But if you feed the hope, the illusion that he's still alive, they will keep on hoping and live a lie. I think it is your duty to protect them from that."

She wasn't going to talk to stupid Aunt Aranaz. She was her father's daughter. She should have been Stadholder herself, not scraggy old Auntie.

Aranaz opened her mouth, but closed it again. The look on her face chilled Hilm to the bone. She swallowed. Now Aranaz would sentence her to death. The silence lengthened and Hilm fought to stay still, but her feet wanted to fidget and her neck felt hot and damp from tension.

Aranaz finally waved her hand at the guard and the big, callused hand descended on Hilm's arm again. She was going to have bruises. Aranaz told the guard Hilm and her siblings were to be watched at all times. Her voice was so flat and devoid of any feeling that Hilm knew she'd just escaped a dire fate. This muddy child business wasn't going to work for her anymore. If she wanted her father back, she'd have to make Aunt Aranaz take her seriously. If that was ever going to happen, she was going to have to show her aunt she was a force in her own right.

Hilm allowed the guards to lead her away.

***

Firdaus couldn't believe how Ing proposed they enter the city. Through the sewers? Hadn't he been brought down low enough yet? Grumbling, he wadded up his cloak and thrust it in his belt. That was one good cloak that had seen too much travel already. He always wondered why farmers didn't dress better, a cotton apron wasn't that expensive, but now he knew why they chose bark cloth and reed skirts. Farm work, just like travel, wore out one's clothes.

He stood on the sewer ledge and steeled himself to dip his bare foot in the sludge at the bottom of the tunnel. The smell was bad, even for a Wan. Some people apparently still shit on their dead wasters instead of gathering their night soil for the middens. He'd have to inform the Assembly. Or no, he never would, unless he succeeded in regaining his reputation and his throne.

Ing disappeared around a corner, but he heard her splashing just ahead of him. He wished their bedsport hadn't become such a wonderful thing because he suspected that Ing's goals and his own would never match. Wanning all of humanity was out of the question, no matter how much persuasion she fed him. A Stadholder would keep his own counsel and use his subjects as he saw fit, but he felt guilty about deceiving her. The fact that she was almost certainly deceiving him as well made it easier, but not quite guilt-free.

Voices? He halted, straining to identify the sounds. Yes, Ing was talking to someone. Another Wan, he assumed. He splashed harder, inexplicably eager to meet another of his kind. Would he feel as repulsed and alienated as with the Queen Mound? Mound Queen. Something.

The creature that met his eyes was nothing like the Mound Queen or Ing. It was a vaguely human-shaped male, but all over its head fronds waved, branching off in tinier and tinier branchlets, like an underwater mushroom transplanted on a goat's head. Its face was delicate and symmetric, but its ears were pointy and grew into the waving horn-fronds.

It executed a perfect bow to Firdaus, with an old-fashioned but beautiful flourish. Firdaus automatically bowed back.

"Greetings, Stadholder," the creature said with a melodious, multi-layered voice. What a singer he would have made.

"Kem

Weaver of hearts

You have woven me into a sash

You wear it around your hips like a trophy" the thing sang with a voice that Firdaus knew, a voice that played a glissando of shivers down his spine.

It was one of his own poems, written in the first throes of his love affair with the beauteous and bountiful Kem. He hadn't written a scrap of poetry in weeks. Must be a side effect of being Wanned. But that voice! That was Haroon 'the Voice' Chatbaneson!

"Haroon?" he stammered. "Is that you?"

The Wan creature bowed. "It is indeed!"

"But how... you died when I was a little boy! I remember hearing you sing at my twelfth birthday!"

"Don't be dim, Firdaus," Ing cut in. "It's not that hard to understand how he survived, isn't it? He was Wanned. Someone took a shine to that voice and preserved it for eternity."

Firdaus' mouth dropped open from the sheer enormity of that concept. It went against everything that he held dear. A person wasn't a fruit to be preserved, however brilliant his singing. It was revolting.

Ing raised her eyebrow. "It wasn't me. Although I think it's a very good idea."

Firdaus stalked closer to the pair standing there shining white in the dim sewer light. Ing looked like she'd been laundered too often, tall, thin, a little unusual around the eyes, but dip her in a vat of onionskin dye and she could have been anyone. Haroon looked like a fairy-tale creature, and no amount of painting or disguise would make him blend into a crowd.

"How come your head is like that? Is it a disease?"

"Ouch!" Haroon said. "Tread on my heart, will you? So handsome and yet so brutal! I grew these myself. Took fifteen years and a lot of effort, I'll have you know. Made myself a little taller too, but these babies are the main attraction. Touch them. Come on, you know you want to! They're very soft and sensitive." Haroon lowered his voice and jiggled the fragile fronds.

Firdaus knew when someone outmaneuvered him and gave in with as much grace as he could muster. He lifted a hand to the white antlers. "Oh, they feel like velvet. No, softer, like..."

He stopped. He didn't want to flirt with Haroon, good memories notwithstanding. A fellow who chose to look like something from a horror story had to be mad.

Haroon cackled and blew Firdaus a kiss. "You got it in one! I'll let you in on a secret. I feel like that all over. How about you try that out someday, hey, when you're a little less bowled over by my stunning beauty?"

"Maybe later," Firdaus said. Maybe.

"Haroon was the greatest lover of his times, don't you remember that?" Ing said and took Firdaus by the hand.

You're a great lover but hands off my sport buddy, interpreted Firdaus. That was fine by him. His days of sporting with men were long behind him, and he wasn't in a playful mood.

"Walk with us, Haroon?" Ing asked.

"No thanks, I'm meeting someone. Catch you later,

hey?"

Firdaus watched Haroon duck and disappear into a downward-sloping side tunnel. The tunnel mouth looked organic, as if it had grown from the tunnel wall instead of having been hewn out. Inside, the walls felt velvety to his touch, almost powdered, different from the hornlike hardness of the living sewer. Just like the body of the Mound Queen. Yet he felt none of the dread he remembered from his visit to that distant entity.

"Why would he make himself look like that?" Firdaus asked as they walked on.

"You don't think it's pretty?" Ing said. "I do. Besides, from what he tells me, there are side benefits. He's made the whole thing extremely sensitive, if you get my drift. I think he tried his whole body, but that made normal life impossible. He couldn't even wear a loincloth or a cloak without getting constant orgasms."

"Normal life," Firdaus sputtered. "This is what you call normal life? You've been spending the past four-hundred years right here, in a sewer, with a collection of freaks? What did you people do, Wan every better than average performer and artisan? You're insane."

"Don't foulmouth it until you see it," Ing said, unperturbed. "We take a right here."

Firdaus splashed on behind Ing, knee-deep in the cool but filthy water, because he had no better place to go. This wasn't how he'd imagined coming home. He'd known with his head he wasn't going to take the city by storm, at the head of an army of mighty Wan warriors, but the sheer enormity of entering up the backside of the city only hit him now, right in the gut.

And worse, the city itself wasn't the home he'd been dreaming of. When he'd gazed down upon the city from the pass, his heart had burst from his chest in desperate longing for his beautiful white city. It was fragrant, warm, and full of people living and talking and singing and squabbling. But that image of safety was false. In reality the city clung like a tiny mollusk onto a giant sea creature, in permanent danger of being battered to a pulp against the rocks of fate. Shucked off in a twitch of impatience. Or destroyed by the wanton malice of a rival, the Queen Mound. He had no idea how he would prevent either of these futures from happening, and how Ing's dodgy plans might help or hinder him. But he would. Somehow.

"Haroon is an important supporter of my plan," Ing said in an undertone when they had moved out of earshot. "He leads a group of Wan who are composers, painters, in general the people who've adapted the best to their new life. He accepts my reasoning and agrees that humanity should be Wanned in toto."

It made sense that the artists were the ones who liked the Wan life. They lived for their art, and being Wan gave them an indefinite extension to practice it. But who would look at it? Their fellow Wan? Or had they found secret channels to sell their work via regular merchants? Maybe the Wan already produced a part of the city's arts and crafts exports instead of people. A disturbing thought. But one that also led to the supposition that the artists would be feeling the trade slump, and might listen to new plans instead of destroying the fabric of human society.

He trailed his fingers over the lukewarm walls as they walked. The sewers, unnaturally smooth like everything the Ancestors had made, opened up into an enormous, vaulted chamber. Firdaus expected every sound to boom and reverberate off the walls, but instead a curious hush descended. His glance skimmed over unidentifiable shapes huddled against the wall, white figures working the stone with adzes and chisels, alcoves that seemed lived in, with pallets and clothes racks and stools.

A low singing insinuated itself into his consciousness, raising the hair on his skin. He craned his neck, and the source of the music seemed to be a net stretching the width of the ceiling. It was translucent, with bladders of air at the intersections of its strands. The bladders trembled, and he decided that they were the ones to produce the sound.

"That's one of our oldest inhabitants," Ing whispered. "He's changed himself very much from his original shape.

He was a Ghast, not a Wan, but he fell in love with the human voice and dedicated his life to emulating and surpassing it."

Firdaus supposed there was a kind of beauty in being able to practice one's passion into eternity, but he didn't feel the slightest inclination to follow in its footsteps. Not that it had feet. He shuddered. The strangeness of this creature was far off on an inhuman scale. At least Haroon, strange though he might be, was still human, with human desires. No, Haroon was a Wan. He shouldn't keep forgetting that. A centuries-long lifespan would change a person. Not immediately, maybe, but eventually. Compared to everyone here, he was still a child.

Ing led him to an alcove. The walls were shelved from top to bottom, overflowing with baked clay tablets, papyrus rolls, vellum scrolls, wax tablets and cloth hangings covered with strange signs. Drawings of plants and funguses and mushrooms done with miraculous detail and color were pinned against the ceiling. On the floor was a luxurious carpet, its deep reds and blues depicting a repeated pattern of strange beasts and flowers. It tickled soft and tufty against his feet.

"You can sleep, if you want to," Ing gestured.

Her bed was made up with the royal luxury of white linen sheets and a kind of rug over it, suitable, it seemed, for colder weather than even this winter had seen.

"I'm going to call a meeting, so you can be introduced, and meet our allies. We'll need to move quickly."

The bed looked soft and inviting. He might even sleep a bit. But what he wanted most was to find his children, sniff up the scents and sounds of his birthplace and think over what he was going to do.

He stretched out on the bed, projecting the picture of a weary man about to fall asleep. The soft pillows smelled of Ing, cardamom and clove. Ing eyed him greedily, and he let his eyelids droop. She bent over him and kissed his brow. "I'll be back as soon as I can, but it might take a while. Be good."

"Hmm," he murmured, as if half asleep.

Firdaus stood up the moment Ing left. He needed to get out. He paused in the middle of the central chamber, trying not to look upwards to the spidery creature singing over his head, now ululating like a mourning woman, then barking like a bullfrog. Which of the three tunnels to choose? And how to find his way back? He returned to Ing's alcove and rummaged in her chest of drawers, an incredibly fancy thing made entirely out of priceless wood with metal handles. The cost of all that wood was staggering, confirming his suspicions about her wealth. Had she brought it with her on her journey from her home isles?

Yes, as he had expected, she had writing tools. He took a flask of red ink and a brush. He'd be like the old story of Hanas and Garetha, leaving a trail in the marsh to find their way back home, only he'd use paint instead of ricecake crumbs.

He picked one of the two entrances he knew he hadn't arrived from, and marked it with a dash of paint. There. Cautiously, he made his way through the faintly glowing tunnel, marking it every two dozen steps or so.

He compared the skin of his own arm to the substance of the tunnel. They seemed identical. The floury substance that had covered his skin the first few days of his transformation had changed to a pearly, ivory sheen, shinier in some spots than others. The inside of his arms, where he brushed against his own flanks, and the spot he rubbed against, were polished to a high gloss. If he wished, he could shine himself up like a chandelier, all sparkly and pretty. He touched his hair. It was matted and filthy and hadn't been braided in weeks. He added a bath to his list of things to do.

But first, he had to get out of here.

***

Ing breathed in the scent of home. The smooth sewer tunnels had been dug out of the mound's living flesh, and she'd never understood why the mound had tolerated it. She dragged her fingernails over the smoothness, trying to get a few grains of mound dust under her them, but the walls remained inviolate.

She entered another chamber, home to some of her acquaintances. She wouldn't call Eyo and Ade friends, even if she'd known them for centuries. They'd chosen to fuse together as one entity. Ade's thick squat body was welded to Eyo's slender one, at an angle of ninety degrees. Presumably so they could still have sex? Inexplicable. In her youth, science was proud of its ability to separate two people who'd accidentally been born like that, by surgery if necessary, by gene therapy if possible. Eyo and Ade might separate again, one day, if they wanted to, but they'd stuck to this strange merger for nearly a hundred years now.

"Comrades," she nodded.

"Mistress Ing! We wondered where you went. Did your mission succeed? Will the Mound Queen help us?" Eyo lisped.

"She will."

"And what would Mother Doughy say to that?" Ade grumbled.

Ade's broad head and thick neck, as befit a man of his heroic build, turned to the fragile little stem that held Eyo, who must have been related to Nefertiti in some way. Their double-thick middle leg twitched. Ing never knew if that meant that one of them was fighting for control, or if some kind of internal massaging was going on.

"I don't know yet," Ing admitted. "I wanted to talk to you guys first, so we'd be stronger when we talk to her."

"I'd be careful about that," Eyo said, with a melting glance into Ade's eyes. "She does have a big stake in it, and I don't want to think what she could do to us if we muddied up her clear pond."

"I think I can persuade her to stay out of it," Ing said, taking note of the look that passed between the two lovers.

They were potential dissenters, feeling strong because they were together, and she needed to keep an eye on them. With Firdaus not yet completely convinced and committed, her group of supporters wasn't as solid as she'd hoped. She'd have to invest a lot of time in re-recruiting people who could have remained backstage if she'd had Firdaus on her side. He seemed satisfied enough, and reduced her to quivering jelly on a nightly basis. But instead of becoming more pliable because of their regular flesh exchange, his mind remained out of reach.

And then the City Mound itself, Mother Doughy as they styled her. How much did she know of what happened in her belly? Ing had always presumed Mother couldn't or didn't listen in to the Wan's words, but she had never been able to confirm that. If Mother Doughy knew about Ing's visits to the Mound Queen, surely she would have consumed Ing long ago?

CHAPTER 12

The tunnels had no plan Firdaus could discern. He wandered on, marking the walls, and so far he hadn't encountered one of his own marks again. He was still walking away from the chamber. He crossed a few inter-sections, some peopled with what might be statues or immobile Wan, some empty.

His ink was running low, and he had no idea if he was any closer to an exit. He must have been nearing the surface since every tunnel sloped slightly upward. All this wandering made the city seem bigger than it really was; he imagined himself spiraling like a crazed woodworm. Now what? Maybe he'd better head back before Ing found out.

Something moved behind him. He turned around. The tunnel he'd come from was gone.

The faint glow from his hands lit nothing but smooth ivory wall dusted with a mauve sheen. He closed his eyes. He should have paid more attention instead of standing here silk-gathering.

He turned back to where he'd been going. A barrier had risen there, too. His chest constricted. Trapped.

No. He couldn't be trapped in, that was impossible. This was oldstone, too hard for the hardest obsidian to cut through. The Ancestors had built it with their magic. He pivoted on the balls of his feet, refusing to give in to the idea that the walls were closing in on all sides. An incipient scream lodged in his throat. What would happen to him? Would he be crushed like a bug? Would it eat him whole? Could he eat his way outside? The scream threatened to burst out and he swallowed it down. He couldn't end like this, this close to his children, caught in the guts of a giant living prison.

The tunnel trembled, moving perceptibly, about to swallow him. He beat on the encroaching walls, kicking them until one of his toes broke off. A strange sensation shot up his leg, like the sympathetic ghost pain you felt when someone else hurt themselves, but not truly pain. Prophet. He was in the guts of a creature that was going to eat him. He snapped up the toe and gulped it down.

"Help!" he screamed. "Ing! Help! It's going to eat me!"

An orifice opened in the wall. "It talks at last. I thought I might be eating a silent walker after all. What do you call yourself?"

Firdaus pressed his back against the side farthest from the talking hole, trembling from head to foot. "I'm F-Firdaus. And you are?"

"I am the mound you have built your city on, once-human. What's your excuse? Why shouldn't I eat your information, when you have rubbed away so much of my substance over the years?"

It took him a while to collect his trembling wits. "You could have eaten the Wan living inside your belly long ago. Yet you don't. You must have a good reason for that. Is it that you like humans, like your sister in the Maze? You have learned to use sound, after all. Must be a nice change after all those millennia of eating silent stupid walking paradiles."

"I see you've eaten Ing. Her brain is sharp, and she never seems to dilute. Such a pity she chose to keep walking around! What a rival she would have made."

"You know Ing?"

"Of course I do," the voice rumbled. The orifice lengthened and then curled like a banana. A smile?

A blob formed above the mouth and then two dimples that deepened into closed eyes. They tore open, rock chips flying around. The chips dissolved quickly into the floor he stood on. Firdaus' feet did a little cringing dance before he told them to stay put. If he was going to be eaten, nothing could stop the Mound creature.

"Ing came to me many generations of human spawning ago, some time after she and her companions arrived in their hard shells. She was white as a paradile, and yet her inner self was still human. I had not thought such a thing possible, because you do not smell at all good to me, with your muddy skins and water-black eyes. I ate some of her, because she was defenseless and lost, but her flesh was so interesting that I returned mass to her."

Rock ground, and more outline swelled, like an emerging relief sculpture. "Hard work to make a voice and a face," the creature complained. "But I do it gladly for the amusement you humans afford me. Such thoughts! Such will bent on shaping the world to serve your fragile meat. I love it. And Ing is unique. Her mind showed me the place you humans came from. I wish to go there. Ing wants to return too, and she has told me of her plans to accomplish that. She seems to count on you to help her in this, so tell me, will she succeed? Am I shooting my spores in a strong current or will they fall on rocky ground?"

Firdaus leaned against the curving surface. Its temperature was the same as his skin, hard yet comfortable to the touch, like a peach that isn't ripe yet. "I don't know if I should talk to you about Ing's plans." Should he just tell all to this strange creature? Surely not. Whatever Ing was planning, he owed her loyalty, or at least caution.

The walls reverberated with the creature's speech. "Yes, yes, caution is good, sharing information is better. I offer you a bite of my flesh, so you can know I'm speaking sincerely. I could make any sound I wished to, and you none the wiser, but flesh doesn't lie."

No reason that couldn't be a lie, but Firdaus was inclined to accept the statement.

"I agree, lady mound, but flesh can omit, can it not?"

"Indeed. The art of flesh, as we mound sisters use it, is to compose a poem of such information as can be arranged in beauty and sent out to each other. We would not want our poems to be contaminated by useless thoughts of whitefish eating or birds pecking at our skin. But it isn't an art for the newly born, young one."

He'd figured as much. If Ing had learned this art, she

might not be able lie to him directly, but she could leave out whatever she wanted to.

He bowed in the direction of the orifice, although he assumed the presence of the mound mind was all around him, that he in fact was leaning against her skin or her intestines right now. "I will gladly offer you a token of my good will, lady mound, but I would speak to my children first."

The rock around him sighed in gratification. "Such an interesting poem, the poem of parenthood! Give me a tiny taste of you right now, that I may experience it in full richness."

"Will I still feel it?"

"Indeed you will. Your whole body is suffused with your essence, isn't it? A bit of it will not go amiss."

Firdaus positioned his right hand on his left hand's little finger. It wouldn't be hard, to snap it off and feed it to the creature. Who knew what he could gain besides its good will? It went against the grain to break off his own finger, although he'd done it for Frog without thinking twice. The Mound Queen had demanded a similar tax, but with her he'd gotten away with giving an already broken-off limb. His whole body tensed in expectation of the pain it knew would come. His mind tried to know better, but it faltered and failed against the certainty of the flesh.

Hesitation would get him nowhere. He pushed the tip of the finger backwards, too slow, pressed harder and twisted. Firdaus extended the tiny morsel on his palm.

"You want me to make a hand? A lot of trouble for such a tiny bit!" the mound grumbled.

Firdaus took a hesitant step forward and deposited his white fingertip, the nail ragged and dirty, into the stone aperture. The mouth slammed shut a fraction of a moment after he'd retracted his hand.

"Yesss..." The voice hissed through tiny slits in its eyeballs. Firdaus stomach heaved at the wrongness of it and he had to turn away from the sight.

"Such depth of feeling. Your procreation is a quick process, but you manage to cram much emotion in such a short time. I revel in its taste. Accept this poem from me."

The white maw gaped open again and a tiny round pearl lay on the rocky tongue. He took it gingerly, afraid to crush it, but it wasn't as friable and light as he'd expected. It lay smooth and heavy in his hand, and it seemed to him that the flesh on his palm started to curl and rise around it.

He felt much less fear and revulsion, hidden in the bowels of his own city, than he had inside the Mound Queen. Was it Mother Doughy's less threatening personality, or was he getting used to being a Wan? He lifted the perfect little sphere to his mouth and sucked on it. It dissolved on his tongue immediately. He tried to keep his wits about him, experience whatever might come consciously, but he could feel his sense of self recede even as he grasped at it with outstretched hands.

The surface of the sea curved glassy smooth above him, smoother than the ocean floor, scattering the light from the cloudsky in a thousand directions. He strained upwards to it, harder and harder, like an endlessly growing erection. If he could breach the rind of the sea, he would gain release. His tip became thinner and thinner and the momentum was receding. One paradile length more, yes please, more! He thrust through into the warm dry air and spouted his seed into a thousand directions at once, heaving, gaping, turning himself inside out until he could feel himself thin and collapse, dying, back into himself, spent, finished, satisfied.

Firdaus picked himself up from the floor. A wetness against his thigh made embarrassingly clear how intensely he had lived through the poem.

"Well?" the voice thundered into his sensitive ears.

If he knew one thing, it was to praise an artist when they'd bared their soul.

"Magnificent, mistress. Master. Intense, vivid, memorable. How did you come to think up such a picture? Did you imagine it or is it real?"

"Hmmm. I have never quite understood the concept of imagination. How can one dream of something one doesn't know will happen?"

His rusty poetry skills would come in handy here. "Not every whitefish becomes a paradile. Not every paradile a mound," he improvised. "Yet they must dream of it, don't they? Even though it will never happen to them."

"I like the taste of your thoughts. I must ponder on this. I will expel you where you need to go, and then you must visit me again soon."

A tunnel opened just left of the mouth and Firdaus took a step towards it. He turned his head to say goodbye, but the rudimentary face had already smoothed out into faceless rock.

***

Frog floated on a mass of weeds, sunning herself in the hazy cloudlight. Suddenly, her makeshift bed undulated with the aftermath of a heavy blow. She stiffened and closed her eyes to concentrate better on the sounds and sensations of the island below her. Another. Thump. Two close together. Thump thump. The sounds approached fast. She rolled behind a clump of reeds, immersing herself in a low depression filled with water. The light magnified the yellow, eight-fingered leaves that grew under the surface, pearled with little air bubbles, home to a whitefish that came out to nibble at her. Frog filled her skin with 'go-away!' and the creature tumbled head over tail back into its lair.

She inched her face up, taking care that she remained flush with the pond's surface. Her nose sucked in the information that bobbed in the air, and she smelled the distinctive, alluring scent of the Wan, only different. The stompers must be Ghast. Many Ghast. Ten. Twenty. More. She dove under again. If she could smell them, they could smell her. She hadn't sighted them yet, but their footsteps rocked the floating marsh in a heavy, continuous beat, all the more ominous because it was so irregular.

Frog waited. The clear mirror of the surface an inch above her face trembled and smoothed out again, trembled and smoothed out. Suddenly the shallow pool seemed

like a prison, a trap. If she was discovered, she couldn't run
or swim anywhere. She shot up like a surfacing behemoth
and swiveled her head wildly to check for the proximity of
the Ghast.

She had underestimated how far sound traveled.
There, a hundred yards away on the narrow strips of land
left behind by peat cutting, the Ghast lurched and
shambled towards her. Their lumpy white forms moved at
different speeds, in different directions. Most of the Ghast
were stunted or lopsided or bent like wind-blown trees.
They narrowly missed each other every plodding movement, mysteriously correcting their divergent angles so
that they moved step by halting step in one direction.

Towards White City, glowing on the horizon.

Frog watched, unable to tear her eyes away from the
weaving, mushroom-colored army. A foot like a tree trunk
lifted slowly as a Ghast angled its body. It followed the
falling foot forward without bending its knees or swinging
its arms like humans did. These creatures had never had to
run after their food.

The thumping of their feet was random, as if the
Ghast intentionally refused to march in step. Thump
thump thumpity thump. Thump-Thump.

Then, in an unexpected moment of complete concord, fifteen feet clumped down at once. Frog's pool
slopped over as the ground dipped under the combined
weight of the Ghast.

She had no doubt they were heading for the city, and
that they could be up to no good if they came from the
Queen Mound. She had to get there first and warn
Firdaus. Warn the villages full of fishers and rice farmers
and peatcutters and reederers between here and the city.

The purpose in her heart was growing every day, it
seemed. She wasn't big enough for a purpose like that; she
was only Frog. But she had to try. She'd been touched by
the Stadholder and that meant this was the duty she owed
him.

If it meant going into the big scary city to find her
Stadholder, she would. If it meant killing that terrible Ing

woman who was making him do things he didn't want to do, she would. No matter what her Ancestors, who she had never been able to honor because she didn't know their names, would do to her in the afterlife.

In the distance lay White City. One day soon she would be standing before its walls.

CHAPTER 13

Firdaus walked where Mother Doughy's tunnel forced him to go. The floor sloped steeply in a different direction from the one he'd been going. The tunnel's scent moistened and muddied. The walls burst open above him, and the influx of fresh air brought a whiff of brine and mud to his nose. Where had Mother Doughy brought him? Firdaus inched his head out of the hole. Just outside the East Gate.

It was possible, even likely, that Hilm and her maidens would be washing clothes or themselves by the stream.

He wrapped himself in his old cloak. The mud under his feet provided the means for a simple disguise; he covered his feet and legs, his arms up to the elbows in orange mud. The court maidens would never look twice at such a filthy farmer fellow. He clambered over the irregular mud heaps and gullies ringing the wall, working his way up to the washing stones and bleaching meadows. Giggling and splashing carried on the wind. It didn't sound as if a lot of washing was getting done.

Straggly brushes and stands of high grasses dotted the stretch between the walls and the stream. Firdaus went down on his knees and crawled the rest of the way. A high gust of laughter wafted past. Hilm. His elbows gave out without warning and his face landed in the mud. He hugged his ribcage in an attempt to mitigate the joy and grief that battled for victory in his heart. His beloved daughter. She lived. She was well. She was laughing.

He hadn't thought further on how to contact her. He could hardly rise from the marshes like a beached behemoth. There, the last clump of yellowed grass. He slithered over to it. He covered his face with more mud, and drew his cloak over his white hair.

Now to catch her attention.

"Great lady!" he called out in a quavering voice. "Help an ailing beggar out? A touch of your divine hand will cure my ills!"

A tall figure detached itself from the colorful gaggle of girls splashing in the shallows, their skirts lifted high enough to show the dance and wiggle of their satiny behinds. His daughter dropped her skirt and shaded her eyes with her hand. She dripped with sashes and jewelry, her arms ringed with bracelets to the elbow, bells jangling about her ankles, her slender neck bowed down with wooden and metal beads. Firdaus peered to make out the colors of the sashes, and thought he recognized the emblems of powerful courtiers and Assembly Members. As if she was being wooed. Had Aranaz made her heir?

He called out again. Hilm sent off one of her maidens with a flick of her hand. Well, well. Authority had come easily to her.

The girl trod up to the plants Firdaus was hiding behind. "What do you want?" she called out.

"To look upon the face of your fair lady," Firdaus said in his most pitiful voice. "I'm an old man, sick and down on my luck. The shine of her countenance would make my last days bearable."

The dramatic lines were from a well-known play. If he was lucky, the girl would know it. Only in the play, the man hiding in the bushes was the princess' suitor. Much more likely to inflame the imagination of a giddy teenager than a boring old father.

The girl skipped back to Hilm and they conferred with much giggling and whispering. Firdaus had no idea if Hilm would make the leap to her father crawling back to her from the marshes, or come out flattered by a suitor.

Hilm took a few steps in his direction. The girls followed, until Hilm ordered them back with a sharp word. Firdaus held his breath. Had she guessed? Hilm knew the play as well as he did.

She clasped her hands before her bosom in a theatrical

gesture. "Say, good fellow, who are you that you accost me in this uncouth manner?" Word perfect.

"A miserly beggarman, good lady. Let me gaze upon the cloudshine of your beauty, give this dying old man a last moment of pleasure."

She stepped closer, waving her arms like a drama player. "I dare not, good sir, for fear you will abduct me to your realm, or offer me rapine."

"Closer," Firdaus quavered.

Hilm smiled over her shoulders at her maidens, winked more or less in his direction and plucked a flower from her headdress. "Silly," she hissed. "We don't want people to know, do we?"

She offered the flower with a coy flick of her hand, forcing him to lean forward.

Firdaus plucked the flower from her hand, exposing his muddied forearm, clearly showing the white where the mud had dried up or fallen off.

Hilm uttered a muffled scream and clapped her hands before her mouth. "Abba! I thought... I thought... never mind."

So she had a suitor, his little girl? He had no right to the pang he felt at that thought. He'd left her, involuntarily, but still, he'd left.

"Sh, not so loud. I'm back. Where can we meet?"

Hilm plucked another flower so she had an excuse to bend over further. "Let's meet tonight, after cloudwane, in the house Ali Mumtazson bought for you in the Dark Quarter. Do you know it?"

Her presence of mind made a father proud.

"I'll find it," Firdaus said. "But not tonight, tomorrow night. How is Boon? The others?"

"Fine, fine. I'll tell you tomorrow. Go away now. You can't be seen."

***

Ing exhaled a long, unnecessary breath when the last of the old crowd Wan left her alcove. She just couldn't understand the way people changed their minds all the time. She'd got them to agree with her, after years and years of talking and sharing flesh. She went to the country for a couple of weeks and suddenly they were starting to waffle, have second thoughts, move away or disappear. So disheartening.

She'd expended all the extra mass she could spare to persuade them back into the fold, and she would have to regain some of that mass soon or she'd have nothing to negotiate with.

It was good of Firdaus to have made himself scarce, because she didn't need the distraction, but now she wanted him back. Where had he been all this time and what had he been doing? Well, trying to get a peek at his precious kids, that wasn't so hard to imagine. She did hope he'd been a little circumspect. Aranaz would certainly kill him now, if he tried to come back. The new Stadholder disliked losing face.

She stacked her extra stools under the desk. Her eye fell on a pen that seemed to have moved since she saw it last. She'd left Firdaus alone here for a bit. Had he been snooping? Not that she'd blame him; that was exactly what she would have done herself. She checked anyway for the few possession she'd always hung onto, her primitive backup memories, her watch. They were fine. She unpacked her mother's green porcelain vase from its cottonwood nest inside a bamboo box inside a padded wooden box and set it in place. It was unharmed as well.

Someone politely scuffled his feet to announce his presence. Firdaus.

"Good morning," she said.

"I'm pretty sure it's late afternoon," he said.

Ing flapped her hand. "I don't hold to the upside weather when I'm down here. Who cares? I feel depleted. You feel up to sharing?"

He didn't immediately offer a bite of himself, which stung a little. "I haven't been eating that much myself," he said. "What else can we eat? I don't feel up to wrestling a paradile."

"You could go tell the story of your Wanning to an audience," she said. "That generally gets good revenues."

"You think?" he said. "Isn't it the same for every-body?"

Ing rolled her eyes. "That could be said for most of literature, movies and everything else that isn't factual, and still people gobble it up. I think it will pay handsomely and if not, what have you lost? An hour of your time."

She offered him a drink from her amphora, but Firdaus made a face after one swallow. "Did you refresh that since we got back?"

"No. Should I have?"

"It's not fresh, Ing. It tastes spoilt."

Ing shrugged. "We can't get stomach bugs or anything, so why care?"

She got one of those looks of his. Culture-gap looks. She'd been living here for four hundred years, and he for twenty-seven or so, but he was so sure he knew best. But when he put his hand on her hip, she forgot all about that flash of irritation. This was his talent. She was still grateful to poor dumb Frog for giving her the notion of bedding him.

He smiled at her, and the idea that he might actually like her for herself was so powerful that her limbs turned to water, and she led him backwards to the bed with the mass depletion forgotten. Sex, or bedsport, as the natives called it, was food for the soul.

***

Firdaus scrutinized the Wan seated in the underground amphitheatre, row upon row of white-skinned shapes, pale and bulbous mushrooms blooming in a huge cellar. The wedding cake tiers that graced the sloping walls dwarfed the big table in the middle into a tiny bench. The man he'd met in the sewers, Haroon, perched on the top tier like a poisonous toadstool, his wrinkly fronds crinkling and swaying in an invisible breeze. Many of the faces tickled his memory in some way. Ing had said that these people were the recently Wanned, meaning in his or his father's lifetime. So many more than he'd expected.

Ing had invited the Wan to a banquet in Firdaus' honor. The table was empty of foodstuffs or plates, and he wondered what they would eat, and what they would eat from. Maybe everyone would bring his own plate and knife, like in a trading caravan or on a ship.

Ing gestured him to the head of the table. The walls, the floor, the benches, all of it was Mound substance, so he was in effect sitting on the person he'd spoken to yesterday. Would she assimilate information from his buttocks? He might as well assume she was listening in.

Why would people voluntarily live their lives underground, divorced from day and night, away from the seasons? He liked to get out and see what the weather was like, dry or rainy, the cloudsky high or low, threatening mist or heat prostration. How would a person know what to do, if he didn't know the season? When to sow, when to plant, when to harvest? He knew, rationally, that these people didn't need to, but it felt like a barren, inhuman existence.

His neighbor touched him diffidently on the arm. Firdaus flinched away from it and then smiled wider than he'd intended, to assuage the guilt. Instead of a creepy Wan she was a small, anxious-looking girl of about twelve, a little younger than his own Hilm. It was just that they seemed so alien, so pale, so smooth, bleached of all color and humanity. Ing had the same creamy cast of skin, but at least with her he knew the seams and cracks of her personality, enough to make her human.

And he knew himself. He wasn't altered just because his skin and hair had. He really ought to try to do all these creatures the courtesy of supposing the same.

"Good day, little one," he said, "My name is Firdaus."

She grimaced and quickly hid it behind a small pale hand. She'd filed or grown the nails into sharp curved claws. A kitten, then, who behind her fluffy, timid exterior would be all sharp thoughts and bloodlust. "I'm Amrit. I know who you are."

Firdaus remained polite. He was surprisingly annoyed at her recognition of him. He'd never before wanted to be one of the crowd. "You do, hey, sweetheart? I would say we're all equal here under the ground. Stripped of our former lives."

Her eyes narrowed. "Don't talk to me like I'm a child. I'm older than you are."

He recoiled. "Sorry. You just look so young..."

"I think you will find that how we look means different things to us Wan. As you said, stripped of our former lives and habits and expectations. For example, now I don't have to bear fourteen children and die a worn-out husk like my mother. I can spend all the time I like on my pottery."

"Oh," Firdaus said, inanely. He'd never considered that point of view, and it disturbed him to hear it from someone who looked so young, even if she wasn't. "I've got twelve children, and I've never regretted any of them."

Amrit rolled her eyes at him, reserve forgotten. "You don't have to carry them for nine months, get ripped open bearing them and have them drink you dry for years on end."

"So you do have children?"

"I had one child," she said. The barriers slammed back in place behind her eyes.

Firdaus didn't care. "What happened to that child when you were turned?"

She glared at the trespass against common politeness. "Just because you are a Stadholder, doesn't mean you can be rude to me now!"

Firdaus laughed. He liked her spirit. He could never rouse to a meek woman, although he knew it would have made his life immeasurably easier. Half his time had been spent wrangling with forceful women over children and living arrangements and the freedom to take other lovers.

Ing's hand landed on his shoulder like a hangman's. "Please pay attention, Firdaus. The banquet is about to start. And my speech."

Ing, jealous again? It flattered and alarmed him both. He'd figured he was her toy, her political plaything to use for her crazy scheme. Now that his eyes had been opened, she'd been behaving more and more like a proprietary lover since they'd left the Maze. Wanting to sport with him all the time, crying in his arms. How strange. He prided himself on knowing people, and he would never have pegged Ing as the loving kind. Something had changed her, and although he might fool himself and say it was for the love of a good man, he was sure it wasn't that simple.

It made him look up to her with compassion and his answer was kinder than it would have been. "Of course, Ing. You go ahead and I'll be glued to your lips like a child to his mother's teat."

Ing took up a place in the middle of the amphitheatre and cleared her throat. "Dear people, the day we've been working towards is at hand. Our numbers have grown, and our influence on trade and craft has never been greater.

"Now is the time to take back the city. The Dark Quarter is ours! People will get used to us again. All of you here still have living relatives. It is your job not only to open up shops and ply your wares and services, but to woo your brothers and sisters and children back. They must get accustomed to seeing you as people. I suggest that some of you return to less alarming exteriors."

Firdaus winced. She'd had them at the Dark Quarter, but now they were slipping from her grasp again. He figured Ing had been grooming him to be her spokesperson, and now he knew why. His eyes met Haroon's.

Haroon snorted and jingled the little gold bells he'd festooned around his antlers. "Are you kidding? My patrons loved me for my outrageousness when I was alive. I'm not going to bland myself down to a nobody again. Take it or leave it."

Ing's smile looked forced. "I strongly suggest you do so. Don't look to me for help if you get mobbed in the Stadholder's Plaza. Let us start the banquet, dear friend. Be the first to receive a morsel."

"I think not," Haroon said. "Have a taste of my opinion instead."

Why had Ing called this a banquet? He saw no food, and it resembled one of Firdaus' old assembly meetings. Including the snarling and the posturing.

He stood up and gestured to the dim amphitheatre around them. "Let us take back the day, friends. Why should we cower in the darkness, in caves, when there are plenty of houses standing empty?"

"Why should we hide in the dark Quarter?" a goldsmith challenged him. "I need light for my work. I want a house with working glowapples!"

"Then I suggest you work your ass off until you're wealthy enough to buy a house in Crane Quarter," Ing snapped.

"I for one agree with you," Firdaus said, bending forward to look at the portly goldsmith. "I miss the sounds and smells of day, and the seasons. I don't even know if the dry season has begun yet. We will take over the Dark Quarter. Hard work and luck will take us further!"

The goldsmith stood up and bowed. "It's an honor, sire. Thank you for your support." He walked over to Firdaus and looked at him expectantly.

"Give him a piece!" Ing hissed near Firdaus' elbow.

Banquet. Now the meaning dawned on him. Of course. Mere talk would never do to turn these people into his allies. He would have to deliver more tangible persuasion. It wasn't like sharing with alien beings like the Mounds. Those present had been human themselves. Had they once been as reluctant as he was to offer his own flesh, in public?

He broke off a finger and offered it to the goldsmith. It felt like releasing his last foothold on humanity.

The man scarfed it down and presented him with an ear in return. "I don't like to regrow my fingers, your highness," he said. "As an artist, I need my hands to be as old as possible."

The ear-scent urged him to eat it. Firdaus swallowed the gristly swatch, its message of submission and support. It flared up briefly and dissolved, completely unlike the powerful conversion that had followed his flesh exchange with the Mound mothers. He was starting to grasp the rate of exchange. The dominant flesh subverted what it ate. The goldsmith's submissive flesh accepted the message of

Firdaus' persuasive finger.

People, almost half of the Wan present, were getting up and crowding around Firdaus to be acknowledged by him, offering him their flesh in homage. Firdaus watched the abstainers from the corner of his eye. He wished he had a better feel for the size of the Wan population.

Under Ing's fretful supervision, Firdaus accepted the gifts and allowed them to nibble at his fingertips. He consumed as many offerings as he could on the spot, since smelling other Wan led to the desire to eat them, but still a pile of morsels in different shades of white grew on the table in front of him. He'd ask Ing what to do with it; should he keep it for later or distribute it amongst his followers? If he kept eating like this, he'd turn into a Mound himself...

The Wan who had received his flesh joined him at the empty table, and politely exchanged opinions with their neighbors. Fingertips, pinches of fat from their midriffs, earlobes, and so on. The equivalent of table conversation. The mix of Wan and human customs blended the mood into an orgy of mellow and togetherness. If Wan were like people, and he felt confident that they were, in spite of the more unusual aspects of the banquet, this would be the moment to speak.

Firdaus caught Ing's eye and nodded. Ing squared her shoulders. "Fellow Wan! I give the speaking gavel to Firdaus, once Stadholder of White City! Listen to what he has to say!"

Firdaus climbed on the dais and surveyed his new subjects. Here he was, back in his own city again, about to re-conquer it. It was strange and yet familiar to take the gavel from Ing's hand and thank her.

Her face looked clenched and fierce but triumphant. He could only guess at the inner battles raging within. To hand him control of her followers, with no strings attached —that spoke of great trust. Or mad singlemindedness. He didn't want to think too deeply about it. Not now.

"My dear fellows, we have already set out in broad strokes what we will do. The Dark Quarter will be ours.

We will form households, so that we may be strong and not alone when the..." His voice faltered. How did the Wan refer to their former fellows? "...the other inhabitants of White City try to drive us out. Remember, defend your new house and your right to set up trade there, but do not anger or antagonize the others."

"The Mud People! Down with the Mud People!" someone cried out. Someone who'd not taken his flesh, he guessed. Abstainers might become a risk factor.

Firdaus put on his sternest face. "No! I will not brook talk like that! We were once like them, and if we want to live and trade among them, we must set these thoughts aside. No matter how you have been treated by them, and believe me, my own sister wanted me killed—we must not act upon those feelings, because that will only lead to open war."

The loudest protestors left the amphitheater. Firdaus took care to remember what they looked like. He glanced at Ing, and she nodded at him. They weren't seasoned campaigners together, so he could only hope she knew what he meant. Keep an eye on them, not kill them. He'd have to trust it and check on it later.

"Is there anything one of you wants to say? Anything I have left out?" he asked, surveying the curd-white faces turned up to him.

Haroon stepped forward, his antlers jingling wildly as he made his way down to the bowl of the amphitheatre. Firdaus couldn't recall Haroon taking flesh from his hand, so he tensed in anticipation of the man's words.

"May I speak, sire?"

"Go ahead, Haroon," Firdaus said and smiled down at him. That was the way to speak up in an Assembly meeting. An excellent thought, if he said so himself. He should form a banqueting committee and set a protocol, to avoid unruly mass meetings like this in the future.

"I am a singer, as you all know. I can't set up a shop to trade my craft, and let's assume I won't be invited to many wealthy houses in the near future. How can I then contribute to our presence in trade and craft?"

"A good question, Haroon," Firdaus nodded. "What we could use is an inn, I think. A wine shop. Which sells water for us, and wine for the rest of the citizens." He was running out of polite ways to refers to humans. "Where you may sing. Is there anyone here who is familiar with running an inn or bar?"

The Amrit girl stepped forward. She looked even tinier and younger standing up. "My family ran an inn out in the Maze, long ago. I'm willing to try, but I will need help from adult-looking people."

Silence from the gathered Wan.

"I shall help you out to start with," Firdaus said. "However, all of you will think of comrades who might be suitable for this venture, and who could be persuaded to join us here."

Ing frowned at him. Did she think he was demeaning himself by taking on a position? He thought otherwise. Just as a Stadholder would pitch in with the planting and the sowing, to show his subjects that he was one of them, so this would work to his advantage. People would feel free to divulge their troubles to them while he was polishing glasses, and he was confident that the position would become so desirable that people would be vying to take it on.

"Thank you, comrade," he said. "Now, people. It's no use talking and not acting. We're not just planning to take over the Dark Quarter someday. That day will be tonight. We will meet at the Dark Quarter gate at clouddark!"

The cheer echoed back and forth from the low ceiling. "To the Dark Quarter!"

CHAPTER 14

Firdaus skulked off in his own personal tunnel, in a hurry to meet Hilm before he and the Wan would congregate toward the Dark Quarter. This time Mother Doughy disgorged him not at the East Gate, but inside a house. This confirmed that she was eavesdropping on his conversations, and knew what he needed. It was a terrifying thought. She must remain his ally, or all their lives were forfeit.

He was looking at a disused kitchen, great swathes of dust everywhere, broken stools, dead food vines lacing the walls. Probably the Dark Quarter.

Voices murmured from another room. Firdaus crept out of the hatch as silently as he could and tiptoed to the door opening, careful not to rattle the bamboo beading. A sagging bamboo closet showed him its rotting interior, and a stripe of sunlight over the bare floorboards reminded him he had no idea how much time had passed in Mother Doughy's thrall.

"Let's go, baby," the voice of Ali, his treacherous milk-brother said. Who was he talking to with so much familiarity?

"I'm just finishing up this letter, Ali. Don't rush me or my marks will get all smudgy."

Firdaus stuffed his fist in his mouth. Ali and Hilm. This couldn't be true. He'd almost not minded little Hilm having a lover, but not, never, ever, Ali. Rather the whole of the Sheriff company than that little bastard.

Were they alone? Would it be safe to make his presence known?

"Hilm, I don't think he's been reading them. Look at

them. Gathering dust, and none of them moved, let alone read. You should give it up. He's either dead, or never coming back."

"Don't be an idiot," Hilm said. That was his girl! "The island isn't that big. One way or another I'm going to find out. Now go away. I don't want you hovering over me while I write."

Ali and Hilm were alone. Not a single extra shuffle of feet or exhalation, no rustling of curtains or leather mail. Firdaus waited, glad he didn't need to breathe. Finally, Ali allowed himself to be sent away, after some sickening, wet sounds that made Firdaus gnash his teeth. The curtain rustled. Ali's footsteps receded.

Firdaus coughed and stepped into the room.

Hilm reacted so slowly, liking moving through butter. She wrestled free of desk and stool and pumped her legs in a parody of running. She landed in his outspread arms with a thump and climbed up his body like a little girl. Her hot face dug in his neck and wet splatters rained on his skin. She trembled and sobbed in his arms, and all he could do was hold her tight and let her ride the storm out.

"Abba," Hilm mewled.

"Shush, honeyheart of mine. I'm back now. I won't go away again." He was shocked to hear how hoarse his voice sounded.

She struggled out of his embrace and set her arms akimbo. "Why did you leave? You shouldn't have left us! We were all alone!"

Firdaus tried to gather her back in.

She thumped on his chest. "No! I'm mad at you! You're not supposed to go anywhere!"

"Sweet carrot, you know Aunt Aranaz would have had me killed if I hadn't escaped. Don't be mad."

Hilm stuck out her lower lip but allowed herself to lean against him again. "You could have snuck back."

"I have snuck back. Here I am." A tide of apprehension rode up from his guts and clenched his voice to a squeak. "How are your brothers and sisters?"

Hilm reached up to his cheek to cup it. "Don't make

that voice, Daddy. Boon is fine. As fine as he gets in summer."

It was his turn to bury his face in Hilm's mint-scented curls for a moment, just to regain his composure.

"I want to see him. I want to see them all. Arrange it for me. Or should I ask Ali?"

Hilm's glossy cinnamon face darkened and she crossed her arms between their bodies. "Don't look to Ali for that, Abba. Look to me," Hilm said with emphasis.

He took a step back from her, his hands still on her narrow shoulders, to take stock of her.

She had grown. Not just in height, although she would be a very tall woman before she was done growing, but in breadth and curves and in wisdom. The expression in her eyes took his breath away. She was a woman. A future Stadholder, no doubt about it.

"I'm so proud of you, daughter. I will make you Stadholder of this city one day."

Hilm tossed her hair and looked him straight in the eye. "I know I will be Stadholder. Aunt Aranaz has no heirs of her own. She needs me. But I'm glad you're back, Abba. Your support would mean a lot to me. Even if you can never be Stadholder again, you still have the wisdom to advise me."

It took Firdaus all his self-control not to gasp at this outrageous statement. In one sentence, he'd been shoved aside as a useless old dodderer and even tossed a stick to worry his remaining teeth on.

"What did you have in mind, daughter?" Firdaus asked, determined to keep his face bland and all his options open. He wasn't obsolete and useless yet, prophet take the uppity little chit! Of course she would be Stadholder, but after him, not instead of him. She was all of fifteen summers old. "Think on your plans first. You are young yet to take on the mantle of Stadholderhood. It weighs heavily. I'd rather you had a few years of careless youth yet!"

"I know, I know. All the other girls are playing around, taking lovers, finding their vocations. I'd prefer to have a few children before I start ruling, but I have no choice."

"We'll see about that. Abba is not too old and dim-witted to help you, my dearest. I have new, powerful friends, who can help me regain the throne."

A fleeting frown crossed Hilm's bronze forehead, but it was gone before he could be sure of it.

"Abba. We should talk about this more, but I have to go back, or aunt Aranaz will get suspicious."

Then don't dally with propheting Ali Mumtazson, but he strangled the words before they could escape. "What date shall we set for our next meeting?" he asked, trying to convey with looks alone that he wanted her without his milkbrother anywhere near her. There was no way to be sure. If only he could just feed her a fingertip... But no. The notion of seeing his beautiful, glowing daughter turn white as milk was enough to curdle his good mood at once. Never!

"At cloudwane tomorrow, Abba," Hilm promised. "Right here. And if he feels good enough, I'll bring Boon. Kiss me?"

He kissed her smooth forehead, the blood-warm, living skin throbbing faintly under his lips. So beautiful, so wise and thoughtful. A true future Stadholder.

After Hilm left, pulling a hood over her face and walking with such obvious stealth that Firdaus had to suppress a laugh, he fell on Hilm's letters. They lay neatly stacked on a rickety table, in order of writing. The first one read, "Three days past First Rice Planting. Abba, I miss you. Why haven't you returned yet? Awayo has three new milk teeth and Hussein is weaned. Boon sleeps all night without coughing. Kisses, your loving daughter Hilm."

"Tenth day of First Rice Planting. Aunt Aranaz says you are dead. Please come back and prove her wrong! Your loving daughter Hilm."

His sister had a lot to answer for.

He took stock of Ali and Hilm's secret meeting place. This house, the very one he'd once asked his milkbrother to find for him, was not homey, with its straight oldstone walls instead of the curved glossy surfaces of the palace. But he'd rather live here than in the belly of the City Mound, however well disposed to him she'd shown herself so far.

He supposed he'd better go back to Ing and the Wan, to head the march out of the Mound's belly. Ing would throw a fit if he wasn't at her heels like a good gosling. The moment wasn't ripe yet to strike out for himself. He needed more information on the Wan themselves, and on the habits of Mounds. Maybe Mother Doughy could find out if and when the Queen Mound would move against the city.

***

Firdaus headed the trek upwards, accompanied by Ing. She pretended to follow him, but she knew the way and he was acting on subtle cues from her. His chest tightened with anticipation. On the one hand, he felt sure no one on the surface could possibly know the Wan were moving into the Dark Quarter. On the other, he could hardly imagine that it was going to go off without a hitch. Other outcasts, thieves and adulterers and craftsmen working outside of the guilds, had surely seen the Dark Quarter's potential? Everything hinged upon the Wan's good behavior and slow acceptance by the mud people.

He looked around to smile encouragingly at his followers, and try for another headcount. Forty, fifty people at most. A goodly amount, certainly enough to foil the scant amount of Sheriffs that usually patrolled the city by night—because what did they need guarding against? The singer Haroon's absurd antlered head kept striking the tunnel roof. If the antler's fronds were as sensitive as the man had boasted, he must be in agony...

The tunnel ended in a narrow shaft rising straight up to a grated exit.

"How are we going to get out?" Firdaus asked.

Ing showed him the stick she'd been leaning on. It boasted a double hook at the end.

"Watch me."

She hoisted the staff and pushed the hooked ends

against the grate. It lifted with some effort. Firdaus took over from Ing, and with his greater height and strength managed to flip the grate over. That had been well planned. Ing was good at this kind of stuff, in her own way. She could set up meetings, define goals, procure the right tools. She just needed a leader to implement her ideas, because as soon as she opened her mouth, she antagonized everyone. It was hard to imagine someone living for four centuries and not acquiring some skills in that area. She must have resisted learning them, or maybe she'd given them away as soon as she noticed her personality had mellowed. Although her attitude to him was as warm and sweet as melted goat cheese.

"You first," she said. "The Stadholder's lot."

"I know."

He wedged himself in the shaft and worked himself upward limb by limb. He was stronger than he'd ever been, or maybe just lighter. He climbed out, the last reddish rays of the cloudlight caressing an empty square. Rotted greens and other market offal covered the white-caked mud. From the smell of it, passers-by used it as an improvised latrine. He could easily orient himself by the achingly familiar skyline of the city, the crazy zigzag shape of the palace, the towers on the four corners and the Singing Tower in the middle.

This had been called Nightlight Quarter before it had become the Dark Quarter. In the alleys leading off the square, darkness had struck already, and not one glow-apple or rushlight was visible anywhere around him.

"Come on up," he called down. "All is well."

Firdaus stood aside and watched the white tide overflow the empty plaza. Small groups of people separated from the crowd and walked purposefully to square-front locations, others headed off to the borders with Crane and Cloud quarters. There the most popular shops were located; closest to the populated quarters and therefore attracting the most traffic. That is, if anyone ever dared to set foot in a Wan-owned shop.

Prophet. And what about prices? He hadn't mentioned them in his speech and they only now entered his mind. A Wan craftsman didn't need to pay for food and midden removal, wouldn't have children. They could ruin the human tradesmen if they asked lower prices for their wares. What had he done? Had he set a stream of events in motion that would hasten the downfall of his city? This must be one of the things Ing had thought out and not mentioned to him. Prophet, prophet, prophet. He'd have to walk by all of them and remind them of the notion that ruined people make bad customers. He couldn't believe he was spouting Ing's opinions; he remembered how he'd felt about Black Shore village's new docks.

***

Two figures greeted him from the door opening of the meeting-place. Hilm, of course, but she had Boon with her! The boy he'd left too weak to sit up straight. Boon looked skinny but hale, with two spots of healthy deep color in his face. He coughed, but then smiled and held out his hands to Firdaus.

"Boon! My boy!" His chest and throat were too full of feeling to say more. He hugged the slender body to his chest and thanked the Ancestors for allowing him this moment.

Boon nestled his head against Firdaus' midriff. "Abba! We missed you so much. Aunt Aranaz keeps telling us you're dead, but Hilm said you weren't. I was so afraid she was wrong..."

"Aranaz wasn't lying, children," Firdaus said. "She thought I did die or at least, I vanished into the Maze."

Boon's eyes grew big. "Did you have adventures like Simad?"

"I did, Boon my sweet. The lady Ing and I traveled through the dangerous marshes in our little boat, every moment of the time wary of the horrendous paradile that infest these waters!"

Boon took a deep, fascinated breath, which ended in a prolonged bout of coughing. Firdaus held him, but his eyes met Hilm's worriedly. Should she have dragged him here? Hilm shrugged. What Boon wanted, Boon got. Everybody was aware he might not live long and spoiled him mercilessly.

"A paradile ate my foot, son! Bit it clean off!"

Both children looked skeptically at his perfectly ordinary-looking feet.

"Don't make up stories if we can see they're not true, Abba," Boon said. "Think of something better."

From outside, a sudden crash of footsteps made them all freeze up.

"What was that?" Firdaus whispered. "Hilm, were you followed?" He thought of a worse alternative. "Did you tell someone?"

"Of course not! I know better than that!" she said.

"Not even...?" He couldn't bring himself to utter Ali's name. He should have wrung the little bastard's neck yesterday evening.

"No! You think I'm stupid?"

"Not now, honeyheart. Shush. Let's get into the kitchen."

Firdaus swept Boon up into his arms and walked backwards to the kitchen. He wasn't mistaken. That was the sound of wooden boots tramping up. Aranaz either had Hilm followed or Ali had gotten suspicious...

"Get down there!" he whispered to Hilm. "Yes, there. Do it now!"

Her face scrunched up in protest, but she seated herself on the edge and slid down. Firdaus stuck his head down the toilet and called down to Hilm, "You catch Boon! Here he comes now."

He'd only just managed to wring his shoulders through the propheting narrow tube when he heard a man's voice call out. "They're in there! I saw Lady Hilm go in there!"

Firdaus pushed the children ahead of him, but they hung back against his body, afraid and out of their depth in the dark tunnel that smelled of Mother Doughy.

"Don't be afraid, children. This is where the Wan live," he whispered.

They clung to his hands and shuffled fearfully forward into what seemed to his eyes a dimly lit tunnel, but must be pitch dark to them.

He cleared his throat. "Now, where was I. Ah, yes, when the paradile had eaten my foot."

"It's not true," Boon said in a reedy voice.

"Children, believe me, cross my heart and hope to die, it really happened. But it grew back. Wan don't bleed, Wan don't feel pain, and if someone bites our foot off, we grow it back. And my friend the lady Ing, to whom I will introduce you, dove into the dark waters of the Maze and killed the paradile!"

Boon stroked Firdaus' arm with a reverent little stick finger. The boy felt warm and clammy. He must still be running a bit of a fever, even in high summer. Firdaus pushed the thought away and continued his story. "Of course, I ate the paradile."

"Ew!" they said in unison. "Paradiles smell bad!"

"Oh, really! As if you've ever seen one up close!"

"Everybody says so. Anyway, they are haram, daddy, you mustn't eat haram food!"

Firdaus looked grave. "I can no longer hold to the law, my children. The only food I can eat is haram."

Boon's whole body twitched, and Firdaus knew it was only with great self-control that he didn't cringe away from his father.

They reached the great hall that contained Ing's alcove. Firdaus knocked on the wall to announce his presence. Ing looked up, frowning, from her tablets.

"Children, let me introduce you to mistress Ing, my friend. Ing, these are Hilm and Boon, my oldest children. Aren't they tall and handsome?"

Ing bared her teeth at Hilm and stared hard at Boon. "Ni hao, children."

When Firdaus saw Ing's less than welcoming expression he felt a little sliver of warning run down his spine. The great mass of Mother Doughy pressed down on his shoulders. Why did he feel he'd just exposed his children to enemies instead of friends?

He put his arms around the children's shoulders and

hustled them away from the alcove and Ing's displeased eyes.

"You haven't changed, daddy," Boon giggled. "Kem used to look exactly like that when we disturbed you."

Firdaus didn't often think of Kem's dark, bountiful flesh anymore. No use pining after what one couldn't have. Frog, and now Ing, had replaced her companionship and sharp tongue with their own flavor of personality. The Wan were as diverse as real people were, and he didn't feel as lonely and bereft as he once had. He still wished he could have all his children by his side, but acceptance of some of the changes had definitely set in.

Boon never forgot the thread of a conversation. "But if you eat haram foods, won't the Ancestors be angry, Abba?"

Firdaus had lost the comforting faith of his child-hood, when he'd been sure that his Ancestors were looking after him, riding on the cloudsky. "I don't know, Boontie. If they are, there is nothing I can do about it. I can't eat the halal foods anymore."

"No meat?" Hilm said.

"No."

"So you couldn't eat us if you wanted to?"

Firdaus gaped. "Is that what you thought? That I might eat you?"

"No, of course not," she said. "I know you. You are my abba and you would never ever harm us. But that is what people think. Kem tells everyone she was in deadly peril the last time you visited her, and how brave and steadfast she was in refusing you her bed!"

Oh, that was just perfect.

"Those are silly stories, children, told by people who've never talked to a Wan in their lives. We have white skin, and we don't get sick or die, but we can only eat whitefish and paradile and..." Firdaus halted. He wasn't quite ready to explain the reciprocal cannibalism thing. That was a bit too gruesome for their little ears. He would tell Hilm someday, she was a woman now.

"The Wan never get sick?" Boon said in a wistful little

voice.

    A cold finger walked down the ladder of his vertebrae. He pushed the thought that threatened to form words firmly back down. No. No way, ever.

CHAPTER 15

Ing waited for Firdaus to return to her alcove after he'd escorted his children outside, the tubercular boy and the sharp-eyed girl. He didn't look as happy as she'd anticipated.

"What's the matter?" she said.

He shrugged.

A ping of intuition sounded. "You think the boy is going to die?"

"Don't say that!" he barked and fussed with his still unpacked roll.

"Throw that nasty thing away," Ing said when he fished out Frog's worn bed mat. "You don't need it anymore."

He growled and turned his back on her. But she wouldn't let herself be deterred by moods like that. "About the boy. He doesn't need to die. If you Wan him, the disease won't bother him anymore."

"Don't be ridiculous! I wouldn't condemn my own son to this existence!"

"What's so bad about it? You can have a long and fruitful life. And if living underground bothers you, find a house in the Dark Quarter and take part in normal everyday life. The people will get used to us. They better, because it's the only way they'll survive."

"He's a child," Firdaus said with emphasis. "A warm-blooded living child, who needs years to grow into adulthood. Not a thing to be turned at a whim, like you turned Frog. And look what became of her! Lost in the Maze. Maybe dead by now, eaten by a paradile."

Ing refused to think about Frog and what had become of her. "You knew her for a week, tops. She was just a servant. Let's not talk about Frog, but about saving your child. You know what kind of disease he has, don't you? It's likely tuberculosis. Or something autoimmune. He'll die of it. Look at him, how small and thin he is for his age. He won't survive this winter."

Firdaus stood up, threw his hands in the air as he started to speak. His elbow caught a vase, her most prized possession, lugged along across light-years and centuries. It tumbled in slow motion to the floor and smashed into dozens of shards. Ing burst into tears. She didn't understand why; anger would have been more appropriate. The clumsy fool. Her mother's vase, made by hands ancient even in her mother's time, a symbol of an ancient culture on a vanished planet. Out of her reach forever, like so many things she desired.

Firdaus apologized and gathered her in his arms. She could still smell the taint of the children's human sweat. This was Firdaus at his best, comforting women and children, regardless of provenance.

"Don't ever mention this again. Promise?" he murmured in her ear.

She nodded. It was always best to seem to agree. She wanted to agree, a weird and unsettling urge, and the sobbing didn't seem to want to stop... what was going on with her? She'd never felt this way before. Not in a very long time, certainly.

The closest thing to this peculiar state of mind she could remember was the crush she'd had on Gavin Park in eleventh grade. She and her father had come to live in the US because he had a guest professorship, and the Korean-American Gavin had been so much cooler than any of the boys back home that she'd nearly swooned when she passed him in the crowded school hallways on physical presence days.

Ing leaned her forehead against Firdaus' smooth, broad chest and knew she was doomed. Firdaus was the new Gavin. The revenge of Frog. Frog would be cackling in her marshy grave if she knew that Ing loved Firdaus with squishy gooey feelings. Ing hadn't felt like this in four centuries and she hadn't missed it. The reason why was clearer than ever. Saving humanity required a ruthless head and a steady hand. How was she going to manage that if her knees shook every time she beheld this amiable giant?

And nothing much had changed. She knew how to make love to him, but she still had no idea how to talk about her feelings. Blurting it out, I think I love you, was still a really bad idea, right? Or did people just say these things?

She tried to remember if Frog had shown her feelings to Firdaus. As far as she could remember Frog had just lain down next to him and shoved her hand under his loin-cloth. Talking was too much of a hurdle, but that example she could follow.

***

Firdaus kicked the wall of the prospective inn. He didn't know what good it would do, but it was a gesture other men made when they inspected a new house.

The goldsmith he'd talked to at the Wan meeting walked by. The man pulled along a little boy. Firdaus greeted him politely and looked for Ing. His head snapped back to look at the child so hard it ached. The boy was human. He was crying.

"Goldsmith! Wait!"

The man halted and smiled his obsequious smile. "Good cloudwane, Majesty. How may I be of service?"

Firdaus crouched down and smiled at the little boy. "Hello there. My name is Firdaus. What's yours?"

The boy stopped crying for a moment, hiccupped, and went off into mindless wailing again.

Firdaus stood up. "Why is he upset?"

The goldsmith pouted and his floury belly shook in agitation. "He's just being ornery, sire. He'll get used to his new life soon enough. He's my new apprentice. My cousin's grandchild."

The boy cried harder and suddenly doubled over, vomiting. The Goldsmith yanked him away from his feet. Firdaus had seen those thick, pink clots before, coming from Frog's mouth as her body voided its last human flesh.

The boys' skin was speckled with paler areas like a spotted goat.

"You turned him? What for?"

The goldsmith looked at him as if he was insane. "I need an apprentice, Majesty. I can't do all the work in a shop myself. He'll be well looked after."

"He's a little boy!" Firdaus yelled. "Are you out of your mind, condemning a child to this existence? Did you ask his permission?"

The goldsmith crossed his arms. "Well, excuse me, Majesty, but nobody asked my permission to be Wanned. Why should I have asked him?"

"Because you know what it feels like to be turned into a monster. The perfect reason never to do it to anyone else."

"I never," the goldsmith bristled. "Who do you think you are, to question my actions!"

"Someone less foolish than you. You've just endangered all the Wan in the Dark Quarter by this thoughtless deed! What will the citizens think?"

The goldsmith blustered a bit but Firdaus knew there would be no more resistance. Now he just needed to find a way to pound it in all the other Wanned heads.

"I'm going to take him with me," Firdaus said.

He took the boy's hand and walked off. Should he have foreseen this? He didn't know the other Wan, but Ing could have warned him. Tonight he would walk a circuit of all the Wan aboveground, and talk to them again. Feed them his flesh. He patted his midriff. He would need more extra flesh if this was to be his life.

Firdaus laid the little boy on the bed in his new house in the Dark Quarter. Although he'd acquired it less than a day ago, the house already felt like coming home. And since he took care to enter it only from the sewers, Aranaz wouldn't know about it yet. It was in a good spot, too, close to the Stadholder's Plaza, next to an empty house the little Wan innkeeper had appropriated. Perfect. He just had to keep his children away from here, because Aranaz kept a close eye on them.

Now what to do about the boy? Maybe his family

would take him back, but that would be cruel. He'd be different, he'd never grow any taller or... that wasn't certain. If he wanted to, and ate enough, the boy's body could grow. Firdaus wondered why Amrit the innkeeper chose to keep the body of a little girl. Maybe she had a lover who liked his girls young?

He stared at the boy on the bed. He wasn't falling asleep as Firdaus' own children would have done, lulled by the safety and warmth of their father's presence. The child was shivering in the new strange environment, feeling miserable, no doubt, eyeing Firdaus' every movement warily. Rescuing children, not as simple as one might think.

Firdaus went over to the divan and cleared off the junk that had already accumulated during his brief stay in the house. Prophet, he'd like a bath. That was another business some Wan was going to have to run. A bathhouse. Baths were the essence of civilization. But how would he ever heat enough water to have a nice bath without servants and a whole array of kitchen fires? He'd have to settle for a sponge bath for now.

He lit a fire in the kitchen with the few mysteriously left-behind blocks of dried peat and tried the tap. No water came out. Great. The Dark Quarter didn't support glowapple vines anymore, and now it was out of water. Nobody was going to contest the Wan the right to stay here. The Wan didn't need to wash as much as the humans, but they did need to replenish moisture. And the arak-house needed water to serve the Wan, water to brew ricewine for the human customers, not to mention the huge quantities of water the dyers and virtually all craftspeople would need.

He raked the fire and trudged back to the main room. He sank on the divan with his head in his hands. No water. How would he ever solve that?

A tentative touch startled him. "Are you sad?" the little boy said.

He looked even more dappled and white-freckled than before, but his eyes had clear whites.

"Yes," Firdaus said. "There is no water and I don't know how to fix it."

"Is it your job to fix the water?" the child said.

"No. Well, maybe. If there is no one else whose job it is, I have to find someone who can do it."

"Oh." The boy stroked Firdaus' hair. He must have learned that from his mother. "I could go to the fountain and get water for you. I do that sometimes for mother."

"Won't she miss you?" Firdaus asked delicately.

The boy's lip trembled and he looked at his white-freckled hands and the big white spot growing outwards from his right armpit. "Uncle said she wouldn't want me in the house anymore if she knew I was going to become a whitey."

"Did she say so?" Firdaus said, easing the boy on his knee.

The boy didn't answer but trembled against his chest. Under Firdaus hand, his shoulder blade fluttered like a broken wing. The boy's sour smell of vomit and sickness and fear rose in Firdaus' nose and his eyes prickled from it.

"Do you want to go home?"

"I can't!"

"What if I take you?"

A waft of heavenly fragrance announced Ing's arrival. The boy wrinkled his nose and hid his face in Firdaus' chest. Ing entered. Her otherworldly beauty, the soft shine emanating from her tall slender body illuminated the room and stirred a response deep inside.

"Hey. Isn't he a little young for you, Firdaus?"

The off-hand cruelty jerked Firdaus out of his burgeoning arousal faster than a dash of cold water. Ing was as mercurial and unpredictable as the tide, especially lately. He suspected he simply hadn't known her well enough to gauge her moods previously.

"The goldsmith abducted this boy from his mother and infected him. What can we do to ban this behavior and punish the goldsmith?"

Ing threw herself on the bed and laced her arms behind her head. She shrugged. Her small breasts jiggled.

"Paora? He's okay, you know. Why punish him? Isn't this what we want to happen? Increase the amount of Wan in the city, and gain acceptance."

The boy sat frozen on Firdaus' lap. He consciously willed his body to relax. "Gain acceptance, yes. Increase the amount of Wan? I think not. You told me yourself the birth rate was declining. The last thing we should do is cull the young."

Ing sighed. "I don't know why I keep explaining things to you. You never seem to grasp the essence of what I'm saying. Humanity will die out. Period. The only way to survive is to become Wan. I have mitigated my plans enormously through your input, you know. You made it clear to me we'd face culture shock and anarchy if we did it all at once. This taking back the Dark Quarter thing is brilliant. But we shouldn't lose sight of our main goal."

Firdaus wanted to hurled the nearest object at her, but the trembling boy on his knee forced him to take deep breaths and calm himself.

"Abba?" Hilm's voice said from the door opening.

He hadn't even heard her coming. Them. Boon peeked over his sister's shoulder. Firdaus felt like screaming. How had they found him? Now he'd have to move again, because he was sure Aranaz had them followed. Didn't they know better than to walk around in broad daylight? He threw Ing a look intended to convey they would continue their argument later.

"Good cloudwane, lady Ing," Hilm said politely. "Hallo there. I'm Hilm. What's your name?"

The boy clasped his hand around Firdaus' thumb. "Ulio, Milady."

"Nice meeting you, Ulio. This is my brother Boon," Hilm said, and her eyes raked over Ulio's skin in a manner that reminded Firdaus of his sister Aranaz and Ing both. It chilled him to the bone.

"Abba, we have to talk," Boon said.

Firdaus looked at his son's face, surprised. Boon was doing the talking? Maybe Hilm had committed some trespass and he was supporting her.

"Abba, I'm sick. Even though it's summer, I'm not feeling good. I'm never going to get better, am I?"

Firdaus throat closed up. Ulio softly stroked his forearm. Firdaus wanted to gather Boon in his arms, but he didn't know how to do that without hurting the other little boy.

"You don't know that. Maybe you will get better."

"It shouldn't be red lung," Ing said, "because that's not a sickness we brought with us, but I have to say, it looks uncannily like it. In that case, he's not going to survive. And you should separate him from your other kids because he might be contagious."

"Shut up, Ing," Firdaus bit out.

Boon approached and set his hands on Firdaus' shoulders. The palms felt clammy and too warm.

"Abba. I don't want to die. Make me like *you*."

CHAPTER 16

Torches flickered like orange feathers in the gray dawn gloom, one or two reed islands away from Frog. She heard voices, too far away to make out words, but the undertone was excitement and fear.

Frog would have preferred to stay away from settlements. She didn't want to remember the life she'd lost, but the inhabitants of the Maze needed to be warned against the Ghast. The creatures would pose a threat not just to the city, but to all the villages they must cross to reach it. She'd crawled from island to island, slipping soundlessly through the watery channels. She crouched down in the reeds to observe the torchbearers unseen.

The people sitting around the fire were all men, easy to identify by their low growling voices, although once or twice one of them shot up high into the squeak of adolescence. They were arguing about something. She peered ahead to where the torches smudged the morning sky with black fingerprints. A clot of men eddied in the middle, scuffling, maybe holding down someone? A wordless cry of scent billowed out and the taste of it was sharp in her mouth. Another of these creatures. A Ghast, that's what it must mean.

She clambered up. She must look a sight, without even a cloak to cover her unsightliness, but it couldn't be helped.

"Good fellows, be careful of that creature!" she cried out. "He can't be killed with blows, and he will escape if you do not bind him tightly!"

At the thin sound of her woman's voice, a few men flicked her a glance, and then started at her appearance.

Two of them came forward, brandishing the smoking torches in front of them, not to light them, because the cloudsky gave enough, but as a defense against her. They gaped at her mismatched arms and the bite out of her breast. Without her purpose glowing strong and firm in her chest, she couldn't have withstood their gazes.

"Otter! Look over here! What are you? Who are you?"

"I am Frog, good fellows, a woman fallen on bad times. A creature like that maimed me and left me for dead. That's how I know how to deal with them."

"Look at you," the biggest one said, looking her up and down with a snarl of disgust on his face. "You're white as hulled rice. You're one of them!"

"Good sirs, believe me, I am not! I was a woman until I was turned into this color. Ask the creature on the ground, you will see it cannot speak, doesn't have a proper mouth or a tongue!"

After a long hard stare, the men allowed her to approach. They gave her a wide berth so she could have a look at the Ghast struggling on the ground. It was still bound, with a snout like a paradile and white eyes that glared at her. It sniffed when she came close, and she could feel the hunger for her flesh exuding from every pore on its skin.

"Kill it by cutting its arms and legs and head off," she said. "Otherwise it will slip its bounds by gnawing off a hand or a foot."

"I've seen the likes of her before," the foreman said boldly. "Only less ugly."

"If you wish to be a good and loyal citizen to the Stadholder, you must take these limbs to the city and give them to him, to warn him of their coming."

"Him? Your news is old, sister. The Stadholder is a woman."

"I meant the old Stadholder. The rightful Stadholder."

The joking and chatting fell silent. "What are you talking about? The Stadholder's dead."

"You're wrong," she said. Talking was hard, and becoming harder. The scent from the Ghast writhing in the soggy rushes at her feet unsettled her. Eat me or be eaten, that scent said.

"He was changed like I am, on the outside. But on the inside, he is still your Stadholder. And if you don't care who is Stadholder, consider helping your friends and family. These creatures are deadly. Kill it and keep an eye open for others of its kind."

The foreman kicked the fallen creature. "Dangerous? It threw a whitefish at us, that's all. It kicks like a donkey, but it's just butt-ugly. Like paradiles, they look creepy with those giant mouths, but they never really bite."

The creature had no whitefish in its hands now. "Has one of you ever been bitten?" Frog asked.

"By what?"

"By the whitefish. That's how I got changed into this. A whitefish bite."

Murmurs started up among the throng of men. "Whitefish don't bite."

"If you frighten them enough, they will. When a person gets bit, they turn white. But they might go mad or kill themselves," Frog said. This was so hard. She had to get them back to killing the Ghast. She needed that flesh, so badly.

"Good idea, love. Look at you now. That's no life, looking like that. You're too creepy to keep around."

"Don't talk about me like that. It's rude," she said as firmly as she could.

The men started turning away.

Frog called out the only name she'd heard. They needed to listen to her. "Otter! I know what the creature wants! Otter!"

One of the men turned back irritably. "What?"

Frog cringed at his snap.

"I'm sorry, lady."

He was kind, after all. Not Firdaus-kind, but more well-spoken than most men. The man was grizzled, and even older than Firdaus, close to forty maybe, but she liked his wide shoulders and his knotted muscles. She wasn't a giddy girl anymore, to be swayed by nothing but a smooth face and snaky hips. He looked like a good man, and if she wasn't a woman with a purpose, a woman who loved her Stadholder, she might have offered him bedsport.

She sighed. He'd never look at her now.

"I know what the Ghast wants. It's on its way to the city to destroy it! Kill everyone it sees. And it has many dozens of siblings sent on the same road. We have to warn the people in the city."

Otter gaped. "Are you mad? The city is a week of travel away! We can't leave our peat. People will steal it and all our work will be for nothing!"

Frog sat back and thought. Otter scratched his head and gave the Ghast a pensive kick.

"You could take me to the next village?" she asked. "You owe it to your neighbors to warn them against this danger."

"Do I? Stuck-up farmers, they are. Treat us like dirt. Won't let us near their daughters."

Frog didn't blame the farmers. Their daughters wouldn't have good lives with peat cutter children in their bellies, although the thought stirred a corresponding interest in her own loins. What appealing prospects did Otter hide under his flimsy grass skirt, a girl might wonder? Not her, though. She was for Firdaus, and Otter would never consider a whitey.

After a long, silent consideration and much lip-pulling, Otter nodded. "What you say makes sense. We can't take you to the city, though. There's peat needs cutting. But we'll take you to the next village."

He kicked the writhing Ghast harder. "Is any of you women going to chop that thing up or what?"

The Ghast roared soundlessly out of its malformed mouth, producing nothing but fearful scent. Could it understand human speech? Frog decided she didn't care. She grabbed a machete from the ground and hacked at one of its lumpy arms. They looked short and funny, and the hands were more like claws. It could never wield a tool with them. The machete, a length of bamboo set with obsidian blades, was too shallow to cleave the thick arm properly, and Frog lifted it for another blow.

"Hey. That's men's work," one of the fellows said. He looked pityingly at her mismatched arms, but wasn't brave enough to touch her.

Frog handed the machete over and the older man hewed off the leg she'd started on with one powerful sawing stroke. She doubted that the Ghast felt pain. She didn't, that was for sure. The other men joined in with the hacking and the sawing and soon enough the Ghast was nothing but a twitching mass of white limbs. Disconcertingly, the head still moved and the mouth opened soundlessly.

"Is it dead?" the grizzled man asked.

"No," Frog said. "They don't die so easily."

***

Firdaus froze on his rickety divan. Boon's words echoed in his head. The weave of the silk cover dug in the back of his thighs. The boy on his knee grew heavier and heavier. Time stretched out in gummy strands imprisoning the whole room in its web. Boon's hands pressed on his shoulders, too light and hot to be real, Hilm's eyes, Ing's sneer, the little boy's unstoppable trembling.

"No." His voice sounded hoarse and strange, like a paradile barking. "This isn't life, Boon. This is nothing. We're remnants of life, pretending we're still here, but there's nothing we can do that makes it worthwhile. We can't eat. We can't have children. We can't feel."

"Abba," Hilm pleaded. "Please. That's not true. You can still love. You love us. You love your lady Ing. You can still lead your life."

His life? His life was travesty. A never-ending play filled with shallow replicas of real people, while his true family drifted away from him on the currents of time. The currents whose ebb and flow he'd lost, cast as he was into unchanging flesh. "Don't give me that crap. I know you would never take that road, but it's good enough for Boon, right?"

"He will die, Abba."

"I know I won't be able to have children, father," Boon

said in his breathless little voice. "But I won't have them if I die next winter, will I? Do you think I can enjoy my food now? If I chew, I feel like I'm choking to death. I have to choose between eating and breathing. I know I won't be able to live in the palace or become Stadholder if I'm changed, but I don't care. I just want to live.

"Abba, please. I'm sure I can find someone to help me, but I want it to be you."

Boon stood before Firdaus. A row of skinny ribs was visible between the folds of the cloak Boon was huddling in, even though it was midsummer and sweltering. His skin wasn't shiny and brown like Hilm's, ripe as plum sap squirting against your teeth. It was taut and dry and flecked with dusty particles, tinged with lilac undertones like a body-wide bruise, the color deepening in the circles under Boon's eyes. His teeth were yellow, his gums bled, and his breath guttered. A scent of sickness wafted from him even now, when he should have been well, because it was summer. Boon was the one case you could argue in favor of Wanning.

It broke Firdaus' heart. "No," he said. "Better to be dead than a thing like this. Ask me anything, Boon. Anything, but not this. I can't do it."

"I will," Ing said.

"Ing, leave the room right now," Firdaus said, without turning his head away from Boon. "Take Ulio to his uncle."

He was too bludgeoned by Boon's request to regret letting Ulio go. He couldn't save everyone. Not even every child. "Better the evil he knows, I guess."

"Abba, please listen to Boon," Hilm said.

"The answer is still no, as you should have guessed," Firdaus shouted.

"But Abba, why?" Hilm ran up to him and wound her arms around his neck, looking up at him with the sweetest, meltingest look from her big black eyes. "It would mean so much to me to have Boon by my side, Abba."

"And for that you'd condemn him to a life as a Wan? A fine sister you are!"

He peeled her arms off and slumped back on the

divan, staring into nothing. The children talked in low voices among each other. He caught Ing's name among their whisperings and knew he couldn't rest yet.

"Children!" he said in his sternest voice. "Come stand before me. I want you to swear that you will not act against my will on this."

"Abba!" Hilm fired up.

"Shush. You are a child yet, and Boon will be one for several more years. You must trust my judgment in this, Boon. I know you want it differently, but believe me, I know what I'm talking about. I'm only trying to protect you from a disastrous choice."

Boon's eyes filled with tears. Firdaus steeled himself against his own rice-pudding heart. If he indulged Boon now, he'd be helping the boy destroy himself. He couldn't let that happen.

Hilm crossed her arms before her chest, crushing her bandoliers. Kem's weave, Firdaus saw. Water colors, to counteract the fire in her personality. Hilm would need Kem's favor to become Stadholder.

"Hilm. Daughter. Give me your promise," he said. He would not budge. They must be made to understand how seriously he took this.

"Boon. Give me your promise."

"Father. I will do as you tell me to," Boon said, his voice trembling and breaking. "Please, Father. I don't want to die."

"I am so, so sorry, my son. I wish there was something I could do to change your health." Tears ran down Firdaus' cheeks. Knowing you were inevitably going to lose a child was worse, in some ways, than actually losing one. You could adapt. With babies you never knew if they would survive, but to lose a wonderful son after only twelve years of life? Hilm's only full brother? It wasn't to be borne.

His chest heaved in a sob and Hilm and Boon enveloped him in hugs. "It's all right, Abba, we understand. We don't want to make you sad. I won't do it if you don't want to," Hilm and Boon babbled against his chest, and he coursed his hands through their hair, curling strongly in

Hilm's case, hanging limp and greasy in Boon's.

"I love you so much, my dearest children," Firdaus said. "Please know that."

The dawn chant cut through their huddle like a knife. The children started, and their wise, sad faces changed into those of guilty truants. "Daddy, we have to go back! Otherwise Aunt Aranaz will ground us! Bye!"

Firdaus wished he could shake off this mood like they could, like ducks shook off water. The children's feathers were still coated with the grease of innocence and childhood. Prophet knew he wished it would never wear off, but inevitably, it would. Strange enough, the tour outside the city with Ing and Frog had made him feel like a young man, carefree, looking no further than a good place to sport with his lover and a nice meal. Here in the city the full weight of his responsibilities had thumped back on his shoulder again, and he felt almost old. He could only hope his wisdom would prove sufficient to face all the challenges that would come to him.

***

Ing slid away from the door just before the children came galloping out, calling out to each other, until after twenty yards the little boy had to stop and gasp and be half carried by his sister. They seemed happy and relieved, although she had gotten the distinct impression Firdaus had refused permission to Wan the boy, whose name she couldn't remember.

She debated going back to him, but that would make it pretty obvious she'd handed the goldsmith boy off to someone else and had listened in. She ambled off, blinking in the roseate glow of early cloudlight. Enough to do without Firdaus. Let him run his colony of surface Wan, she'd tackle the other groups that still lived in the deepest heart of the City Mound.

She lifted a grille in the corner of a deserted mews and slipped inside. Mother Doughy generally didn't shift the old sewer tunnels about much. Ing had never figured her out, but she didn't seem to carry a grudge. If someone had built a city on top of her head, and dug channels through her flesh, Ing would have killed them all, but Mother Doughy continued to take it in baffling equanimity.

Ing went deeper and deeper into the city's guts, sliding down steep tunnels until she was below sea level. Here in the dim coolness of the Mount's heart, no outside light penetrated and sounds boomed through the friable mound flesh like surf pounding a beach.

She entered the low wide hall where she always approached Mother Doughy. The size of the hall seemed designed to crush the human spirit. The ceiling nearly brushed the top of her head, and Firdaus would have had to crouch. It was so wide that the ends could not be seen. Ing trusted Mother Doughy not to trap her in her belly, as she never had done so before, but Ing still had to force herself not to continue on all fours.

She arrived at the rough outcropping of rock, like an unfinished statue, that generally housed Mother Doughy's consciousness. Or maybe her mind was everywhere, but this is where she'd fashioned a mouth and eyes to facilitate speech with the Wan. The face projected crudely from the white rock, a blob of a nose, two eyes haphazardly placed above and to the right. A wide, disconcerting gash for the mouth. The hair grew back into the rock, and the body was nothing but a protruding boulder. Flesh, Ing knew, but it still looked like rock to her. It was harder and less breakable than her own flesh, although she could smell the similarities.

The mound personality had no reason to pretend to have limbs or breasts; she wasn't a woman in any sense of the word—the Ghast were genderless. But Mother was the name the Mound had given herself when they'd first met.

"Mother?" Ing called out. "It is I, Ing. I would like to speak with you."

The stone face ground to life. The eyes snapped open, and the mouth inhaled to inflate its bellows or whatever it used to produce sound. Ing had never been permitted to learn.

"Mistress Ing. I knew you had returned. Why did you

not pay me a visit earlier?"

Ing gnashed her teeth. She'd never known the extent of the Mound's knowledge of what transpired in its body, so she'd conducted her affairs with some circumspection. "I was busy, Mother."

"You are telling the Wan to move out. Why?"

"We want to live like the humans. See the cloudlight, conduct business, ply our craft."

"The concept of craft has never ceased to amaze me. I could understand it of the humans, who after all cannot change their bodies, but why do Wan insist on making things? They don't need them."

"Humans and Wan need to make things or grow things to feel happy," Ing said tersely. She wasn't in the mood for a long discussion about the differences between the two races.

"I think of it as making poems outside their bodies. With sound or wood or cloth. Am I right?" the stone voice rattled.

Ing had always surmised that Mother D. couldn't distinguish between qualities of sound. She had managed to teach her the right volume, but she seemed impervious to the difference between singing and talking.

"Right enough," Ing said. "What I wanted to talk to you about... Will you send some of your walkers to live with us in the Dark Quarter?"

"What I wanted to ask you, Ing, is what you and the Queen Mound have plotted?"

"What?"

Ing sweated and fidgeted as she tried to think of a plausible answer. Mother Doughy couldn't know of the Queen Mound's plans, could she? Ing herself took care never to think of the vague notions she had of those plans.

Mother Doughty would probably ask to share flesh. Ing told herself she didn't know the plans, that vague guesses weren't knowledge. Mother had cottoned on to the intriguing facility humans had of saying one thing with sound and another with flesh. So far Ing seemed to be the only creature on the island to have the facility to lie by omission. As far as she knew.

"The Queen Mound didn't inform me of her intentions."

Mother Doughy produced a grinding noise from her unknowable innards. "Quite. Did you inform her of your intention regarding your fellow humans?"

Ing was about to ask the creature how it knew, but then she realized it would have overheard every discussion she'd had with her fellow Wan, for the past centuries.

"Yes."

"I am thinking of disallowing you entrance in my mound, Ing. I knew you were of the Queen Mound's flesh, but you seemed unaware of it. Now I see that she does have your loyalty."

Ing's thoughts skittered in all directions like startled cockroaches. Any other moment she would have been ecstatic from the information and what it implied. She was from the Queen Mound's flesh? What did that mean? That the whitefish who had bitten her so long ago was related to the Queen Mound? And apparently Mother Doughy could distinguish somehow between walkers. Possibly between whitefish and paradiles as well. She should have known that there would be some kind of competition going on, but she'd never realized there were distinct differences between two competing individuals. Her kingdom for a gene sequencer.

Firdaus. She'd Wanned Firdaus with the wrong whitefish. If only she'd known that its lack of allure indicated a different lineage. Her stomach heaved from her own blindness.

"You are not speaking, Ing. Are you creating a new thought inside you? Let me taste it."

She would never give the old monster the satisfaction of having surprised her. "I didn't know you could tell walkers apart. Does that go for whitefish and paradile as well?" Ing asked.

"Of course. But stick to one taste per poem, Ing. I don't like it if too many thoughts are mixed up at once." It almost seemed as if Mother Doughy rumbled in disapproval.

"What?" Ing stammered.

"My walkers will feast on the Queen Mound's, Ing. And then they will return to feed me. If you taste of betrayal one more time, I will consume you."

The ceiling lowered down at Ing. It could descend on her faster than she could run, and anyway, that wouldn't make any difference. She was inside the monster's stomach, wherever she went. Pink streaks wound over the ceiling and the walls, just like she'd seen in the Queen Mound. A shocking color in all the whiteness, but only visible after a long while of adjusting to the dimness. Nor-mally she would have asked about them, so many things about the Ghast still being a mystery, but the only thing she desired now was to get outside. She's always hated the gray after having grown up under blue skies, but right now, the cloudsky beckoned like a symbol of freedom.

"In a few years' time, all the humans will be Wan," she gasped. "You would be able to exchange flesh with them at your desire."

"Would there never be new humans again?" Mother Doughy asked.

"No. The humans are doomed, anyway, Mother Doughy. Their numbers are dwindling and the crops are failing."

"This is not the only place that has humans, Ing. Did you know that? My sister mounds send me flesh to tell me of humans on other atolls."

Ing shrugged, and then hastily voiced the thought. It would be disastrous if Mother D ever learned to read body language. She better not play Rosetta Stone. "It doesn't matter." She didn't have time to waste on temporary solutions.

"I must suck on your words a little longer, Ing," Mother Doughy announced. "Your plan has much flavor, but I taste impurities that must be explored. I will not eat you yet, but you must not act before I give permission to do so."

What? The big lump of mushroom brain was giving

her orders, now? Ing thought not.

She bowed, a reflex from her youth. "Yes, Mother Doughy." She sent all the obedience and blankness of thought she could muster to her ring finger and extended it to the stone mouth.

Mother Doughy bit down hard. Ing listened to the crunching with panic buzzing around in her head, which she could not show, not ever again, not inside the Mound. When the sound ceased, she crooked her hand automatically for the trade. How many of these transactions had gone on? Too many to count, though fewer and fewer as the centuries ticked past. Talk had more and more replaced the exchange of flesh. Mother Doughy was learning. Was she learning too much? How intelligent was she? She'd shown more awareness of the outside world than Ing had ever noticed before. She really didn't need complications at this stage.

The nugget of Mother Doughy's flesh exploded in her mouth with textures so overwhelming she reeled from the impact. Giant white golems browsed through her mind and stomped with concrete feet on her innermost thoughts. Ing gagged and retched to rid herself of the flesh, but it had dissolved instantly on touching the inside of her mouth.

The white shapes split in half, and again, and again, and Ing whirled everywhere to gather her precious memories to herself. She pushed the golems away, but there were so many, eating away at her best-kept secrets. She mustered her strength and willed them to dissolve.

She found herself sobbing on the floor of the long low cave, with the statue of Mother Doughy looking down on her impassively. Her own hand had dug deep into the flesh of her left breast, as if she was digging for her heart. Nonsense. She no longer had a heart. Nothing, no mind attack could take away her determination to save the world. If Mother Doughy thought Ing would bend to her suggestive flesh, she was wrong.

But she had definitely gained a new adversary.

CHAPTER 17

The new Wan bar was a makeshift affair, with chairs and tables they'd scrounged from deserted houses, no decoration, and no glowapples or running water to make things easy. The floor was dirt, straight on top of Mother Doughy. He'd walked on tiptoes at first, so as not to tickle her scalp, but familiarity was eroding the new habit before it could settle.

The main room was occupied by a few groups of Wan, but it still sounded hollow and new. They needed wall hangings, a fireplace, more stuff. More people.

The door opened and… *something* walked in. Firdaus first noticed the change in atmosphere and then the newcomer. It sat down on the floor.

Firdaus and Amrit the little innkeeper stared at the strange creature on the floor. Why did it do that, because there were plenty of seats free. It was a strange Wan, thickset and stumpy, with oddly short arms and legs. The creature sat squashed on its peculiar long torso, like a clay toad made by a clumsy child.

"You know him?" Firdaus whispered.

"No. Never seen him before. It's not a Wan. It's a Ghast. Let's hope it's one of Mother Doughy's walkers, and not some stranger. I'm not serving it. I don't want to exchange flesh with it. Who knows what it thinks about?"

Firdaus bowed to the creature crouching on his freshly rush-strewn floor. "Greetings, stranger. How may we serve you?"

It opened its lopsided, lipless gash of a mouth, and emitted a few sounds.

"They never speak," Amrit said.

"This one does," Firdaus said. "Excuse me, good sir or madam, could you please repeat that?"

"Ah-eh."

"One cup of water for the gentlebeing," Firdaus called out to Amrit.

She shuffled backwards to the water vat, keeping a wary eye on the thing on the floor. Firdaus had found a human baker willing to sell water from his tap to a Wan. It solved part of their water problems, at least. Running a meeting place had taken priority over bathing, for now. He dipped himself in the muddy waters of the harbor now and then, but it felt like he'd relinquished an important part of his civilized self.

He grabbed the nearest chair and sat down on it slowly and demonstratively. Then he held out another chair to the creature. It rose and inspected the chair. Then it folded its body down on it. Disconcertingly, its head now faced backwards. It hadn't quite managed to copy him, but it was a good first attempt.

Amrit offered it a cup of water, but its hands were unable to grasp it. It had a few stumpy claws but no opposable thumb.

"Amrit, a saucer?" Firdaus said, when she stared and giggled.

She brought it, and the Ghast dipped its small head over the bowl while she held it and slurped the water up, although Firdaus didn't see a tongue.

"Amrit, why are you acting like this? You know how humans treat us, there's no reason to treat the Ghast badly."

"They're not people, Firdaus, not like us. They can't talk. They're Mother Doughy's."

"They can talk with their flesh, right? Would it be polite to exchange some?"

Amrit drew her lower lip to her chin in disgust. "Feel free to do it. I'll be serving our real guests."

Her small hips swayed over her short legs as she stomped off to the group of music lovers clustering around Haroon, in a corner by the window.

Firdaus pulled up his chair to face the Ghast. "Can you understand speech? What do you think about our city? Wouldn't you like to live above ground? Maybe Mother Doughy can make a few airy caves with lots of daylight."

The creature stared at him, its head swinging weightlessly like a poppy in the breeze. Firdaus stared back. No answer came forth. He decided to try it the traditional Ghast way. He broke off a fingertip and offered it to the creature. It opened its mouth eagerly. Firdaus was a little disconcerted, but then he realized its hands weren't made for picking up things. He placed the fingertip on his palm, and slowly picked it up with finger and thumb, showing the Ghast the pincer movement a human hand could make. No reaction. It wasn't as smart as a human being, he figured. More like a paradile, although its public behavior hadn't been overtly threatening.

He stuck the pearl of flesh into the mouth. The wide gash clamped down, barely missing his fingers, and the creature's eyes fluttered and sank closed. No chewing. Its head went down. Was it falling asleep? Had he killed it with his fingertip gift?

No. The creature rose again, its eyes glistening. It lifted a hand and clicked its crude claws together. Hey. It was thinking about pincer movements, right? It broke off the whole hand and presented it to Firdaus. Only a lifetime of court training gave him the wherewithal to accept the generous gift. The creature stood up and bowed to him. Firdaus, stunned, eyeballed the pale, heavy paw in his hand.

"You really are a Stadholder," Amrit's voice said by his elbow. "That thing bowed to you!"

"Politeness, you know. Pays off," Firdaus said.

Amrit humphed.

The door slammed open with a loud bang. Firdaus looked up, prepared to greet another newcomer, but nobody entered. Instead, a fireball shot into the room, landing in the middle of Haroon's clique.

An admirer's clothes caught fire at once, and the man made it worse by standing up, shrieking, running blindly hither and yon and not giving anyone the chance to douse the fire.

A second fireball.

An arrow hit Firdaus' thigh. Firdaus gasped in surprise, but it didn't hurt. It galvanized him from his shocked paralysis. He dove onto the screaming, burning Wan and tossed him to the ground, rolling him over with his foot until he'd quenched the flames.

"Shut the door!" he bellowed. "Amrit!"

Several more flexible Wan had run to the windows, which had no shutters. "City men, sir, armed with cudgels and torches."

Firdaus crawled to the window. Less than a dozen men stood there, a few torches among them, a few clubs and ulama paddles. Their faces dark, they swung their weapons and milled about as if unable to stand still from excitement. Angry, fearful men. Aranaz must have sent them. If Firdaus and his Wan went out, a fight was inevitable. Firdaus ground his teeth. Whether the citizens acted on their own or were sent by Aranaz, the message was clear. No Wan allowed aboveground. Not even in deserted and ruined inns.

He would not yield. Aranaz could, and probably would, chase him out of his successive houses, because of his children, but he would not give in to this kind of public harassment.

He ordered the Wan present to douse the fires with water and sand buckets.

"Stay inside! I don't want an open fight, don't give them any excuse to get violent."

"They don't need excuses, Firdaus," Haroon said. "They already are violent."

Firdaus curled his lip at him. "Who's a carpenter? We need bamboo doors and shutters."

"Those will burn," Haroon pointed out.

"Thank you. Indeed they will. But at least we will not be visible to any passers-by."

As if on cue, the Ghast, who'd stood by silently during the fracas, disappeared into the ground. Firdaus goggled, but then reviewed the event in his mind. Mother Doughy had opened a private entryway for her walker.

Maybe he and his Wan could ask her for an exit inside the inn. That way, they wouldn't have to appear outside. Then again, that would defeat his whole purpose in re-integrating the Wan back into city life.

Firdaus ordered his people to stay put and not to engage with their attackers. Dusk fell, and after a while, the angry citizens ran out of ammunition or got bored. They left with some final insults and promises to return.

Amrit planted herself in front of him, shook her braids backwards and tore off an ear without batting an eyelash. "Here. Accept this from me. Think of me when you get back your power." She held out the grisly curl of cartilage. Gracious she wasn't, but it would do. And at this rate, he'd have a Stadholderly belly again in no time. A little buffer for when he needed persuasion.

He hesitated. He was still reluctant to gobble this stuff up in front of everyone, but it would be rude to refuse.

Tribute. He was becoming a Stadholder again. He touched the Ghast hand to his lips, recoiling from the alienness it exuded, and then chewed on Amrit's ear. It held grudging admiration and a few snippets of her former life.

***

The water clock on the tiled counter of the bar plopped softly. Firdaus rose. Time to go check up on Boon. In spite of the still-hot late summer weather, Boon had gotten another cold. He was sniffling and hacking his lungs out on Firdaus' ratty divan. Boon had gradually stayed longer and longer over the past few weeks, until he'd been too weak to return home, and Firdaus was glad of the boy's company. At first, he'd feared he'd have to be constantly on the move every time Aranaz discovered his new lair, but he soon learned that, as long as he didn't take Hilm home, Aranaz didn't care. Boon wasn't important to her.

Life was not bad, for now. He still ached for his other children. Particularly for the older ones like Gül and Ichiro who might think he didn't love them anymore.

As he left the inn's square, he thought he saw a glimpse of Ing disappearing around a corner, but the figure didn't react when he called out. He'd chosen the noon hour to return home, because most of the angry and suspicious mud citizens would be taking their siesta. When he arrived home after the hot trudge through the deserted streets, Boon was alone. On the table stood a mysterious contraption built out of hollow bamboo lengths, connecting pots and pans and beakers.

"Where's Ing?" Firdaus asked. "What's that? One of those projects you two are so busy with?"

Boon flapped a weak hand. "We were going to start an experiment, but then she suddenly ran off. She's so easily distracted."

That wasn't something Firdaus had noticed before, but if Boon said it, it must be true. Boon had a mind like a paradile tooth. The questions he'd asked ever since he could talk were always posers. Firdaus had few answers, but Ing, to his surprise, was spending a lot of time with Boon. The things they talked about were completely incomprehensible to him, but as long as Boon was happy and occupied, Firdaus had no complaints.

Boon coughed and wheezed to catch his breath. "She was here because she'd seen a Ghast in the street and ran away to hide. Abba, why can't she go back into the Mound to pick her stuff up?"

"What? What's that about not going down? First I heard of it." Firdaus frowned. He'd noticed Ing was curt, not eager to make love, but at the same time, she'd been needy and clingy. He had no problem sleeping chastely plastered up against her back if that's what she needed, and he'd been too busy being Stadholder around the new Wan Quarter to pay close attention.

"You know," Boon said and tried to sit up so he could talk easier.

Firdaus rushed over and helped Boon arrange the cushions.

"She misses her things," Boon gasped out. "She wants

to show me some writing she did, but she says she can't go down there anymore. Can you help me go pick it up?"

Help him, Boon was a fine one to talk. In his present state, the boy would collapse before he reached the front curtain. Of course Firdaus would go and arrange for a couple of Wan to pick up Ing's belongings. And after that, he would corner her and find out what was bugging her. He'd been ignoring her, really. Rolling into bed without more than a few perfunctory words. That was going to change.

"Sure, Boontie, I'll see to that, don't you worry. We'll get you those scrolls and pictures so you can be just as brainy and talky as she is."

As long as it lasts, Boon's eyes said. Yeah. He knew that. The little boy, with heroic self restraint, never once mentioned his desire to be Wanned again. One might call it manipulative, but Firdaus admired his reticence.

A shadow darkened the door curtain. Firdaus pulled Boon against his chest in a protective reflex. "Who's there?"

The figure didn't answer but stepped into the room, shrouded in an expensive blue linen cloak from head to toe.

Aranaz, who else?

Behind her, two bulky guards took position on either side of the door, and behind them another person stood, invisible but for his shadow on the floor. Aranaz polished her nails on her bandolier, the only way that she ever expressed tension.

"Firdaus," she said.

She used to call him brother. That would be admitting weakness, he supposed, after all she'd exiled him within minutes of finding out his secret.

"Sister," he answered.

"You weren't supposed to come back." Aranaz could strip emotion from her voice like a trained singer in an Ancestor play. "You must cease to meet Hilm. Don't make me regret my generosity in exiling instead of executing you."

Boon coughed, managing to make it sound derisive.

"I will allow you to leave in peace. If not, I will be forced to take drastic measures. However. I will allow you the company of Boon. With regard to the circumstances."

"Don't worry, Naz, me and my fellow Wan only want to live in peace in the Dark Quarter, which was deserted anyway. I'm not trying to take my place back, or asking to allow the Wan to live anywhere else."

When he heard himself say that, he liked the sound of it. A slow-growing acceptance of the Wan was in many ways preferable to the chaos and danger of a coup. The reality, however, was that the citizens feared and resented the Wan's coming. Probably would have even without Aranaz' meddling.

Aranaz raised a thin black eyebrow. "The citizens of White City disagree with you, brother. And I will not stand in their way. Things could, however, be even worse.

"Go away. Take Boon. And don't even think of saying goodbye to the younger children, Firdaus. It'll be kinder in the long run to let them forget you."

Boon waved his hands in agitation, but he couldn't find enough breath to speak. Firdaus assumed the boy meant to disagree. He concentrated on what Aranaz wasn't saying. She hadn't mentioned his children for nothing. She was threatening him with their lives. He held his gaze to hers, hoping she would read steadfastness in them and not his soft heart already preparing for loss.

Aranaz nodded infinitesimally to Boon. "Nephew."

"Aunt," Boon answered.

Aranaz frowned, as if she suspected he was making fun of her, but she let it go and swept out of the room without another word to Firdaus. When her shadow had retreated from the door, Ali's voice started up. Aranaz and her yapping little dog.

"Abba!" Boon said. "We're not going to leave and let Hilm become like her, will we?"

Firdaus fondled Boon's lank hair, desperately touching the one child he could. "Of course not," he lied.

***

Firdaus needed to confer with Mother Doughy. He lowered himself into the sewer opening in the kitchen. It was getting tight, due to all the tribute the Wan seemed intent on paying to him. He increased, while Boon decreased. Boon's summer cold had progressed into something worse, a deep wet cough that made Boon's sides and back hurt and kept him from sleeping. It kept Firdaus from sleeping too, but the worry about Boon's health would have done so anyway.

What if he relented and allowed the boy to be Wanned? Was it cruelty to let the child die? Firdaus shook his head, although no one saw him as he trudged through the tunnels. He would remain firm. It was one thing to be Wanned at his own ripe age of twenty seven, a middle-aged man with a life and children behind him, and another to let it happen to an eleven-year old child. How would Boon grow up if he never knew the care and worry of love and children and the frailty of his body? Look at Ing. The woman had lived for four centuries but she was crazy as a loon, and emotionally no older than Hilm. He had no doubt that she loved him in her way, but something about her was so wrong that his own feelings waxed and waned.

The wall ahead of him exploded in a bubble of bulging flesh, cutting him off. Firdaus staggered and placed his hand to where his racing heart would have been. How long would it take him to lose those automatic gestures? Maybe he never would.

An aperture formed in the blob. "Firdaus Stadholder," it grated, before it had even formed eyes.

It had other senses to identify him. His own hand knew with tingling certainty whether it touched human or Wan flesh. With a creature as vast and ancient as this Mound, who knew how much she could sense while he walked through her body?

"Mound mistress," he bowed.

"You may call me Mother," the voice boomed back.

Firdaus flinched and clapped his hands before his ears.

"Apology. I will adjust the volume." She continued in a softer voice. "My walker returned with a glowing taste of your flesh," she said. It said.

It took Firdaus a moment to understand what she meant. "Oh. The Ghast who came into the bar for a drink. Glad to have been of service. Is he your child?"

"How could I have had children, Firdaus? I am still here."

That was too obscure for him. He'd leave that one for the likes of Ing and Boon.

"Are you in agreement with Mistress Ing's plans?" Mother asked.

"Not as far as I know of them," he replied sourly. "I don't understand why she thinks we should Wan everyone. What's the point of life if there are no babies, no change? People aren't meant to exist forever."

"Indeed. Neither are we Ghast. We are sporulated, we grow, we combine, we settle down on a good spot and grow as big as we can. That is good, that is the right order of things. To continue on forever without ever sporulating would be wrong. Unnatural."

"Hm," Firdaus agreed politely.

"But I have eaten many Wan thoughts, and I understand that humans are different. I like the flavor of that difference, you know. It would be bland and tasteless if that uniqueness were to be smoothed out. And even if I myself won't taste it in centuries to come, I wish it for my offspring. That is why I am warning you. The time of sporulating is approaching rapidly."

Now he would have to ask. "Sporulating is when you bear children?"

"It is when I scatter into a million tiny bits, some of which will grow into power, others will be consumed by their siblings. It happens to all the Mounds at once, and that time is nigh."

"So you die, and your children live?"

"They aren't children as humans make them. They are tiny seeds, and they will have to make themselves. Until humans came, we always did it the same way. First a spore, then a worm eating its host, then a whitefish, a paradile, if the fish managed to eat many of its siblings, then a walker, and for a very few, the Ones Who Walk No More. Such as I," she ended with false modesty.

"So you're expecting?" Firdaus said. He checked the walls for signs of bulging and extra shine, but they looked as floury and pale as ever.

"That word has no taste for me."

"Up the spout? Bun in the oven? Baby in your womb?" Firdaus said.

"Ah. The flavor releases now. I do not make little copies inside before releasing them into the world. I will open up and release my spores, spending myself into them. Can you taste this explanation?"

"Nope. Yeah. Like a puffball? One of those things we used to kick as children?"

The moment the words escaped his mouth his mind played an enlarged version of that event, projected on his own city. Houses being blown hundreds of yards into the air, people flying helplessly, everything of beauty destroyed, Stack Palace, the Singing Tower, the Physicians' Temple. The four Quarters. He couldn't make himself feel it. Something as big as the city ought to be forever.

"My mass is many thousands of times greater than that strange plant." Mother said.

"Of course, of course," Firdaus said. "You are the greatest mound I've ever seen. I bet you're bigger than the Queen Mound! You certainly have more presence."

He didn't even need to pay attention to have the platitudes roll out of his mouth. His city! His people! If it was true, what would happen to them without houses and a place to live? Would the survivors be forced to toil in the marshes?

"I suspect my roots go much deeper than hers. After all, isn't she perched nearly on the skirt of the mountain?"

"I always thought so. So did I hear you say you are all blowing together? Both mounds?"

"All the mounds in all the land will blow. All will be eaten by the spores. All. The spores can even eat the green stuff humans brought. They can eat the human walkers on two and on four legs."

Firdaus' head reeled. He hadn't even adjusted to the idea of the mound blowing up, which could only mean his town would be in ruins, but this was worse.

"Eating?" he said. "Eating everything? How many spores?"

"More than there are rice plants in a field. More than there are humans on the land. Like raindrops in the sky."

"But... but afterwards! How will the land look afterwards? If they eat everything?" Firdaus cried out.

His tongue went on asking, but his mind flailed helplessly around in his skull, seeking escape and finding none.

"The marshes will be empty and barren for a while. Then the seeds that have found no host will bloom as plants. The worms will eat each other and become whitefish. When there are no more worms, the island will flourish again."

"It won't work like that for humans," Firdaus said bitterly. "Or their livestock or their crops. And all the halal plants will just be gone."

"This is likely. That is how I remember it from my time as many worms. Together these little memories give a strong enough flavor to tell you about it."

"Thanks for the warning. But we will all die. We must leave the city. No, there's no point. We will die anyway without food."

Firdaus sank back against the Mound's wall. "Food. Where can we hide the animals and food and seeds for the next season?"

"Do humans not have stored seeds in the vessels you came in?"

"Vessels? But storing seeds is an excellent idea. I wonder why Ing isn't planning for this, instead of for our lack of babies?"

"She doesn't remember. She was the first human to get bitten after she and her people arrived in the saucer boats, that are now stacked on top of me, and in the fear and the panic she lost her memory. I don't know what happened to her in all those years afterwards, but what I ate of her mind convinced me she was potentially dangerous to me. To all the Ghast. Someone who is that knowledgeable about life would find a way to destroy us to save humanity."

"You ate that much of her? No wonder she's nuts. Somewhere, somehow she must remember it, and that's why she feels this absurd urgency. Which is not so absurd anymore."

"I cannot say. What do I know of the workings of the human mind? I ate many of Ing's thoughts on the matter, and she tells me you humans have layers in your mind and hidden corners and forgotten memories. I am not like that."

Firdaus wasn't in the mood for an Ing-style discussion. "I have to go now, Mother. I have to think. I have to devise a plan to save everyone."

"Don't tell Ing about it."

"Maybe. We don't have boats, though. I don't know. I can't think. Goodbye."

He wandered back the way he'd come. This was the end of the world they'd talked about. He saw no way out. Everybody would die. Boon, Hilm, the other children.

Everyone.

CHAPTER 18

Frog waited for the peatcutters to sleep. She needed to fill her belly and she didn't think it was wise to eat in front of the men. The smell rising from the lumpy Ghast limb was indescribably attractive, not like Firdaus but like Ing, both repellent and alluring, a strange mix that made eating even more urgent.

The soft sounds of the three peatcutters settling into sleep around the banked fire reassured her that she wasn't alone in the chirping, sighing night. She remembered how Firdaus had reacted to eating great gobbets of paradile, and she didn't want to be helpless in the grip of Ancestors knew what strange feelings and thoughts. She wouldn't have contemplated eating the Ghast if she didn't know she needed the mass to repair her wonky arm and shoulder. It would be no good to come to Firdaus looking like a monster.

The cloudsky wasn't completely dark yet. She should wait, but the spicy, powdery scent wafting over to her was mouthwatering. Curried rice and cinnamon, butter and honey, all wrapped into one. Her mouth watered and her limbs twitched with the desire to tear straight into the Ghast and stuff her mouth with the godlike food. Her whole body knew with absolute certainty that she was meant to eat this.

When darkness had settled, she crept around to the bound lump by the fire. The thing that exuded the delicious cardamom and asafetida fragrance writhed its limbless torso. Not dead, as she had foretold. The head had reattached to the body. It stilled its movement and stared at her with white eyes as big as her palm. It resembled a paradile, but it wasn't. Its jaw was wider than a man's, and its severed arms and legs were like a man's, although short and stumpy. Frog crept closer. Ropes bound the thing's body, and the wriggling was aimed at escaping those bonds. Its jaws worried at the rope around its thick chest, stretching its neck or hinge into an impossible contortion.

It didn't see her as a threat, she guessed. It made no sound. Maybe it couldn't. She'd certainly never heard a paradile growl or bleat or croak like her namesake.

Before she could think about it, she dashed forwards and grabbed a limb for herself. She lifted the heavy lump of thigh to her face and the smell slammed into her nose. She could feel her jaws widen and bite deep into the crumbly yet firm flesh. The taste raced through her veins like ricewine and the earth rose up and hit her in the back of the head. She couldn't move, not a finger, yet her jaws remembered how to bite and chew, bite and chew.

The Ghast was a walking emissary of the Queen Mound. The Queen Mound had given it and its siblings a clear command to travel to the other Mound in the South. It was to eat as many of that Mound's walkers as it could, and to hold whitefish against any mud people it encountered.

Frog spat out the last bite and vomited. Nothing came out, but her body remembered vomiting and bucked and heaved pointlessly, and even produced copious fake sweat for a while.

She fell forward awkwardly on her uneven fists and growled softly at the Ghast. What was she doing? She was no wild creature, she was just Frog. She shook her head and inspected the chewed arm. Had its flesh made her feel like that? If she had a knife, she would have sawed off a chunk to bring with her, but she couldn't carry a whole limb. It weighed more than a grown man's arm. And the peatcutters wouldn't understand.

The creature regarded her with unblinking eyes. Now it truly saw her. She'd bested it! She suppressed a guffaw of triumph. The creature batted at her with its stumpy hip. It was offering her another bite?

She knew it must be so. She bent forward and nibbled off a bite from the stump, preparing herself for the attack of wild and inappropriate feelings that would storm through her as she chewed. Instead, she sensed only subservience and a strong yet humble desire for an answering gift of flesh. She almost held her finger against the wide, lipless mouth, but she deliberated first. Why give a dangerous creature like this anything? It was obligation, that's why. An exchange of politeness among equals. It made sense. But it wouldn't get as much as it had given. Frog broke off the tip of her little finger and offered it up against the creature's face. A fissure opened in the cheek and the little bead of flesh disappeared.

The Ghast looked up at her and Frog stared back. What did it want? Except freedom? She wouldn't set it free, though. She owed the men more than she owed this creature. She slid backwards, not wanting to leave her eyes off the thing. It resumed its writhing and now started on its arm stump. Maybe it would free itself before the men woke, maybe not.

It was the hour before cloudwake. Her rapture, though poor in new insights, had taken away several hours of the night.

The Ghast flesh confirmed that others of its kind were converging onto the city, intent on murder and destruction. The Queen Mound's evil shone through in every action. Frog could understand the rivalry between the two Mounds. She imagined they were like two male swans fighting over territory. They would want the best food, which meant as many Wanned humans as possible.

***

"Abba?"

There Hilm was, at last! Firdaus shot up from the couch, mouth open to yell at her for taking hours to answer his message, but rattling breaths from Boon's divan stopped him short. He tiptoed towards Hilm, a finger on his lips, and motioned her outside.

"It's too hot to be outdoors," Hilm complained.

She looked more like a woman every time he saw her.

"Did you get out unseen?"

"I think so, but Aranaz was in a big flap when she got back. Did she actually talk to you? Why are you still in this house? Where are we going?"

"To the new bar."

"The dark Quarter has a bar?" Hilm's nose wrinkled. "What do Wan eat and drink? Babies? Each other's piss?"

Her light-heartedness grated on him. Boon was dying. His city was going to be destroyed, and he was in no mood to pander to a fifteen-year-old's sense of humor. Hilm should find a lover and get pregnant. Parenthood was a great way of growing up fast. He recalled the first feel of her wriggling, delicate little body after his first lover Halma had expelled Hilm from her womb in blood and pain. She'd felt like a lukewarm sac of slippery sausages, then she'd looked at him with those deep filmy newborn eyes, and life had never been the same.

They arrived at the bar and Firdaus waved a hand to Amrit and the ever-present cluster of Haroon and his cronies.

Hilm stared. "What kind of creature is that? What's that on his head?"

"The famous singer Haroon. He sang at my twelfth birthday," Firdaus said. He waved Amrit away. "I have something more important than Aranaz or Wan occupying the Dark Quarter. Did I tell you about the giant Ghast creature I saw on my travels? Shaped like a bald mountain rising from the marshes, white as salt?"

Hilm nodded.

"Our city is built on just such a mound."

Hilm's eyes went straight to the floor, where her dusty bare feet were resting on the floury surface of mound substance. "You mean we're standing on a Ghast right now?" she whispered. "Can it hear us?"

That hadn't occurred to him yet. "I don't know. Could be. The good news is, she's friendly to us. Which is why she warned me that she's about to blow up in the agony of her labor: she will die as she pushes many thousands of young from her womb."

"Blow up? But what about the city?" Hilm said, still whispering.

"The city, beloved daughter of mine, will be destroyed. No house will remain standing. We must evacuate the people."

Hilm half-rose from her chair, but Firdaus pulled her down again. "There's more. The Ghast young are tiny worms that will burrow into anything living and eat it from the inside out. We have to find a place to hide the people, all the livestock, food, seeds for planting after it's over. Nothing alive will be left on the island. Not the marshes, not a goat, rice plant or mulberry tree."

Hilm began to cry. "Abba, why are you telling me this? And shouldn't we get back to Boon? I don't want him to die alone."

"I don't want him to hear this, sweetheart. I don't want him to be afraid."

Hilm's tears fled and her round-cheeked face flushed with anger. "He's already afraid, Abba. He's afraid of dying."

The knot of Boon-related misery in Firdaus' chest twisted tighter. He knew Boon was dying. Hilm knew Boon was dying. Did they have to talk it to death? "Let's not go into that now. We're talking about saving our people from a horrible fate."

"Can't we kill the creature? Can't we save the city?"

Firdaus shook his head. "I don't see how. If you can see a way, I'm willing to try it, but I really doubt it. Let's focus on saving the people. For that, we need Aranaz. We must convince her of the danger. If she won't help, we'll have to remove her from office. Somehow."

Hilm shook her hair off her face, her tears and anger forgotten. She laid her hand on his, sweaty auburn on cool dry white. "Let me talk to her. I think I can convince her."

"Exactly. You prepare her, and then I come in to tell her..."

"No," Hilm cut him off. "Abba, I know you mean well, but the time to step back into the limelight is not now. Aunt Aranaz and the Assembly won't listen to a Wan. I have to do this. I have a plan. Trust me. I've been talking to a lot of influential people, and I know they will back me."

Firdaus sat back. How had this happened? Hilm had yanked the rudder of their plan out of his hands and steered it to a point on the horizon slightly beside his own. He didn't relish the sensation.

He became conscious of the silence in the water bar. He hoped he hadn't been talking too loudly. His fellow Wan would be told about the impending apocalypse in due time. He was their leader, and he wouldn't shirk that responsibility, but in his heart he was still a father first, a leader second.

The eyes of the small crowd weren't on him, but on Hilm. She was, he realized, the first mud person to enter the bar. He might as well introduce her.

"Amrit, Haroon," he called out, "I want you to meet someone."

***

Stadholder Aranaz sat ramrod straight on her throne. The leather bands didn't creak as much as when her father had sat on it, Hilm noticed.

"Dear niece. I have been grieved to learn how irresponsibly you behaved in visiting your... the Wan person."

Hilm looked her aunt straight in the face. She was going to let her have her say. She was no longer a grubby teenager in the shortest of aprons, her hair swirling down her back. Today she was dressed in a sari made out of a dozen costly silk strips, her arms ringed by countless bracelets, wooden ones from the woodworkers, bone and ivory ones, reed ones for the basket makers, gold and silver and copper and stone. Her hair had been piled up in a regal knot, trailing pearls and silk tassels. Her appearance, decked out in the visible symbols of the people she represented, would do the talking for her.

Aranaz softened her voice. "But that isn't what I wanted to talk to you about. We must set that aside and grieve for my beloved brother only when the city doesn't need us. It needs you, Hilm. The people need you. You know I have no heir."

Hilm lowered her eyes. This was what it was all about. She shook her braids back with a tinkle of tiny bells, but her hair was still when she finally spoke. "What are you asking me, Aunt?"

Aranaz leaned forward like a bird of prey. She'd grown thin, lately. Spidery fingers rubbed against each other with a dry, papery sound. The many cares and responsibilities had her aunt sprung taut like a bow about to be loosed. Good. She deserved it.

"We are family. I believe with all my heart that you are Firdaus' daughter, and not some other man's," Aranaz said.

Hilm nodded her thanks about this formal acknowledgment, her eyes never leaving Aranaz' face.

"I am willing to adopt you as my heir," Aranaz said, slow and formal.

Hilm's eyes shot to the scribe who was furiously recording this statement on clay.

"Yes, niece, I am not playing with you. The scribe will write it on clay, to be baked as soon as it's dried, a second scribe will ink it on parchment even today, and a Stentor will call it out on the Stadholder's Plaza, to make the customary three records. Do you accept?"

Hilm's eyes met her aunt's. Power was finally in her grasp. Her aunt might live long, as barren women often did, or she might not. Hilm would be in a position to protect and help her younger brothers and sisters, and possibly even her father. She was sure Aranaz knew exactly what she was thinking, but it didn't matter. Aranaz would only respect her the more for it. If only her aunt hadn't deposed her father, Hilm might have supported her rule. Aranaz was no fool.

"I accept your offer, Aunt. I will be your heir, and so will my heirs after me." She held her breath to see what Aunt Aranaz would make of the last stipulation.

Aranaz smiled. "I accept your terms."

Hilm hadn't named her children, but her heirs, meaning that she was free to name one of her children or friends as heir if she chose to do so. Did her aunt not care? She wouldn't be so foolish to name Firdaus and commit political suicide, anyway.

Aranaz lifted a hand and the quick shuffling in the corner meant the servant on duty had received her request.

Within moments, a series of trays was carried in, displaying the best high summer had to offer. Paper-thin slices of dogfish, leaper, and candied eel, luscious greens highlighting the flesh-tones of the fish. A thin glass of arak to accompany the repast, suitable to signing an alliance between rulers.

Hilm waited until Aranaz had tasted everything first. Proper etiquette, for sure, but she wouldn't put it past Aranaz to poison her. After all, it was one of the things she'd considered doing to Aranaz, only it would have been bad public relations to do it right now. Aranaz must mean her offer.

"To Stadholder Aspirant Hilm!"

"Thanks, dear Aunt! And now I want to run something by you..."

***

Firdaus hurried back home. Hilm's words about Boon dying in his absence had struck him like a fist in the gut. The wheezing fluid rattle that greeted him when he came back was a relief. At least Boon lived.

He bent over his son. Compared to the sight of Hilm's glowing cheeks and lithe limbs, the bluish tone in Boon's pale lips was a shock to behold. How could Firdaus have let him sink this far towards death? The boy could hardly eat, hardly breathe, couldn't walk anymore and talked in monosyllables. He had days left, if that.

He cupped Boon's cheek. It no longer felt soft and feverish; the skin was rough and cool to the touch. He'd left it too long. His own stubborn, pointless righteousness appalled him. Of course he would allow Boon to be Wanned. What else could he do? The boy had a right to live. He was too young to die. Frog's life had been destroyed when she'd been Wanned, killing any chance she had of having babies of her own, but Boon wanted to be a Wan. His lively curiosity would keep him alive and interested for centuries to come.

Boon could still be Wanned. What were a father's objections against the life of a precious child? They were nothing. Nothing at all. He would give in and save Boon's life.

Firdaus' legs wobbled from the tension that flowed out of them and he sank on his knees beside the divan. Yes. His decision was made. And because he'd left it so late, he was now in a tearing hurry. Where to find a whitefish before Boon gave up his last breath? Prophet. He remembered Mother Doughy's words. It had to be the right whitefish, or he'd condemn Boon to be an ally of the horrid Queen Mound.

No time to lose. But he dithered, torn in an agony of indecision. If he picked Boon up and carried him to Mother Doughy, Boon might die from the exertion. If Firdaus left in search of a whitefish, Boon could die in his absence.

He staggered outside into the blinding afternoon glare and sank on his knees onto the dry hot earth. He lowered his hands and forehead in supplication. "Mother Doughy, can you hear me? If you can, please help me! I need one of your whitefish to Wan my son, who is dying. Please hear me."

Did he feel the earth ripple under his hands? Did a sensation—he wasn't sure if it was taste or touch or smell —assure him that it would be done? He couldn't tell. He rested his face on the blistering ground, feeling the cloudlight burn on his back, the drowsy sounds of the city-wide siesta in his ears, murmuring voices, footsteps a few alleys away, the clatter of tools and the mooing of buffalo. The day wheeled away underneath him like a cart creaking under its own weight. He wanted to sink bodily into the earth below him, earth that wasn't earth but the body of a mother-thing, to be consoled and subsumed, all his worries eaten away, but he couldn't, he didn't, not with the slow rasping and gurgling of Boon's breath in his ears a few feet away.

He should get up. Sit the boy upright, pat on his back

to loosen the fluids, moisten his lips with a sponge. Something forced him to wait, to lie here supplicant under the baleful glare of the white sky. He let go of himself. He lay in broken pieces waiting for the mercy of an alien creature, and it was so peaceful not to be Firdaus for a while. No decisions, no responsibility, no sorrow. He remembered the little boy that had been Wanned by his uncle. Ulio. Maybe he could be Boon's playmate.

Uneven footsteps approached. The scattered bits of Firdaus rolled over and clicked back together. He pushed his upper body off the ground and shaded his eyes to look at the thing shuffling near. It was a Ghast. Was it the same one he'd seen in the Pompous Paradile, as the Wan Bar had been renamed?

It stopped a few feet away from him and executed a clumsy bow, bending at an unnatural place high up its lumpy torso. It held out a hand.

Firdaus got up and stepped closer. In its white claw it held a floppy whitefish that wriggled and bit at the air. Mother Doughy must have sent it.

"Thank you," he said to the Ghast. His voice sounded like someone had sandpapered his throat.

The creature bowed again, turned around and walked off. Firdaus stared at the toothy thing in his hand. So this was it. His son's savior. His brain floated like a feather on a cloud, oblivious of all that roiled beneath the cumulus cover, his head scoured clean of worries and feelings. No doubt they would return at some point, but he entered the house with steps as light as a dancer's.

He would save Boon.

CHAPTER 19

The paradile grinned at Ing, chewing on the hand she had fed it. She recoiled from it in shock. What? What? Why was she feeding a paradile her own flesh?

It was dark, the muddy pool she knelt by flat as a sheet, not a flicker of light anywhere. A nasty, earthy taste slithered around in her mouth. She lifted her hand to wipe her face and found strands of slimy weed trailing from her mouth. Apparently she had eaten a bit of paradile, too. The paradile swallowed her wrist with a convulsive movement and arced back into the lagoon with a great splash and stink of stagnant water. It was the same taste she had in her mouth, rot and slime and small dead things.

She stood up, reeling, and tried to orient herself. An orange flame high in the sky must be the Singing Tower. She was just outside the Marsh Gate, the North Gate. The whats and wherefores of her being here felt absent. She'd probably just fed them to the paradile. Something or someone, someone big and old and white presumably had summoned her here. Or she had just sent it a message.

Her mind wasn't her own. The Queen Mound owned half of it, and Mother Doughy had plowed through the rest with alien furrows.

Ing wiped a drop of salt from her eye. She should tell someone about this. Ask for help. She trudged toward the gate.

***

Ing sidled into Firdaus' house. Although smoke hung all over the city that morning, she'd already smelled that he was home, but if she was in luck, he might be sleeping. She couldn't say why she felt so wary in his presence. Part of her longed for nothing more than to sob out her troubles on his chest, but something compelled her to keep silent about it. It was like being mentally ill and knowing it, and by your very compulsion being unable to check into the mental ward.

Boon's labored breathing wheezed around the room, which was disordered as always. Maybe Stadholders were so used to people picking up after them that they couldn't learn to be neat.

Firdaus wasn't sleeping. He sat motionlessly on his bed, legs crossed beneath him, staring into nothing, his hand clenched around something she couldn't make out.

Ing hesitated. She couldn't remember what she'd come here for. Mother Doughy must have messed with her in some way, because she couldn't seem to keep a thought straight in her head for more than three minutes flat. She'd found herself talking to empty walls once or twice, or people shouting at her for no reason she could understand. Everything was slipping from her hands. Her friends avoided her. She wasted time counting spider webs and nothing was the same. Except Firdaus.

Firdaus' head jerked up and fixed her with a disconcerting wide-eyed stare. Too late to escape now.

"Ing," he said, as if tasting the word in his mouth. "Where have you been? Boon missed you this morning."

She didn't even know what day it was. A glance outside confirmed it was past noon. "I haven't been around?" she asked, and grimaced when she heard the lost little girl tone in her voice.

"Not really," Firdaus said. "You've been sleeping here occasionally, but I don't think I've woken up beside you even once."

Ing shuffled her feet. She didn't know what to say. She would like to curl up to him right now, but he seemed so far away on the bed, and the expression on his face was daunting.

"What... what's the matter? Boon's sleeping," she said. Not dead, she meant. But he must know that if his ears were still working.

"I have to leave here," he said. "But Boon's sleeping so peacefully. I don't want to disturb him."

"Where are you going?"

"I don't know. Inside the mound maybe. We're not safe as long as Aranaz is set on burning down the Quarter."

Aranaz was burning down the Dark Quarter? How could she have missed that? No, she had smelled the smoke. She wasn't nuts. Just distracted.

Firdaus got up and started pacing, carefully avoiding her and the scattered pieces of furniture and discarded clothing. Somebody should really start up a laundry-service, but how, without running water? Ing grasped her laundry-thought with both hands and clung on. That was a good thought. A normal thought. She still had it, some-where. She wasn't going to be fazed by Mother Doughy's tricks. Maybe she should go back to the Queen Mound to get fixed. No, that was out too, although she couldn't at this very moment remember why.

She staggered to the bed and leaned on her hands. Why should she leave here? She didn't want to leave Firdaus. She needed him for her plans, and her plans had to take place right here, where the most people were.

An edge of Firdaus' wrap, wafted up by the ferocious speed of his pacing, brushed the back of her thighs and she quivered in a rush of arousal. If they could just sport for a while, exchange flesh, she just knew her mind would clear up and they'd be fine again.

Ing grabbed Firdaus' arm on his next passing and forced him to halt. She looked up at him and smiled as appealingly as she knew how.

"Come to bed, honeyheart. Let me take care of you."

Firdaus stroked her hair, but his eyes were shadowed as he looked down on her. "Now?"

"We'll be silent for Boon," she whispered and clasped her arms around his thighs. "Please?"

If anyone had told her a year ago she'd be begging a guy to bed her she'd have laughed in his face, but here she was, begging away, and feeling not the slightest shame.

Firdaus sighed hard and released his muscles so quickly

that he fell hard against her and they rolled on the bed, tangled in each other's limbs. Close-up, he smelled of sorrow and secrecy.

Her hands roamed his back urgently, seeking purchase on his skin, grabbing thick folds of it and releasing them again, restlessly. Ing was afraid she might cry, again, and held on tight to her worries.

"Calm down, calm down," Firdaus murmured. "It's all right. I've got you."

"No, it's not all right. I've got to tell you," she said, and then wasn't sure what she wanted to tell him.

She found the sleekness around his middle and kneaded the new soft flesh like bread dough. As long as her fingers were busy, she could keep her limbs relaxed. Firdaus pushed her thighs open and searched for her flower. She whimpered wordlessly and he stilled her faint cries with his big hand. Of course. The boy. He never forgot about that damn kid.

"It won't be long now," Ing said softly. The kid must be drowning in the blood pooling in his damaged lungs.

"If you had seen Boon earlier," Firdaus asked, his voice so twisted and knotted that her own throat hurt in sympathy, "Could you have helped him?"

Ing shook her head. "No, he needs antibiotics, if it is the disease I'm thinking about, which I have no way of finding out. And the most advanced medicine would be too late by now. He'd need a lung transplant."

Firdaus wouldn't get most of that. She'd miss Boon, whose mind was as interested in the cogs and levers of the universe as her own. In time, she could have taught him to think like a true scientist. Too bad he wouldn't live. She could still Wan him on the sly. No, she'd have to abide by Firdaus' decision or lose any chance of his support.

Ing's spine curled, her body bucking with the release of joy, and she sat straight up, overheated and disoriented. What the hell was she doing here? She had an insurrection to run, information to gather, no time to waste on bed-sports.

Firdaus' eyes looked back at her, strangely tranquil in

his shadowed, grooved face. What was he thinking? What had they been talking about? A painful, sawing rattle from behind the divan answered that question. Of course he was suffering over Boon's death bed. Poor kid.

Firdaus sighed long and hard.

"I love you," she breathed into his ear, her voice wound up like a piece of string. There. That was said. Whatever would happen, would happen.

And something would, although she couldn't remember what or why.

***

After Ing had dropped her message of love in Firdaus' ear, she bolted like a muskrat burnt out of its hole. He stared after her retreating form, her shoulders hunched and her hands wringing. What the prophet had happened to her? Floating in and out, leaving things halfway?

But today he was grateful for her rapid exit. She hadn't asked him any questions he didn't want to answer and had allowed him to bury his fears in her needy flower. Firdaus stretched, grabbed a random piece of cloth and tiptoed over to Boon. Did he imagine it or was Boon's breathing easier? He touched two fingers to the fragile little wrist, and in spite of the audible breathing, he was still relieved to feel the fluttering heartbeat.

Mother Doughy had come through for him. The big question now was, what would she demand in return? He didn't really worry, though. Boon's life was worth his own, if the worst came to pass.

A shadow darkened the door. "Enter!" Firdaus called out. So much for secrecy. Did everyone know where to find him?

It was a messenger, carrying a tablet from Hilm. "Dear Abba," she wrote. "I have come to an agreement with Aunt Aranaz. We are planning the big event together. I may not be able to come see you anytime soon, but please inform me about my brother Boon. If he should become worse, I want you to send a courier before it's too late. Your loving Daughter, Hilm Halmasdottir."

She still used her mother's name, hadn't exchanged it

for Aranaz's, in spite of the political advantages of the latter action. A subtle sign of her continued allegiance to him. He hesitated. The courier was waiting for his answering tablet. Firdaus thought about keeping silent about his capitulation to Boon's wishes, but after some contemplation he quashed that base urge. Hilm had acted out of love, and he was supposed to be older and wiser than she, and not exact petty revenge by keeping her in the dark about Boon's health.

"Dear daughter," he scratched back, "Boon's health seems to be taking a sudden turn for the better. It's too soon to be completely certain, but I personally feel he will recover completely. Your loving father, Firdaus Eyvindursson."

He handed the tablet to the messenger and returned to the pleasure of watching his son enjoy untroubled sleep. Boon had been an early and underweight baby, his hands not the fat cinnamon shrimp of Hilm's newborn hands, but little claws so frail and translucent Firdaus had almost been afraid to touch him. He'd carried baby Boon next to his warm belly almost non-stop, only handing him to his sick mother for breastfeeding.

Maybe that why he'd always felt closer to Boon than to his other, robustly healthy children, all ten of them.

Firdaus softly sang a song under his breath, a baby song he'd used to sing to all his children when they had trouble sleeping or were sick. It was about a little white sheep that strays from the flock of black sheep, and as white sheep are wont to do, got into mischief. Finally she returns home, having dyed herself black in a puddle of tar. All ends well.

Firdaus stroked Boon's hair, and imagined he felt more spring and life in it already.

"Abba?" Boon whispered.

Firdaus felt his face breaking in a wide smile. "Boon! You're awake!"

"I feel so strange," Boon whispered. "Am I dying?"

"No. Not dying, not today!" Firdaus sang.

Boon blinked his yes, stretched his twiggy little hand

out in the faint light from the doorway. "I'm still brown, Abba. For a moment I thought..." he shut up and lifted his chin bravely. "Never mind."

Firdaus took both the cold skinny hands in his big one. "Boon. I apologize for being such a bad father to you. If I had been able to make my mind up sooner, you wouldn't have had to suffer as you have these past weeks. Can you forgive me?"

"Abba! You mean I can become Wan?"

"I have made you Wan already, my son. You've been bitten, and in few weeks you'll be changed completely."

Boon's head sank back against the pillows. His lips pressed tight and his ribs bucked. Trying not to cry.

"Dear son, please go and cry if you have to. Tears will no longer sway my judgment, because it's already been swayed. Forgive me for choosing this for you. You understand you won't grow like a human boy would, that you will never have children?"

Boon smiled. "I don't think I like girls enough to make babies, Abba. So that's alright."

"Aren't you a bit young to be so sure about that?" Firdaus said. Boon shook his head. "I've always known it was boys for me, Abba. That's okay, now, because Hilm will have lots of babies, and my brothers will too."

Firdaus sighed. A last worried knot loosened. What if Boon had changed his mind, after all? You never knew with children. And, for sure, at some point in the future Boon would hold it against him, if his life didn't turn out as he'd wanted to. Children always blamed their parents for everything, until they became parents themselves and realized how hard it was to shape another person's life.

***

Frog inched closer to the fire, in search of warmth. Her flesh didn't need it, but her tired mind did. The peatcutters and rice farmers retreated from her in an eddy of fear. The ones seated closest to her sat hunched, defensive, the threat of her presence curving their spines and clenching their fists.

She knew the only thing keeping them here was their

even greater fear of the thing trussed up against the mulberry tree. She didn't like it, though. It felt too much like being excluded out of contempt, even if the reason was the complete opposite.

The grizzled leader of the peatcutters, Otter, cleared his throat. "Honorable Loach, chief of Red Rice village. We have brought you this woman, Frog, to warn you against the coming of many Ghast."

Frog knew what she looked like. The terrible white-eyed face with crazily curling hair she glimpsed in still pools was one thing, but her arms and body just would not become normal and the same on both sides, although she'd eaten sufficient Ghast meat by now to make up for the loss of flesh.

The chief chewed on his thin, silky mustache and contemplated Frog from the corner of his eyes, while pretending to stare into the fire.

"What is that woman?" he asked. "We know of such, who steal the souls of our beloved kin and haunt our fires. Who's to say she isn't one such?"

Otter coughed and looked away from Frog. Was he going to sell her out while she sat right here? "She warned us about one of them. She knew how to tie it up so it couldn't escape. They gnaw off their own hands rather than stay bound."

Chief Loach nodded sagely, as if he completely understood those words. Frog doubted that. Mallard's father Loon had been just like that, he never understood anything new until it had been pounded into his face several times.

Otter spoke again, after a polite pause to give the chief a chance. "She also knows how to kill the creatures. You have to hack them into small bits, and wrap the pieces in green leaves. That is the only way they will not rise from the dead."

A collective quake went through the men seated around the fire and they slid their eyes away from Frog.

Chief Loach coughed and in the silence that fell, he waved a grand gesture to the group of men huddled around the fire, encompassing the invisible green fields that lay around them. "What use do I have of such knowledge? What need do I have to know of such creatures? This one you brought with you, and the woman, are the only ones I've ever seen."

"My grandfather saw one, far away across the river, when he was a boy," Otter said.

A polite but disbelieving silence followed this statement.

Frog cleared her throat to indicate that she was going to speak. The chief's lips thinned. Frog guessed that his wives and daughters never spoke up. She never had, when she'd been Mallard's wife, but now she had to.

"I have seen many dozens of these creatures. They will pass through your fields on their way to the city. I'm the Stadholder's servant, sworn to help him in any way I can, so I travel to the city to warn him against this band of evil beings."

The fire crackled and threw up sparks, and the man sitting on Frog's right twitched in surprise.

"So?" the chief said. "Pass through, and do not trouble me with your awful face. As long as you stay away from my daughters and my rice."

"That is not enough," Frog said. "These peatcutters are honorable men, and at my request they have helped me. They have taken me to your village, and when they leave, they have agreed to warn two more villages on their way back to the peat marshes. They will pass White Rice and Hull, and take my warning there."

"And you will go with them," the chief said. It wasn't a question.

Inside Frog, something that liked to obey men, and village chiefs especially, quivered in agony.

"No. You will listen to me, and you will take me to Black Rice. And in your turn you will warn two villages, one lying close to Black Rice and one more westerly from here. I think they are called Threshing and Oldfield."

The chief pulled at the poor stringy mustache so hard that Frog feared he would pull it out altogether. A lot of men in this village had his look, a bit like Ing around the eyes, hair less curly than most people, and skin more golden than brown. Pretty men, but still the best-looking man she'd ever seen was tall Stadholder Firdaus, with his full lips and big nose and tightly frizzing hair. Nobody could compare to that.

"Why? I have crops to tend, houses to repair, ducks to smoke. Wives to chastise. Why would I listen to a white woman who reeks of barrenness and disobedience?"

Frog bit her lips. He was right to chide her for disobedience, because who'd ever heard of a woman traveling alone? She had to be a runaway or a cast-off. But she wouldn't let it matter. Her purpose was clear.

"I said it before: this is my task. The Stadholder rules us all, and he needs to know about these creatures so he can defend his city. Don't you owe your neighbors the warning? Don't they have the right to hide their daughters from these creatures?"

She crossed her fingers behind her back for telling this lie. Eating the Ghast had told her of their goals, the Queen Mound's goals. She didn't quite understand how fighting the other Mound would involve killing all the people, but she did trust the information she had eaten. The Ghast substance did not lie.

Chief Loach shifted on his heels, and she bet he was wishing he hadn't convened all the village elders to talk with her and the delegation of peatcutters. If he'd been alone, he could have safely denied her request, but now his honor was at stake. His men shifted and mumbled among each other, and Frog knew she'd won the day.

"Your warning is received in thanks," Loach said stiffly. "I will ferry you to Black Rice, and two of my most seasoned men will go out to warn the neighboring villages."

Roughly translated, this meant that he'd send a couple of oldsters he wouldn't miss too much in the coming harvest. Frog didn't mind what kind of men he sent, as long as they passed the message along.

"You will ask Black Rice to pass along the warning to

the southern and eastern villages," she said. "And help me negotiate another passage closer to the city. I must travel faster than the Ghast that are now stumbling towards us, even as we speak."

The younger men threw frightened looks over their shoulders behind them. Loach's neck corded in restraint.

"We thank you, mistress Frog, for your kindness in warning us. Let me escort you to your boats, master Otter."

Otter didn't move an inch. "We gratefully accept your escort, after we have seen off our trusted companion Frog."

After this, Frog wouldn't be surprised if they killed her the moment she was out of sight of Otter and his burly wifeless men. No sane famer would go up against them, but once safely away, Loach might still decide to shrug off his promises and her dire warnings. Nothing much she could do about that now. They would discover she wasn't to be killed as easily as a straying wife.

CHAPTER 20

Midsummer Fair day dawned hot and overcast as always. Ing needed to replace her supplies of vellum for writing and clay tablets to bake into backup copies, and she was hoping to find both in the stalls filling Stadholder's Plaza from corner to corner. But Aranaz' Stentors had announced that the Fair crowds would receive no free food from the palace, and added to the lack of foreign traders, it might be a subdued affair. But it would still be fun, and she could walk around by day, because nobody looked twice at a stranger during the Fair.

She crossed the Plaza, keeping to the long shadows of the early morning, and seated herself on a bale of tanned fish hides in Fishmonger Alley. With her cloak over her white face and hands, and her feet tucked under the frayed hem, she expected to evade attention.

People streamed in from all over the city, dressed up in their best loincloths and jewelry, glad to leave the protective clothing of their professions behind. Troops of skinny farmers from the rice paddies further in the marsh, whelkers and froggers, reederers and leatherers and potters. She wondered if they were feeling the decreasing fertility. She wanted to ask them if they ate a lot of whitefish. A face jerked back from her in an exaggerated rictus of fear. Ing stumbled, crudely yanked from her deep thoughts.

"A Wan, look, a Wan," someone muttered behind her.

Her hands scrabbled for her cloak. When had she put the hood down? It was broad daylight. How long had she been standing in the middle of the Plaza, daydreaming? She lifted her cloak over her head, but a dozen pairs of eyes stared right back, a miniature crowd in the making.

This could be a good moment to sneak away from Stadholder's Plaza, before the mood turned any sourer. Fishmonger Alley led further into the Crane Quarter and the docks, and she'd have to cross Stadholder's Plaza to get back to the Dark Quarter aboveground. Ing spotted an abandoned house, hoisted herself over a crumbling window-sill and slid into the house. The upper story's floorboards had been stolen long ago, and she could see through the supporting beams into the open sky. She jumped up and dragged herself onto a beam.

When the cloud cover brightened, the invisible sun rising overhead, Ing climbed upon the second story windowsill and counted the people milling below. Three or four thousand, she estimated. Lower numbers than she would have thought. Had people stayed home or had so many died over the winter? She wished Aranaz would do a census. Too many faces had the bluish hue of whitefish eaters.

The babble of the growing crowd outside swelled to a roar. Fishwives tumbled into the house below Ing, shriek-ing curses at each other, lugging as many baskets of fish as they could carry, against the backdrop of the crowd's ominous rising buzz. Ing bit down on a giggle. They were fleeing the impending outburst, straight into the arms of a monster.

The people outside yelled and surged mindlessly back and forth over the square. Ing could smell the rising excitement, sweat and excrement and rotting fish guts churning themselves into the heady soup of rebellion. Bread and games, eh? With rice so scarce, Aranaz should have offered them games. Hung a few criminals on the palace steps. Nothing could broach the stacked landing saucers of the palace towers, of course, certainly not a mob armed with wooden or shell knives, but Aranaz' reputation might not survive this fracas. Interesting. Ing figured she'd better get out of here, save her own skin.

She balanced over a support beam to the other side of the room. The hallway was solid oldstone slab, and she

crossed to the window on the other side, which unfortunately overlooked a courtyard. Damn. She didn't want to
be here all day. She crept down the stairs, hoping to sneak
out in the melee and find an underground entrance
somewhere near, but one of the fishwives spotted her.

"Hey! You there! What do you think you're doing,
hey? Stealing our fish that we've worked hard for! Hey?"

The fishwife thrust a hand under Ing's unprepared
nose. The hand reeked of countless layers of fish grime,
thick with scabs and old cuts. "Honest working hands! Not
mincing about in fancy robes!"

She yanked Ing's hood down and shrieked like a
teakettle, stumbling backward and oversetting one of her
precious baskets. Silver-gray smelts slid out and flowed
over the earthen floor.

"Wan! She's a Wan!" the fishwife shrieked, and the
other women in the room gaped and pointed or screeched,
depending on their proximity to Ing.

Damn.

Ing backed off, trying to pull her hood over her face
again, but the fallen woman surged up and held on to Ing's
cloak with vindictive determination. Ing grabbed the edge
and fought for possession of her wrap, but the damage was
done. The thin worn cotton slid further off and revealed
Ing in all her white-skinned glory. The women stared.

"She's got no hair down there!"

"Look at her little breasts! She's got no kids for sure!"

"Hold her, hold her," the fallen woman yelled, alternating between grabbing after her strewn smelts and
trying to get up on one knee. "Bring her into the street!
She has to pay for our Stadholder!"

"Oooh! She the one as ruined our Stadholder?"

A little obsidian knife struck Ing in her upper arm. It
stung, a ghostly memory from when she could feel real
pain, with real nerves attached to real skin.

"Let go of me, or I will infect all of you, and your
children and your children's children!" she said in as
menacing a voice as she could manage.

The room emptied within seconds. They'd be back

with their husbands, but Ing had a few moments to make her escape. Damn those superstitious fools! She grabbed her cloak and ran across the courtyard into a random empty apartment. In the kitchen, she yanked the cover of the convenience. The sewer was dead but out of use, and any smells had long since disappeared. She wriggled her way down the narrow and mercifully clean sewer channel and dropped down into briny water.

***

The second day after his Wanning, the day of the riots, Boon coughed out so much of his lungs that Firdaus thought he was going to die after all. Why was it so hard for Boon? He himself had felt weak, yes, but at times it seemed Boon might die of the Wanning process.

The third day, Boon's skin was dappled like a fawn's, and the fourth day he was starting to pale to ground ginger. His breathing was normal, his hair curled gold, and Firdaus had never seen Boon's eye whites so clear.

"I'm going up to the palace and visit Hilm," Boon said.

"I'm not sure about that," Firdaus said cautiously. "She might be scared of you."

Boon inspected his brightening skin seriously. "You think I can still pass?"

"Maybe at cloudwane you still can. If you stay out of the rooms with a lot of living glowapples."

Boon nodded. "I know I'm a Wan now, and that I have to live underground. I just want to say goodbye to the others."

Firdaus' throat clogged up. "Boon, we're not going to be able to stay in this city for ever. The Mounds are going to blow up, and take all the houses and the palace with it."

Boon goggled. "But Abba... how do you know?"

"I heard it from the Mound Mother herself. I'll introduce you to her. Now that you're a Wan, you're going to have to meet a lot of new people."

Boon skipped next to him, holding his hand, and Firdaus was reminded of how young the boy was. Actually, he seemed younger today than he had in years. Knowing that he was going to die soon had aged him prematurely, and it was incredibly rewarding to see him shed those heavy years.

Firdaus looked for the entrance he'd taken with Ing. Not three steps inside stood an enormously tall and wide Ghast. Firdaus' nose suggested it was the Ghast he'd met twice before, but he couldn't be sure.

It ambled forward on its thick legs and dinnerplate feet. Boon hid behind Firdaus' thighs with a squeak. The Ghast sniffed them both deeply and stood aside to let them pass.

"Abba! Am I going to look like that, too?"

"Only if you want to, Boontie."

Boon mused this while they climbed downwards into the guts of the Mound. "What do you mean by that?" he asked at last. "Could I make myself grow taller?"

"Yes, if you got enough food."

"I'm not hungry," the boy said, surprised. "I never saw you and Ing eat. Don't you have to eat?"

"Yes and no," Firdaus said. He'd gotten used to this aspect of Wanning now, but he felt reluctant to explain it to his son. "People will give you stuff to eat and you will know stuff they know. It's very interesting."

Boon's eyes got big and he stumbled over nothing, rapt as he was in his own visions. "I could maybe find out everything Ing knows."

"That would certainly be very useful," Firdaus said, but immediately he felt ashamed. He didn't need to drag Boon into his doubts and complicated feelings about Ing.

"She knows everything about plants and animals and she explained to me about Pythagora. I want to be just like her when I'm a grown up," Boon said.

"I don't see why not," Firdaus said. "But stop dreaming for now, because this very moment right here is interesting, too."

He entered the round chamber where he'd spoken to Mother Doughy before. Surprising, that she had kept it intact. Was it his imagination or did it smell a little different, though? Almost cheesy or rotten-fishy, with a salty undertone. Boon gripped Firdaus' hand hard, and Firdaus rejoiced in the strength of the thin fingers.

"Mother? Are you in?" he said for lack of anything better, and decided he needed to devise a protocol for politeness to mounds. "Are you receiving visitors today?"

Stone eyes ground open and Boon gasped, leaning his head against Firdaus' side.

"I haven't thanked you, yet, Mother, for your kindness to Boon. I'm more grateful than I could ever express. If I can ever do anything in return?"

"A taste of the gratitude would be very much appreciated," Mother Doughy said. "And this is your making? Who has only half your substance? Such a wasteful way of procreation. I myself prefer better odds. All my seed is an aspect of my present self."

It was like talking to Ing, half the words didn't mean anything.

"His name is Boon, and he would have died without your gift," Firdaus said with a flourish.

Firdaus hauled Boon forward, intending to order the boy to say something appropriate, but Boon didn't need any goading. He made a beautiful bow. "Thank you, Mother," he said in his reedy voice. "I am very grateful for living. There is so much I don't know yet. How old are you?"

"Ah, hm," Mother rumbled. "I cannot taste that flavor."

Boon looked disappointed. "How come you can talk?" he said. "Do you have lungs? Do you need to breathe? Can I see your tongue?"

"A little Ing in the making," Mother Doughy said. "Firdaus. There is one last thing I must tell you about Ing."

"Okay," Firdaus said. "Go ahead. But maybe first tell me if you know when you're going to blow?"

"I feel it will be soon," she said, "but I can't be precise. All of us must be ready, and when the scent in the air is thick enough it will happen. It is not yet."

"But when? How many days?"

"I cannot give you that flavor. The idea of precise numbers Ing has explained to me many times, but I cannot taste it."

"More than my fingers?" Boon said and waggled his hands in the air.

"Well. Yes. I think so. I will know it when I know it, and then you will have less than a day to leave here."

"We're going to have to start the evacuation now." Firdaus said. "I wish I'd heard something from Hilm already. She was going to convince Aranaz."

"I said I wished to talk about Ing," Mother Doughy cut in. "Cease your pointless branching off."

Someone was getting very bossy. And since said someone was as big as a city, and they were dwelling inside her body, Firdaus shut up and listened.

"Ing is planning to turn everyone into a Wan, as she has been turning Wan for centuries now. I tolerated that, because she gave me interesting new flavors. The ones she chose were always new and complex tastes. However, I like humans. I wish them to continue. We must stop Ing."

The ball of anger building in Firdaus' chest was sudden and harsh, burning its way out of his mouth. "Ing Wanned everyone? What are you saying? She's the cause of all this?"

"Ing was the first human to be Wanned since your people arrived on my world. It broke her mind, and destroyed a thing she carried in her head that held many memories. But, being Ing, eventually she recovered and found out how it had happened. And being Ing, she tried it out on others."

Frog's sweetly adoring face sprang to mind, alternating between its brown and its ethereal white version. He should have trusted his instincts then, and killed Ing instead of allowing caution and expediency to rule him. Firdaus measured out his words carefully. "Do all the others know about this?"

"No," Mother Doughy said. "That is why I am giving you this morsel of information, for you to consume as you see fit."

"I see fit," Firdaus said grimly. "Oh, I see fit to use it!"

Boon looked up at him, stricken. "I'm sure she meant

well, Abba! Ing is just curious!"

"Boon, my boy, it's not right to be curious at the cost of someone else's life, is it?"

"No," Boon said. His head hung, and the ebullience he'd displayed for the first time in years evaporated.

"Ing has just entered me," Mother Doughy said helpfully. "If you wish to act on this morsel, I will direct you both to the same chamber. I advise you to wait and listen before you act."

***

If Mother Doughy thought she could disable Ing with a brain virus, she better think twice. Ing would just fetch her stuff, hop in and out of her alcove and never return.

Ing inched her way to the narrow tunnel. It had been in the same place for centuries now, and the once-smooth walls had dried out and felt velvety, almost crumbly to the touch. Maybe Mother Doughy didn't remember this tunnel. Maybe she couldn't feel and hear everything through the old, decaying matter making up the tunnel walls. They had the same pinkish striae she'd noticed in both Mother Doughy and the Queen Mound, and she was guessing it was a sign of age. Maybe Mother was dying. Maybe Ing should start stuffing herself and become a mound in her own right. The past weeks' wandering tired her. She felt old, and her brain was as full of holes as old cheese. Even that feared future seemed like a well-deserved rest now.

The tunnel narrowed further, and after a hesitation, she went in feet forward. She'd never liked small, enclosed spaces, and this resembled her nightmares rather more than was comfortable. The tight fit of the walls forced her shoulders to hunch. Suddenly, she shot loose of her footing and whooshed down into the darkness. The walls became smoother than glass under her fingers and it was like a swimming pool slide without the water. She landed hard on her feet in a large, echoing space and closed her mouth with a snap when she heard her own surprised, frightened yell echoing off the walls. Phew. That was scary. She'd never known this tunnel to get so steep. She must have ended up in a newer part without realizing it.

She did a few cautious steps forwards and realized she was inside her old friend, the amphitheatre. It seemed dimmer than normal, and while her eyes adjusted only slowly, her ears picked up the slow susurrus of people talking, shifting on their asses on the hard seats, rustling with clothes, patting their hair, shuffling in. Her people. Her Wan. Long, long years had gone into the making of this moment, and her heart swelled with pride or joy or some such sissy kind of emotion. This was the triumph of planning and hard, cold, shiny science.

She could still be a scientist, even without computers with bigger brains than all of humanity combined. A scientist could make calculations on clay tablets and vellum scrolls. A scientist could build her memory palace brick by brick, until she had enough incontrovertible evidence. And when that moment came, that scientist would take action. She hadn't planned this exact moment, to be sure, but she would seize it.

Ing checked the number of people present. The filing in slowed to a trickle. It was enough. Time to start.

"My dear fellow Wan!" she said and paused a beat or two, so everyone could murmur a greeting in return.

"We have long prepared for this day. Some of you are old and wise, and others are younger, with more fire in your bellies than us oldsters. But together we have one purpose! We're going to save ourselves, and everyone in this city. We're going to protect them from famine and disease and old age. No longer will we have to watch our loved ones die. We will be the forerunners of a new era.

"We're going to go out tonight and turn everyone into Wan. Away with suffering and hunger! Away with death and forgetfulness!"

The feeling in her heart spread throughout her whole body and it was as if she was putting her fingers directly into people's minds. Communion, that's what it was. They were right there with her. It felt great.

She threw her head back and flung her arms up. "We will rebuild civilization! We will relearn technology and one day we will return to the stars!"

The silence that fell after her last words was different from the awe-struck silence that had counterpointed her words before. This was a dull hard silence that bounced the words right back into her face.

Ing blinked. What had happened? There, the older Wan, her friends, to whom she'd given many times her bodyweight in persuasion, the younger Wan, still clinging to their human forms. There, Mother Doughy unexpectedly protruding from the wall. Firdaus, and Boon standing next to her. Boon? Standing? She peered harder and he seemed different, more vibrant. His eyes looked straight at her, big and shiny and full of tears and reproof.

The look from Boon's eyes was like an electric shock. What was he thinking?

Everything that had happened the past few weeks dropped back in her mind with a resounding thud. She'd been insane, roaming the streets babbling to herself. After Mother Doughy had given her something to eat. Mother Doughy had betrayed her, fed her commands that were eating at the very foundation of her sanity. It was practically a declaration of war.

Her skin contracted in a million goose bumps and her lips went numb. Firdaus and Mother Doughy. Firdaus was going to betray her. She had to stop him from speaking. She stumbled down from the platform, trying to get down to the amphitheatre floor, but a thousand arms stopped her and two thousand feet tripped her and bodies hemmed her in, dampening even the sound of her frantic shouts.

A light glowed down from the chamber's ceiling, illuminating Firdaus from above. Ing choked in indignation. Mother Doughy was helping Firdaus! Not fair! She'd known Mother much, much longer. Firdaus wasn't bright enough to understand what she was accomplishing here. She needed to get out, warn the Queen Mound that now was the time to act, to repay her promises.

Firdaus lifted his arms and everyone fell silent.

"Friends! Listen to my words. Yes, we are here to save humanity. We are here to save ourselves and our fellow human beings. We are here to save them from the great danger that is coming upon us in the next few weeks. I'm not talking about hunger and disease. We will deal with that wave when we meet it. I'm talking about the Mounds becoming ripe and blowing up in millions of spores. We have all kicked puffballs in our youth. Mother Doughy is going to become a giant puffball and burst open.

"Picture this in your minds for a moment. The city we are standing beneath will be destroyed. All the buildings will be destroyed. Our homes here inside Mother Doughy will be no more."

Firdaus paused. "Do you understand what I am saying, my friends?"

Ing could have burst like a puffball herself. How did he know this? She'd spent centuries trying to find out the last piece in the puzzle of Ghast reproduction, and she'd gotten nowhere. Both Queen Mound and Mother Doughy had clammed up whenever she brought up the subject. The discovery should have been hers!

Firdaus answered the Wan's questions and went on with his speechifying. Ing didn't listen anymore. Not fair. This was Nobel Prize material, if they still had those back on Earth, and if old Earth still existed, and now nobody was ever going to know about it. This explained everything. The bareness of the planet on the pictures they'd used to pick it out, and when they landed it hadn't been bare at all.

Firdaus was talking about the spores eating everything in sight. Yes, yes, that fit in with her hypothesis. The spores would have to be omnivore to have any chance of survival. Then they'd become the worms she found centuries ago, but hadn't seen in a very long time. The worms grew into whitefish, who'd been becoming scarce of late, some of whom combined into paradile.

Everything was falling into place.

"We have to hide from the spores!" she shouted.

Firdaus glared at her. "That's what I was just telling everyone, Ing. We need everyone here to help. My daughter Hilm and Stadholder Aranaz are leading the evacuation on the human side, but I urge you to work together. And nobody gets Wanned. I want you all to promise that. Wanning can be a solution if someone's dying from a disease, like my son Boon. But it's not something you can do to another human being without asking."

Ing snorted. Firdaus was trying to cram several agendas down their throat in one fell swoop.

Unfortunately, a beat of silence had fallen after Firdaus' words, and her snort echoed through the chamber. Unnaturally so. Mother Doughy was doing something to the sound, Ing was sure. A creature as smart as Mother Doughy, with time on her side, would be able to study sound like no one else once she'd understood its importance and uses.

"Yes, Ing, I was waiting to hear you say something on the subject of involuntary Wanning. It is you, isn't it, who Wanned everyone who is standing here today?"

All hell broke loose. People rose and shouted at her until she saw only wide-open mouths and furious faces. Judging her.

She didn't even get the chance to defend or explain herself. "Hey!" she shouted as hard as she could, but the wall of sound of nearly a hundred Wan talking all at once on top of their voices was hopeless.

"Silence!" Firdaus shouted, and of course they all shut up for him.

"I'm asking you once more, Ing, are you the person who Wanned everyone here without asking their permission? So that without your interference no Wan would exist except yourself?"

"Well, hey, it's not as black and white as that," Ing said, but her voice trailed off into nothing. "We should talk about this at some other time. When we're not in the middle of a crisis."

The crowd undulated, an eye blink, and bore her on top of their hands towards Firdaus. They dropped her on the floor at his feet, and she just couldn't get her feet under her. The ground shook and trembled and heaved and she kept falling flat on her face, until she gave up and kneeled.

"I'm sure the occasional whitefish would be stupid enough to bite a human being, you know."

"Why did you do it, Ing Gioksdottir? Why?"

"My name is Giok Siu Ing. I did it for science. I needed to know more about Wanning. How had it happened? How does it affect the average person? How does it affect extraordinary people?"

"Did you not pick out all of these people here for their special gifts? Didn't you pick out the artists and the thinkers and superior craftspeople?"

"I guess. Not everyone has the inner resources to withstand living forever, you know. It needs strong, intelligent people with intrinsic motivation."

"I don't know what that means, Ing, except that you have just admitted to Wanning everyone here." Firdaus paused.

Ing stared up at him, unable, even now, to keep her eyes away from his noble face, with the great prow of a nose and the crinkly hair like a halo around his head. The skin she'd kneaded with her hands, the rod that she had tasted and taken into her flower. Her man. Whom she'd foolishly confessed to loving. And this was exactly how she had always been treated when she had loved before. She'd been a fool. Betrayed as usual.

Firdaus' silence went on. Most of the Wan stared back at him, rapt with attention. Sheep, they were no better than sheep, to be swayed by a noble face and a deep voice. Cheap rhetoric.

"What does Ing deserve in return for her deeds? How do we judge Ing?"

Another, terrible silence fell, a silence as deep and menacing as the cold black of space. Ing searched the crowd for friendly faces. Some of them must be her supporters, surely? Ing's throat contracted and the squeak that came out of it echoed around the chamber, amplified by Mother Doughy's acoustic tricks.

A formless shout shattered the silence into a thousand growls and yells and the crowd surged in on Ing. The claustrophobia she'd experienced before in the tunnel was nothing compared to this. She was pressed on from all sides, compressed into a tiny cube of Ing. Nails peeled at her skin, hands tore at her hair, teeth clamped down on her fingers.

She tried to shout but her voice was gone. She tried to crawl but she had no knees. She tried to beg for mercy but she had no hands to clasp in supplication.

CHAPTER 21

Frog waved goodbye to her last ferry, a little wobbly as her feet touched dry land once more. The dignitary who'd given out warnings to the next village ducked and pretended not to have seen her. The rowers paddled furiously, their faces scrunched up from the effort.

With each successive village, her task had gotten harder. Without Otter the peat cutter boss and his belief in her story, it had been more difficult to convince the chiefs and headmen of the other settlements.

Nobody had ever said it was easy to have a purpose. The brave Stadholder daughters in the story, who escaped their evil stepmothers by climbing down on a rope of their own hair, rescued a Stadholder son from a giant behemoth and lived happily ever after, never had to do difficult stuff like this. They had their brave Stadholder by their side, and magical swords, and armies. She was just Frog, who'd never had to speak up in an Assembly before, and it was harder than she'd even imagined, because she'd never bothered to imagine it. All she'd ever wanted was a baby, not public speaking.

The pirogue fled from sight into one of the thousands of hidden channels and creeks of the Maze. Frog's goal was the shining white city in the distance. She looked up at the dyke bordering the Maze, the Road on top of it. Long ago, she had travelled that road with the trader, and a tremor of remembered fear and misery tiptoed up and down her spine.

It was no use standing there, being afraid. Frog rearranged her new reed mantle around her shoulders, although the fresh, still-moist knots chafed a little. But she'd wanted to look her best and had stayed up all night weaving a new apron and elbow cape. It had plumes of maroon-flowering reed heads that bobbed when she walked, and clusters of red berries to add a festive touch.

She climbed up the grassy slope to the road. She took a deep breath and set her first step on the road to White City. Nothing happened. No angry traders sprang up to lead her away in chains, no hordes of Ghast, no uppity city women looking down their noses at her. She could do this.

A speck appeared on the far horizon. The stench arrived before the sound did, and Frog recognized a midden wagon. Before she could decide what to do, her silly scaredy legs had carried her down the slope, back into a stand of tall fern trees. Her knees knocked with fear. This was a sign that she wasn't meant to walk on the road after all. She would humbly make her way at the foot of the dyke. It was good enough for her. Wet feet had never hurt a person before, except that some people got foot rot and smelled bad. But then, she hadn't had a sniffle or sore back since she'd turned into a monster.

A troop of messengers stamped by, overtaking the midden wagon, sweating hard as their well-shod feet ate the road pace by pace. On her other side, small skiffs shot out from the edge of the city, all headed for the marshes. A lot of activity. Maybe her warnings weren't needed anymore? Some dignitary had taken it upon himself to warn the Stadholder? That would be a good thing. Not a disappointment at all. It wasn't her wish to shine, it was her wish to serve Firdaus. She must still make her way to the city, because she couldn't stop those runners and ask them their business. They were highly trained in secrecy and speed, and were sworn to let nothing halt them.

Frog righted her shoulders, which kept hunching down, trying to be invisible, and squelched on over the muddy skirts of the dyke. It was so funny that people stayed up top, because in the first ten steps she spotted about a dozen edible plants, and yummy fat frogs hopping in and out of little pools. If you sucked on those grasses they were sweet, and giant dockleaf made good hats. Look at them up there in the hot morning light, sweating, their mouths dry, while she was having a perfectly good walk down here in the shade with nice cool feet.

***

"Abba! Abba! Stop them! They're killing her!"

Firdaus looked down on Boon's face. His feelings plummeted down from their judgmental place and landed with a sickening thud in his belly.

He couldn't let Ing be torn apart and eaten. He would have to be quick, though, to save even a little snippet of her. She'd disappeared under the heaving mass of death-white limbs and her voice had stilled beneath the roaring of the angry Wan.

"Stop!" he shouted, using his best Stentor-voice. "Stop right now!"

The second time his voice miraculously caught some kind of natural echo and thundered down on the growling mass like an avalanche.

The group splattered outwards like a boil bursting and Firdaus sought Ing. Was that her? That hump of white stuff? It didn't have arms or legs or breasts or...

Firdaus pushed Boon behind him. "Don't look, son. Don't look."

He had to look, for Ing's sake. He slammed down on his knees and lifted her up by what he thought must be her shoulders. Prophet, he'd never seen anything like it. He could do nothing for her right now. He cradled Ing against his chest. Maybe she could feel his skin against hers and get some comfort from it?

The faces of the Wan nosedived from their delirious, vengeful high, turning to shock and guilt. They were his first priority. He had to mitigate the aftereffects of their cruelty, or the whole society of Wan would fall part.

"You have exercised your judgment on the woman Ing. I call this sufficient punishment. Now lay down any flesh of hers you haven't eaten, and step away from her body. It's enough. You are done. Your judgment was harsh, but you must forgive yourselves for what you have done. Put it away and don't think about it anymore."

He paused. The faces surrounding him showed confusion and doubt. They needed more.

"I condone what you have done here. I forgive you."

That was it. The shock fell away from the white faces. Soft talking started up; people began breaking away from the back of the group.

Firdaus raised his voice. "Do as I have told you. Go and perform the tasks you were given. Go."

He stroked the featureless bump that had probably once been Ing's head. "I need three volunteers to see to the lady Ing's remains."

"I volunteer," Boon said in a voice as fragile as a blade of grass. "She was my teacher. Is she dead?"

"I don't know."

Boon stretched out a trembling finger to touch the knob on Ing's shoulders. "Bye, Ing. I wish you could have taught me longer. There's a lot of stuff I wanted to learn."

One by one, the remaining Wan stepped up to Ing's body and deposited at Firdaus' feet the bits and pieces of Ing they hadn't consumed in their rage. Amrit offered up her shawl to gather the clumps of dry white Wan-stuff in.

"At some point, Boon, you could eat these morsels of Ing's knowledge," Firdaus said softly. He wished this moment could have been postponed until Boon was older, or at least a bit more used to the idea of being a Wan. He just knew that he couldn't afford to let the opportunity to preserve some of Ing's knowledge pass them by.

Boon's face wrinkled up in disgust. "That's gross. I'm not going to do that."

"It's what the Wan do. I heard Ing explaining it to you."

He held up a fingertip under Boon's nose. The boy's eyes glazed over and he licked his lips. "It smells so good. But I don't want to."

"Think of it as knowledge, not as Ing. She has no use for it anymore."

Boon took the fingertip from him and stared at it, mesmerized, as it trembled on his palm. With a visible effort, he put it on the checked cloth with the rest of Ing's crumbs.

Firdaus held on tight to Boon, nodding brusquely at the three Wan who presented themselves as pallbearers. Two people whose names he didn't know, and Haroon, one of his beautiful antlers hanging at half-mast. Damaged in the scuffle, probably.

"We'll take care of her," Haroon said. "Unless you want to..."

Firdaus got his point. Yes, that is what a conqueror would do, but he really didn't want to consume Ing's thoughts. Prophet knew how they would change him, and he was done with changing for a bit.

"Take her, then," he said.

Haroon unwrapped his artfully draped sari and covered the largest lump of Ing's remains with it. Something inside Firdaus balked at the thought of so much precious food being taken out of his reach, but he denied the impulse. The heap of nibbled bits and pieces was still getting higher. More people having second thoughts about consuming the thoughts of someone they had reviled. Very sensible. He set Boon to gathering the small bits.

Maybe, one day, if he had enough of his life, he'd hold a banquet and allow his children and subjects to eat him, as a last tribute to being a good Stadholder. Wouldn't it be a great way to end one's life? If one had enough of eternity?

***

Firdaus was still surveying Ing's possessions when Hilm found him. In spite of Ing's betrayal, Firdaus still felt responsible for picking up Ing's precious records as he'd promised several times.

"Abba."

Firdaus turned and blinked when he beheld his daughter. "Daughter! I hardly dare hug you because I'm afraid I'll spoil your beautiful dress..."

"Don't be silly, Abba," Hilm said, but her embrace was markedly less tight than usual.

"I take it you succeeded with my sister?"

"Yes. She offered me the position of Stadholder-

Aspirant, as I had hoped."

"And now you're laden with tokens of support from the guilds," he said, admiring.

Hilm raised a royal eyebrow. "Hardly. I collected those before I went to my dear aunt. I didn't want to be beheaded or poisoned. She knew when she saw this that she couldn't get around me."

"Hilm, you scare me. When did you become a politician like that?"

"When I was head of our house, because you were gone and there was no one else to look out for my brothers and sisters."

Boon entered the alcove with his tally-tablet ready.

"Boon-tie!" Hilm shrieked and for a moment the mask slipped. "You did it! You're alive!" She embraced him hard.

Boon went on collecting Ing's notes and scrolls in baskets, noting them down meticulously on his tally-tablet. They mattered to him, so Firdaus could leave him to it with a clear conscience. They'd be stacked in the Dark Quarter awaiting evacuation.

He gestured Hilm to sit down on Ing's fabulous carpet. "So, daughter, Stadholder of the city, tell me about your progress."

Hilm composed herself just so, her skirts elegantly baring a painted foot in a dainty sandal, spine straight, hands folded in the gesture of determination and strength. "Aunt Aranaz was easy to convince. She's the one who's been haranguing the Assembly about ignoring the signs of change and she's set several projects in motion. She's been building ships. One of those ships is being sent out to warn the other islands."

"Ships? I had no idea Aranaz was a supporter of mine," Firdaus said. If only she'd supported his ideas when he was still Stadholder.

Hilm frowned at him. "Aunt Aranaz is no fool, Abba. If they don't survive, to whom will we trade our goods?"

Why had Aranaz opposed him so hard on these issues, thwarting his every attempt, only to adopt them the moment she kicked him out of the picture? Power, that was why. That was Aranaz' focus in life, as it would never be his. His core was family, love, peace. Things worth fighting for.

"I argued for two ships, but we settled on this compromise. The remaining boats will be used to ferry people to the villa and the caves below it," she said.

"How are you going to seal them off to protect everyone from the seeds?"

Hilm grimaced. "We set the reed-weavers to creating screens that we will coat with wax and clay, but it's going to be impossible to seal off everything. We might have to ask the elderly to serve as a safety layer."

"Prophet, Hilm. That's cruel. They will be eaten."

"If you have a better suggestion, Abba, I'll gladly consider it," Hilm snapped.

She'd make a terrific Stadholder. Where had this frightening woman come from? She didn't take after him, that was for sure. Her mother had had Boon's kind of smarts, but this determination was more of an Aranaz thing.

"Good. We Wan are emptying our homes here in the mound, and we will follow the citizens in small boats of our own. I trust there will be no problem about mingling with the mud people?"

Hilm composed her face. She was going to say something he didn't like, he guessed.

"Abba, we cannot mingle the Wan and the real people. That would only cause more riots and fights. The people are getting wind of our preparations already, and they're panicking. Please believe me when I say I would grant your request if I could. But it's impossible."

"Daughter," Firdaus said formally, "You wouldn't have this vital information if it wasn't for us. For me. I ask of you that you acknowledge that debt."

"Father, I will do anything you ask but this. I will grant you official right to the Dark Quarter, I will allow you trade with normal people, but we can't have you frightening the women and children."

"Grant me ownership of the Dark Quarter? Oh, that's rich! It's going to cease existing in a few weeks. No, daughter, this is one thing I'm going to insist on. Show yourself with me in public. Shake my hand. We will set up a stall of our goods on Market Day, and you will buy something from a Wan. Is that understood?"

"Aunt Aranaz won't accede to those requests, Abba," Hilm said.

"Think about it before you ape her inflexible stance," he said. "She would have killed me that day on the Plaza. She would kill to become Stadholder. Is that the woman you want to imitate?"

Hilm's face crumpled and she hiccupped once before she got hold of herself and smoothed her features. "I'll discuss it with her. And I'll do as you ask. I would never deny you, Abba."

"I should hope not," he grumbled.

But he relented and tousled the one free-dangling lock of her hair. Hilm squeaked and tried to evade his hand.

"Do you know how much time it costs to get myself done up like this? And how much it weighs?"

"As a matter of fact, I do know. You see, once upon a time, I was Stadholder of a city myself," Firdaus replied.

"Fine, fine, point taken. I have to go now, Abba. Is there more information I need for the evacuation?"

Firdaus thought hard. "Did you send messengers to the villages? Over the ridge?"

Hilm nodded at every item on his checklist. "Yes. We've invited the Maze villages to evacuate to the city."

"Prophet. What will we do about food?"

Hilm shrugged. "We're ordering them to take all their stores, to take seeds and seedlings, their livestock... we need them, Abba. Anything that survives will save a citizen from dying of starvation."

"You're right. Ancestors! How will we manage this, Hilm?"

"I delegate the responsibilities and hope for the best." Hilm spread her hands. "There is no way I can oversee all of it, or Aunt Aranaz could. The Assembly members are run off their feet. The guilds are all in action. Everybody has tasks and deadlines. It's huge. I mean, what to take? All our beautiful merchandise? Or choose food?"

"Food," Firdaus said. "Merchandise can be made again."

"Not all of it. Silks and jewelry? They can never be duplicated."

"Metal and pottery can be stashed," Firdaus said. "The seeds won't eat them because they're not alive."

"You're right. Oh Abba there is so much to decide! It drives me nuts! How did you do it?"

Firdaus shrugged. "I was Stadholder in the last days of a prosperous time, when everything ran without me. This is a completely different thing you're doing right now. I wish you luck. We better get started."

***

Light slowly bloomed over Ing's covered face, until she closed her eyes to shut out the brightness. She was on a boat. Why? What were they doing to her? She remembered speaking to the gathered Wan, but, after that, a blanket of forgetfulness covered her memory. And now she was here, swaddled, blindfolded, being rowed away somewhere.

"Help!" she cried. "Help me! I'm a prisoner!"

Nobody answered. Voices murmured softly somewhere ahead of her. She'd never felt this helpless before. Tears leaked from her eye. What had happened to the other one? Ripped out in a fight? She couldn't move her limbs.

She ebbed back and forth into oblivion, and woke up with a jolt when the boat hit something hard. Voices called out to each other, but she seemed to have lost the ability to understand the words. She was roughly grabbed and tossed onto something hard that smelled of peat and rotting vegetables.

"Help!" she cried, but her mouth was crushed by the cloth over her face and the sharp-smelling moist stuff that seeped through it.

"It's a waste to leave that boat here," someone said.

Ing twitched from the surprise of suddenly under-standing him and the closeness of the voice.

Something hard kicked her and she screamed from shock, though not pain. Why had they abducted her? Why did they hate her? The voice seemed familiar, but like her recent memories, she couldn't seem to retrieve its owner. The drawers of her memory were empty or stuck.

The soft soil of the island shook and someone cursed. Splashing faded out of hearing. She was alone. She tried to roll over, scream, but nothing worked as she thought it should.

They could at least have uncovered her face, the miserable bastards. Ing screamed. Fuck the world, fuck fate, fuck her own failing memory. She wouldn't be vanquished this easily. She was Ing. Nothing could take that away from her. It didn't matter if she didn't quite remember where she was and who she had been. She was still Ing, and nobody ditched her on a wobbly island. No-body.

She opened her mouth and set to work on de-molishing the cloth pressing against her face.

CHAPTER 22

Firdaus was about to hurry off in search of a few spare Wan to help with the evacuation, when he remembered the lace adorning the tunnel ceiling above him.

He halted and craned his neck. There, a few slender strands curling in a corner. "Friend Ghast on the ceiling," he started lamely. "Can you hear me?"

"Firdaus," a thin eerie voice sang out, a voice like a bird, without human vocal chords or a ribcage to give it depth and volume.

"How are you going to leave the Mound?" Firdaus asked.

The thing sang a few notes.

"I need your help. Can you ask a few strong people to help Boon with packing Ing's stuff?"

"Firdaus," the voice warbled.

He decided to take that as a yes.

Outside, in the noon sun, Firdaus strode through the curdled crowd, cleaving the stream of people in two. The heat squatted on his shoulders like a monstrous hangover. The sky above glistened like a week-old fish, squamous, multi-hued, about to go off in a spectacular cloud of stink.

His height allowed him to see over the churning mass of citizens trying to exit the city through four narrow gates, one of which was unusable because it led only to the docks. All the ships and boats and rafts were long gone, requisitioned for the foodstuff transports. Another gate led to the Marsh, where nobody wanted to go.

People looked up at him and tried to steer around him, but the pressure was too great and they were forced to brush close by. Firdaus greeted those he knew by name and some of them were brave enough to answer him back. It was a risk, showing his white self in this unstable crowd, but he didn't have the time to crawl about underground.

The din of creaking cart wheels, haranguing mothers, crying children and gulls screeching doom overhead was deafening, made worse by the teams of Stentors calling out the evacuation warning every quarter hour, so nobody would be forgotten.

The Stentors were hoarse, and it didn't look as if anyone was staying behind. Panics crashed in waves through the crowd. But since nobody could go anywhere, the surges of fear died bloodily against the walls of the South Way.

Firdaus couldn't guess how many people were trying to leave that day. The last census of the city had been in his father's time, and had hung on the wall of the Assembly chamber ever since, tallying 10,000 people. Twenty years later, he doubted that number lived in the city. Possibly, the census had been polished up to a more pleasing number. And that meant how many people leaving per gate at the same time? Not enough room. This wasn't going to work.

The crowd's mood was getting to him. The fear of being trapped, of not being able to take your loved ones to safety. He had no way to speed up the exodus or make things easier.

He spotted his daughter Hilm standing on the lower palace balcony, overlooking the road leading from Stadholder's Plaza to Crane Gate. She was frowning, peering into the crowd, saying something he couldn't hear.

"Hilm!" he shouted.

She found his eyes and lifted her arm, beckoning him towards her. Firdaus wrestled through the thick porridge of non-moving people and finally managed to squeeze himself into the palace. The auditorium, situated in the lower, broader part of the building, brimmed over with courtiers fidgeting in their silk skirts and fancy bandoliers as they lounged against the walls or sat on the floor. Someone must already have evacuated the furniture.

He climbed up the stairs and found the upstairs chambers much cooler and emptier. The perks of being Stadholder Aspirant, he supposed. He waved at his daughter.

"Where's Boon?" Hilm asked.

"Seeing to Ing's papers," Firdaus answered.

"Papers?" Hilm sniffed. "I can think of better things for him to do."

Firdaus shook his head at her. "Hilm, he's a little boy. He'd be helpless in this crowd. And yes, those books could mean our survival. Ing was a very old and very wise woman."

Hilm sniffed again.

"You didn't know Ing in her better moments. I miss her already."

"You miss... that?"

"A little more respect for your elders."

Hilm fingered her turquoise and teal bandolier. "I do. I have great respect for Kem, and she respects me right back. I couldn't have confronted Aranaz without her support."

"That's good. I was afraid she'd be angry at you for my sake."

"What did you do to her then? She doesn't know about lady Ing, does he?"

"Hilm, she kicked me out of her bed the moment I turned the wrong color. Let's say that cured me of her."

Hilm shrugged. "Fair enough."

At the door to the plaza, the door guards were speaking to a slight white person, barring his or her way with their spears.

***

The caul around Ing's face parted with a disappointing raspberry. The cotton had been soft and rotten. She shut her eye, afraid of blinding it with the glare of the low-hanging gray clouds. A good thing it wasn't a bright day, because it was going to take her longer to free the rest of her body.

She wiggled her hand, but nothing showed up in her peripheral vision, just a vague ripple in the cloth where her belly should have been. Why couldn't she move her head?

With heroic effort, she managed to get her chin out of the cloth. Pink, for crying out loud. She'd been kidnapped and tied up in pink. It was like a bad movie. Why couldn't she see beyond the small hump she glimpsed below her neck? She couldn't feel her legs either. If only she could see it better!

Slowly, the folds of faded pink cotton came into focus. It was a little bit weird how she floated above her own face, but that worry was for later. She discovered she wasn't bound, just mummy-wrapped in the cotton cloth, all bundled up and twisted in strange shapes. That must be why she couldn't feel her left hand and her legs, they were wrenched out of shape, nerves pinched or damaged. Or maybe she'd just been stunned.

The first priority was obviously to get away from her straitjacket and assess the damage later. If she rolled to the left, she would unwind like a silkworm being freed of its cocoon. No use waiting, then.

She clenched her teeth. They felt funny and ridgy. She shelved that concern next to the other ones she was saving up and made like a worm.

Argh! Now her face was pressed into the sucking moistness of the ground she lay on, and she couldn't breathe. If she panicked now, she was going to die. No, that was the panic speaking. She didn't need to breathe, she didn't have a nervus vagus anymore. She twisted again, as hard as she could. Her face rolled free again and she suppressed a sob of relief. Hysterics, shelf two, for later, when she was out of this jam. This temporary setback.

Her eye recuperated only slowly and she swiveled it until she found the now bigger blob of pink. It was working! Her vision was still funny and off, though. Depthless, which must be because of her other eye being swollen shut. Or something. No use dreading worse options.

She rolled over again, squinting her eye and mouth shut at the intrusive tendrils of ochre moss and turned onto her back. The sky swung back and forth in a disconcerting after-wiggle. Must be the absence of bracing from her hands and feet, which were too stunned to do their jobs. The ground thumped. And again.

That hadn't been her. Right?

She panned her eye hither and yon, but she could see nothing except the pink blob of her own still shrouded body, and green and yellow blocks of color that she assumed were vegetation. The only thing she could do was unroll further, because she would sure as hell be helpless if whatever it was found her trussed up.

Roll. And roll again.

Still only a slight movement in her one hand.

Sidewind. Hump like a caterpillar.

The skin of her back landed in squishy wetness, flopping partially free of the cotton. Ew. Was she lying in a bog or something worse? It was hell not knowing.

She lay still, listening, feeling with her whole body for the next shudder and thump from far away. When the thump came, sounding as if it was ten feet from her ear, she was unable to stop herself gasping from shock. The thumping stopped.

Ing bit her lip to stop herself from crying out. She was discovered. Who were they? Why were they approaching? She'd already been abducted; they might be her rescuers. Why was she feeling this unnamed dread? Something lurked under her memories, hidden deep in the septic tank of her brain, and in spite of her fear for the stench that might escape, she started tugging at the cover. She needed to know, whatever the cost.

The thumping started up again, softer and more deliberate.

***

The clouds overhead brightened into the gray glare of day. The light lit up the city a few thousand steps away from Frog's position below the dyke, and when it touched the top of a white spire, the most beautiful singing started up. A male voice soared high into the clouds, darting and tumbling around the center note in an orgy of joy. She caught only a few words, but it was an ode to the greatest Ancestor of all, praising his greatness over and over again. Her heart ran over with inexplicable joy. The buff walls and pink roofs were so grand and majestic that the biggest, widest-horned woven halls of the villages she knew paled beside it. Boats swarmed at the mist-shrouded feet of the city, ox-driven carts listing from the tall piles of stuff on top crept over the road. There sure was a lot of activity around a city, even at this hour.

Frog swallowed. She couldn't go into something that grand, she just couldn't. She was too small beside the sheer size of the city, the amount of people and wealth it must harbor. She was like an ant carrying a bug twenty times its own size on its back, for the good of the colony. But she must push down her fear and get her burden to the Stadholder. She took one step forward. That wasn't so bad.

From the corner of her eyes, she caught a flicker of color, and at the same time a distant, irregular thumping of heavy feet. The Ghost! This close to the city already?

She looked around wildly. The morning haze over the marshes obscured all but the closest details. There, that flash of color again, closer to the ground than she had imagined. A bright pink piece of cloth lay on the ground, fluttering with helpless movement. Her heart swelled up and slammed into her throat. A baby. A helpless, abandoned baby in danger of being smothered in its mother's wrap!

Her feet were flying before she could even think of what to do. Not a moment to lose. A sweet little baby, all alone in the world, with only Frog to save her. Maybe the mother was dead and even if she wasn't, she'd abandoned the helpless scrap. That mother had lost any rights she ever had over the baby, and it would be absolutely clear that it was Frog's to keep. She jumped over narrow channels separating the small island from each other, sharp reeds and grasses raking her calves, but she didn't care.

"I'm coming, I'm coming. Don't be afraid, I'm going to help you!" she shouted and then could have lopped her tongue off. Shouting wasn't going to pacify a baby. She would croon soft songs to it; hold it close against her breasts.

She flew over the last channel separating her from the

struggling child. The Ghast hadn't sped up, maybe because they hadn't seen her? From her encounters with them, she knew that sight wasn't always something they used, or knew how to use well.

She skidded on the slippery mat of rotting, half-submerged weeds and fell hard on her ass and the back of her head, wetting the dangling strands of her cape and probably damaging some of them. No matter. Rescuing the baby was all that counted. She rolled over and crawled the last few feet to the struggling thing. It was white, as white as a Wan, a very lumpy, misshapen baby. Maybe that was why the mother had abandoned it. She would love it, because she knew what it was to be different and unloved.

"Baby, sweet baby," she crooned in her lowest, most intimate voice, "don't be afraid, I'm going to help you, I'm going to hold you, I'm going to feed you," on and on in sweet nonsense syllables whose meaning didn't matter. The child would feel the intention behind the words and be comforted, she was sure.

The baby twitched under her hands, heavy and too solid for a child's body. It had to be at least two years old or even older, but it was curiously helpless and its arms and legs were ludicrously short. It was a really ugly toddler and it glared at her with its one eye. Frog swallowed. Was it an evil child? No normal child had a look in its eyes like that. It was a dwarf, an evil dwarf. A white Wan dwarf.

"Shut the fuck up," the dwarf growled from the circular hole that was its mouth. The words came out garbled and mashed, but Frog twitched at something familiar in its tone.

"Who are you? What are you?" Frog asked.

She stretched out her arm and touched the bald, too small head to reassure the thing.

"I'm... I'm..." it ground out.

"I'm Frog," Frog said. "Can I help you with anything?"

"Frog! Frog!" The thing's mouth exploded in a spittle-missile of utter derision. "You're fucking Frog?"

The lump of a body bucked off the ground in its involuntary expression of disgust.

Frog knee-walked backwards a few paces. The thing was clearly insane or maybe just vicious by nature. Not a sweet baby or helpless toddler. It was a full-sized torso, with a strange small head no bigger than a grapefruit, and with no legs and one hand attached to the shoulder like a flipper.

Did she need to help this... thing? Not really. Nobody could expect her to give up her mission for a foul-mouthed dwarf.

The face writhed and stretched and snapped back as if bugs were crawling under the skin. When it settled back in repose, it opened two malevolent eyes at her. The new face in miniature was one Frog remembered only too well.

"Ing?" she stammered.

"Yes, Ing. What are you doing here? Have you come to taunt me? Did they send you to finish me off?"

Frog embraced her own ribs to still the heaving of her lungs. She tried to make a sound but couldn't. When at last her mouth erupted, it was with a growl of rage.

She would now finish what she hadn't managed to do when she was first Wanned. She opened her hand wide and plunged stiffened fingers into Ing's eye. Ing's mouth screamed a shrill keen of terror, but Frog paid her no mind. Ing had shown no mercy when she ripped off Frog's arm and breast. Ing had eaten them with relish while Frog looked on.

Frog clawed the eyes into her mouth and her head exploded with visions. A bright light splattering across a peculiar flat blue sky, square things flickering at her, Firdaus' ecstatic face, her own hands scratching endless marks across reams and reams of paper, year after year after year.

Frog was an old hand at this now, so she shoved the dreams aside and grabbed more fistfuls of Ing flesh and stuffed them into her mouth. It widened to accommodate both hands.

Ing's body writhed and stretched and grew flaccid hands that pawed at Frog. Frog ignored her. She ripped off the most well-formed hand and set it aside, on a patch of green herbs. How useful that she knew the right way to disarm a Ghast! Ing was no better. And besides, where was Firdaus? No doubt Ing had betrayed him like she had betrayed Frog. Frog grabbed Ing's neck and one shoulder and tore the torso in half. Strong, but also fragile. She ripped off flesh from belly and flanks, a spidery foot that tried to grow away, a hand sprouting from the shoulder blade. Ing just couldn't grow defenses fast enough and Frog wasn't going to let her go. Ing deserved to be punished. It was fate, the hand of a kind Ancestor of Firdaus who was helping her.

Coincidence, a strange voice echoed in her head. Ancestor my ass.

Frog paused with a piece of neck hanging from her mouth. Could she wrestle those weird demons to the ground? Yes, she could, she answered herself with confidence. Ing was a pitiful thing. She'd easily eaten half of her.

You become what you eat, the voice said with a sneer. Sure you want to risk that?

Ignoring the voice, Frog discovered that if she placed a piece of Ing on her bare thigh, her own flesh opened up and assimilated it. That was useful if you were in a hurry.

She grabbed the remaining pieces of Ing, still about half of what she'd been, but now ripped apart in five-pound chunks. The Ghast were stumbling closer. They could smell her now, and she had to move fast. They didn't deserve Ing. Ing was her prize, hers and her alone.

CHAPTER 23

"Hilm!" A high voice sounded from the open doors. "They won't let me in."

Hilm gestured to the guards to allow Boon into the courtyard.

"The tunnels widened to let Ing's wooden chest through, Abba! Isn't that creepy?"

"You shouldn't have ventured through the crowds," Firdaus said. "I told you not to."

"But I have an idea! I had to tell you!"

"Go on. We're all out of good ideas," Hilm said, and waved towards the people inching by behind Boon, shuffling step by step towards the gate.

"The palace towers. Ing told me they weren't always a palace. The saucers were boats she and her people arrived in. I think I know how to make them fly for a little bit and take more people to the caves!"

"The palace towers? How could the palace possibly fly? Don't be silly!" Hilm said with the deadly scorn an older sister has for a younger brother.

Firdaus fingered his chin thoughtfully. It was a crazy idea. But maybe this was the right time for crazy ideas.

"Tell me how you would do it, Boon-tie."

"We have to get to the saucers and look for the... thing. Where the buttons are."

"Buttons?"

"I can't explain it very well. There are buttons you push and then the whole saucer can fly."

"So we should start at the top," Firdaus said. "Or the whole palace will topple onto the people down there in the square."

Thinking as one, the three of them craned their necks upward. On top of the oldstone foot of the palace, the nine saucers balanced in two improbable stacks of rounded shapes. Enormous things easily a hundred yards across.

"Fly? Really?" Firdaus said, awed in spite of himself.

Boon nodded. "Didn't you eat any memories of flying from Ing?"

Firdaus shook his head. "I have memories from the saucer insides, when they looked different, with odd-looking people walking around in them. With pale skin and blue eyes, or people looking like Ing but with black hair and white skin. Ghosts."

"I think they were our Ancestors. Like the friezes in the Physician's Temple. Let's go, Abba!"

"I'm going with Boon," Firdaus told Hilm.

"I can't leave here," Hilm said with no small dose of jealousy.

Firdaus and Boon took the precious wooden stairway to the first saucer, keeping their heads covered so Aranaz and the courtiers massing in the auditorium wouldn't spot them.

"Where are the little ones?" Boon asked.

"Hilm is sending them in the first convoy to the Villa," Firdaus said.

"Good."

They climbed up the rickety ladder to the next level, swimming against a stream of servants carrying goods of all kinds on their backs. The reflected heat from the smooth, charcoal-colored surface made even Firdaus feel hot; the palace was a heat trap in summer. The stairways and balconies bristled with pegs to hang hammocks on, and they kept stepping over abandoned heaps of bedding.

For several layers of saucer floors they could walk around the palace on the spiraling stairways, but for the last level they had to cross the top floor, once Firdaus' own quarters.

The rooms were empty, of course, since Aranaz and Ali had his stuff thrown out. He better take a good, long look at the city. It would be the last time he ever saw it.

"It's beautiful, isn't it?" he said.

The city looked strangely serene from up here. The white walls, the roofs lying red and friendly like a child's toy under the hot sky, with the people crawling like a plague of locusts through every plaza and street. The Dark Quarter was empty; the gate there opened only on the marshes, and that was not a place anyone wanted to be just now.

"Abba! Look!" Boon said from inside.

Boon wasn't troubled by sentimental goodbyes. Was it just childhood, or had he made them a long time ago when he thought he was going to die young? Never mind. He had work to do.

Boon was trying to pry one of the beautifully worked wooden panels off the walls.

"Hey! That's antique scrollwork. Careful."

"Abba, it's going to blow up anyway. Help me get it off, because I know it's behind there."

Firdaus broke off a finger while wrenching the panel loose and absentmindedly fed it to Boon.

Behind the panel they discovered a peculiar piece of wall decoration. It was glossy, and lukewarm to the touch like wood, but had a different echo to it when you rapped your knuckles on the smooth surface. It had square glittering bits, and many knobs and buttons of different colors. Little black print pictures, and some baffling commands in almost illegible, spiky script. "Hot", "Blue", "Halal", "Haram". Odd.

Boon put his hand on one of the hard-edged jewels and touched a button. A red light flashed so bright Firdaus involuntarily yelped.

Boon rolled his eyes. "It's cool, Abba. This is what's supposed to happen. I just don't know why it says I'm not allowed."

"Because you're not Ing," Firdaus guessed. "What is it? The Spirit of our Ancestors?"

"I think so. It's a servant of Ing's."

"What do you see happening? Is this chamber going to fly up into the heavens? Or the whole palace?"

"Just this bit."

Firdaus tried to picture it in his mind, but he couldn't make the disc fly up. For one, it had no wings. His thoughts showed him his old room toppling down into the square and crushing his toiling people like ants.

Boon touched several more knobs, but nothing happened like the red flashing light. His shoulders sagged. "I don't know what I'm doing wrong, Abba. The memory isn't sharp enough. It seemed like such a good idea."

Firdaus rubbed Boon's neck. "I still think it is a good idea. Just think hard, son. There has to be a way. We have to get everybody out of here faster."

As he looked down from the saucer balcony at the heaving mass of people on the Square, Firdaus caught sight of a tall Wan woman staring upwards at the palace. He almost lost his footing and had to grab a banister. The woman couldn't be Ing. Although they could use Ing's knowledge right now, it would still be a bad thing if Ing had managed to survive whatever Haroon and his buddies had done to her. A very bad thing.

Still, his feet picked up speed as he slid and wrung himself back down the stairs past and through the slow snake of trudging servants. Ing? Here?

He burst through the dim, stuffy heat of the auditorium onto the over-bright, even hotter Stadholder's Plaza. The moments that he used up fighting his way through the throng were like a nightmare, where your feet just don't seem to be able to get a move on and something is almost upon you. The air was stifling with the dust of a thousand feet and stank of a thousand armpits.

The woman hadn't moved from her spot. Her face swung unerringly in his direction. Firdaus stopped, pierced by her pale citrine gaze.

It wasn't Ing. Not with that face, those breasts. His palms tingled, remembering cupping that soft flesh. The face was Frog's, or almost Frog's. The look in those eyes was not Frog, the straight hair and the height were not Frog's, and yet. And yet.

"Majesty," the strange woman said with Frog's voice.

"Firdaus."

She walked into his arms and his whole body leapt to meet her skin. Her scent entered his nose like an arrow of longing and his eyes closed, reeling with confusion. She smelled of Frog, and Ing, and other things. Her crudely woven cape scraped harsh reed tassels against his chest, mingling with the soft stroke of her straight milk-white hair, hair you could use to paint poems on your beloved's skin.

"Frog?" Firdaus said, disbelieving his own words.

Her face lit up in a smile as bright as the cloudrise.

"But... what? How?"

Her fingers dug in his back muscles, kneading the skin mercilessly. An Ing habit, his back told him. But her face smiled with a very Froggy nose-crinkle. "She didn't kill me, as she thought, leaving me inside the Mound. I crawled out and lived. I followed you here."

"Who killed you? Tried to kill you?" Firdaus asked, although the answer clenched like a fist around his heart.

"Ing," she said.

"But she couldn't kill you again, could she? You're a Wan."

"She wanted something of me," Frog said.

Her features were impossible to look at for long, still didn't fit smoothly over the picture in his head.

"She tore off my arm and shoulder and breast, and left me to be eaten by the Mound Queen."

He could believe that of Ing, sad as it was.

Frog stepped closer, the disconcerting smell that was part Ing crowding in his nose.

"You know what she wanted of me, don't you? She wanted the part that knew how to attract a man. You."

His hand closed around a smooth soft shoulder, in lieu of breasts, the flesh he really wanted to touch. Her nipples kissed his chest. Firdaus licked his lips. He was drowning in the shimmering commingled scent of the two women, fighting to keep his nose above the surface, fearing the predators lurking below. How strange that he was reacting like this to Frog, who was after all, only Frog. Just another girl. But his body was telling him with blood and heartbeat and swimming innards that she meant more to him than that. Or was it Ing he was reacting to?

"How did you find me here?" he asked.

Frog shook her head and the tips of her hair lashed his arm like silk ropes. His skin goosebumped in response and he took another step closer. They were standing thigh to thigh, belly to belly now.

Frog smiled and reached under his wrap. "Firdaus. Take me now," she said.

Her directness was even more devastating now, here, standing in the merciless light of the day, humanity sweating and cursing and toiling all around them, than it had been in the secret darkness of the Maze by night. He wanted to push her up against the nearest wall and ride her to oblivion.

"Frog," he rasped out.

She splayed her hand over his right nipple, rubbing it in slow circles that were invisible to the passers-by. Or so he hoped.

"I missed you," she said. "I came to be with you. And to warn you about Mistress Ing and the Ghast marching on the city."

In his heat and lust-dizzied state, mindlessly pushing his hips against her prickly reed apron, it took a while for the words to reach his brain.

"What? Ghast?"

"Yes."

The breath on which that word rode pushed straight into his heart. Ghast coming, why Ghast? The Queen Mound honoring her promises? They hadn't killed Ing soon enough, apparently. When had she signaled to the Queen to start the attack? Never mind now. He needed to stop it.

Frog's presence had blown all worries from his mind like so much chaff on the wind, but now they came tumbling back. Good. Because this was not the moment, nor the place, to forget himself in Frog's sweet flower.

"Maybe you can show me your palace," she said.

Firdaus stifled a surprised guffaw. Maybe she thought the city always overflowed with panicked crowds. "Not now, Frog. The city is in shambles. Can't you see? Everybody is trying to get out before it blows."

She shrugged. "It's not always like this?"

"Prophet, no. The Mound is going to blow up, like a puffball. We have to flee and hide from the voracious seeds it's going to spout. And now we know, thanks to your warning, that the Ghast are coming. I only have time to save my people, Frog."

She nodded with quick understanding, so like Ing that he recoiled from the sudden look in her eyes.

"Who are you?" he said.

"Frog, of course," she answered, but her eyes shifted away from him.

The clues clicked together in his mind like tongue and groove. "You found the remains of Ing, didn't you? You ate some of it, right?"

Frog lifted water-clear eyes up to him. "Yes."

But for the defiant lift of her chin, he would have left it at that. "How much?"

Her full lips trembled but her voice was steady. "All of it."

"Prophet."

He hadn't realized he'd stepped away from her, leaning into the press of people walking past.

"Now you hate me," she said sadly.

"No! It's just... Ing left a bad taste in the mouth of many people here."

She nodded. "I knew that. She was my enemy. But I won. I ate her. Her evil thoughts only trouble me, not you. Nor did those Ghast win her as spoils. I did it to serve you."

Her hands fell limply by her side, and everything drooped that had waved proudly only moments ago.

Firdaus clasped those long-fingered, capable hands, nothing like Frog's stumpy callused working mitts, and pressed them gently. "You will serve me, I promise. You did me a great service already. If Ing had been eaten by those

Ghast, Ancestors know what would have happened. She knew so much. But now you can serve me because of those memories. Come with me!"

He grabbed her hand and started to pull her to the palace. Hope bubbled inside him. If anyone could unlock the secrets of the flying magic, it was Frog.

"I need your memories!"

He could see she didn't understand yet, but her mood lifted immediately in response to his, following, as Frog had always followed. He could almost believe that Frog had the upper hand in the unlikely mixture of the two women. Ing never followed, Ing led, and didn't even look back to see if anyone was coming after her. She had probably never cared.

***

Frog's heart sang, her skin jubilated as her feet followed her Stadholder into the Palace. The noise of so many people was like frogs croaking out their mating call on a spring evening, but then magnified a thousandfold. The heat! The glare of the clouds in this strange, dry place. Her feet were caked with dust, her mouth parched from lack of moisture, her eyes prickled with the strange odors and salty winds that blew here. It was nothing like she'd imagined. She'd thought a city was like a village, with bigger halls of woven reeds, taller plumes, bigger boats, fatter people and more children. This rocky dry place was stranger than hanging like a paradile underneath an island.

Firdaus tugged her on, forcing the stream of people moving down to part for him. They shied away from him, but not as fearfully as she was used to. She saw more Wan dotting the brown and black mass of people, like white roots in a mash of broiled meat. They got more personal space than the average bronze, bistre, or mahogany person, but not a lot. She predicted that in a day or two, habit would have replaced fear.

The alien thought retreated into the background, leaving Frog gasping. Creepy. It was like the voice that told her not even to try to get Mallard's attention, or to stay away from Firdaus' bedmat. Not to be trusted.

The palace towered over her like an angry mother-in-law when she entered its unknown darkness. Those few moments before her eyes adjusted, it smelled like a reed long-house after a long winter of being cooped up like ducks in a pen. Whew.

As she followed Firdaus, the room left an impression of fat, sweaty people in eye-blindingly colorful clothes. That was how she'd imagined a city, not the dun colors of the real one, bleached of color by relentless salt wind and bright cloudskies. Did it ever rain here?

They went up ladders that were hewn out of rock, a strange sight inside a dwelling. Another room full of people, although much less crowded than the one before. A tall, beautiful, haughty-looking girl beckoned to Firdaus, who obligingly veered off course to meet her. Hot needles of jealousy stabbed through Frog. This must be his new mistress.

"Hello there. Introduce me, Abba?"

"Frog, this is Hilm, my oldest daughter, Stadholder-Aspirant and Heir to Stadholder Aranaz."

Who the prophet was Stadholder Aranaz? Firdaus was the only Stadholder she needed to know. Oh. His daughter. She had a sweet smile, and she looked like Firdaus must have before he was Wanned: tall, mahogany-skinned, staring coolly at Frog past a high-bridged nose. Such a beautiful and regal girl.

Frog stammered something inane. She was a servant and didn't know how to talk to glittery people like this, especially this young woman with dark eyes so wide and piercing, seeing everything a person thought. She'd make a bad enemy.

"We met on my journey with Ing," Firdaus said.

Ha, the hateful voice whispered. He never even mentioned you. He loves me.

He loves me! Frog answered, and then backpedaled in shame. It doesn't matter who he loves. I live to serve him. That is enough.

You actually believe that? the voice sneered. Fool.

"When are you leaving? Time to get out of here. I trust you to look after the babies," Firdaus said.

"Aunt Aranaz has asked me to accompany her to the villa," the daughter said, looking shifty.

"Do you think that's wise?" her Stadholder asked mildly. "The people would be better served if you two weren't in the same place when the spores strike."

The daughter sighed. "Abba, I have to. She has the little ones."

The big hand enfolding Frog's clenched tight, hurting her. Did men yearn after their children as much as women did? Frog thought they must. The two tall people, one white and male, the other brown and female, stared hard in each other's eyes. They looked very much alike in spite of the color difference. The tension snapped and Firdaus turned away from his daughter.

"Come," Firdaus said, tugging Frog along.

She came. She'd follow him anywhere. They crossed the room, went outside again, so high above the ground that she closed her eyes from fear of following her gaze down there, tumbling like a swallow that had been hit by a merlin, spiraling down, down, until it hit the ground, dead as a stone.

"Come!" Firdaus said, curter now.

Frog inched outside, and saw that he was pulling her toward another stair, a wooden one, this time, the cost of that much wood boggled her mind, but her feet remained rooted to the floor. No, it wasn't the floor, it was the roof. She swayed.

Don't be a sissy, the voice sneered in her mind. Here, let me do this.

The world tilted, swirled, she was no longer teetering on top of the world but standing on a low roof about to climb higher into the palace proper.

She followed Firdaus silently. Were they going to his room to have bedsport? That was an excellent idea, but it still seemed somehow unlikely, given his frantic demeanor and the threat against the city.

Random Ing thoughts kept floating to the surface. So

Mother Doughy was about to explode? Fascinating. She'd never been able to find out just how the Ghast reproduced. What a privilege to be around when it finally happened! Her mind spun around the fabulous notion. Like a puffball, Firdaus' excellent analogy. The interesting thing was that it happened only once in hundreds of years. Mother Doughy, what would happen to her? Reproduction for the Ghast was death. Not a petite mort, but a grande mort. No wonder she'd always refused to talk about it.

While she mused, they ascended the spiral palace stairs to the very top, a saucer she'd never entered since they'd been stacked on top of each other and turned into a monument first and a palace later.

Firdaus pulled at her arm and showed her the vista of the green Maze over the balustrade. Frog clung to his solid presence, dizzy at first, but then her eye caught a white clot eddying slowly towards the city.

"Firdaus! The Ghast."

They didn't move like people, in a coordinated group, in one direction. A part of her imagined letting chaos theory and mathematics loose on the Ghast movement, and another part remembered their smell and their taste. They wandered off hither and yon, bouncing off obstacles, rejoining the group, turning back.

But always the group relentlessly converged upon the city.

CHAPTER 24

The moment Frog stepped off the wooden stairway spiraling around the palace and went inside the topmost saucer, a wash of memories obliterated her sight. All the paraphernalia of the court's habitation had been stripped away, laying bare the gray ceramic walls with their hand-grips and closed storage lockers, instrument panels and printed evacuation procedures on the wall. It looked like a ship's bridge again, except for the twining wisteria and clematis. The contrast between the vines, listless in the heat, and the pristine high-tech interior was painful. So much knowledge lost, so much time passed by.

"Frog," Firdaus said, and the thought slipped from her grasp.

"Don't call me that," she said between clenched teeth. "Now I lost the memory."

Firdaus' eyes were piercing and clear as glass daggers. "What should I call you then? I need those memories."

"I don't know. Fring? No, I take that back. What do you need my memories for?"

"Boon says this thing once possessed the magic to fly. We need it to evacuate more people. Will that work?"

She thought wildly. "We could ask Mother Doughy to collapse the supports below the walls and the houses you want to disappear? Or, um, gather brimstone, charcoal and saltpeter? We could make powder to blow the gates up."

"How long would that take?" Firdaus asked, his voice pinched with anguish.

Frog's heart swelled as she thought. She was helping him by speaking the inner voice out loud. For him, she would tolerate the strangeness that at times took over her thoughts. Anything to help her Stadholder.

"Too long," she answered herself. "How long do we have before Mother Doughy gives up the ghost?"

Firdaus shrugged. "I don't know exactly. Maybe weeks, maybe days."

A thought dropped into her mind like a stone into a pond. "Damn. Those pink streaks. I should have seen that, of course they are the warning signs for reproduction. Did Mother Doughy say anything about the Queen Mound going to blow, too?"

"Yes, she did. But that's not our concern. We need to get the people out of here."

"Christ. What will happen when the seeds blow? Will they darken the skies?"

"They'll eat anything that lives," Firdaus said. "If we don't seal ourselves away, we will all die."

"You will anyway," Frog said absently. "Without crops and livestock."

"We're taking all that. Some of us will live. Now stop thinking about death and destruction and help me fly this thing!"

"Right." She walked up to the instrument panel and put her palm on the security screen. It flashed red.

"Shit. It doesn't recognize me. Of course it doesn't, because I am not identical to the Ing I once was."

"What?"

"It knew the whorls of Ing's original flesh, when she was still human. I don't have fingerprints anymore."

***

Hilm cast a last, longing look at the palace towers, two stacks of discs thrusting stubby fingers against the pale cloudsky on top of a squatter, wider adobe block. She wished she could go with Boon and that odd woman who reminded her a bit of Ing. Flying sounded like a lot more fun than directing the evacuation. She'd given the order of Raid Alert to the Singing Tower. Now she needed to gather up her brothers and sisters and take them to safety.

She dragged herself into the big anteroom, which was full of frantic people packing and running up and down like crazed chickens. Two Sheriffs closed the doors behind her, cushioning the din from outside into a surflike murmur.

"Leave those open, please," Hilm said. "It's too stuffy in here already."

The Sheriffs looked at her, at each other, and then switched on their thousand-yard stares. Their spears clicked on the hardened mud floor and their legs eased into a holding stance. They weren't seriously going to disobey her, were they?

"Come, my dear," her aunt's voice said from behind her. "Let us confer."

"I only have a moment, Aunt; I've got a ton of stuff to do. I'm taking my brothers and sisters to the villa myself."

Aranaz smiled at Hilm and put a hot, insistent hand on her arm. Hilm figured she owed her aunt the attention. It was a stressful time for all of them.

"Come, sit down," Aranaz gestured and Hilm sank down in one of the woven leather chairs that had come from her aunt's quarters.

"No need to pretend anymore, is there?" Aranaz said with a peculiar smile that Hilm knew in her gut meant bad news.

"Pretend? I'm not sure about that. We need to set an example," Hilm said and tried to look grave like a true Stadholder-heir. "We don't want the people to panic."

Aranaz kept her dark eyes steady on Hilm. Aranaz seemed to have lost weight in the past days. The impending disaster must be taking its toll on her as well. She wasn't young; she must be at least thirty or thirty-five years old, older even than her father.

"But we know that there is nothing to panic about, don't we, dear niece? We know that it is a ruse, thought up by my devious brother."

Hilm's mouth fell open. What the prophet? She struggled to maintain her composure, but she knew Aranaz would read the shock and horror on her face. Something wasn't right about this conversation.

"No, that's not true, Abba would never deceive me. He

knows—"

Aranaz' hand cut Hilm off in mid-sentence. "Don't bother to lie to me anymore, young lady. I have seen through you. You and your father have set all this in motion. There is no threat." She stamped her feet on the floor. "This is earth. This is no person or puffball. Firdaus thinks he can drive the true people from the city, that he can drive their rightful ruler off. And once we sit shivering on the beach, without our possessions, he will lead his army of Wan in here and conquer the throne!"

Aranaz threw her head back and laughed. "But I'm not a fool. What did you think, that you could lie and scheme and sneak about and clamp my Ali between your legs so he wouldn't betray you? Ali is mine, loyal to the bone, and he and I together know everything about your deceit."

In spite of the room's stuffy heat, Hilm's skin contracted into a tight hard sheath around her bones. She was hot and cold at once. What had her aunt planned against her father? She had to warn him. She half-rose from her chair, but another Sheriff she hadn't noticed pressed her down with the haft of his bamboo spear. All around her, the buzz of people went on unceasing, as if they were deaf to the terrible words Aunt Aranaz had spoken.

Hilm cleared her throat. Aranaz' raptor gaze made it hard for the soothing words she needed to come out. "Please, Aunt, believe me. Father and the Ghast Mound are telling the truth. The cataclysm is at hand. I've seen the Mound, spoken to it; I've even gone into the tunnels beneath our feet. I trust my father. He's only trying to help you."

"Ha. If you speak truth, my brother is even viler than I thought him to be. He deceives even you, his own child. I know better. He's conspiring against me, and has ever been."

Hilm sagged against the leather backrest of her chair, trying to find some kind of support. "What will you do? How will you stop him?"

Aranaz uttered her mirthless laugh again. "I don't

need to do anything. Nothing is going to happen. When the days pass without any kind of disaster, the people will start to doubt. They will see my courage and steadfastness, because I will not leave this palace. I will remain here, in full view of the people. And when they come back with their tails between their legs, I will graciously allow them back into the city again."

Hilm took a deep breath. "Aunt. I can't force you to leave. But I fear the disaster that is coming, and it is my duty to take my kin to safety. The nurses and children are waiting for me."

The spear across her thighs did not lift.

"Aunt?"

"You and your siblings will remain here. The family of the Stadholder can't be seen to leave, you understand that." Aranaz' gaze left Hilm as she commanded a servant to bring her and the heir refreshments.

Hilm swallowed. She would die here, with Aunt Aranaz and the servants, and worse, so would the little ones.

***

After delivering the news about the fingerprints to Firdaus, Frog looked around the saucer. It seemed to him that she found meaning in the patterns of orange blinking lights and steady green ones.

"Amazing. The cooling system still works. The lights. So there still is energy. I wish I was an engineer, because when there's energy, there's something you can do with it. Hm."

She rubbed the skin of her upper arms thoughtfully, as if she was cold. Maybe she was. Firdaus had almost forgotten how wonderful it was to sleep in a cool room on a hot summer night. He wished she would stop stroking herself. The effect on him was the same as if she was actually touching his flesh, which was straining against his old cotton skirt in an embarrassing way.

"Abba! I have an idea!" Boon cried from the door opening, stripped even of the bead curtains that used to shield it.

Firdaus coughed. Saved from embarrassing himself by his darling Boon. "Boon, this is Frog, a young woman from the marshes whom I hold in high respect. She has consumed a lot of Ing's knowledge, so she might be of help to you with the flying magic. Frog, this is my eldest son Boon. He chose to be Wanned when he was dying of a deathly disease."

"Greetings, Stadholder Boon," Frog said shyly, bobbing a clumsy curtsey at Boon. "You are quite tall and grown already. Do you have younger children, Firdaus?"

"I have twelve children," Firdaus said proudly. "The youngest is five months old."

Frog's face softened and her eyes grew big. "You think I could see him? I would love to see all your babies."

Firdaus' heart ached for her. She'd never have a baby now. Maybe, someday, some human woman would let her take care of one, but that day was not in the near future, he suspected.

"Frog, let me hold this idea up to you. If the shiny device there reads Ing's fingertips, maybe some of us Wan can remember what her fingertips were like, and make ours like that? Some of the Wan here in the city have changed their own bodies. I haven't tried that yet, but I know it can be done."

Frog fired up into a typical Ing thinking pose, pacing, pulling at her nose, jabbing her finger at Boon as she spoke. "I should be able to do that. I ate a lot of Ing stuff."

Firdaus thought about it. "Can you and Boon continue here? I have to go do something about those Ghast. And soon."

Frog frowned. "Of course. Boon, maybe close your eyes and concentrate on Ing's fingertips? And so will I."

Firdaus watched Frog crumple up her face in concentration. She was Frog, and then she was not Frog. The back and forth between the personalities was dizzying. He wished he had the old Frog back, or the old Ing, but this peculiar two-people mixture was too muddy a taste for him.

Before he climbed down, he threw one last look at the

white cloud of his enemies, approaching slow but sure. His heart skipped a beat. On the horizon, far behind the first wave, he beheld a second dirty white blot coming his way.

***

Firdaus found the closest of the Stentors who perched on a stone pedestal on every corner of the Plaza and at every Quarter entrance and Gate, intoning out the Evacuation message. This meant that Hilm hadn't gotten the new orders through to this Stentor. Firdaus better give him the order.

Firdaus yanked the Stentor down from his man-high post. When the Stentor, a tall, lanky fellow, saw who was hauling him down his face went gray and his legs went out from under him.

"Have mercy, sire, have mercy. I have three children, please don't eat me."

Normally, Firdaus would have felt frustration at this evidence that his pro-Wan propaganda hadn't reached this important functionary, but he had no time for that.

"I have work for you, new orders from Stadholder Hilm. Call the Sheriff Alert, tell them to gather at the North Gate."

The man stared, his mouth working around his tongue without producing sound. "In the Dark Quarter?" he stammered out.

"Yes. Danger from the Marsh."

The man straightened fractionally. "A raid?"

Did the Stentor need to know more? No. "Yes, a raid. Now hurry!" There hadn't been any raids on the town in generations, not since the new wave of rice farmers had supplanted the rogue fishers and hunters who'd supplemented their livelihood by raiding. The raid call must have been kept in the Stentors' repertoire.

Still the man dithered, waving his skinny limbs around and scratching his hair. What was his name again? Rodman?

"I'll never reach the Singing Tower through the throng, sire."

"Then don't go there. Do it from your perch. Can't

you signal your man on top of the tower to take up the call?"

Rodman nodded, and kept nodding while he clambered back on his Stentor's station. Once he'd risen upright, his nodding and trembling ceased. He stood tall, feet planted almost on the edges of his raised post, took a deep breath and set his stomach muscles so that every ridge stood out from under his skin.

Firdaus clapped his hands to his ears to protect them against the incredible volume a Stentor could produce.

"Guard Alert! Guard alert! All guards to the North Gate! Raid! Alarm! All guards to the North Gate!"

The people around Firdaus didn't react much. Their tight faces and slow shuffle didn't change, and Firdaus figured it was for the best. They had to save themselves and their families, and they hadn't yet understood that there was more than one contender for the position of White City's worst enemy.

He took a deep breath, the Stentor still roaring away over his head, and threw himself into the fray. He was going in the opposite direction of the crowd's movement, and because everybody was jammed together like pinky fish in a barrel, they couldn't see him coming and anticipate. The crowd flowed into the gap he left behind, but it was still almost impossible to push forward. People stared like oxen, dumb with terror and hopelessness, unable to think two seconds ahead and lean a few inches to the side so he could pass.

Every step seemed to take forever, and all he could do was struggle on, blind without news from the Singing Tower, hoping he'd be on time to lead the Sheriffs against the Ghast. Even from far away and high up, the wallowing, lurching gait of the white enemy had promised a horrendous fate to anyone who happened to be in their way.

"You there, you look like a big strong fellow to me. Follow me to the North Gate! There's a raid. Grab a cudgel or a torch and follow me! Get your friends, too!" he called out to a likely suspect, a man as tall as himself with hands the size of baskets.

The last resistance, a fat man refusing to move his belly out of the way, suddenly vanished and Firdaus stumbled into the dusty deserted street leading through the Dark Quarter to the North Gate. A pang of recollection held him for a moment, no more, but then he thrust it. No time for vengeance. He would have to lead the very men who held him at spear point, and he'd have to make them follow.

***

The anteroom, once a cool and impressively high chamber where her father doled out judgment, contracted into a cramped prison. One that was jammed full of people growing hotter and more uncomfortable by the minute, their preparations for flight halted.

Hilm couldn't even crawl into a corner and concentrate on her own thoughts. Aunt Aranaz kept her close, and directed a steady stream of words at her.

"I have no choice, you know. Mark my words and remember them well. A ruler must always give the example to the people, no matter how difficult. If they see your courage, they take heart. If you save yourself first, so will they. You see? You see how we have to stay here to show the people we are sure nothing is going to happen?"

And so on, in an endless litany of the same sentiments in different words over and over again. Did Aranaz even believe in them? Or was she convincing herself as well as Hilm? Hilm couldn't tell. Even she wasn't completely sure anything was going to happen, but evacuation seemed like a small price to pay for survival.

Two Sheriffs in front, two behind her seat. Her brothers and sisters huddled on their nurses' laps or played on the filthy throne room floor. The windows were high, designed to let in light, not heat or dust, and certainly not meant as exits. Escape was impossible.

Thunder rumbled.

More thunder. Hilm's chair shifted. Something large and wooden crashed in a hallway. A fine mist drifted down from the ceiling. She tasted dust. The palace was shaking. But not by a force from below, as she'd expected to happen sometime soon. From above. Was her father up to something?

The thunder subsided. Sea birds started screeching again.

She checked the high windows, but the grey cloud-light shone the molten metal of noon. Next to her own chair, Aranaz' bloodless hands squeezed the carved wooden arms of her chair so hard Hilm expected sap to squirt out. But her aunt didn't say a word. As if by pretending the rumbling and the shaking hadn't happened, she could will the world to stay the same.

Hilm caught the eye of one of the guards behind her chair. She tried to look young and helpless and sweet. "Please, I'm afraid," she said. "I want to leave here. What if we're trapped?"

"That trick, my dear, only works for a brief while," her aunt said. She regained some color and leaned back with a show of nonchalance. "Much better to work on stratagems that last one a lifetime, even after one's youth and beauty have gone."

The guard's lips twitched.

Hilm suppressed her snarl and presented an unconcerned face to the world. It was difficult; the hard seat pulped her buttocks and she had to pee.

She rose. "Aunt, I have to go."

Aranaz twitched a finger, and two more guards materialized out of the crowd.

Great. Hilm thought of summoning two of her own women, as was her right as Stadholder, but no. This way she could probably get them to leave her alone in the compost room.

They threaded their way through the smelly throng of people, all feet and knees and buttocks, fires being stoked right on the floor to boil water; babies, trash, packs and bales and squawking chickens. Aranaz was nuts. She was killing these people just by locking them in like this, no need for cataclysms whatsoever.

The bathroom was blessedly empty. "Sheriffs, give me privacy," Hilm said with a gesture she copied from Aranaz.

Sweet little girl hadn't worked; she might as well try out her aunt's advice.

They hesitated, but they turned away and allowed her to enter on her own. The bead curtains wouldn't hide her from them if they really looked, so she had to act fast. She took a deep breath and clambered onto the composter seat, feet dangling to the inside. It had worked in the Dark Quarter, so why not here?

She pushed herself off the edge and plunged down into the depths of the waste-seat.

***

Firdaus picked up speed and ran through the pale streets, empty now that he was in the Dark Quarter. The air shimmered with heat, and the crowd behind him growled like a vast and distant beast. The narrow alley widened onto the broad street leading the North Gate. The houses and shops lining the sides were empty, shutters hanging crooked. Not a sound could be heard in the dusty, hot street but his own panting and the slapping of his feet. At the end of the street loomed the tall double doors of the Gate, thick half-round slats of bamboo over triple-enforced wicker. He slowed down when he saw they were still shut.

A single Sheriff hove into view from a side alley, his face hot from running, but his cudgel in its back sheath. Not like a man expecting serious trouble.

"Hey!" Firdaus shouted, waving his arms. Prophet. He'd come as he was, empty-handed.

Above and behind him, the Stentor on duty at the Singing Tower broke out into a copy of the first Stentor's chant. Good, but a lone guard and one ex-Stadholder would do little good against a score of lumbering immortal warriors.

Firdaus loped up to the gate. Little groups of Sheriffs jumped off roofs or shot out of alleys. Firdaus named them silently, Temudzhin, Sala, Henk, Wesli, Keiko. Good boys all. Mostly young men with sun-darkened cheeks, innocent in their very brawn and swagger, some older men, solid and assured in spite of thicker bodies and slowed reflexes.

He strode in before they could gang up on him. "Listen up, men. We're up against a horde of Ghast coming in from the March, with orders from the Queen of the Ghast to kill on sight. They're hard to kill. You can put away your slings and bows and spears right now. The only way to kill them is to dismember them or set them on fire. Team up with a friend, and never go up against one alone. Each pair must grab a Ghast at two ends and tear him apart. Go for the head first, so he won't be able to see for a bit. The legs next. Questions?"

"Aren't you one of them?" a bold young Sheriff said.

"Yeah, why should we listen to you?" another one chimed in.

The gate shuddered from a resounding crash on the other side. The Sheriffs looked at each other and then back at Firdaus, more respect in their eyes now. Another teeth-rattling crash. The Ghast were trying to get through, not over. So far. If enough of them massed against the gate, they could use each other as climbing posts. Clang.

"What's that?" the first Sheriff asked, less bold now.

"Those are the Ghast. They are strong and inhuman, and they will continue harrowing the gate until it fails."

"What do we do?"

Firdaus imagined the possible outcomes. The gate would hold. The gate would hold but the Ghast would crawl over it like ants. The gate would break and they'd have to fight the Ghast in the streets of the city, hampered by fleeing citizens everywhere.

He spoke before he'd realized he'd made a decision. "We open the postern gate and slip out. We have to keep the Ghast out of the city, so we'll engage them outside the walls. Follow me."

They trooped up against the door, flinching every time a blow landed on it.

"Once you're through the gate, move away so the next man can get through," Firdaus said tensely. "Wait for that man, then two of you grab a Ghast and dismember him. And so on. Remember, they are strong, and nothing will stop them except death!"

The Sheriffs swallowed and puffed up their chests. Firdaus pretended not to see their fear and inexperience. It was one thing to nab a belligerent drunk with a stick or toss a stunned and sick man into the marshes, but fighting an enemy intent on killing—none of these youngsters had even seen a raid. The only practice they had was hunting, fishing, and the ulama court.

He picked out the youngest and most scared little Sheriff. "You there, get on top of the roof. Get a fire going, shoot at the Ghast. Throw us burning brands."

Firdaus whirled around at the others still awaiting orders.

"Henk and Temudzhin, open the postern gate. All of you, pair up and be ready."

He positioned himself, ready to barrel his way through a wall of Ghast.

Another slam of a heavy body against the gate. The bamboo didn't split, but the ancient withy and rope lock burst apart. A thick white limb thrust through the gap between the doors, could be a head, could be an especially crudely formed arm. It nosed ahead, questing. If it was like him, it could smell his presence. Firdaus could almost taste the Queen Mound's poem in his mouth again, a heavy, dank emanation that clashed with the human smells in the city. It tasted of rot, of anger and destruction.

Sheriff Quan hacked the intruding limb off before Firdaus could open his mouth. Good. It would lift their spirits. "Remember!" he shouted. "In pairs. Take off their heads. Tear them in small pieces. Temudzhin, take point."

Sheriff Temudzhin wrenched open the postern gate and ran through, pike first.

Firdaus shooed the Sheriffs through the low postern gate one by one, wincing at the shouts and the sound of blows. When about half had gone through, he threw himself into the mêlée.

CHAPTER 25

For a brief moment, the narrow wastepipe clamped around Hilm's shoulders, but then she fell free into empty air, straight into a gooey sludge of human excrement. Stink jumped up from it. The walls of the sewer tunnel arched high above her head. This was a living composter tunnel, busy eating all the goodness from the waste to keep itself alive. The smell was overwhelming, stomach-turning awful. Her feet went into the waste to the ankle and her flesh crawled at the touch of excrement. Too late to turn back, though. She slithered away through the disgusting brown carpet and turned the first corner she found. The sludge became drier, crisper, and within a dozen steps she trod on harmless, sweet-smelling compost.

Would the Sheriffs guess she'd jumped down the composter if they checked out the bathroom? Probably. She'd better get away from here. No, not away. She couldn't leave her half-brothers and sisters. If possible, she even ought to save all the citizens still left in the city.

She'd played in these tunnels a lot when she was a kid, when they stank less, but she'd never entered through the palace composter. She just needed to find her bearings. The tunnel sloped upwards. It had to lead into the palace itself. From there she could exit through another waste-seat and do the clever thing she would think up any moment now.

The runner of compost turned into smelly goo again. A few turns later, light struck the tunnel from above. Another waste-chute opened up in the ceiling.

If she'd still been the stick-thin girl of only six months ago, with no breasts or hips to speak of, she would have been up in that tunnel in an eye blink. With her new curves, and muscles slack from months of lounging on sofas and plotting politics instead of playing Raiders and Sheriffs in the mud, it wasn't going to be easy.

She jumped up, hoping to find some traction on the insides of the shaft, and her fingers caught on the edge. She banged against the wall when she came down and landed on all fours in the sludge. Biting her lip to keep from crying, she scrambled back up. She wasn't a little girl who would go blubbing for help to the nearest grown-up. She was the Stadholder Aspirant, the Heir, and she was the adult who needed to save the little ones.

She jumped again. Her nails stabbed into the side of the tunnel, dug in, and managed to hold on for several seconds. She shot loose, and landed hard on her back and shoulders. Just bruises. She had no choice but to get up. Under the coating of sludge, her fingertips were covered with pale putty. Something softer than the side of the tunnel, the living tissue of the waster above.

She clawed back up. Her thighs shook from tiredness, and her hands flexed only reluctantly. Her shoulders were on fire. She had one good jump left. This had to be the one that stuck.

Again. She jumped up, dug her fingers in the wall of the shaft so hard pain rayed up from her broken finger-nails into her wrists. She swung her legs up and jammed her knees into the sides just when the first hand broke loose. This was good. She was getting there. Humping her back like a caterpillar, she wormed herself upwards with her knees until her shoulders joined her legs in keeping herself into place. Now she would go and find the little ones.

* * *

Firdaus and the Sheriffs stationed themselves in a half-circle around the postern gate. Roughly two dozen Ghast turned from their attack on the main gate to harry the Sheriffs. Right outside the great North Gate the ground sloped down to where the lake had been, and now treacherous mudflats extended long fingers between the water, edged by reeds and young willow shoots.

Their most important goal was to keep the postern closed. Prevent the Ghast from entering the city. The men in the outer ring held the Ghast at bay with stout blows of their cudgels and ulama bats. Firdaus counted until all the Sheriffs had joined the circle. The younger men clutched their clubs and danced from one foot to another, eager to start attacking.

Firdaus stationed two older men to guard the postern gate. "Defend it with your lives. If the Ghast threaten to enter the main gates, sound the alarm."

To another trembling youngster: "Start another fire. There's plenty of last year's reeds to use, and some willows right there. Make us long, burning brands." A safety measure, in case the other Sheriff couldn't fulfill his mission. Some men cracked under the responsibility.

He turned to the rest of his men, a scant two score, up against double that number of Ghast. "Our task is to draw them away from the Gate. Engage them in the open field, but don't stray too far away in case they break the gate, or if Antjil gets the fire going."

***

"Now what?" Boon said. "If we can't get the saucer to fly, how can we help Abba? It's our duty to protect the people."

Nobody had ever protected Frog, except Firdaus. It made sense that he'd protect everyone, not just her. It was a big burden, though, protecting the people. She'd wanted to lay her burden down at Firdaus' feet, and she figured that when she met him she would be done. Finished. But burdens, apparently, never finished. That was why Stadholders were special people, she guessed. Not everyone was made for burdens like that. Frog wasn't, and from the resonance she felt from the floating ghost in her head, Ing wasn't either.

But she'd have to step up anyway. Circumstances had turned her into somebody who was close to Stadholders and shared their burden.

"I think we should help your abba before we help the

people," she said. "The saucer may not fly, but we can try to crash it on top of the Ghast. That'll stop them."

She pictured it only after the words had left her mouth. Like stepping on the Ghast with a giant foot. It might work.

Boon's eyes sparkled. Of course, he was a little boy. Boys loved crashing and destroying things. "Yes! Crash it! I like that!"

She almost laughed. Using a delicate piece of machinery like the landing craft to smash one's enemies? A fitting end to the colonists' ambitions. And yet she wanted to preserve the precious relic with all her heart. How would she get off this planet without the landers? Frog shook the strange thought away.

"How will we know where they are?" Boon said. "It's getting dark, and by cloudrise tomorrow they'll be everywhere in the city."

"Turning people," Frog said. "The Queen Mound is going to convert as many humans as she can. Wan of her own flesh. I don't see how that will help her though, if she's going to sporulate soon."

"I thought Ing knew the other mound's reasons," Boon said. "Ing was in her pay, did you know that?"

"That's awful," Frog said. Where was that knowledge when she needed it? The memory popped up in its entirety. Yes. The Queen Mound wouldn't want her to hinder the Ghast but to help them. She might as well crash the saucer on the Palace Square and nobody would be the wiser. Not even Firdaus or Boon.

"Or it could be sheer spite, I bet. Like when Abba was sporting with one of the servant girls, and the other one who he'd sported before tried to kill him and cut off his balls. If she couldn't have him, she didn't want the other girls to have him either."

It was bad enough to think of Firdaus sporting with Ing, but countless other girls more beautiful than she was? It wasn't fair. He didn't love Frog. He'd fled from her as soon as he could. Her life was for nothing. She might as well do as the Queen Mound wished. The praise and love she would get from that huge creature would be immense, better than anything he could give her.

Boon put his hand on her arm. "Don't look so sad. I'm sure he'll come around. And if we kill those Ghast, he will be really grateful, too."

Frog looked down at the cold little hand on her arm. White on white. Firdaus' child. Boon was only a tool in her hands, just like his father. Frog studied her fingertip. Boon said she had the most of Ing inside her, and he'd fed her his own memories of Ing's hands. She willed her skin to form ridges exactly like the ones Ing's had once possessed. She didn't know if Wan retained a memory of their fingerprints. Even Ing had never been able to answer that question, having only primitive means of finding out.

"Are you ready?" Boon asked.

She shrugged. "As ready as I can be."

He gestured towards the instrument panel, a king inviting his subject.

Frog suppressed a smile. She wasn't going to fight him for dominance. Or maybe he thought she'd eaten his mentor and held it against her.

She waggled her hand at him and pressed it against the security screen. For a second or so it seemed she was through but the lights flashed red again. Her spine sagged into a defeated curve. She'd been so sure Boon's idea would work.

Her eyes met his. "Sorry," she said.

"That's okay," Boon answered.

He was such a sweet and well-mannered boy, although she wished he'd been smaller so she could have cuddled him and sang him songs. Frog froze in mid-thought. What was she doing? She'd been about to betray this cute little boy, not to mention the man she loved. Those Mound Queen thoughts needed to be out of her head right now. She forced the treacherous thought down into her left hand, into the pinky. She'd break it off as soon as she could without Boon noticing.

"Do you have smaller brothers and sisters?" she asked.

"Abba already told you," he said.

Of course Firdaus had. Her brain just wasn't working very well at the moment. She sighed and swung her arms to release tension.

"We'd better get out of the city, then," she said. "Unless you have something else up your sleeve."

"I promised Abba I'd do this," Boon said stubbornly. "Give me the knowledge to make her finger pattern. I'll try it."

"If you wish," Frog said. "I've eaten more of Ing than you have, though."

He frowned and stuck out his chin. Oh, that still hurt. She shouldn't have brought it up. "Don't be mad at me," she said. "I'm not going to hog Ing's knowledge. You're welcome to share it. I'll be your teacher, just like Ing."

Boon sniffed, but the stiffness of his thin little body relaxed a bit.

Together they walked back to the instrument panel. A memory popped up to the surface of Frog's brain like a dead fish going belly-up. "I have to speak to the magic. And use my fingers."

"You have to say a magic word? Do you know it?"

"Not a magic word. Just her name. Ing's name."

"Does she have a name? Is she of noble birth?"

"Not like that. Where she comes from, they name people differently. Watch and be very silent."

Frog knew it was going to work. She just knew. The knowledge shone like the sky on cloudlit nights.

She worked a change in her throat, positioned her right hand on the panel, leaned forward, and spoke in Ing's crisp voice: "Giok Siu Ing."

**

The Sheriffs at first sent heavy blows to the Ghast heads, which would have killed or incapacitated a human soldier, but the Ghast absorbed them easily.

"Watch me," Firdaus shouted. "This is how you kill them!"

Firdaus paired up with a Sheriff. They each grabbed a lumpy Ghast limb, digging their fingers in the powdery, friable top layer, which puffed out defensive scent. "Now!"

Firdaus shouted. He and the Sheriff pulled. The limbs came off, but the armless torso still moved and swayed, eerily soundless.

Firdaus threw himself at the head and tried to screw it off. The white Ghast stuff under his hands slithered away into another shape. A mouth on its hide opened against Firdaus' arm and raked his skin, sending warning signals down his non-existent spine. The bites didn't hurt, and he didn't lose much substance, but he wrenched the creature off and threw it down into the mud.

The Sheriff he'd paired up with got a kick in the head from one of the thrashing legs and went down. Another Ghast joined in. Firdaus climbed on the too broad, asymmetrical back of the new Ghast and dug gobbet after gobbet of flesh out of the neck and the head. The cinnamon smell that rose from the springy, dry stuff clogged his nose and urged him to stop and eat it. Still it moved, trampling the Sheriff beneath its plate-like feet.

They were losing, losing badly. Only a few Sheriffs still standing, three or four Ghast converging on each of them. Firdaus' ears roared painfully. Maybe he'd been hit on the head, but would that even affect him, Wan as he was? He ploughed through mud, blood, and Ghast mush. The red of the blood shouted at him, and the mingling of disgusting and mouthwatering smells made him queasy.

***

Hilm's head emerged into darkness. The lack of visual reference made her dizzy, and she closed her eyes a moment, listening to the steady drip of water. Inch by inch she emerged from her cramped cocoon and slid out when gravity pulled hard enough. Finally, she could relax. She unlocked one arm, slowly, but she lacked her normal muscle control and the arm jerked to the side.

She screamed, throwing her head back, but her overtaxed muscles jackknifed her head back onto her chest. Slowly, the cramps and twitches in her limbs eased up, and she sank down on the floor like a used-up dishrag. She hadn't exited on the main floor as she intended, but on another layer of tunnels beneath the palace. She'd have to find another way up.

Hilm rose and walked on. The faint sprinkle of light from the airshaft faded. The only sound was her own footsteps. The tunnel sloped down, again. Were these even the same tunnels she'd played in as a child?

Her hand touched roughness. She halted and carefully walked her fingers around the perimeter of the rough patch. It was a hole, not an airshaft like the palace had, but something irregular, chewed-feeling. Rats. Or maybe it was part of the mound creature Abba said the whole city rested upon. Her hand quested inwards, trembling, expecting to be bitten by a burrow creature inside. She felt nothing but a slightly cool, crumbly surface.

Should she go in? She didn't know where this tunnel led. Maybe outside, to safety. She couldn't take that option, because of her duty to Gül and the other children. But then, wandering around in sewers wasn't so great either. Time was passing. Was it still morning? Abba was expecting her, but he wouldn't be back to get her if she didn't show up in time. His duty was to the citizens.

She had to choose.

She went in.

***

Screaming. Two Ghast pulled at one Sheriff's arm. Firdaus blinked and blinked, as if blinking would set the world right, but the enemy kept trying to kill his man. The Ghast were clearly intelligent, learning quickly from their opponents' tactics, but they still knew nothing of human-kind. One blow to the head would have dispatched the tortured Sheriff, but the Ghast kept trying to tear his arms from their sockets. If only Firdaus could spare a moment to think, there would be an advantage there.

Firdaus ducked and ran as two Ghast converged upon him. He was more flexible and changed course more easily. A dazed Sheriff, a brawny fellow no more than fifteen years old, clambered to his feet. Firdaus grabbed him by his sweat-moist, solidly human arm and dragged him to a lone Ghast still trampling a long-dead bloody smear on the ground. "Legs first!" he shouted.

They barreled into the cool hard substance of the Ghast and threw it down. The young Sheriff grabbed a foot like a tree trunk and yanked it one way. Firdaus grabbed the other, more slender foot and pulled the other way. The leg came off with hardly a sound, like breaking off a mushroom stem. A slitted mouth clamped on his calf, but the Sheriff came over and stamped down on the neck, tramping it into a lumpy white mush. Not that it breathed like a person, but the neck came off.

A flicker from the corner of Firdaus' eye caught his attention. Fire, at last. He waved over the hesitant Sheriff who held several burning brands, bristly makeshift things that wouldn't hold out for long. He grabbed two brands, handed one over to Sala who'd lost his cudgel and thrust the other one straight into a Ghast face. The brand hissed and fizzled, at first, but then with a whoosh the Ghast head exploded in a wet splatter of Ghast stuff. A rain of scorching remnants fell on Firdaus and leopard-spotted the grass around him.

He checked to see how his Sheriffs were faring. Not many left standing. But an armless Ghast was tearing the limbs from another Ghast with its snake-deep jaws.

Why?

CHAPTER 26

The navigation panel in the saucer lit up like fires at dusk, tongues slithered in and out, eyes blinked. A creature waking up after a long, deep sleep.

Frog's eyes slid to Boon. He was staring with rapt eyes at the panel, his fingers twitching with eagerness. Frog figured they didn't need fingers to steer the craft.

"Land us on top of those Ghast north of the Dark Quarter," she said.

"Destination unknown. Scanning," the wall answered.

A picture formed on one of the smooth wall surfaces. It made no sense to Frog at all, but then she blinked, and suddenly she was looking down on the city as if she was standing on the balcony. She thought she could even see the white fog of Ghast-shapes swarming, massing at the old Nightlight Gate, now Dark Gate. Or she could just let the saucer fall where it would, destroying everything in its way. Frog ground her teeth and hid her hands below her shoulder mantle. Snick, there went the evil pinky and the sneaky, slippery thoughts she'd stashed there. She tossed the offending object into a corner, and pricked a good obedient finger on the exact spot on the map where she wanted to go.

"There. Land there."

A string of numbers came up on the screen. "Please confirm."

"Confirm," she said.

"Projected time of landing?"

"Now. At once."

"Unable to comply. Seatbelts aren't fastened."

Frog's brain supplied a picture of a seatbelt. There was

nothing like that in the room. No seats, even, just discolored spots on the smooth gray floor. The seatbelts? The statues of Firdaus' ancestors that graced the Physician's Temple wore them like bandoliers. They'd have to risk a rough ride without seats.

"Um. Emergency override. Seats damaged," she said.

"Confirmed."

The saucer shuddered. Frog's head filled with disaster scenarios. Thanks so much, Ing. The craft might be so firmly attached to the stack of saucers that it would attempt to take the whole palace up in the air, and the engine would burn out. The energy cells might have run down. The flight sensors might be broken.

The saucer lurched and she fell against Boon, squashing him on the floor.

***

He blinked mud out of his eyes. Something touched his hand. A Ghast pulled him up with a reed-thin appendage growing from its empty shoulders, its hand-thing sending messages of shy friendliness. Firdaus grabbed the limb and hauled himself up. Was it a trick to get him off-balance? He jerked himself loose and sprang aside.

Something was still attached to his arm. The Ghast. It brought its head close to his arm and licked it. It broke off its new thin limb and offered it to him.

From the corner of his eye, he saw the other Ghast lumbering about, doggedly sticking to their destructive purpose. The Ghast by his side waited, giving every appearance of docility. This was the first Ghast he'd torn the arms off, he remembered now. It had clamped its mouth on his bicep and ate a bit of his flesh. By eating from him, it had become his, converted by his dominant flesh. Firdaus broke off a finger and fed it to the creature. He ate from the arm it had offered him. The Ghast stuff oozed submission, joyously assimilating Firdaus' point of view.

Firdaus awoke from his brief dream with a jolt, full of purpose. He ran off, breaking off another finger while he ran and rammed it into the mouth of the nearest Ghast, who was in the process of ripping off a yodeling Sheriff's arm. He didn't stop to check if it worked. Another finger, another mouth. There, three Ghast converging on a slender young boy, who must have survived so far by dodging his attackers. His thumb, this time.

Prophet, how was he going to break off the fingers of his other hand? He stuffed his hand in his mouth, yanked, plucked the finger from his mouth, fed it to the nearest Ghast. Repeat, yank, repeat. He had no fingers left. It didn't matter, he could grow new ones. He rammed his fingerless stump into the mouth of the next one, felt a great lump breaking off, dragged his arm back and turned to another Ghast. No, that one was his own, he recognized it by the dangling finger-thick limb. It was feeding lumps of itself to a new Ghast. Good. Were they all following his lead? They were. A few converted Ghast flailed around, maybe the ones that had gotten pinkies; others were feeding their brethren hunks of white meat.

Firdaus stopped and bent over, resting the ragged stumps of his forearms on his knees. It wasn't as comfortable and easy a fit as with real hands. The stumps slid off. And why was he resting? He wasn't out of breath. He'd just given away so much of himself he was reeling from the loss of mass.

"To me! To me!" he yelled.

His Sheriffs came. The Ghast he'd charmed into becoming his allies by dint of eating his flesh perked up their heads and flocked over to Firdaus' side as well. The Sheriffs bristled and gripped their weapons.

"They're on our side now," Firdaus said.

"How will we tell the difference?"

"They won't try killing us."

Only a handful of the Ghast were his, several recent converts already turned back to the Queen Mound's side. Still, he had a fighting chance now.

"My Ghast," he said. "Convert the Queen Mound's walkers, or kill them, whichever is easier."

Had they eaten enough of him to understand spoken language? He entertained no more than a moment's doubt:

his Ghast swiveled on their plate-like feet and stormed as one into the greater mass of enemy Ghast.

He'd managed to ward off the Ghast attack. The battle was over. He never wanted to live through something like that ever again, but he had won!

"Sheriffs, to me! We have won the day! To me! The Ghast are no longer a danger."

A joyous sight, Ghast feeding one another bits of themselves. One by one, the enemy Ghast ceased their blind trashing and turned on their former comrades. Ghast broke away from battered Sheriffs like piecrust from the filling.

The pent-up tension left Firdaus' body in a long sigh. He found a Sheriff lying prone on the ground, and knelt stiffly to check for vital signs. One by one, his men limped over to him and watched the body of Ghasts halt and stand at ease with their faces in Firdaus' direction.

Sheriff Sala helped Firdaus stand. His knuckles itched fiercely, already growing new fingers.

"What happened, my Lord?"

Firdaus contemplated a long explanation, but discarded it. "They surrendered."

"What should we do with them?"

Firdaus opened his mouth, with no idea what he was going to say, but snapped it shut again. The Ghast were turning away from him. They broke ranks, drawing to two sides, leaving an avenue of sight cleaving through.

At the other end of the lagoon a flurry of white running shapes closed in fast. Firdaus slapped his forehead. He'd seen them coming from the Palace roof, but he'd forgotten all about them.

The second wave of Ghast, twice as large as the first.

***

"What's happening?" Boon moaned. He clung to the floor, hiding his face from the wildly tumbling cloudscape visible through the door. Below Frog, the white and red city whirled around itself, a dizzying merry-go-round of Palace, Temple, Tower, Dark Quarter, Palace.

Ancestors. They hadn't closed the door. She should

have been a little less congratulatory and a lot more careful.

"Permission to close exits."

"Doors!" Frog screamed from the floor. "Close!"

She'd used her own voice, not the dispassionate Ing voice. Would the magic creature in the saucer comply?

Her stomach flopped into her toes for a long agonizing moment and Boon clawed his hands into her thighs. What was happening? Her guts flipped and lodged in her throat.

***

The Sheriffs gasped as they beheld the fresh troops behind their former foes. The world fell silent. The moans of wounded men, the fluting of the sea wind around their ears, Firdaus knew these sounds still reverberated in the air, but his ears couldn't process them. What to do now? He felt depleted and weary, he had only half his men left, and less than complete confidence in the flesh-bought loyalty of the converted Ghast contingent.

He forced his sagging spine to straighten and took a deep breath. He coughed, cleared his throat. He got out the words he wanted at the third try.

"Sheriffs of White City. We have vanquished the vanguard of the Ghast Army. We are hurt and tired and we deserve to lie on silk couches and drink chilled sorbets from the lips of wide-hipped houris. But it is not yet to be. There is one more task that awaits us. We must protect our city from the main army."

Henk, the Sheriff standing closest to him, bit his lip and blinked his eyes to keep the tears in. Firdaus clapped a stump on his shoulder.

"Don't be ashamed of fear or weariness. We're all weary. We all fear the outcome. But in spite of that we're going to give all to keep these monsters from our wives, our mothers, our children."

Most of the Sheriffs managed a ragged cheer.

Sala wanted to push through the mass of converted Ghast, but Firdaus stopped him. "Wait, Sala. Let them take the brunt."

Firdaus swallowed. They were doomed. Utterly doomed.

He could not hope to feed an army that size. Unless. Unless he offered himself up as a sacrifice. Yes. That was the only course.

He elbowed his way through the Sheriffs and forced his tired legs to pump harder. He ululated a yodel he hadn't known his lungs could produce.

"Heya, Ghast, here comes Firdaus, harbinger of your end!"

They'd tear him apart and devour him. If this was his last act for his city, it was worth it.

***

Frog hung from the ceiling with one hand, but her face was squashed against the saucer floor. Her stomach lurched even as she thought, "But I have no stomach!" The ceiling banged against the back of her head and her arm folded double.

"Landing site not available," the ship's voice said.

Her tongue stirred around against the roof of her mouth, looking for purchase. What did that mean?

"I think it means there are people on the ground," Boon said.

"Humans or Ghast?"

Nobody answered.

"You have to ask the ship," Boon said helpfully.

Frog reined in her temper and managed not to snap at him. "Ship, show video of landing site."

"Image quality low."

Frog corkscrewed her head around until she located the upside down video screen. She saw two blots of white, one speckled with brown, one uniform. She could only destroy one of them.

"Ship, emergency override. Land on biggest group of alien life forms."

With a deafening thud, she and Boon flipped up and landed again so hard her face must be etched into the floor. Pain invaded her body and all went black before she could even scream.

***

A thunderclap boomed over his head.

The world darkened. He looked up. The sky barreled down on him like a fist of wind.

With a last mighty effort, Firdaus leaned into the wind, clove it in two and ran away from his position between the two Ghast armies. His room, the saucer, the palace fell out of the sky. Mud churned and spouted up even before the thing hit the ground, splattering his men and the Ghast with gray slime, red blood and black mud.

His ears throbbed with bells and drums, a wall of sound traveling through the earth and turning the mud to jelly. The saucer bottom hit the upturned faces of the second wave of Ghast. The world lightened to a gasping void that roiled with black and grey clouds. His teeth clacked together so hard his jaw hurt. He sat down involuntarily.

Firdaus staggered upright, swaying, shaking. Water streamed from his ears and let in the world of sounds. His feet squishing in wet moss. Distant thumps. He smelled something burning, something wet, and, after some blinking, the low-hanging curling clouds connected with the burning.

He shook his head and the world made more sense. The saucer! Frog and Boon had saved them! The saucer lay crooked on top of the destroyed Ghast, bigger than it had ever seemed before, sunk half in the mud. Red and white streaks marred its smooth anthracite surface. He just stood there, staring like an idiot. Where were his Sheriffs? Had the saucer killed all of them, not just the Ghast?

No, he saw movement. He ran off towards the mash of black heads and brown limbs, splattered with orange mud and scarlet blood. His Sheriffs lay dazed or stood swaying, disoriented and deafened by the smoking hulk of the saucer. He didn't see any movement inside. Had the impact killed his beloved Boon and Frog?

He picked his way to the saucer. It lay still, exuding great heat and smelling like an empty pot left on the fire. He rounded the saucer, careful not to tread on his people's blood, or on the Ghast snippets that writhed and tried to take new shapes. His old bedroom door gaped open.

He went inside.

Frog hung from one endlessly long arm hooked over a ring in the ceiling. Her face was slack. A heap of white in the corner must be Boon.

"Boontie! Baby, wake up?" he said gently as he knelt near the tangle of knees and elbows.

"Abba?" a little voice said. "Did I do it? Did I help?"

"Of course you did, darling. You and Frog are heroes. You squashed those terrible Ghast like beetles. Can you get up?"

Slowly Boon uncoiled himself, limb by limb. Children, even Wanned children, were like putty. Nothing fazed them for long. Firdaus turned to Frog, who was stirring vaguely, trying to move but hindered by her arm.

"Frog. Your arm has grown long and thin. Can you move it?"

She shook her head. "Firdaus! I mean, my lord. Did we succeed?"

"Indeed you did! Come, let me help you. You're a hero now. You killed most of the Ghast."

Tenderly, he lifted the poor arm off the hook. It flopped down on the floor.

"Is it very ugly?" Frog asked.

"Not at all, my dear. Why did it grow so long?"

"The acceleration," she said vaguely, rubbing the arm and pushing it hard against the socket. It was shrinking in length and filling out to its normal circumference already. "No seatbelts, or seats, for that matter." The words were Ing's, but the feeling behind it was all Frog.

"Your hands!" she exclaimed. "What happened?"

"Casualty of war," he said, trying to sound nonchalant. "They will grow back again."

"Do you need my flesh? Here!" She broke of half her hand and fed it to him.

He accepted gravely. She must have lost the little finger in the fall, but the ring finger and middle finger made a great snack.

Firdaus clambered out. The wounded Sheriffs moved slowly, unable to recover from the blow and the aftermath as fast as he had. He still didn't know when the blow-out was going to come, but they were hurt too badly to make it to the caves on their own.

He leaned his elbows on the saucer floor. "Frog? Did you break the chamber or will it still fly?"

Frog looked around with a frown on her face. He longed to smooth it off with a tender finger, possibly even kiss it, but he feared there would be no room for getting to know her again anytime soon.

"It doesn't seem damaged. Why?"

"I want you to ferry the wounded Sheriffs to the caves. I must leave you and get there in great haste myself, now that the Ghast are no longer a threat."

Frog peered over his shoulder. "Why are they leaning on their elbows? Are they copying you?"

"I think they are. Let's hope they won't be following me around like little ducklings."

Frog smiled a tiny smile. "Must you go now?"

"Yes."

She bit her lip but nodded. "I accept this task from you. I will bring the men to the caves. Where are they?"

The surviving Sheriffs gathered, leaning on each other, subdued, a mass of cuts and bruises and broken limbs. None of them had escaped unscathed. Nevertheless, their spines straightened and their faces brightened. Firdaus hadn't counted them before the fight, but now less than a dozen remained standing. Two more staggered up.

"We won!" bold Quan said. "Sire, we killed them all!"

CHAPTER 27

From his perch on the gunwale of the overloaded boat, Firdaus looked at his rapidly receding city for the last time. The singing tower and the palace towered high over the red roofs and white walls of the four quarters.

From here, only the most southern point of the town was visible, with the elbows of the palace just sticking out beyond it. No change yet. He hoped that Boon and Ing would manage to join him soon. Thousands of people were still within the town walls, and the population kept swelling from the farmers and fishers, reederers and peat-cutters coming in from the Maze.

He lowered his gaze back into the boat. The little boy on his lap was fast falling asleep, lulled by Firdaus' inhuman calm. He missed cuddling his own children, and he hadn't seen the little ones or their mothers since he was exiled. They might not even remember him. He'd never have another baby now. He would have liked to give Frog one.

The steersman rose to direct the disembarkation. The oarsmen stowed and secured their oars, then jumped in the sea to receive the bales of goods and the children in their arms.

Firdaus shouldered his pack and trudged through the wet sand to the entrance of the caves. A harried clerk told him where to unload, and he threaded his way through the chaotic mass of people and goats and ducks and chickens and children running and playing underfoot. People hardly looked up as he passed, already inured to his pale strangeness. Or too numb to care.

Firdaus set the heavy pack down. He paced the black

sand, wishing that he could sit down somewhere, but the rocks were as sharp as if they'd just been thrust up by mother earth. If it had been white instead of black, the cave exit could have been the mouth of the underworld, ready to swallow up the evil and the haram. He'd qualify, all right.

"Firdaus," a rockfall voice scraped.

He jumped. Behind him stood a Ghast, but one such as he'd never seen before. A giant child had slapped it together out of wet clay, leaving it scaled with fingerprints as wide as palms. It was twice as wide and deep as most of them, and almost as tall as Firdaus. Its scent, unlike its looks, seemed familiar.

"Are you Mother Doughy's walker? Have we met before?" he asked.

"In a way." Rocks tumbled and slid in an approximation of laughter. "She made me out of the walker you knew. You can talk to me as if I was all of Mother Doughy."

"How can you be Mother Doughy? She's bigger than a whole city. You're not her child, are you?"

"No, she's about to sporulate. Those will be her children."

Firdaus opened and closed his mouth and looked the Ghast up and down.

The Ghast's limbs weren't as haphazardly placed as on most of them. Mother Doughy had attempted to mimic human symmetry. If it had had hair, and a decent sari to cover the bulges, it might have looked like a prosperous if ugly washerwoman.

"But what are you then?"

"Think of me as an emissary," the unlikely mouth rumbled. "She put as much of her into me as she could. After long deliberation and weighing of all the pros and cons she composed the poem of my flesh."

"Er, yes. What a magnificent epic it is, Madam."

The Ghast fixed a disconcerting, globular eye on him. Firdaus smiled tightly and hoped humor, like symmetry, was too new for it to have fully grasped it yet.

"But I thought all the Ghast would die when the young

came out and ate everything in sight."

The Ghast nodded, so human and pensive a gesture that Firdaus' respect for Mother Doughy grew even more.

"That is the essential spice in this poem. Mother Doughy, me, and all my walkers will blow up or be eaten. But I don't want to die. I don't want to have to start all over, only a grain of me ending up in a new mound, waiting centuries to find enough intelligence to appreciate humans again. I don't want to miss anything that happens in the meantime."

The coin dropped. "So you are going to hide out with us, and gain a head start on all your competitors! How clever! Such foresight. Mother Doughy, you have my utmost respect."

"Thank you. And I mean that to all of humanity. I do have fragmentary tastes of former existences as mounds, and never before have I enjoyed myself so much. Humans are so entertaining. "

"You call me human, and yet humans think of us as Wan, as dangerous, frightening monsters who eat children."

"Details, details. The color of your soup may be different, but the taste and texture are identical!"

"I feel the same as before, true," Firdaus said. "Are you the only Ghast to think up this notion?"

"I am. Walkers are smarter than paradiles, but Mounds are many times smarter than Ghast. I'm not just a walker, Firdaus. I'm filled to the brim with every poem and notion Mother Doughy thought relevant. She meant me to make alliance with you, in the hope that we would be of use to each other."

"I have a feeling you will be," Firdaus said. "I thought I'd miss Mother Doughy, so this is good news. What is your name?"

"That is a thing that I am not equipped for. I know who I am, but names are so human. I haven't been able to think of anything I wish to be called."

"Hm. In human life, mothers and fathers name their children."

The Ghast sighed. "Even the words mother and father

give me a thrill. So alien. Unique!"

"When I was a Stadholder, I was the father of my people. Would you do me the honor of allowing me to name you, Mother Doughy's emissary?"

The Ghast could not show emotion like humans, but it dipped its lumpy, misshapen head towards Firdaus. The enormity of his request suddenly gripped his throat. What if he made a huge gaffe and gave her, him, it, a name that was all wrong? For all he knew, it might use it for centuries. This Ghast would survive, even if humans didn't. This was a weighty moment.

"I will call you... wait. Do you want to appear male or female?"

The Ghast slaked a sigh of delight. "Oh, can I? I pick... I pick... I can't change over if I don't like it, can I?"

Firdaus pondered that. "You know, I think one could. If you're able to mold your form you could change your face and add some breasts if you wanted to be a girl after all. Start over, as it were."

It was a stirring idea. If he had enough of being Firdaus, he could become Firdausia. Of course he'd be a noticeably tall woman, but he'd just give away some mass and make himself shorter. Oh, what was he thinking? If, if, if. First he and the rest of humanity would have to survive the coming blowout.

"I name you Giok Doughyson."

Why had he used Ing's father's name for the creature? Too late to withdraw the impulse now.

"Doughyson," the Ghast said. "That sounds very human. I like it."

Firdaus lifted his hand to clap Doughyson on the shoulder, but then thought better of it. "About Mother Doughy. Do you know when she's going to blow?"

"Soon."

"That's what she's told me. I need more than just soon. How long beforehand will you know?"

"At noon. Are you ready?"

No. They were not ready.

***

The tunnel floor gave slightly under Hilm's bruised and scraped knees. It didn't smell the same inside the Mound as before. She rapped her knuckles on the wall every few yards. "Mound person? Are you in there? Can you help me?"

Her limbs trembled and shook, and it wasn't just fatigue. She'd never been as afraid as she was now. Some gut instinct told her she was in the bowels of a giant creature, and she'd never get out. She knew in her head it wasn't true, that the creature was wise and her father's ally, but her hindbrain refused to believe it.

Tap tap. "Mound lady? Please answer me. I'm in a hurry. I have to save my brothers and sisters."

Something rumbled. "Firdaus' pup. Save them from me? You wish to devour them yourself?"

Hilm was too afraid to feel relief. "Mound mother! Please, I need to get to the throne room in the palace without anyone seeing me. My aunt is holding the little ones hostage."

"What is an aunt?" the rumble asked.

Hilm could have beaten her head against the walls. "My brother's sister. His rival. She wants to, to eat his children."

"Ah! Naturally. I wouldn't want my greedy sister the Mound Queen to eat any of my spawn. Firdaus is my ally. His sibling must not win! I will make a tunnel for you. But you must hurry. I'm up the spout, I have a bun in the oven, and will spawn soon. My structure is no longer sound; my roots have begun to withdraw into my belly. Keep talking so I will remember you are there."

"Y-yes," Hilm said. In spite of the promised help, the mound's words weren't reassuring.

"You mud people need more light?" the thick clotted voice asked from somewhere else.

"Thank you, I would," Hilm said.

The world split asunder with ominous shaking and thundering. Hilm closed her eyes against the bright stripe of light pummeling her. It couldn't be good, opening up a fissure a hundred yards deep to give her light. The mound's judgment smelled off. When her eyes had adjusted to the light, she was surrounded by mottled pink cake dough that disintegrated at a glance. Speed seemed a very good idea. She crawled on in the tunnel that opened up before her. The walls closed behind her, and slid right up to her back, exerting a pressure that at first seemed gentle. Then the slope steepened, the tunnel-hand on the small of her back pushed harder and she slid head over heels down.

"I apologize for the unseemliness," the walls ground and creaked out. "There is much haste. Now you must climb."

Hilm dug her hands into the softening stuff and hooked her way up.

"Look," the voice said. "These smell like you and your father. Are they his offspring?"

A narrow tunnel opened into the throne room, about two feet above ground level. The morning light had progressed, but not by as much as Hilm had feared. Unless she'd spent a whole day underground.

She looked straight at a group of playing children, watched over by tense mothers. She ticked them off, yes, Gül, Ichiro, Heike, Awayo, Osma, Zuzana in her mother's arms, the other ones peeking in twos and threes from behind their mother's skirts.

"That's all of them. I think," Hilm said.

She tried to count, but she was too frazzled, the children moving around too much.

"Tell them to run fast," the mound said.

The floor opened up beneath Firdaus' children and former concubines.

***

Firdaus' head nearly exploded from the many tasks that demanded his attention. If the mound was about to blow, they had far less time than they hoped. Only half the city was inside a cave, a quarter was on its way and the stragglers were still trying to get out. The caves he'd seen were already full with people. They needed more shelter. Frog and Boon were gathering up the wounded and the stragglers. He could only hope they would make it in time.

The signalman stationed on the roof fanned his fire to a roar. Signalmen were Stentor guild members, presumably the ones with weak chests.

"Wait a quarter and then repeat the first message," Firdaus commanded. "Then add a warning at the end. Keep repeating it every hour."

"Sire," the signaler coughed from his own fire. "I can do that, but I don't think there's anyone to receive the signals anymore. I can only hope someone knows how to read the smoke signal, and is looking this way."

Boon probably could read signals, Boon always read everything and knew stuff like that. But would he look?

He would have torn at his hair or beat his chest, but a ruler shouldn't give way to his emotions like that.

"Boon knows everything. And Frog is no slouch either, with all that Ing knowledge in her head. They will look."

The Ghast put a palm, rough as a scab, on Firdaus arm. "Who has eaten much of Ing?"

"Frog. My friend from the marshes."

"We must be alert to the possibility that she is under compulsion from the Queen Mound, like Ing."

A ring of cold tightened around Firdaus' heart.

"You think? How can you tell?"

Doughyson made a peculiar rolling movement where people had their shoulders. Maybe he meant to shrug, but body language was not the Ghast's strong point, although Firdaus had no doubt that a century or two would make him master of it.

"There is a subtle difference in smell. Every Wan or Ghast is made up out of thousands of components," the Ghast explained. "These components might or might not be from the same mound, but the Queen of the dominant mound exerts a pull at that walker. Her charisma is so great, that we can't but do as she wishes."

"So would that go for me as well?" Firdaus asked.

The Ghast shut its mouth and looked Firdaus in the eye. "Mother Doughy, the city mound, is your ally. Take my assurance that we both have nothing but the welfare of humanity as our main interest."

Firdaus put the thought aside for now and strode over to the balcony. Black Crag cut off most of the view to his right. He could only see the tip of the Signing Tower and a tiny sliver of palace from here, but he couldn't stop staring in that direction. Boon had to get the message that was even now puffing up in gray clouds into the sky. He had to. Firdaus hadn't let him turn into an abomination just so he could perish. And Frog.

He'd fled from Frog's earnest avowals of love and chosen this place, the farthest he could get from her, to think it over. He'd liked Frog well enough. At some moments, he'd almost loved Ing. But the moment he'd seen the Frog-Ing mix bounce up to him, his heart had flipped and his guts had fluttered with expectation. He'd just known he could love that woman, though he didn't know her.

And now he wanted the new Frog by his side, and not just for her Frogness. It was Ing that made up a large part of the attraction of the new Frog, the Ing who always had the most peculiar answers to everything: theories, prophecies, interesting angles of thought that no one else had. He missed that aspect of her.

He sighed and leaned his back away from the tantalizing view of the city, so near and yet so far. Part of him wanted to see what happened when the destruction hit, and another part wished to hold on to his memories of the city.

The Ghast loomed over one of the servant girls suckling her child. She sat, sunken in the breastfeeding stupor he remembered from his past consorts, paying not the slightest attention to the monstrous clay idol inches away from her.

Doughyson caught his eye and ambled over. "Fascinating. What kind of information does the mother feed the child? The secrets of sound and movement?"

"It's just food," Firdaus said. "They have no teeth yet."

"Hm. Resembling one of our stadia," the Ghast mused.

A movement in the corners of his eye.

The resonance of a hundred drums rolled over the water.

It was time.

CHAPTER 28

A new, odd sound filled the air, higher and different in frequency from the low rumble of the breakers. Like a migrating beehive, but magnified a thousand-fold.

The blowout had begun.

A pink finger thrust into the air above the city, listing slightly to the right from the sea wind. The pink flower bulged. The wind smeared pink over the whole sky, but new clouds of fuchsia roiled up from underneath, keeping the rose of smoke firm and wide. The middle of the city bucked up, lifting its spine like a caterpillar of stone buildings, forming a hump that split apart at the top. The Singing Tower leaned to the left, farther and farther until it broke off and slid down in a shower of white stone. The Physician's Temple broke into two jagged pieces that fled from each other in a widening V until gravity got a firm grip on the top levels and yanked them down. White clouds boiled up from the city, cupping the pink cauliflower in the sky with white hands of steam and stone. Silently.

Firdaus turned away. He couldn't bear to look at his beloved city's last moments. Broken, erupting with boils of spores and sea water all over. Ruined. Gone.

The sound reached him heartbeats later, buffeting his back with slaps of thunder. He wiped at his eyes. Just fluid. No bitter salts in Wan tears.

Far below him, the beach trembled under his feet. The sea receded from the beach, laying bare the steep black slope hurtling down into the deeps, strewn with shells and twitching fish.

"Look!" Doughyson said and pointed his too-short

arm away from the city.

"What? Those birds?"

"That's not a bird," a servant girl said. Her voice was thick with awe. "That's the palace! It's flying!"

"Magic. Ing's magic."

"This is how Ing's Ancestors arrived here," Doughy-son said. "Mother Doughy remembers the vibration in the air against her skin."

Firdaus fought to keep his footing as the whole sleepy roof-population rose as one to gawp at the flying saucer. What was keeping it in the sky? He still had no answer to that question, except that Ing and Frog and Boon caused it.

Screams of panic rose from the beach below. A few bathers, probably hoping to catch a shellfish or a shrimp, came splashing in from the widening beach.

"On the beach? She's going to fall on the beach?"

"If it can fly, why couldn't it land?"

"It has no legs to perch on," someone pointed out with relentless logic.

The saucer dropped down with relatively little fuss, as if it was as light as a feather. A second later the sound of the splash rang in his ears. The saucer floated silent and heavy on the waves, the charcoal surface gleaming wet. People spilled out of it, staggering, supporting each other. Brown people. The wounded Sheriffs. Then a small white person. Boon! The sight of his son released Firdaus from his paralysis. He ran down the villa stairs to the beach, more than a hundred yards below.

The very last person to come out was Frog. Firdaus met her halfway down the stairs. He scooped her up in his arms and hugged her hard.

"I was so afraid you wouldn't get here in time!" he said as she pressed her face into the hollow of his neck.

"Nothing would stop me from coming back to you," she said simply and once again, his heart bucked at the weight of her words. Frog had no subtlety or subterfuge. She meant what she said, and her honest gaze demanded that he reciprocate.

"I'm happy to see you, Frog," he said and her relieved smile was enough reward for now.

***

An avalanche of screaming people, elbows, toes, noses, baby bottoms tumbled over one another, coming to a smacking halt a little ways below where Hilm crouched.

The crumbling gap sphinctered tight, shutting off the screaming from above, and the light.

"Silence!" Hilm yelled, while her eyes adjusted to the mysterious half-light in the tunnel. "We must escape from the city. It's going to blow up. Pick up your children or your little brothers and sisters, and run after me!"

"It's not true!" Hanako screamed. "Firdaus is wrong! I'm not going anywhere!"

Hilm scooped up Osama, ordered Hussein to climb on her back and grabbed Heike's hand. "Run, children, run! Gül, carry Ayodele."

Hilm staggered forwards under her load, checking over her shoulder if everyone was following. Gül, always serious and obedient, followed right on her heels, her green eyes big and scared.

"Hanako!" Hilm called out. "Think of your children. I'm taking you to safety." She had no time to stop and persuade the silly woman. Hanako stood frozen in indecision, her baby in her arms. Every time Hilm looked back, she receded further.

"You smell bad, Hilm," Gül said.

"Better stinky than dead, honey."

The floor tilted into a gentle incline.

"Walk faster, children!' Hilm said. "Mound, are we going fast enough?"

No answer came, but the tunnel floor sloped down more steeply and the walls closed in on them.

"We can't walk faster," Hilm panted, her face to the ceiling. "They are too little. Mother Mound, push us out, spit us out as far as you can!"

The mound substance behind them roiled and approached faster. "Hold on, children, hold on to me!"

The children converged on her, little hands on her

arms and legs and skirt and hair, and then the mound gathered them up, rolled them into a porcupine ball and hurtled them through the darkness. Ten heartbeats of wailing, crying, wriggling children clinging to her, then a circle of light raced towards them and ate them up.

They fell onto the rocky slope in a great squirm of bruised flesh. Hilm fought free from her own hair and the slippery little bodies, wet with sweat and snot and tears, and checked out where the mound had deposited them. On the slopes just above the city's roots, juddering white and pink just below them. Half an hour's walk for an adult to the villa over the rocky goat path. With barefoot toddlers, who knew?

"No time to cry!" Hilm said. "Get up, get up, get everybody's hand, we are going to run to the villa. Abba is in there, and he will kiss all your hurts away! Come, you're all big boys and girls, and you have to help the little ones. Ich—No Ichiro. She was sure she'd seem him in the throne room, and surely later in the tunnel? She counted quickly. There should have been nine children, not including baby Waalo with Hanako, but there were only eight.

She fought the urge to collapse in a crying heap. Too late to do anything but save the ones that were here. She didn't look at Gül, Ichiro's older sister.

"Gül, you carry Ayodele on your back, and Heike can hold your skirt."

The path, trodden deep from long-time use by goats and people, was too narrow to walk abreast.

She gathered one child on her back, one in her arm and one on her skirt. "Giovanni and Bao, hold each other's hands. We're princes and princesses, and we are hiding from the dragon in the castle above the city. We will be safe in the villa. Who's going to be the first to get there? Run ahead, Heike, and if you see the villa first you have won!"

***

Firdaus tore himself from Frog's arms and she stood still, the faint ghost of his embrace lingering against her skin. Frog couldn't see the devastation of the city from this spot on the stairs, but the pink finger in the sky thrust itself into the air with frightening energy. The sounds had stopped for a bit, but the sheer hush lent the frantic hurry on the beach an air of unreality. She had to help him. What could she do?

"Get into the saucer," she said to the first woman she met, toiling up the stairs with her slew of children. "You'll be safe there."

Frog searched for Boon. "Boon! Help me get people in the saucer. It's started."

She cast around for the shelters and cave she'd heard about. No shelters, just pathetic low walls of stacked rock on the black powder beach. Caught short. There, the first cave entrance, hidden amidst the whorls and crevices of volcanic rock. The entrance was hardly sealed yet. That had priority.

"Firdaus!" she yelled. "Tell them to get inside and get the caves sealed off!"

What more could she do? She scooped up a lonesome, wailing baby off the sand, only to have it snatched from her arms by the mother a moment later.

"Get inside! Hurry!" she called out in all directions. "Hurry! The cloud will be here in minutes!"

People running inside, check. People clambering back into the saucer, check. Boon. Where was Boon? Firdaus?

She spotted Firdaus' tall white form first. He was stacking up rocks to close the entrance. He needed mud. She scooped up a handful and told everyone she met to do the same. She stuffed handfuls in the cracks between the stones, but it wouldn't stick like clay. What would Ing have done?

Cloth. Steep cotton in mud, to hide its organic nature, and then stuff it in the cracks. "Firdaus!" she said. "Take your clothes off."

"Not now!" he snarled and heaved a giant block of basalt on top of the breast-high wall.

"To put in the cracks. Everybody should do it."

His eyes stared angrily through her, but then he got it and took off his apron. "Women of White City! Give up your cotton and linen clothes to seal the cave entrances!"

He sent runners to the other caves to tell everyone to hurry.

Frog craned her neck to check the progress of the pink hand stretching their way.

"Hurry!"

"Get inside!" Firdaus snapped back.

A Ghast brushed past her, setting another block on the parapet. Frog stared wildly at the rough-hewn face.

"Firdaus, who is that?"

"Get inside!" Firdaus repeated. "I can't think if you're not safe."

Frog floated to the cave on the cloud of these words and walked into a wall of frightened people. The cave was a low, deep space, thirty man lengths deep and forty wide, the walls and floors rough and treacherous with sharp knives of rock. Rushlights and candles lit pockets of the big cave, but the only natural light came from the entrance. The ground was too closely packed to allow open fires. They had to spend days inside here? What about air, food, water? It was a death-trap.

She turned. "Firdaus! Is Boon inside?"

"Yes," he bit back.

The last people working on the cave seal went inside, arms full of muddied cloth and smaller rocks. Frog shook herself out of her stupor and started to plug any hole or crack she could find with sand, stones, clothes, seaweed, dung, whatever was at hand in the cramped conditions just behind the hastily erected wall. As they worked, they closed off the light source and an uneasy darkness descended on the nervous mass of people. The heat from all those bodies was already pressing on her neck like a clammy hand.

Firdaus stepped back and slid his hand around her elbow. The matter-of-factness of the intimate gesture pricked her eyes. She blinked. She was safe. Firdaus was safe. Now all they could do was wait.

***

Aranaz caught the gazes of her guards, one by one, forcing down their tremblings and forbidding their longing glances to stray to the door. The mood in the room was changing; she could sense it. The people, the guards, they were slipping from her grasp.

"We stand fast," she said. "We are the brave and the loyal, and our resolve will be rewarded. Stand."

A tremor rattled the throne room. Plaster dust rained down from the ceiling. A beam of light lit the room from above, where no light had ever shone before. She peeled her hands away from the armrests of her chair and hid them under her now limp wrap. She found a hangnail that needed seeing to. Very carefully, so as not to disturb the smooth fabric in her lap, she started to pick at it.

An hour ago, the south corner of the room had collapsed into a great gap, taking a whole group of children and their mothers and nannies with them. The royal children. It didn't feel like a coincidence. That perfidious Firdaus or his traitress daughter Hilm must be behind it, although she couldn't see how. Perhaps armies of white skinned devils had been digging away at the foundations of the city for weeks now. She wouldn't put it past him.

The odor that rose from the hole wasn't so easily ignored. Inch by inch the people had crept away from it, so slowly that she could never catch any of the culprits in the act of moving. The pit was now surrounded by a great swath of empty throne floor. Aranaz wanted to scrub her nose clear of the insidious smell, something sweet and rotten and feminine, as if every woman in the room had started her courses. She knew that if she coughed or rubbed her nose or stood up to stretch her legs everybody would bolt. She owed them her protection. She'd soil her wraps rather than abandon them to their own fears.

A deep phlegmy cough reverberated through the earthen floor. A child wailed. One of her guards' spears tapped out a little tattoo on the floor.

"Stay still," Aranaz hissed. "You're frightening the children."

Another wet, bone-rattling burp. Aranaz floated in the air for a moment and then her chair legs clicked back onto the floor. She swallowed. She thought she'd closed her eyes, but she met the gaze of her chief guard. The whites showed around the black and his teeth chattered.

"They're trying to get us to cede the palace," she said. She nodded. A great notion. She hadn't known until she said it that it must be true.

A soft rushing started up behind her. The cords in Aranaz neck twitched as she forced herself not to look. In the end curiosity won out.

The edges of the cleft in the throne room were softening, crumbling inwards, almost liquefying. The stench boiled out in thick, pink clouds. People coughed and yelled and stood up, against her express orders. It was almost satisfactory to see them stumble and fall.

Her right foot slapped down on the floor. Her whole weight was on that foot now. How could that be? The guard leaned on his spear to keep from falling. Falling how?

Her right buttock slid off the chair, and no matter how much she was determined not to leave the royal dignity of her post, her arms flailed around for purchase. For one teetering, incomprehensible moment, her eyes were level with the high-up window slits and then the pink maw rushed to embrace her.

Aranaz stuffed her hands in her mouth to keep the panicked screech in. She and the hot undulating yawning abyss met in a wet, crunching kiss. She said farewell to the silver sky that shone uncaring through the gaps in the roof. Her eyes closed and her arms folded on her chest as became a dignified Stadholder corpse.

Hard objects punched her, as if she were a piece of beef pounded by a butcher. It wrenched humiliating groans and cries from her. She prayed her subjects and her ancestors would not hear her.

Would they lay her out on a bier and burn her in state? Would there be anybody left to take care of her body?

She could let go now.

A burning heat scorched her belly and her limbs swam and kicked like a frog in boiling water. Every opening in her body widened and screamed in agony. A blinding light enveloped her, and strange sensations raced through her innards. She was falling. No, flying. Her eyes opened and below, her beloved city contorted in its death throes, roofs popping like waternuts in the fire, towers crumbling, strange fires and smokes belching and farting out of inappropriate holes. She looked down into the mouth of the beast.

She rushed towards the sea, but the sea ran away from her. Would she always meet rejection? Soft sand rose up to meet her, turning out to be not soft at all.

The last thing she heard was a snap, like twigs breaking.

***

Hilm halted and looked back at the city. The ground below shook, eerily silent. Hilm counted three heartbeats before the roar arrived. The Singing Tower shivered and then folded gently to one side, sliding down on itself, disappearing into bulging mushrooms of smoke. The Palace Stacks, strangely symmetrical, still held, but where was the top saucer? A cloud of dust began to roil over the red roofs. Chunks of white city rock fell down and slid into the sea, churning into a white and green rosette. The sound arrived with a rumble that made her belly ache.

"Are we stopping?" Gül said.

"No. Go. We have to run faster. The dragon is coming."

Hilm's feet bled and her thighs felt like sacks of rice. They had to be close. The noon light glared down on them, the heat like a millstone. The baby in her arms, wailing for milk and a change, kept slipping down her exhausted belly.

There. The villa.

The world tilted and smashed her against the rock. The children cried harder.

She forced herself upright and walked on. She pushed Heike. "Walk on! We're almost there."

"I can see the villa!" Giovanni's flute thin voice called from ahead. "I can see it."

Hilm's head craned back, as if forced by unseen hands.

A plume of pink pointed into the air straight above the seething, swirling hole where a moment ago the city had stood. The sea rushed in, a boom of sound reached her.

"Run!" she screamed. "Run!"

Her aching legs pistoned up faster, fueled by fear. She bent down, scooped up another toddler in her free arm and ran, no longer checking if the child clinging to her skirts could keep up. She passed Gül, Heike, Bao.

"Faster, children, faster."

There, the villa. Someone held the door for them. Hilm fell inside, cool marble against her hot and aching knees, shoved one, two three, four children in waiting arms, turned back to check if Giovanni was inside too. The heat and the ominous booming outside where like a wall keeping her inside the cool safety of the villa.

Three more.

"Help me get the children!" she yelled to the people behind her.

She ran back to Gül, grabbed the baby from the girls' arm. "Grab my hand!" She sprinted back, Gül's body trailing like a scarf from her hand. Seven down, one to go. Where was the last little one?

There, Awayo, at least a hundred yards away still. His fat little legs tottered over the heaps of rocks, his face smeared with black dust and tears, his arms held out for an adult to pick him up. The pink cloud overhead lunged closer, spreading with frightening speed, the reverberation of rocks and rushing sea receding so she only heard Awayo's sobs.

Hands pulled at her. "Stay inside!"

She fought to get back out. "No, no, my little brother, I have to get him."

"Too late," a blunt male voice said. "Look. I'm closing the door now, with or without you."

CHAPTER 29

Firdaus figured it had to be day, because a vague gray ambience hung about the cave that made it possible to light fewer lamps. The half-light picked up the whites of eyes and the flash of teeth, a drop of moisture on a white Wan arm. Humps of people in tightly rolled cloaks were nearly indistinguishable from the boulders that lay scattered through the cave.

"When do we leave, my Lord?"

"Soon," he answered.

"My Lord, how long? My daughter is crying."

He was hot and clammy with sweat, so that every speck of dirt clung to him.

"I wanna go home!" A little girl cannoned into him and clung to his thighs. Her cloud-soft hair tickled his knees, a fat cheek coated with snot kissed his hand.

Rushlight flickered over towering antlers. Haroon. Firdaus couldn't believe he was looking forward to seeing the singer, in this sea of humanity churning with petty strife and fear.

"Haroon. Just the man I wanted to see."

"Firdaus! You changed your mind about that promise, I bet!"

Firdaus was flummoxed for a second before he remembered the promise he'd tossed Haroon's way. He chuckled to cover his embarrassment. "Not now, for the love of prophet, Haroon! It's crowded and smelly in there, and I wouldn't be able to enjoy your beauty the way it deserves."

"Good save," Haroon said. "Don't sweat it, little Firdi, I won't hold you to it. Got plenty of women hanging around you already, don't you?"

"If you're talking about my daughter, you dirty minded bastard, hands and mouth off her."

"I've been talking to your son," Haroon said with a snicker.

Firdaus clenched his hands into fists, but willed them to relax. "A little young for you, maybe?" he said.

"Not to worry, I'm just baiting you. Go on. No need to be polite to me. Sow concord and peace with your deep voice and your big feet planted firmly on the earth."

"Actually," Firdaus said, "I have an idea."

Twenty minutes later, he leaned back into Frog's arms and rested his weary head on her soft bosom. The melodious strands of one the city's oldest lays drifted over them, and the angry buzzy undertone of the voices in the cave quieted to the occasional murmur. Everybody knew this music, and if Haroon would stick to his promise to lay off the incendiary verse or bawdy ballads, all would be well for a while.

Until they could leave the cave, and then the real problems would begin.

Firdaus woke up with his face in something filthy and a searing, pulsing pain leaping from his right shoulder down his spine. No—not pain. A damage signal. He rolled over and burnt his hand on glowing coals. Prophet. Where was he?

Someone screamed and for two whole seconds he was fumbling on the wrong shelf for the voice's identity. Then the memory slammed back. The cave.

"Help!" someone bellowed. "To me! To me!"

Firdaus cursed the darkness that prevented him from doing anything. His hand stung and he remembered the fire he'd almost rolled into. He grabbed the nearest person and snarled at him to rake up the fire.

"Fire! Rake up your fires! Light your lamps! I need to see what is happening!"

Gratifyingly quick, light sprang up all over the caves, but it wasn't as effective as he'd hoped. The darkness was now dotted with reddish islands of light, but it made the blackness between seem deeper and more impenetrable.

A bloodcurdling sound exploded from someone's throat, a man's death scream.

"Help! It's killing me! The monster killed my friend! Aaargh!"

The darkness was like an enemy, preventing him from doing anything. He plodded as fast as he dared towards the sound, head thrust forward, hands out in case he stumbled into a stalactite or over a sleeping child, blind and helpless as a mole.

***

Why were her hands full of ripped-up clay-soaked cloth? Hadn't she been putting it in the cracks before? Frog shook her head to clear it, but the chaos inside had infected even her perception. Her mind's eye flickered with flames and screams, spikes of red and searing hot sounds.

Someone grabbed her mental withers. Right. She had to put the cloth back in the cracks. Why had she taken it out in the first place? Those people were screaming because the spores had managed to come in, and she was helping to stop it. Right?

Again she found herself pulling the stuffing out instead of in.

What the hell was going on? No wonder everything flickered, she was losing time. She better think fast, before the compulsion or whatever it was took hold again. It was just like in the saucer, a moment of inattention and her fingers went gallivanting off, doing exactly the wrong things.

Ing. It must be Ing. Frog had never had weird thoughts or murderous impulses. It was all Ing.

The hell it was, her thoughts bit back. "I'm no fluffy lamb, but why would I kill the people I was trying to save?"

"Then who is it?"

The thoughts slithered and roiled. Frog dove after them and wrestled them to the ground. "Who?"

A white mound, like a ripe pustule on terracotta skin. The Queen. Of course. The Mound Queen had fed Ing suggestions too strong to resist.

"No, no, she's my ally. What would she gain by killing people? Mother Doughy is her enemy."

"I don't know why. Does it matter? We need to cast those thoughts out!"

During the exchange, Frog's legs had walked themselves back to the compromised outer wall. If she could have stopped the subversive acts by ripping her head off she would have. This couldn't be happening. She'd finally seen love in Firdaus' eyes, and now all would be lost because she was the cause of the screaming and the flames in the background. She'd just crawl into a corner and die.

"No!" the voice in her head said. "Stop whining. You didn't give up before. Help me get rid of her."

"How? I put the bad thoughts in a pinkie, but they're still here."

"Right idea, but you have to think bigger. Maybe a whole arm or leg."

Frog wailed silently. Not her arms! She'd worked so hard to get them back to normal. "Okay. Show me how to do it."

***

"Help me! Where are they?" Firdaus yelled, and helpful hands took his and pushed him in the right direction.

A spray of something warm hit his face and another shriek curdled the fetid air.

Silence fell. Firdaus kept blinking as if that would help him see better.

The caterwauling was getting louder and more panicked as he ducked under a particularly nasty row of stalactites. He hastened as much as he could, navigating in this warren of humps that might be people or bales of grain lit by flickering fires or rushlights, spears of rocks ready to pierce his guts at every step.

"Help! Help! It's eating him!"

Grisly suspicion gripped him in the balls and stopped him in his tracks. This could only mean one thing. Spores had gotten inside somehow and were rampaging through his people. But how?

Firdaus turned his head and bellowed into the darkness. "Doughyson! Come over here, we need you!"

He forced himself to go on. His skin shuddered with revulsion and fear. This was a danger to Wan and humans alike. He had no idea how to fight a spore. How big was it, for example? Would he be able to see it?

A fleeing man crashed into him and almost caused him to tumble onto a nearby family and their dung fire.

"Stop!" he called out after the man. "Tell me what's happening!"

"Something is eating that man, something inside him!"

The man stumbled, saved himself by windmilling, and ran on, sobbing, into the darkness, out of Firdaus' sight.

Firdaus shuffled on as fast as he could, hands out before him, cursing the darkness and his own reliance on glowapples. A vine would take weeks to grow from a seed; his people would be long gone by then. Or dead. There had to be a solution that worked better than the pitiful rushlights. Only nobody had taken the trouble to find one because their houses and workshops were always lit by the Ancestors' glowing fruit.

Someone cannoned into him, then another, and he leaned into the stream of people like into a gale. He grabbed the next person trying to pass him.

"What's happening? Tell me!"

"It's eating us! It's horrible, don't you hear them screaming? We've got to save ourselves, let me go!" The man writhed to get away from him. "Please, sire, be merciful. Let me have my life!"

Firdaus clasped the man firmer. "Start at the beginning. What happened?"

"We heard a whoosh and Salim went over to have a look. And then they got into his eyes, and he started screaming and kicking his legs and peeing himself... his brother tried to help him, but then his own cheeks got itchy, and my cousin Vinnie tore out his own hair..."

"Firdaus," Doughyson's voice said from behind him.

It had never been more welcome. "Doughyson! Did you hear what he said? Is it the spores? What can we do?"

"We have to burn the victims, and everyone who was standing around, and all their stuff. There is no time to lose."

Without waiting for his permission, Doughyson stooped to pick up a fire basket and proceeded in the direction of the screaming.

"You," Firdaus said to the trembling man. "Pick up a lamp and some flammable stuff. We're going to help your family."

The man obeyed, shaking, but apparently relieved to be told what to do. Firdaus echoed the man's relief. Without Doughyson, he wouldn't have known what to do.

The shouts and sounds of a tussle were coming closer.

"Stop the creature! Kill it! Burn it!" he heard. He was sure they meant Doughyson.

"Stop in the name of the Stadholder!" he roared with his best bellow, but his voice was hoarse from overuse and the close, smoky air smothered his great shouts.

"Help the Ghast! Help my friend and ally Doughyson! He will save you all!"

Flames shot up, licked the roof and added another reek to the already laden air. Firdaus elbowed his way through the heaving throng of people who were yelling at something in their midst.

"Get away from here!" he yelled. "Stay only if you saw what happened!"

That was the bad part about being a king. Sometimes you had to sacrifice the few to save the many.

He forced his way inside.

Doughyson's silhouette was limned against rising flames in all its blocky lumpiness. The screams crescendoed when he tossed a young man onto the fire. The Ghast must be immensely strong. Firdaus found a scrawny young woman frantically scratching her bare arms bloody, and with a quick prayer to the Ancestors he set fire to her hair and dry grass skirt.

Fidaus was about to heave a shrieking old lady into the fire, when Doughyson laid a paw on his arm.

"This one I can save," Doughyson said.

Doughyson grabbed the woman's pulsating arm, pocked with craters spraying blood, and bent his lips to it. The woman screamed and tried to wriggle out of the Ghast's grasp, but Doughyson held her as if she weighed nothing. His mouth curled over the woman's elbow and sucked the arm in.

Firdaus' jaw dropped. The woman's scrawny hand disappeared further and further into Doughyson's mouth, as if he had a gullet as wide as a bucket that went straight down into his stomach. Doughyson's rubbery lips stretched farther than humanly possible, like a snake swallowing a prey bigger than himself, and engulfed her arm. The screaming woman fainted, Firdaus didn't know whether from pain or relief, and Doughyson gently released her from his mouth. The arm looked gray and bloodless for a second, then went bright pink as blood rushed back in. Dark blood pooled in the pocks on her upper arm, and the whole skin looked as if pricked with a thousand little needles.

Firdaus turned away from the old woman when her relatives found enough courage to take her from Doughyson. She'd live, or not, but it was good to see a Ghast active in such a positive way. Where was Frog? Undoubtedly saving mud people left and right.

He went on methodically torching stacks of possessions, meager or rich, pausing only to snap commands. Haul more water, soak the bystanders.

The fire roared, people screamed in the writhing flames, hair singed and fat burned. But Doughyson had done a good job; the alcove was completely sealed in by flames, and everyone and everything inside burned.

Firdaus stomped out sparks, hauled up crying children, and checked them for damage. He tossed a beautiful little girl into the fire; the right half of her head had been completely eaten away. She didn't utter a sound as the flames consumed her.

When he let her go from his hands, it was as if he was sacrificing his own Gül or Heike or Hilm. Curse the day he became Stadholder, and took responsibilities for the lives of other men's children.

CHAPTER 30

"Nothing works. I can't do it," Frog said.

"I can see that. And besides, you don't have what it takes. Poor brave Frog sacrificed a whole pinkie... that must have hurt sooo badly..."

"What are you proposing, then?"

Ing's thoughts felt gritty and forced, as if she was thinking through grinding teeth. "She's too alien. Her thoughts don't work like ours. It's all we can do to keep it together with the two of us."

The Mound Queen's commands didn't use words or images, or even something as recognizable as smell or touch. Her suggestions seeped like noxious marsh gases through and under her feelings, subtly changing them. Fetid mud crept through the foundations of her mind, thoughtful, malicious mud with questing tendrils that rotted everything they touched.

Frog's arm flailed out of her control and jerked her whole body in the direction of the stone bulwark closing off the cave. Frog clamped her other hand over the deserter arm and jammed the twitching limb into a fissure. Anything to keep herself under control.

"What if I just break off the arm?"

"We're not going to be able to drive the Mound Queen into an arm."

"What, then?"

The black rock surrounding her magnified the screams and the crackle of burning human flesh, a background chorus that threatened to overwhelm all rational thought.

"I'll do it. I'll be the glue that holds the Mound Queen

parts together," Ing said. "I'll push her and myself into a tight space and it's your job to get rid of that part. Can you do that? Rip it off and burn it?"

"What part?" Frog asked. Ing had taken an arm and a breast from her last time. This was sure to be worse.

"I don't want to say it, slowpoke. If you know it in advance, so will she. So can you do it?"

Frog pictured herself strong as wood, sharp like stone. "I know it won't hurt, but still. But what about you? What will happen to you?"

"Could be I'm signing my own death warrant. Feel lucky, sister Frog, coz I'm putting humanity first. Here goes. Goodbye."

Frog started and grasped after Ing's dwindling thoughts. Too soon. How would she know when to act? The arm she'd jammed into the crevice slid away from the rock face. It had shrunk itself until it was no longer stuck. Now what? She grew the arm back to normal size, her mind casting about for a sign of either Ing or the Mound Queen.

Her stomach burbled. Her intestines knotted and her distracted mind had her walking towards the latrine pit before she grabbed hold of herself. She didn't have guts any more. This must be a sign of battle. She should be thinking ahead, preparing. Her thoughts felt sluggish and dull. She sensed no trace of Ing's decisive conclusions, they way she plucked facts out of thin air. This was just Frog, who found thinking hard.

She had to be ready to destroy part of herself. The answer was all around her: fire. Firdaus was silhouetted against flickering orange flames for a moment, wrestling a body into the huge fire roaring in the middle of the cave. A good thing some air had gotten in with the spores, although fire would be eating through it in no time. Hey. That was Ing knowledge. She hadn't lost it all. That was good, because she'd be of limited use to Firdaus without Ing's stores of science and history.

An ironwood band squeezed around her ribs. Frog fell to her knees. She couldn't pay any attention to the battle raging in her body; she had to get to a fire. Not the big one, a small one, preferably abandoned.

Her chest burned and fists stomped through her skin from the inside out. Her muscles spasmed and she lost control of her knees and hands, falling flat on her face. Now the internal fight reached her throat. Somebody squeezed her windpipe shut, strangling her, mangling her. She scrabbled at her throat, even while she knew it was futile. No one was here except herself. The crackling fire and panicked shouts receded to the background. All she heard was her labored breathing, the fluting and roaring in her ears, the moans coming from somewhere down her belly. Right. She didn't have lungs; she didn't need breath. As long has she held that thought firmly in her mind nothing would happen to her. There, the fire.

A splitting headache hacked through her thoughts, scattering them around like a flock of birds startled into flight. Squeezed into her skull, the fight seemed twice as intense as it had before. Her skull? Her head? Ing meant to drive the Queen Mound into her head?

That was insane. She couldn't do that. Nobody could rip their own head off their neck! But it was her signal. She had to act now. If she didn't do it, everybody she loved, well, Firdaus, would die. She would die too. Ing was already dead. She had to act. Now.

Frog watched her hands rise to her neck once more, slower than she wanted, but her frantic commands didn't seem to reach them anymore. The lethargic hands reached her throat, lengthened to encompass her neck and twisted.

Noo! Frog screamed from a thousand openings on her skin. She couldn't do it. It was too much like suicide. She lived behind her eyes. It wouldn't work, without her head, she'd be dead as well. Her hands inexorably went on twisting.

A snap like a tree breaking.

A blindfold wrapped around her eyes, her ears went silent, her tongue froze. Her hair floated into space, no longer attached to her head.

Something heavy landed in her lap. She groped for it. She still had hands; they still gave her sensations. She was alive. The blindfold changed into a gauze bandage, like a mist before her eyes. Where was that fire? That orange spot in the mist must be it. She cradled the heavy round thing under her arm, but changed her mind as it grew hundreds of little mouths that sucked and gnawed at her. Rolling would be a much better idea; so her hands only had the briefest of contacts with it. She'd need better eyes for that. Her eyesight sharpened and her point of view rose higher until it seemed she looked at the white floss-haired ball on the ground from a normal height. Everything was white and black now, even the fire. Funny how fire was gray. So counter-intuitive.

The white hair flailed around and grasped at every crevice and pebble it encountered, but the hands, her own hands, she supposed, firmly tapped it forward and corrected its willful swerving. There, the fire.

Frog pushed herself up with her hands, everything different, no balance, and when she felt steady enough, she grasped the squirming, twisting head in both hands and tossed it onto the fire. Dozens of little mouths opened on the face, the neck, shrieking like teakettles. The almond eyes, so white and black against the stone color of the face, stared at her with silent reproof. Frog swallowed in her new throat, she didn't want to check where it was exactly. She'd look worse than when Ing had torn her arm off. Thank the Ancestors for the darkness surrounding the flickering flames.

She poked her thoughts from all sides, but she couldn't find any trace of the Mound Queen or Ing. Good. Probably good.

The fire ate up the hair in a big whoosh, no stink though. Where were all the smells? The fire licked at the cheeks a long time before they began to blister and char. The eyes leaked moisture, and remained lustrous and sad for a long time while the face around it blackened and fell apart. Finally, the eyes caught the edges of the fire and Frog watched them dull and shrivel and fall to ash.

***

When everyone had settled down into exhausted

sleep, Firdaus still stood. He kept hearing the screaming baby, saw the half-eaten faces. He would never sleep again. His heart was bruised and sore. Killing babies, toddlers, what had he become? Killing the Ghast army had been exhausting work, but there had never been any doubt that he was doing the right thing. This was different. Even the conviction that without his actions everybody would have died didn't help the smear of foulness on his soul.

Someone walked into him and grabbed between his legs. In spite of the inky darkness, he knew it was Frog by her clove scent, the cool powdery feel of her skin. His spine arched and his hands sought blindly for flesh to squeeze. He needed to forget where and who he was, what he had done. Frog would help him.

She pushed him up against the wall, lips and hands greedily seeking and finding his most sensitive spots. Firdaus cast about for a place to lie down, but the cave had no free horizontal space. He grabbed her upper arms and twisted them around, pushing her back up against the wall, forcing her pelvis high enough to receive him. Yes. This was exactly what he needed to forget.

Frog crooned strings of syllables at him, nonsense words and love words and bedsport words, like pearls dipped in wine to strengthen the taste. Her words sounded a little mushy as if she'd bitten on her tongue.

"You're my lover. You lifted me up, I'm a Stadholder lover now, Firdaus lover, I love you so much, I will love you always serve you always bear you children love me hard, Firdaus, love me more..."

Firdaus did not speak. His rod and his quivering thighs were doing the speaking for him, slipsliding them to a frantic peak, hurrying to finish before someone disturbed them.

Frog yodeled at the pinnacle of her joy, so Firdaus felt free to let the reins slip and follow her. She slid off him and he leaned into her warm neck, recuperating, waiting until his legs would hold him again without the support of a wall.

Frog lifted shining eyes to him. "My Stadholder."

Yes, he was. It felt right when she said that. Not like the old Frog, humble and craving the smallest drop of his approval. The new Frog was his equal.

"Frog," he said slowly, trying to find the right words, "I'm so happy that I met you again. I think you will be a great help to me, with your strength and your spirit and Ing's knowledge. But you know you aren't beholden to me anymore, do you? You are free to go and love whoever you choose."

Her eyes shone as big as raindrops in the monsoon season, catching the scant light like little mirrors. She looked shiny and new and supple all over, like a just-laid egg. "But I choose you."

They fell asleep together.

***

Frog eased out from under Firdaus' heavy arm and groped for free space on the rough rock of the cave floor. A light flared. The strange Ghast that had been hanging around Firdaus lit her way.

"Thank you," she said. Her tongue still felt a bit new and stiff. She wished she had a mirror, so she could check her new-grown head.

"My pleasure. Tell me, how did you come to be? Did you think you could hide the aroma of the Queen Mound from me?"

"What?" Frog said. Would it never end? The new world was full of love, but it was heavy all the same.

"You are not all of Mother Doughy's flesh. Almost half of you is other. You did not succeed in killing all of it."

"I don't know what you're talking about. Nobody sent me. I belong to Firdaus. He made me his servant."

"He turned you?" the voice like a rock fall said.

"No, that was Ing. But he was kind to me."

"And how did you become commingled like this?"

"I don't know what you mean. I ate pieces of a few Ghast, I hope you don't mind my saying that. And I ate the remnants of Ing."

"Ah!" it said. "That explains it. Are you aware that Ing was following the Queen Mound's suggestions? That you might have eaten those poems?"

Frog shuddered. She couldn't be more aware of that fact. She thought she'd successfully vanquished the Queen Mound's commands, and Ing's ghost with it, and nobody the wiser. She didn't want this Ghast to see through her. She was loyal to Firdaus. It had no right to doubt her.

"No! I would never do that."

The pale round eyes regarded her without blinking. "I will keep my skin alert to any whiff of treachery from you. Stadholder Firdaus is my ally. Humans are under my protection."

This creature was nothing like the walking Ghast she'd spoken to out in the Maze. The force and weight of its personality were like the rock hemming her in. Did it think she had other loyalties? It was very wrong then.

"Who are you?" she whispered.

It didn't answer for a long time.

"Who is it that wants to know?" it asked at last, its regard still unwavering, boring into her, about to touch all her secret shames and fears.

"Frog," she said proudly and lifted her chin: she would not give in to a Ghast, no matter how old and wise. She was the companion to the Stadholder, and it couldn't harm her.

"Give me a taste of you," it ordered.

The words popped out of her mouth before she could think about it. "Tell me how to make a person. A walker."

"A taste first."

Frog broke off her finger and dropped it in the outstretched hand.

The thing popped it into its mouth without chewing and closed its eyes for a moment, as if to savor the morsel.

"Frog. I taste you now. Your flesh is under your control alone," it said. "I will bother you no more."

"Tell me."

"After this is over. You must promise to help me take root."

Frog didn't have to think about that one. "I promise. What's your name?"

"Firdaus gave me one. I'm called Doughyson."

Frog swallowed. She wanted a taste of Doughyson in return. "Give me a piece of you," she said and held out her hand.

"Of course, child. You were made by one of mine originally. See to it that the taint of Ing doesn't spoil your lovely meat."

Frog nodded obediently and opened wide when the thing broke off a knob from its forehead and fed it to her. The essence of something much wiser and older than she was stilled her fear instantly and she crawled back under Firdaus' arm to sleep.

Doughyson's voice woke her up. "Firdaus. Wake up." He shook Firdaus' shoulder.

Firdaus shot up, bumped his head against Frog's elbow, rolled against the rice bale mountain. "What? How long did I sleep?"

"Ten thousand heartbeats, no more. We can go outside now, Stadholder. It's over."

They pushed out the rocks at eye-height, the ones that had been put in last. The mud hadn't even had time to harden. Firdaus crawled out first, as the leader must, to see if it was truly safe for his people. Frog followed on his heels. The bright daylight hurt after the single endless night of the cave. She swayed on wobbly legs, a newborn chick coming out of its warm egg into a harsh world.

CHAPTER 31

Firdaus' first glance found a slice of beach and rock and sky. It didn't seem changed. The craggy cliff and the beach were still black, the waves breaking against the shore still white-capped. He looked closer, taking a few steps forward to check his perception. Under his foot, a white worm wiggled and bit at his sole with a wet urgent mouth. He bent over and tore it loose. He wanted to throw it away, then remembered who he was and ate the tiny creature.

It tasted of nothing. It had no experience or knowledge to impart. It was just food.

The whiteness on the water he'd taken for foam was a teeming mass of tiny wormlets like the one he'd swallowed, crawling and writhing in mindless hunger. He'd better not step into the water. The seas would be like this all over the world, wherever the wind had taken the spores of what had been Mother Doughy and the other mounds.

Maybe the animals that were able to flee to the deepest deeps of the ocean could have survived, but he knew that behemoths needed air every hour or so. There would be none left. He should have ordered the fishermen to catch a breeding pair and taken it into the cave. Same for the halal fish, the prawn, the wild birds. He'd only thought of his domesticated animals, but how would the people live now that the danger was over? Bees, to fertilize the fruit trees and plants. Bugs for the chickens and ducks to eat.

They were doomed. And he could tell no one.

He composed his face and turned toward the cave to wave out Doughyson. He'd told the Wan to go first, to show the people that it truly was safe outside now.

Doughyson came, and then Haroon and the ten other Wan who'd sheltered in this particular cave.

The emptiness of the beach sprung into sharp relief. There should have been boats. The saucer had floated right here when they'd gone in. There was nothing except the unchanging boom of the sea and the clouds glaring down on them. Gulls screeching. Gulls! At least some birds had survived.

The makeshift wall that had sealed the cave for the past few days—a week?—tumbled down, rumbling like Doughyson's voice.

People came out, stumbling on cramped legs, blinking against the brightness of the day, clutching children and chickens and beloved possessions. Firdaus looked up and down the beach. Not all the cave entrances were in his view, but so far they were the only ones to come outside.

He needed to find Hilm and her brothers and sisters. His stomach churned with dread. Had he made the wrong choice? Should he have stuck with his babies and left his people to fend for themselves? No, duty went before family. He had made the choice before he realized what he'd done, and maybe it was better like this. The youngest children would forget him. Ayodele and Gül wouldn't.

This was why Stadholders had Assemblies and Guilds. A city was simply too big to rule on one's own.

Frog came up to him and squeezed his arm. "Go find your children. The babies must miss you. What needs to be done here, Firdaus? Do you want me to find Boon?"

Firdaus straightened. Frog understood him. Strengthened, he issued orders to open up the other caves, to find the boats, to set guards against the teeming sea of white worms. He collected a dozen strong young men to escort him up to the villa, where he hoped to find Hilm and his other children. He prayed they'd gotten away in time.

The group climbed the stairs, two temporary bodyguards in front, two in back, and two on each side of Firdaus. Besides his children, he might find his sister. Aranaz wouldn't give up her throne so easily, and would have been plotting for all eventualities once the danger was over.

Halfway up the steps, he gazed to his left, from habit, checking out his city. He wished he hadn't. Where once the gleaming Stack Palace and the Singing Tower had stood, towering above the red roofs of the white-walled houses, a pool of muddy water churned. The sea had filled the vacuum Mother Doughy's passing had left behind.

Hilm came limping down the stairs, blinking in the sharp white light that beamed down on the devastated beach. Her face was gray, her arms and legs covered with bruises and scabbed-over scrapes.

How fragile a human being was, and how lucky he was to still have her. He embraced her carefully, trying not to touch her poor tender skin.

"We are alive, dearest. Let us thank the Ancestors for that."

Hilm clung to his hand, filthier and more disheveled than he'd seen her since she'd left her tomboy years behind. Her whole body trembled and her eyes were swollen with crying.

"I'm so sorry, Abba," she said. "I failed you so badly."

"What do you mean, honeyheart?"

She fell into his arms and sobbed out loud. "I didn't get them all out, Abba. I tried, I really tried, but their little legs couldn't run fast enough, and I carried them, but Awayo... Awayo was the last and I..."

His eyes misted over and he grabbed Hilm's arm so hard she yelled.

"Awayo is dead? What—how?"

Firdaus' legs refused to bear his weight and he smacked down hard on his knees. A cry tore its way out of his chest.

Awayo, his baby. He could have borne a child's death by misfortune or disease, but being eaten by mindless worms?

"How dare you kill them? How dare you!" he shouted and slammed down his hands on the rock floor. Why couldn't he feel pain, prophet it? He needed to feel his hands hurt to dull the other pain. His ribs heaved and he couldn't catch his breath.

Hilm sobbed uncontrollably, so he forced the question down. He stood up and concentrated on patting her back and keeping his breathing even. "It's all right, baby. It's all right."

Hilm calmed down a little and lifted her chin up to him, determined to tell it all. Firdaus didn't want to hear it, but he knew he had to. He wished he hadn't left Frog on the beach.

"No, it's not all right. Don't forgive me so easily, Abba, wait until I've said it all. Hanako wouldn't leave the palace. So that's Waalo. And then I thought I'd found all of them, but Ichiro was never there. Gül doesn't have a brother anymore."

Hilm's face swam before him. Three of his babies dead. He couldn't bear a loss like that. He just couldn't. He swallowed down his anger. Hilm hung her head before him, devastated. She wasn't to blame. He'd love to blame someone, anyone, but not his brave daughter. He folded her back in his arms and kissed the top of her head. "You've done well, my dear. Later you can tell me how you managed to save so many of your brothers and sisters, but now I want to find them."

Firdaus started climbing again. He heard children's voices from above. His legs tingled with eagerness to find his children and he sped up. Gül, Heike, Osama, Giovanni, Yun, Bao, Hussein. The human bodyguards and battered Hilm struggled to keep up, but he couldn't wait for them.

He leapt up the last few steps and stopped, stunned. On a bier lay two little bodies. He couldn't help checking their faces, although he knew no trace would remain of his poor babies.

"My Lord!" his old Assembly ally, Midwife Meena, stammered. "Your children are inside. These little ones starved."

They should be burned. He wouldn't have to burn his own children. Was that mercy or another load? Bare feet ran up to him and slaps rained down on his shoulders. A woman he didn't recognize.

"It's your fault!" she screeched. "Your fault! You destroyed the city!"

He grabbed her flailing hands. "Good woman. No one is sorrier than I am about that. But I am not to blame."

"Aranaz said you made it happen," the woman sobbed. "To become Stadholder again, to make the people turn to you in their fear. And now she's dead because she stayed behind so bravely."

Aranaz was dead? Of course. Hilm told him she'd stayed behind, but his brain was lagging behind the real world, it seemed. He took a deep breath. So. He was Stadholder once more, albeit without a city. Maybe someday he would care about it again.

"Where are my children?" he said.

Gül slunk into his arms within a heartbeat. She'd hung back, waiting for him to notice her, as always.

"Thank you, darling, for looking after the little ones. You're a sweet girl."

Gül hiccupped. "I'm sorry, Abba. I didn't look after Ichiro properly. Are you mad at me?"

"It's not your fault, sweetheart."

He rose, still holding on to Gül. His knees creaked and his head pounded. Wan didn't grow old, did they? Too bad they could feel grief. He stared at the gray sky over the head of the faceless servants clustering around him.

He would have to grieve for his children later, longer.

He found the once round, but now heavily drooping face of the First Farmer. "My good Acamad. I need to you gather men and..." He swayed. Someone gave him a clay cup of water. "All of you, Assembly members, Hilm. Go forth and help my people. I need a moment with my children."

***

Frog pivoted on her heels, surveying the beach. The black sand was speckled with bedraggled, dirty people who sat around and stared into nothing. Scattered among them were odd remnants of the city, half a roof, a doorway with the bead curtain still in it, a miraculously unbroken pot, the back of a chair, reminders of the awesome powers unleashed by Mother Doughy's demise. A few Assembly members in limp silk scarves were rounding people up and giving them tasks, so she trudged through the deep sands to the next cave around the crag.

The sight that unfolded before her was like an old war movie. The cave seal lay broken before the entrance, and the cave floor and the beach were covered with remnants of people. Some of them were half eaten up; others were still alive, screaming, shapes moving under their skins. A whole cave fallen to the Mound seed. How many would there be? Hundreds, probably. Vital skills lost, genetic diversity endangered. A few men were building a fire and tossing the remains on it. The stench and the smoke made her gag, but she remembered that this was the way the meat always smelled at Midwinter. Like roasting goat. That must be hard on the humans. When she got downwind of the fire, she smelled another rank odor. The gagging sweetness of putrefaction. The seeds must have gotten in days ago if the bodies were this far gone.

She covered her mouth with the remnants of her shoulder cape and walked past, head turned away from the heavily smoking bonfire. Should she tell them to stop the burning? Precious fuel was being wasted. Oil would become a scarce commodity soon. She knew they wouldn't listen to her. Yet.

She found the saucer section bobbing on the waves of the next beach, and Boon sitting on the straw-packed bales that held Ing's stuff. He threw himself in her arms and cried. His standoffishness was apparently a thing of the past. "What's the matter, Boon?"

"I was all alone and everyone was mean and yelled to me and they were fighting all the time..."

"Yeah. That's what happens when people are frightened and have nowhere to go. Come with me, your abba is up at the villa."

Boon hiccupped against her belly. "Are Gül and Hilm okay? And the others?"

Frog swallowed. "Hilm is fine. Come with me."

Together, she and Boon once more ascended the steps

to the villa. Firdaus, surrounded by mud people she didn't know, was busy giving commands, creating order in the devastated world. A green-eyed little girl clung white-faced to his thighs.

Firdaus drew Frog beside him. "Frog. May I introduce you to Gül? She's a very brave little girl who has lost her mother. Gül, this is Frog. You must look after her now, because Frog doesn't know anyone and feels very shy. Can you do that?"

Gül lifted her grubby face up to Frog and nodded. A hot little hand slipped into Frog's and just like that, a pact was sealed.

***

Firdaus smiled. "Come, Frog, I need you."

"I'm here," she said.

He drew her to the edge of the cliff, apart from the servants fussing around. Gül followed silently.

"Frog. I need your Ing thoughts. What do we do? How will we live? We saved seed grain, we saved our livestock. But what will they eat? What will grow in the marshes?"

"The haram species of plants must evolve from the spores, like the paradiles," she said, her voice trembling with the strain of dealing with the data without Ing's personality as glue. "The halal seed grains will be mixed with other seeds from wild plants, they always are. I told people to bring cuttings and clumps of reeds. They will multiply over the years."

He sighed. "I hadn't thought about wild seeds among the grain. But we never took all the plants with us, did we."

"No. We can only hope that bits of roots and buried seeds survived. I'll ask your Ghast if he knows."

He smiled when Frog stood taller and he hooked his arm through hers. "Together, eh, Frog?"

She nodded and squeezed his arm hard.

"What will we do? How can we ever feed the population?"

He could see the ghost of Ing in her eyes as the words tumbled out at once. "We could Wan a group of the population," she said. "The women too old to bear children, whose wisdom we need. Men who have fathered enough children, who are wise and strong."

Hilm ambled over to him, Heike and Osama clinging to her hands. Firdaus kissed them again, assured them again that he wasn't going anywhere. He foresaw many repetitions of this in the future. Hilm looked down on the beach, swinging her head to the right to where the city was.

His eyes misted over and he grabbed Hilm's arm so hard she squeaked. They gazed at the emptiness that had once held their city. When his eyes looked beyond, where normally the green haze of the Marsh hovered, his eyes found nothing but glittering water and dark brown devastation. Several men in the bodyguard cried openly.

"What will become of us, sire?" one of them asked. "Where will we live? What will we live off?"

"We will rebuild. We will replant our crops," Firdaus said. "We will work together and we will survive this."

The man nodded. "Yes. But how?"

"We brought seeds for new crops. But there are hard times ahead, my friends, never doubt that. We must all work together to secure our future."

A ragged cheer broke out among the gathered people. "Stadholder Firdaus! All hail Stadholder Firdaus! Savior!"

Firdaus swallowed. They remembered their love for him again, called him Stadholder, even with his white skin and white hair. He bowed to his subjects, and then turned back to his family.

He checked Hilm's face. A little frown marred the umber skin between her brows, but she squeezed his arm reassuringly. "Don't worry, Abba. You deserve to take the throne back."

EPILOGUE

The orange and black speckled mud steamed gently in the midday heat.

Doughyson halted his shuffling. "This is a good spot," he said. "Running water, but not too deep or too fast. Cloudshine in the morning, shade in the afternoon. My toes are liking the taste of the mud, it has many layers of interest."

Frog could see very little difference from the other sites they'd been looking at all morning. The cloudlight glinted off flat sheets of shallow water, and every sound was distorted and magnified by the heat and the mud lake's mirror surface.

"Firdaus, Assemblymen, what do you think?" she asked.

Meena Midwife, now First Assemblywoman, nodded gravely. "An excellent location, Doughyson, I commend you on your choice. Within easy walking distance of the new town, but not too close."

Frog swiped a bit of mud on her finger. "I perceive now what you mean, Doughyson. I haven't tasted a better spot all day."

"Then I shall proceed," Doughyson said. He tossed away the loincloth he wore as a nod to human modesty, and waded into the mud. He'd gained enormous amounts of weight in the weeks since the cataclysm; he was almost wider than he was tall and could only waddle instead of walk. His growing girth was a bitter inversion of the weight-loss that plagued the humans. It was a good thing he was leaving the new settlement.

Doughyson's thick white thighs, smoother now than

when he'd first been made, stirred wide ripples in the sluggish mud. At ten paces or so from the shore, he turned and met the eyes of the politely waiting troop of humans.

"Well, Firdaus. Here I will take root. I thank you for your kindness and instruction. Perhaps you and Frog will one day follow my example, hey?"

"Take root?" Firdaus shook his head. "I'm feeling much too walkerish yet, Doughyson. I want to see my children grow up, I want grandchildren."

Hilm coughed. Everyone knew she was pregnant, but she was trying to keep it hidden behind voluminous, if tattered, robes.

"Maybe I will take root one day," Frog said. "But not here, in this land." She said it softly, for Firdaus' and Doughyson's ears only. Memories of the rolling dry lands of Ing's childhood plagued her dreams, and she felt a great longing to visit them, no matter the centuries and light-years between here and there. But that could wait until Doughyson had fulfilled his promise to her.

Doughyson squatted down into the mud, disappearing into the thick stuff to his waist. "My toes are becoming roots, Firdaus. Here they will grow wide and deep and mighty."

Firdaus had promised to bring Doughyson ten baskets of white worms per day, the equivalent of the food that he would have gathered for himself as a walker. If Doughyson had had to grow at the normal walker rate, he wouldn't have been able to plant himself yet, since worms weren't sentient enough to come in response to the call of his charisma, and whitefish not yet plentiful. With part of his diet seen to, he could grow roots and become big. In a century or so, he would be a sessile mound about half the size of Mother Doughy. He was skipping several growth stages of his species and getting a head start on his competitors, all thanks to his human helpers.

Doughyson folded his arms over his bulging belly and closed his eyes. He'd told Frog he would keep his arms and his eyes for a few years, until his network of roots had grown large enough to gather information in another way.

More innovations spurred on by the example of human beings.

The Assembly members returned to the many duties of building the new town, while Frog and Firdaus remained by Doughyson's side. When the Assembly members were out of earshot, Frog squatted down and spoke the words that had waited impatiently. "Now tell me how to make a baby," Frog said.

"As I promised, I will," Doughyson said.

Firdaus knelt opposite to Frog. As one, their hands moved to their bellies, where they had saved up extra flesh for this day.

"Take the idea of a new small person into your heads. Imagine how it will smell, how it will move, what it will feel, what its shape should be. Position this idea into one spot on your body."

Frog imagined the soft slack flesh of a newborn against her palm, the scent of milk and baby rising from its crown, a pink little mouth seeking her nipple.

"Take from your flesh," Doughyson intoned. "Then quickly press the torn edges against one another."

She tore a chunk of flesh from her waist, as much as she could hold. By touch, she guided it to the one Firdaus had made. The edges made a sucking sound when they met. Frog took the combined hunk of Firdaus' and her flesh into her arms, her eyes still firmly closed.

The blob of lukewarm Wan stuff squirmed slightly against her hands.

"Will it into the person you want it to be. Expect it to be ready when you open your eyes."

A small hiccup sounded. Something soft flailed against her breast.

"Open your eyes now."

The heavenly scent reached her nose before she could open her eyes. A feeling rose in her throat, her ribs heaved in a sob. The white crown of the baby's head looked moist, and its downy cheek moved against her skin, seeking solace. Tiny white fingers and nails waved aimlessly, like the fronds of a sea anemone. It depended on her and her alone for everything.

Firdaus' deep voice trilled against her neck. "She's so sweet, so little."

The feeling of completion was so immense that Frog couldn't tell where she ended and where the baby began, where Firdaus was or Doughyson, the lagoon and the sky, all meeting in a vast white searing joy.

Her own voice sounded rough and pinched in her ears, not like her own. A new person had been born in this moment, and she didn't mean the baby. "I'm calling her Peony."

A moment of silence. Then Firdaus' voice, still so close to her neck her spine arched in a mindless response.

"What does it mean?"

"It was my favorite flower when I—when Ing was a little girl."

"Peony it is."

They bowed to Doughyson and took their leave.

"Sometimes I wondered how exactly we benefited from dealing with the Wan," Firdaus mused. "It seems Doughyson, or Mother Doughy, has all the advantages and we have none."

Frog looked at the baby sleeping against her left shoulder, its tiny buttocks secure in her hand. How could he even think that? "We are alive. Humanity survived. Who knows, we might be the last pocket of humanity in all the universe. Behind these clouds is the Sun, Firdaus. And stars. One day we might return there and rejoin the rest of the human race. If they still live."

"Eat today's fruit instead of planting your grand-children's orchard, dear Frog," he said.

Frog bent down. The tiger-striped mud surface thrust up a tiny irregularity. She balanced the baby and dug her arm elbow-deep into the mud. "Look!" she said. "Look what I found!"

Firdaus looked at the mud cradled in her hand. "It's special mud?"

"No! It's the nub of a fern tree. A tiny, tiny fern tree. I'm going to plant it close to the edge."

"But shouldn't they all have died?"

"They should have. But this one didn't. This means," Frog went on, waving her free hand excitedly, "that there might be more."

Firdaus sighed. Frog knew he disliked hearing the Ing remnants speak, but she refused to silence almost half of her brain.

"Firdaus!" a voice yelled from the direction of the beach.

Frog took a step to look down the long stairway to the beach. Boon was racing up the stairway as fast as his little legs could.

"Look, Abba, look!"

As one, she and Firdaus shaded their eyes to look to the horizon. Far away, on the line that separated sea from sky, a triangle bobbed up and down, in and out of sight.

It was a sail, coming in fast on the clipped northern wind that blew towards the shore.

Firdaus' voice came out strangled. "A ship! Survivors. But... how...?"

"Humans are more resourceful than I thought."

Firdaus looked deep into her eyes, as he sometimes did when she reminded him of Ing.

Frog smiled. She wasn't Ing anymore. She was something bigger than the both of them. "We'll build a new city, Stadholder. An entire new world."

ACKNOWLEDGMENTS

I'd like to thank for tireless critique buddying and brainstorming: First and foremost: Sylvia Volk; but also Ogi Ogas and Gio Clairval. A one-night read-through and great encouragement during VP by the peerless Jim D. McDonald.

Many people on OWW gave separate chapter critiques on the first draft. Erin Stocks, Josh Vogt, Ruthanne Reid, Kathryn Allen, Jesse Bangs, Terry Jackman, Steve Chapman, Anna Kashina, FRR Mallory, John Horner Jacobs, Rayne Hall, Aliette de Bodard, Simon Rhodes. The Pendragon workshop for the first chapters: Victoria Kerrigan.

My fabulous editor Dr. Bill (Bill Racicot) helped me smooth out continuity and give the novel its final gloss.

And last but not least, my husband and kids for putting up with me, reading many drafts and coming up with great explosion ideas…

ABOUT THE AUTHOR

Bo is the first Dutch author ever to have published a story in the US *Fantasy & Science Fiction magazine*. Her other short fiction has appeared in print and emagazine format. For a full bibliography, see her website: www.boukjebalder.nl/wordpress

Before becoming a writer, she practiced a series of preparatory professions like dishwasher, rowing coach, model, computer programmer, and management consultant.

Bo lives and works in Utrecht, close to Amsterdam.

Other science fiction titles available from
PINK NARCISSUS PRESS

DARKWALKER
A post-apocalyptic crime novel
by Duncan Eagleson
"I love this book from the moment I met Wolf. It's got high-stakes action and great characters without sacrificing any of its wonderful mythical resonance. What's not to like?" —Charles de Lint
ISBN: 978-1-939056-04-7

DAUGHTERS OF ICARUS
New Feminist Science Fiction and Fantasy
"Throughout, the authors explore themes of gender, identity, and autonomy, with characters as diverse as miniature clones, stripper vampires, aggressive mermaids, and mystical crones. Many of the stories focus on gender roles and the pull of relationships, whether parental, familial, or romantic, among all kinds of people." —*Library Journal*
ISBN: 978-1-939056-00-9

IMPOSSIBLE FUTURES
Return to the Future that Never Was!
"This wholly satisfying collection delivers an entertaining, engrossing, even exhilarating reading experience." —*ForeWord Reviews*
ISBN: 978-1-939056-02-3

NARCISSUS IS DREAMING
A science fiction novel by Rose Mambert
"*Narcissus is Dreaming* reminds me of some of the work of the late Theodore Sturgeon, who also dealt with concepts of otherness, loneliness, and the endless varieties of love."
—*Analog*
ISBN: 978-1-939056-05-4

www.ingramcontent.com/pod-product-compliance
Lightning Source LLC
Chambersburg PA
CBHW050700290626
47170CB00016B/2482